"THE PATTERNS
SHOW WHA' MUST BE . . ."

"Vanessa," Christopher said, "if you don't say anything at all, people will hear what they want to hear, and then they won't fear you."

"But the patterns . . . The patterns say I must. They show wha' must be, an' tha's the way it is . . . unless . . . unless . . ." There was a sudden flash of fear in her eyes, the look of an animal caught in a trap.

"Unless?"

Her fear was stark, uncompromising. "I saw them change," she said softly. "The patterns. I didn't think they could change, but when the legate came up to me, I saw them change. He changed them. Everything turned about, an' then there wa' a different future. . . ."

"Then that means," Christopher said, "that maybe what you see doesn't cause the world. Maybe it only reflects it. And the legate changed the patterns because he made a choice. That means you can change them by making a choice, too!"

MAZE OF MOONLIGHT

by

Gael Baudino

A ROC BOOK

ROC
Published by the Penguin Group
Penguin Books USA Inc., 375 Hudson Street,
New York, New York 10014, U.S.A.
Penguin Books Ltd, 27 Wrights Lane,
London W8 5TZ, England
Penguin Books Australia Ltd, Ringwood,
Victoria, Australia
Penguin Books Canada Ltd, 10 Alcorn Avenue,
Toronto, Ontario, Canada M4V 3B2
Penguin Books (N.Z.) Ltd, 182–190 Wairau Road,
Auckland 10, New Zealand

Penguin Books Ltd, Registered Offices:
Harmondsworth, Middlesex, England

First published by Roc, an imprint of New American Library,
a division of Penguin Books USA Inc.

First Printing, March, 1993
10 9 8 7 6 5 4 3 2 1

 REGISTERED TRADEMARK—MARCA REGISTRADA

Printed in the United States of America

To my brave sisters,
Christa and Judith,
who left this world
28 January 1986
seeking the stars . . .

. . . who found instead
the arms of the Mother.

Lors li commence a faire saus
Bas et petits et grans et haus
Primes deseur et puis desos,
Puis se remet sor ses genols,
Devers l'ymage, et si l'encline:
"He!" fait il, "tres douce reine
Par vo pitie, par vo francise,
Ne despisies pas mon servise!"

—Tombeor de Notre Dame

CHAPTER 1

Massing in the east, dark above the restless and bare branches of Malvern Forest, roiling above the distant plains and mountains, redolent of storms, clouds surged westward across Adria like the cold hand of a miser greedy for another gold coin.

Pytor leaned on the parapet of the curtain wall and squinted into the stiff wind. It had been a cold autumn, full of rain, and now, winter having sent in its vanguard of sleet and hail even before the crops had been gathered, the fields were damp, ragged with the marks of a harvest brought in hastily and in the midst of evil weather, turgid and muddy with the peasants' attempts at early sowing. The late afternoon sunlight held no warmth, and these clouds foretold yet another night of cold and damp, a night filled with rain and the drip of water from innumerable leaden gutters.

Worse than in Novgorod. At least there the boards in the street kept your feet dry.

But there was nothing in Novgorod for him save slavery and perhaps death, and if the streets were not boarded here in Aurverelle, he could at least afford good boots. Perhaps that was an improvement. Perhaps that was desirable. Perhaps not. God knew better than he. In any case, it was what he had, and he would have to be satisfied with it.

But he reminded himself that what he had might well not last for much longer, and as he had once walked from Russia to Adria, so he might well have to walk again: from Adria to other lands, other kingdoms. France, perhaps. Or Castile. Or even farther. For though Castle Aurverelle seemed solid and secure, its walls thick, its stores and its armories sufficient to equip and feed a thousand men and most of the surrounding town for a month, it was in actuality tottering precariously between one existence and another.

Castle Aurverelle had no master.

It would have been easier, perhaps, had Baron Christopher simply died in the carnage at Nicopolis. It certainly would have been understandable: most everyone had died, save for the French nobles who had organized the crusade, convinced the two rival popes to pause in their constant exchange of excommunications long enough to proclaim it, and finally led it to bloody defeat in distant Bulgaria. Christopher could have perished in the forest of sharpened stakes that had been planted by the wily Turks to foil the charge. Or fought to the death like Philippe de Bar and Odard de Chasseron.

But that had not happened. Christopher was, instead, missing, and had been so since the battle. Many had died, and a few had returned, but Christopher delAurvre had vanished, and the uncertainty of his fate had placed the entire estate of Aurverelle and everyone in it square in the weighing pan of teetering balances.

Pytor turned away from the battlements. God knew where Christopher was, but it obviously did not please Him to tell anyone. Pytor would have to be satisfied with that, too.

He had almost reached the entrance to the south tower when an apple core suddenly descended like a meteor and struck him squarely on the forehead. He looked up to see a mocking grin from the furry creature that was clinging to an upper crenel by a hand and a tail. Cursing in florid Russian, Pytor looked for something to throw, but the monkey had already vanished with a screech; and so the seneschal of Aurverelle was left to mop his face with a large hand and make his way down the stairs of the tower, plunking his heavy boots down deliberately on each tread, contemplating the satisfaction he would gain from stamping a certain apple-throwing monkey into jelly. If he could ever catch it.

He continued to murder the monkey down to the second floor, and then he gave up and entered the dark corridor that led along the inside of the curtain wall. The wind moaned in the shutters and doors, and he could not help but recall—with a shiver—the story of the village girl who had refused the marriage night privileges of the last baron but one. As a result, Baron Roger had chained her to a bed in an upper room, used her, and left her to starve to death. On days like this, Pytor fancied that he could hear her screaming . . . far away. . . .

Pytor shuddered, stopped at a door halfway along the corridor. Bright lamplight seeped out from beneath it. Did he hear moans? Screams? He banished them with a knock and a shout. "Jerome!"

"Come."

The office of the bailiff of Aurverelle possessed the largest glass windows in the castle save for those in the rooms of the baron's residence, and the light they admitted, eked out this lowering afternoon by the lamps that flamed brightly around the walls, gave Jerome the illumination he needed for his accounts, his tallies, and his records. Headless though Aurverelle was, it lived still, and living for a barony, like living for anything else, involved money, commerce, labor: the greasy and sweat-soaked components of mortal life.

Jerome was old and dry, a Franciscan who had fled a schism-torn monastery. True to the old ways, he kept his vows without equivocation, and his brown robe looked as shabby and worn as his face. "I was just finishing up, Pytor," he said, looking up from his accounting tables. "Is there something you want?"

Pytor stumped over to the bench on the other side of the desk, sat down heavily. "Food," he said.

Jerome's eyes crinkled up in what passed for laughter. "The kitchen, I think, would be more appropriate."

Pytor was used to Jerome's gentle teases. "Not for me," he said. "For our people. You are chief bailiff. You have the accounts. Will there be enough to eat this winter?"

Jerome cast a look at the window. The clouds were still massing, overspreading Aurverelle. "You've been out looking at the fields, haven't you?"

"I've been looking at them for weeks, Jerome. This has been the worst harvest since I took service with the master's grandfather. The fields are wretched, the rains are already washing out the seeds, and . . . well?"

"Messire Christopher's people are loyal," said Jerome. He pulled a roll of parchment from the rack of pigeon holes behind him. "The taxes have come in on schedule, the laggards are few. I can tell you about taxes."

"I don't want to know about what they have paid. I want to know what they have left."

Jerome spread the parchment out to reveal rows of neat columns painstakingly added and totaled and summed into tables with monkish diligence. Here, inked onto the scraped skin of a sheep, were the lives of the commoners of the Aurverelle estate—merchant and farmer, peasant and artisan—their economic existence reduced to a set of figures.

But Pytor found himself thinking that perhaps all of life had become like that: figures, tables, money. The war between France and England had collapsed into a temporary truce not because of any new-found pacifism on the part of either party, but as a result of simple financial exhaustion. And the mercenaries who were no longer paid from belligerent coffers had—simple economics, really—turned to brigandage, plundering a comfortable living from fields and towns already gutted by taxes and tithes. Even the Church had mired itself in questions of profit and loss.

Pytor watched as Jerome passed a finger down a column of figures, mumbling to himself. Was God like that, too? Grace counted out in florins and ducats? Salvation measured by the kilderkin, diker, and cartload?

Item: one Pytor of Medno, escaped stradnik, *now seneschal of Aurverelle. Devout enough, but payments seriously in arrears. Recommended action* . . .

Pytor shuddered. *Few saved, many damned,* the saying went. Who could afford salvation these days?

"What is left?" said Jerome at last. "Probably just enough to squeak through. I've seen a season or two like this in my time. It was just like this two years before the big drought, if you recall, and . . ." He looked up, stared at Pytor, blinked, stared again. "You have bits of apple all over your hair, Pytor."

Pytor drew a hand across his head. The fruit was wet and mealy, and he scraped it off and threw it into the rushes on the floor. "It was the monkey again."

Jerome chuckled. "It got me the other day. Ranulf's boys are still trying to catch it."

"They have been trying for two years now and they still haven't got it."

"Well . . . yes. It's a clever one."

Pytor half turned towards the window. The gathering darkness had dimmed the light. "I wish that the beast had followed its bitch of a mistress into the grave."

Jerome pursed his lips and was silent. No one in the castle disputed Pytor's opinion of the late baroness.

"If it were not for her, the master would not have gone away."

"Yes . . . yes," said Jerome softly. "I know. But Anna was pious, and Christopher was looking for . . ." He lifted his hand, and the parchment rolled up with a dry rustle. He shrugged. "Looking for something. I don't know what."

Pytor ruminated. Then finally: "Food," he said.

Jerome nodded. "Enough. Just."

"Thank you," said Pytor. He stood up.

"I'll have the provosts make inquiries in the villages, Pytor," said the friar. "If there is any distress this winter, we'll hear about it."

"Will we be able to do anything about it?"

Jerome shrugged. "Well, there are no tourneys to finance, no squires to knight, no grand progresses to equip, no wars to be fought." He turned reflective at this last. "At least not at present," he added. "If there is insufficient food to be had from our fields, I daresay food can be bought."

Pytor bowed and turned to go, but stopped at the door. "Have you . . . have you heard anything . . . ?"

Jerome shook his gray head. "No, Pytor. Nothing."

Pytor bent his head. "You know, I have stopped praying for master's return."

Jerome looked startled. "Indeed? But, Pytor, you—"

"I pray now only that he is happy." Pytor lifted his head. "One can be happy in death, you know."

"A doubtful proposition," said Jerome somberly. "You must recall Raymond Diocrès."

"I am an unlearned peasant and a runaway slave," said Pytor stiffly. "I believe my master can do no wrong."

Jerome nodded silently. Pytor left the office and went back into the hall, his eyes aching. It was hard to have hope, harder still to give it up.

About him, Castle Aurverelle was quiet. Gone were the parties, the dancing, the troupes of tumblers who had, once upon a time, come down from the passes across the Aleser to find themselves given a warm place by the fire and a chance to perform before the haughty but gracious baron of Aurverelle. The squires sent for nurturing and training had departed months ago, likewise the girls sent to Lady Anna: those who had survived the outbreak of plague that had taken the baroness and much of the town had gone home.

Stone, and mortar, and the cold slumber of an ancient

keep. Endless battlements and towers and stairs. More armor and weapons than the remaining men-at-arms really needed. More fields than a depleted peasantry could work. More rain (yes, it was drumming on the roofs even now, and Raffalda was bawling for the few remaining maids and kitchen boys to run and fasten the shutters) than anyone could use.

God knew best. Florins and ducats. *Few saved, many damned.*

Dark thoughts, Pytor, he told himself. *Dark thoughts.* The master never liked that studied, Russian melancholy any more than he liked being addressed in the third person.

But the master was gone—there was now no reason to give up any of it—and the dark thoughts accompanied Pytor down the corridors of Aurverelle as he wondered about his master and considered the future.

Aurverelle, deserted and cheerless though it was, was nonetheless one of the largest estates of Adria, and Pytor and Jerome both knew that other barons were already looking for ways to acquire it. There were any number of relatives of the delAurvre line scattered throughout the manor houses and castles of the land, and it would be a relatively simple matter for one of the more powerful of them to make a claim to Aurverelle. All very correct, all very legal, all very formal.

And that would be the end of it. Pytor wondered again about Castile. Franciscans and runaway slaves were not to everyone's taste. It would be a long walk.

As though to defy the sunny land to the southwest, he went to his room and took a thick cloak from the peg, then plunked down several more flights of stairs to the outer court. The rain pounded on the cloak and the mud sucked at his boots as he stepped from the cobbled gateway into the streets of the town, but he hardly noticed: he was wondering—despite his words to Jerome—whether there was still hope, whether he would ever again sleep on the floor in front of Christopher's room in the knowledge that his master slept peacefully and safely in his own bed.

A pair of goats wandered across Pytor's path, butting one another and dipping their heads for morsels bobbing in the mud and sewage that had pooled in the middle of the street. Slaughter time was near, and a pig snorted and rooted its last days away in its mire of an alley. Pytor sloshed past them, turned a corner, and pushed into the fevered light and noise of a small inn's common room. Had he so desired, he could have stayed up at the castle and drunk all the wine and beer that he could hold—drunk himself into a stupor, in fact, as he often did—but the castle was too dark tonight, the master's absence too palpable for him to find any solace there.

Over three years now. Three years and five months. And no word. And Jean de Nevers and Boucicaut, strutting their way through France in their jewels and their finery as though they had won a battle rather than lost the whole campaign, taxing their already starving peasants to pay the ransoms that Bayazet had demanded, acting the courtly clowns—

Grimacing, Pytor slammed the door behind him and threw back his hood just as a burst of laughter bounced off the walls and lingered boisterously among the dark beams of the ceiling. "Come, master beggar," someone was shouting, "tell us of your begging."

"I . . . beg . . ." A thin voice, halting, quavering, and oddly disturbing for that. In the light of the big fire on the hearth, Pytor could see a man as thin his voice, as thin as the japing monkey that still lurked among the slate roofs and battlements of Castle Aurverelle, a man who lifted his hands and waved them about his head as though to gather strength from the smoky air. "I beg to live . . . and I live to beg. Gig-a-gig! God only knows how I have run and jumped from here to the Danube!"

The beggar's sing-songing prattle followed Pytor to a bench in a dark corner. He sat down, signed to the tapster: his usual, dark and ripe with barley and malt and in the biggest tankard in the house. Inevitably, it was the same brew that Raffalda and her wenches had cooked up, so Pytor was paying money for something he could have had for nothing. But he excused himself for his profligacy: he was not paying for beer. He was instead paying for the right to occupy a seat in a wretched room that was *not* in the castle, *not* empty, *not* without a master—and for the dubious pleasure of watching some of the townsmen taunt an old, half-wit beggar.

"And did you see bears?" said Walter, the turner. "Did you?"

"Aye," quavered the beggar. "Many a bear. And lions.

Ho-ho-ho! The arms and shields hang low, and there's many a Christian knight hangs on a pole this evening!''

"You're blaspheming!" said Walter. "The priest will hear about this.''

"No man—ha-ha—can serve two masters . . .'' The half-wit crouched low, then sprang up, shaking as though possessed, his body a gaunt shape against the flames. "But, you know, they follow me.''

"Follow?'' said someone else. "Who?''

"The fiends. The fiends in their gowns and their staves and their turned-up shoes, the ones who play pick-a-back with the popes—there's two, you know.''

"Two?''

"Two popes. One for each side: black and white. But no one knows . . .'' The beggar whinnied like a horse. ''. . . which is which. Or which way the board is turned. And they won't until the end.''

The men who had gathered to hear the performance drew back a little. The schism was not something about which to joke. It had been said that since Clement had been elected in direct opposition to Urban, not a soul had entered Paradise.

Few saved, many damned. As though many would enter Paradise in any case!

Pytor accepted a brimming tankard from the tapster, poked a thumb at the beggar. "Who is that, Ernest?''

Ernest wiped his hands on his apron. "Nay, m'lord seneschal, I don't know. Hasn't said his name. Turned up this afternoon between nones and vespers and hasn't left. Otto gave him some bread and beer for the love of God, but he could surely use more.''

And, true, the man's tattered clothing hung on a frame that was not much more than bones with enough flesh to keep them dangling. His face, where it was not covered with matted beard and hair sunbleached as white as a leper's arm, was burnt almost black by the sun; and his eyes, ringed with darkness, reflected the firelight with a feral madness that had made him the entertainment this rainy night.

"I want to hear more about the bears,'' someone called.

"Do you hear that, beggarman?'' said Walter. "We want to hear about bears.''

"Bears? Ah-oo!''

"Not wolves, idiot." The turner gave him a shove that nearly sent him into the fire. "Bears."

"Bears," said the beggar. "Bearsbearsbears . . . many bears . . . more bears than you've ever seen, master."

"Shut up and show us how bears dance."

The beggar hunkered and slouched and capered before the fire, now and again attempting a hoarse roar. Pytor drank his beer. Rain outside, and loneliness in Castle Aurverelle, and a master gone for over three years. The schism had riven the Church to its core, bad weather was threatening the estate with starvation next year . . . and the drunken laborers of Aurverelle had nothing better to do than to torment a daft old man.

The tapster looked at Pytor and shrugged. Pytor shrugged back. The tapster went back to the counter. Over by the fire, someone had produced an old battered lute, and Walter played the pipe and tabor, and the music echoed and pounded in time to the beggar's dance.

> *The merchant drinks, the student drinks,*
> *The lord drinks, and the lady too,*
> *The sweet girl drinks, and wencher drinks*
> *And so all drink, and drink again . . .*

But the beggar was thin and weak, and he could not play the bear forever. Soon, quite soon, he wavered and slumped onto a bench, covering his head with his hands. "Leave me, leave me," he whimpered. "I'm tired. I want to go home."

"You're not through dancing, bear."

"Leave me. It's too close."

"Dance!"

And Walter and two other men seized him by the arms and stood him on his feet again. The beggar capered for another moment, then collapsed.

"Hey-nonny-no!" he wheezed faintly. "The fiends have me by the tail and the winds blow cold and cracked! The world is crooked, and who'll set it right?"

Walter and his friends were reaching for the beggar again when Pytor stood up. "Enough," he rumbled. "Enough. Leave the man alone." In the sudden silence, he turned to the tapster. "Ernest, give him some supper and a place to sleep. Tell Otto to send the reckoning to the castle."

"It shall be done, Master Pytor."

The men by the fire sat back down with dark murmurs, but the beggar straightened up. Even from across the room, Pytor felt the glitter of his feral eyes, and he shuddered and finished his beer standing. No solace here. It would have been better had he stayed in Aurverelle and drunk himself to sleep in the hall outside the door to the baron's bedroom.

He reached for his purse, but Ernest shook his head. With a nod of thanks, Pytor turned for the door.

Night had fallen firmly by now, the darkness weighed down by the heavy rain, and Pytor had almost reached the castle gate before he realized that the beggarman had followed him, creeping along in the shadows of the overhanging solars and wading through the torrents of muck that poured out of the alleyways.

"Go back," said Pytor. "Go back to the inn. There is supper and a place by the fire for you there."

The man was shivering—chattering teeth, spasmodic jerks of his arms and legs—but he crouched a few yards from the seneschal like a hungry dog and did not move.

"Go on."

"Mastermaster. Oh! How he pinches me! Black and blue I am and—"

"Blue with cold, damn you!" said Pytor, and he would have seized the man and dragged him back to shelter, but for all his cold and weakness, the beggar was nimble enough to dodge away.

"Don't send me back there, mastermaster," he yelped. "They make me dance, they do. They prick me with burning needles and red-hot guilts, and there's no Grandpa Roger to keep them away."

Grandpa Roger? Pytor's eyes narrowed. Baron Roger had been dead for seven years. Was this beggar making fun of the old man? Well, half-wits had to be forgiven. "Come on, man," he said gruffly, for the water was seeping into his boots and his cloak was as heavy as if it had been made of granite. "Come on. I'll take you to the castle. You can sleep there."

"Thankee," said the beggar. "Thankee. I'll sleep by a good fire in the castle, with stuffed shoes and statues all about. Thankee."

He allowed Pytor to take him by the arm, and together they slogged up to the gatehouse. The guards saluted Pytor, but looked dubiously at his companion. "My lord," said one, "have you taken to picking up rags in the street?"

"I myself was a rag in the street once," said Pytor. "Baron Roger picked me up, washed me up, and patched me with Aurverelle cloth. I'm here today because of that. This man is a child of God like you and me."

"But, he's a—"

"Beggar," said Pytor. "Tramp. Commoner. Peasant. Yes, he is all that and more. But as Baron Roger treated me, so I shall treat him."

The beggar had been standing owl-eyed throughout the conversation, but now he nodded and capered oddly. "Grandpa Roger! Grandpa Roger!" He bobbed up and down, splashed through the puddles in an antic dance. "He had the Free Towns in his pouch and let them go again!"

The guards stared. "Forgive him," said Pytor. "He's mad, that is all." He took up a lit torch, took the beggar by the hand, and drew him into the courtyard. Come on, man," he said, "We'll have you dry and fed in a moment. It is lucky for you that Russians have an affection for madmen." But the beggar had abruptly ceased his capering and was walking quietly at his side, head first down, then up, regarding muddy cobbles and tall towers with equal wonderment.

But Pytor found that there was something about the beggar's gait, something almost familiar, that struck him with a sense of unease. And it seemed suddenly not at all remarkable to hear this second set of footsteps—quick and light, even through the rain—blending with his own.

Grandpa Roger? What?

The guards on duty threw open the door of the keep, and torchlight spilled into the night. The beggar blinked. *"Fiat lux!"*

"Now, now . . ." Pytor took him into the vestibule. "Let's get you something warm, for the love of God." He lifted his head. "Raffalda! Where are you? Someone call Raffalda!"

The beggar was bobbing his head. The gaunt irony had left his eyes, and he regarded the room sadly, a little dazed. "Will I . . . will I sleep in my own bed tonight?" he said in a small voice.

"You'll have a straw mattress in the hall just like—" Pytor broke off as though something had caught in his throat, for the beggar's daft tone had moderated, gentled, turned into something else. Something disturbing.

Raffalda's footsteps were approaching, but Pytor held his torch close to the beggar. No, he realized, this was no old man. This was a young man worn by years and deprivation, damaged by pain and travel. Moreover, this was a young man—

Grandpa Roger? His own bed?

Pytor suddenly felt hot, dizzy. He found himself trying to peer beneath the man's sunbleached hair and beard, almost afraid to believe, almost afraid to see. Was it possible? Beyond all hope?

The beggar blinked in the light and studied Pytor's face as earnestly as Pytor studied his. Beneath the dirt and the sunburn, the lines of madness and fatigue, a light suddenly kindled, and he laughed sheepishly and a little hysterically. "Hey-diddle-dee!" he said. "Not one word of greeting for your old cock-a-whoop, Pytor?"

Pytor stared, transfixed. Then, just as Raffalda entered the room, grumbling about bad nights and worse beggars, he thrust the torch into her startled hands and fell to his knees, embracing the beggar about the waist, pressing his cheek against the filthy and vermin-ridden garments, weeping out loud and without shame.

Christopher of Aurverelle had come home.

CHAPTER 2

October. All Hallow's Eve. Outside, snow falling, muffling sounds, muting the scraping of branches across the thatch. Inside, Lake sitting up by a low fire.

By habit and will—not by need—he usually went to bed early, but tonight was different. Tonight, he stayed awake, and if he dozed at all before the flickering coals, it was only for appearance's sake, an attempt to convince himself, despite birth and heritage, that Lake of Furze Hamlet, like any doughty farmer anywhere, could, at the end of the day, feel a weariness that only sleep and oblivion could cure. Humans dozed before winter fires. Humans fell into and fought their way out of dreams that were variously pleasant or disturbed. And so Lake forced himself to do the same.

But though, through self-discipline and work, he had gotten the knack of such things, he did not sleep now, for he was listening for the knock that would come to the door. He would have a visitor tonight. He knew it. He did not doubt it. He hated his knowledge and his lack of doubt.

Up in the wide loft, Miriam, his wife, breathed softly in unfeigned repose, and Vanessa's fourteen-year-old restlessness rustled the straw and feathers of her bed.

Vanessa. Did she sleep? She seemed to. But that, perhaps, was her only normal quality. Lake rose, crept to the stairs that led to the loft, peered up anxiously. It was important that Vanessa be asleep tonight. It was important that she remain asleep. She saw enough already: it would not do at all for her to hear also.

The fire crackled abruptly and sparked once, twice, and the mules and the oxen grumbled sleepily in the adjoining stable as they hunkered down amid dry and plentiful litter. Vanessa groaned softly as though in reply. Lake bowed his head, wondering what she saw in her dreams, frightened because he suspected that he knew.

An hour dragged by. Two. Distantly, he heard the bells
of the Benedictine abbey, and he began to wonder whether
he had been wrong, to hope that the subtle but unmistakable
feeling that had prompted him to remain awake by the fire
was false, the product of worry about himself, his past . . .
and his youngest daughter.

A tapping on the door: measured, light.

Lake stared at the fire. In the corner of his mind, he
detected a barely perceptible glimmering. It was inviting,
gracious. He thrust it away.

Once more the tapping; this time softly, reluctantly, as
though it would not be repeated again. With yet another
anxious glance at the loft, Lake rose and crossed the room,
lifted the bar softly, and swung the door open.

The night was cold and black, but even if the glow from
the fire had not illuminated faintly the gray-cloaked figure
standing in the snow outside, Lake would nonetheless have
seen enough to confirm his feelings and his vigil, for there
was a light about his visitor that seemed to shine from
within. It played softly on his womanly face, and it echoed
the gleam of starlight in his eyes.

"Varden." Lake spoke reluctantly. "I . . . expected
you."

"Be at . . ." Varden hesitated, then nodded slowly. "Be
at peace. May I enter?"

In answer, Lake turned away from the door and went to
stand before the fire with folded arms. Behind him, Varden
entered and shut the door, but though Lake heard the rustle
of a cloak being removed, shaken out, and hung up on a
peg, he also heard enough to tell him that Varden, as though
unsure of what hospitality he might find in this house, had
stayed just within the threshold.

Silence. The crackle of the fire. The scrape of branch
against snow-laden thatch.

"It has been some time," said Varden at last.

Lake did not turn. "Ha' it been that long?"

"Twenty years."

"That's na long . . . for such as you."

Varden was silent. Then, cautiously: "I believe I feel the
years more now than I once did."

Even though his back was turned, Lake sensed his visitor's manner and presence. Slender and straight, arms
folded, eyes troubled, Varden had not moved. It had indeed

been a long time. Lake would have preferred that it had been longer.

"How is Ma?" Lake said at last.

"She is . . ." Varden's voice was suddenly strained. "She is dead, Lake. She died a week ago."

Lake bowed his head, but he could not find the tears.

"We can still do much," Varden continued softly, "but we cannot take away age."

"You never could."

"Not so. Once—" But Varden broke off, stood in silence. "Roxanne believed in cycles," he said after a time, "and in her Goddess, and in death and rebirth. She would not have allowed such magic, even had it still been possible."

Up in the loft, Vanessa stirred again. Lake started, looked towards the top of the stairs.

"But she was old," said Varden. "It was her time, so she told us. Natil and Mirya and Terrill and I were with her when she left. Charity, too." He hesitated. "I . . . I do not know where she is now."

Lake found that his jaw was clenched against tears that he could not, would not feel. Annoyed with himself, he unclenched it. "Well, that's wha' comes o' being human," he heard himself say. "That's wha' comes o' getting old. I'm old myself. Middle-aged, and getting fat and . . ."

Lake turned around, and he saw plainly the gleam of starlight about Varden. His voice caught. He could see it. Of course he could. And he could see what had happened to Vanessa, too. Thank God or the Lady or whoever watched over such as made up his family that it took that taint of ancient blood to detect such things, otherwise . . .

Involuntarily, he looked up at the loft again. No. Never. Vanessa would have a chance. Maybe in a city somewhere, away from her father, away from reminders, even unconscious reminders, of another heritage and race, her symptoms might fade. She might never know what she was. She might never have to.

Yes, he could do that. He could do . . . something.

"I'm . . . old myself," he repeated. "I suppose that's good. I'd have a hard time explaining endless youth as well as everything else."

Varden had not moved. "Everything else?"

"Well . . . the stories, the rumors. They've followed me even here. And I've ne'er learned to sleep very well. People

noticed that, too.'' Lake scuffed at the rushes on the floor.
''It's hard to get away from your birth . . . or your parents.''

Varden's young face turned pained. ''*Lakei—*''

''Dan call me that.''

Varden lowered his gaze. ''And do you hate me so
much?''

Lake turned away, eyes stinging. ''I dan hate you. If I
hate anything at a', I hate what you di' to me. An' so I hate
wha' I di' to Vanessa.''

''I am sorry.'' Varden fell silent again, and when Lake
looked up, he noticed that, in addition to the almost sublim-
inal shadow of starlight that played about Varden, there was
a hint of transparency to him, as though he hovered on the
borders of existence.

He blinked, looked again. It was true. Roxanne was dead,
and Varden, in accordance with the fate of his kind, was
. . . fading . . .

''Cam sit down an' . . .'' Lake's voice caught at the invitation as much as at his realization, but he pushed on
through. ''. . . an' warm yourself.''

Varden hesitated for a moment, then nodded and sat down
on the bench near the hearth. Clad simply in the green and
gray of the shadowed forest, he seemed to Lake a gleaming,
wild thing, as out of place in this peasant dwelling as a fox.
But the firelight only heightened the sense of the ephemeral
about him. Hovering. Only hovering. And Roxanne was
dead. Soon, very soon, only the heritage would remain.

Lake remained standing. Outside, the wind picked up,
and the snow rattled on the wooden shutters.

''I stayed away because I knew your desires,'' said Varden, and if he himself had noticed the transparency, he gave
no sign. ''I came because I gave in to my own. Roxanne
is . . .'' The starlight in his eyes was troubled by grief.
''Roxanne is gone. There are but four of us left in the world.
I . . .''

He bent his head. Lake could not find the tears. Varden
could.

''And so you wanted to see me,'' said Lake.

''It is . . . so. I wanted to see you, to . . . to know that
life continues. Roxanne and Charity speak of the mystery
of the corn, the dry head of seed which appears dead, but
which grows into new life. I need that hope now. So, I

believe, do we all at this time of fading. So I wanted to see—''

"You wan' to know about Vanessa.''

Varden nodded. "I do. I looked. I have seen.''

"I was afraid you'd do that.''

Abruptly, the light in Varden's eyes turned angry, defiant. "Why? Do you not think that I care?''

Lake fought with his own anger, the burst of temper that would have done no good. How could one rage against what had already been done? Roxanne had loved Varden. Other people had loved . . . others. Lake's heritage was shared by many: how was it that he found the temerity to complain? "My other children—girls and boys both—they dan see it. Whatever they've got from you is hidden. An' that's good. But Vanessa: she's . . . taken after me . . . an' . . .''

He whirled suddenly on Varden. "Dan it bother you? Dan it touch you? No . . . it can't, I guess. You're down there i' Saint Brigid wi' people wha look at you wi' belief an' dan hate you. An' you're fading anyway: soon you'll na ha' to worry about anything.'' Varden looked away quickly, but Lake continued. "But Vanessa and the rest, and their children, and their children's children . . . now and again it's going to show up in them, and they'll ha' to fight wi' it, and they'll either deny it, or go mad, or get burned or . . . or . . .'' His hands were shaking furiously, and he clenched them and thrust them into the pockets of his overtunic. "Or they'll ha' it wake up i' them, and then one day, if they've enough o' it, they wan't be human anymore. An' then it'll be all the same for 'em. They'll die anyway.''

Varden did not look up. "And do you wish that I had not loved your mother?''

"I . . .'' How much did Varden's kind feel? Did they bleed? Of course they did. The Inquisition had demonstrated that over and over again. But could they bleed inside? Could they feel that day-to-day gnawing that could turn every hour into a new trial, every careless word into a pang of fear? Lake did not know.

But Varden was weeping silently now: a grief too deep for utterance, a sorrow that struck its roots down into the infinite ages of the past. Did he bleed? Of course he did. Did he feel? Of course he did.

"Forgive me,'' said Lake.

Varden shook his head. "It is I who should ask forgive-

ness. I have troubled you. That was not my intent. It is not
the intent of our—'' Instinctive courtesy made him catch
himself. ''Of my people.''

''We've needed t' talk,'' said Lake heavily, ''if only t'
shout at one another. I guess we've both known that for a
long time.''

Varden nodded.

''You want to know about Vanessa.''

''Tell me. Please.''

''Why? Wha' can you do for her?''

''I would protect her.''

The transparency made a mockery of Varden's words.
Lake glared at him. ''You can't protect her. You can't do
anything for her.''

Shadowed and glimmering in the dusk left by the low fire,
Varden took a deep breath. ''Tell me.''

''She's . . . different.'' Lake spoke softly, unwillingly, as
though his utterance might make more real an already too
real fact. ''The other children, they grew up, married,
started families. Charlotte wa' the last. She's up in Furze
now wi' a hat maker, an' doing well. Anthony lives a few
fields awa'. He's the eldest, ha' children of his own, and
Baron Paul waived the inheritance fees: when I die, he'll
take my fields wi'out cost or question.'' He stared moodily
into the fire. ''All o' them, all quite normal. And then . . .
Vanessa.''

Varden leaned forward, listening.

''She wa' strange from the beginning,'' Lake went on,
just as softly, just as unwillingly. ''Even when she wa' barely
talking, she spoke o' things that set the priest to crossing
hi'self. She'd go an' play with the river as though it were
another child, and she'd talk to birds like she thought they'd
answer.'' Above, in the loft, he heard his daughter stir, cry
out softly in her sleep, fall silent again. ''We tried to ignore
it, but it kept getting worse, and now . . .'' He shook his
head. ''It's as if she in't really one o' us.''

Varden's starlit eyes were intent, fixed. ''What do you do
about it, Lake?''

''Wha' am I supposed to do?'' Lake shrugged helplessly.
''Foster it? It's as though she's old and young at once. She
says strange things, asks odd questions. She's always talking
about the patterns—''

''The Dance.''

"She calls it the patterns. She tells people what's going to happen. She's ne'er wrong. But she dan talk much to me. I can't say but that I dan let her."

Varden looked alarmed. With a guilty glance at the loft, Lake sat down, leaned towards him, spoke earnestly. "I grew up i' Saint Brigid," he said. "They tolerated such things there. It's different now, I'm sure, but of all the Free Towns, Saint Brigid probably still tolerates them."

Varden nodded. "They do."

"They even tolerated Ma, so long as she wa' . . . discreet."

"They did. And they love Charity."

Lake shook his head. "I couldn't stand it i' Saint Brigid. E'eryone knew, an' so I ran awa'. I wanted to be . . . human. I wanted to fit in. I din't want people pointing at me, whispering to one another. *There he goes,* they'd say. *There he is, the Elf-child. One o' us, and yet not.* I ran awa' from that, came to Furze Hamlet here, settled down. I learned the ways, married, had children . . . and now . . . now it's all cam back on me, and it's put us all in danger."

"Does the priest trouble you?" Varden was keeping his voice carefully neutral.

Lake grimaced. "Bonnerel is a good man. At first he spoke o' it as some kind of holy vision . . . like Clare or Hildegard. But he's always been uneasy about what he's heard about me, and he's frightened by what he sees in Vanessa, because she really in't anything like Clare or Hildegard. He's getting more frightened, too, an' he just might do something sa'day." He passed a hand across his moist brow. Someday? Any day. "I can't blame him. She's like sa'thing out o' the forest."

"Vanessa is as human as you."

"Aye, Varden. Tha's it exactly. As human as me." Lake felt the anger rising again. Varden could talk of comfort, could mumble all the reassuring words that he wanted, but that did not change in the slightest the fact that Lake could not look into his daughter's eyes without having his own denials and fears thrown into his face like a bucket of hot pitch. "Tell me, now. How human am I? How much starlight do you see in me? What kind o' fading does such as I face?"

If Lake's words had stung, Varden gave no sign. "What do you intend to do for her?" he said.

Lake stood up, folded his arms, hung his head. "God knows. I dan. I'll think of sa'thing, though. What wi' the schism and all, the Church is turning bad. Gregory set the Inquisition loose on sorcery some years back, and so I'm ha'way expecting . . ." He shrugged. He did not want to say it. Someday. Any day.

But Varden was shaking his head. "The Inquisition has attempted before to make inroads into Adria. It was last directed at the Free Towns, at the instigation of Baron Roger of Aurverelle. It failed."

"That was before I was born," said Lake, "an' people still talk about it as though it were some kind o' miracle. I suppose it was, too: Roger just turned around and let the Towns go. Just like tha'. But times have changed. E'en the Free Towns ha' changed. It could happen again. And in any case, it wan't take a crusade to claim Vanessa, only one frightened priest and a few woman-hating Dominicans."

"And what about you?"

Lake snorted. "I'm nearly fifty. I've lived. I've seen enough, and I'm tired of it. I can leave it." He felt Varden's starlit eyes. Fifty years? Compared to a lifetime measured in eons? Varden had watched the making of the world, and here was Lake insisting that his own tastes had become jaded after only fifty years.

But Varden said nothing. He did not have to. The transparency about him was eloquent enough.

"But Vanessa is young," Lake forced himself to say. "She dan deserve that." He shook his head, covered his face with his hands. "My God, she's fourteen. She should be married by now, or at least we should be planning it. But no one i' the village . . . I mean, wha' man in his right mind—"

"Would you . . ." Varden spoke slowly, hesitantly. "Would you let me see her? Perhaps—"

"Stay awa' from her," Lake snapped. Varden was silent, and Lake looked up at the loft uneasily. "You've got to understand," he said, his voice a taut whisper, "you are as you are. That's all. But Vanessa and I . . . We're struggling just to be human. It's na simple in this world. We ha' to fight for it, and it hurts us." The starlight gleamed in Varden's eyes, and Lake's voice shook. "Maybe it will kill us. I dan know. God knows."

"Or the Lady."

Lake nodded, torn between beliefs, between races, between worlds. "Whate'er, Varden."

Silence again. Finally, Varden nodded and rose. "Forgive me for troubling you. Do what you think is best. Roxanne is gone, and I begin to understand now that my work is done. Indeed . . ." He shook his head sadly. ". . . I wonder whether I have not marred as much as I have made."

"You dan know?"

"Everything is fading. We do not see as we used to. The world is for men now."

Varden went to the door, cast his cloak about his shoulders; and Lake wondered whether he was now seeing the wall behind him as though a thin veil, whether the shadow Varden cast had lightened from black to gray. Fading, like all his kind, leaving a shadowy legacy behind that, with time, would itself fade into the mortal blood of the world.

But a thought seemed to strike Varden, and he returned to the hearth as he unfastened a chain from his neck. A pendant in the form of a moon and a rayed star swung flashing in the dull glow of the fire.

"Give this to Vanessa," he said. "Tell her its origins or not as you think best. But—please—give it to her."

Lake took it as though it were a serpent. "And wha' can this do for her?"

Varden shrugged. "A sign," he said. "Perhaps a token if she ever needs one. Or, if not, a bauble to catch the eye of a husband." He smiled thinly. "The hand of the Lady be upon you, Lake."

And then he opened the door and was gone. And though Lake looked after him, it seemed that Varden's form and the gleam of starlight that veiled him faded long before he had gone far into the falling snow. The road was suddenly empty and silent and dark. All that was left was the cold, and the night, and the snow.

Fading.

Lake closed the door, barred it, and banked the fire carefully; and then he climbed the narrow stairs to the loft, undressed, and crawled under the thick comforter next to his wife. Miriam smiled in her sleep and snuggled closer to him, shifting her head from the feather pillow to his strong shoulder; and he wrapped an arm about her as though to shield her from Varden and all that he represented, as though to gather into his embrace all the mortality and humanity to which he could make some small claim and hold it up as a bulwark against the comforting, frightening, dangerous, immortal light of the stars.

Miriam, at least, was safe: peasant born, stout, smiling, and happy. Vanessa, though, sleeping uneasily a few feet away, tossing amid visions of patterns and futures, was another matter. Well, at least she could sleep. At least she had that much.

The pendant burned in his hand like a latent stigmata. He resolved not to give it to her. Not tomorrow, at least. Perhaps someday, but not tomorrow.

Roxanne was dead. His mother. And now Varden was gone to whatever fate folded soft wings of oblivion about those in whom the immortal blood of the Elves ran pure.

The tears finally came. Truly, he was alone now. "The hand o' the Lady be upon you too, Da," he whispered, and then he forced sleep to accept him.

CHAPTER 3

"He had the Free Towns in his pouch and let them go again!"

Christopher, or rather, the outward semblance of Christopher, crouched in the windowsill of his bedroom, his back to the shutters, looking, Pytor thought with a pang, like nothing so much as the escaped monkey, save that the monkey was as hairy as a devil and Christopher had been subjected to as much of a shave and a haircut as the castle barber could manage.

Eyes wide, the baron fixed his gaze on Pytor. "What do you want now? You want to prick me with needles? Fry me in pans? Oh, a soft prison is a hard bed indeed, when you've seen your friends cut up like capons!"

Guillaume, the castle physician, entered the room behind Pytor and shut the door. He examined Christopher from a distance. "Not much better, is he?"

"No," said Pytor heavily. "Not much better at all."

"To be expected," said Guillaume. "Can't have everything at once. Takes time. Took three years to get him this way: three weeks isn't going to fix him."

Pytor was wringing his cap in his hands. "I should like it very much if we saw *some* improvement."

Christopher bobbed his head like a brain-damaged hawk. Guillaume chewed over his answer. "Hard to do anything. Won't lie down, won't take his medicine. Get rid of his fever, he'd do better. Could tie him up and dose him, I guess."

"Tie up the baron of Aurverelle?"

Guillaume shrugged. "They tie up the king of France."

The physician was right, but Pytor was uncomfortable with such extremes. Perhaps he was a little afraid of Christopher—what would happen if the baron abruptly recovered his senses and discovered that he was bound?—but he admitted to himself that it was more likely that he did not want to confirm the seriousness of his master's condition. To have to tie him up would say, unequivocally, uncompromisingly, that, yes, Christopher delAurvre was mad, totally mad, and would best be chained to the rood screen in the chapel with a cross shaved into his hair.

Christopher pointed at the two men and giggled, then whooped, then waved his arms and growled like a bear. "Grandpa Roger knew what to do, didn't he? He planted peach trees!" More giggling, more growls. The baron seemed torn between despair and hideous amusement.

Pytor winced. "Isn't there anything else we can do?"

"Tried them. He threw things at the musicians. Tore the clothes off one of the tumblers. Frightened Efram and the lads near to death when they tried to sing. The books say happiness. I'm not one to contradict the books. But if he won't take it, he won't take it."

"Happiness sounds like a good idea," Pytor agreed. "He has not had much happiness these last years."

"Hard trip. Had to be."

Pytor nodded, but Christopher's repeated mention of his grandfather had made him suspect that there was more to the baron's condition than was immediately obvious. "Yes," he said. "That too."

With a sudden leap, Christopher launched himself from the windowsill and threw himself on Pytor and Guillaume. His fevered madness lent him strength, and as neither the seneschal nor the physician were willing to use much force against him, he easily tumbled them to the ground.

But an attack was not what Christopher appeared to have in mind. He left the two men sprawling, and his hands, trembling as though with palsy, went to the door latch, lifted it . . .

. . . and then he was off running down the hall, howling, with Pytor and Guillaume right behind him. Barefoot, Christopher pattered down the rush-strewn hallway, leaping over chests, vaulting balustrades, descending stairwells hand-over-hand rather than on his feet. Pytor shouted for guards, but the men of Castle Aurverelle were no more willing to use force on their baron than was he, and so Christopher gained the front door of the residence and bounded out across the court.

Wondering only for a moment what idiot had left the door

open, Pytor plunged out into the November cold. The wind smelled of frost, and the eaves and ledges of the castle were dripping with icicles, but he did not have time to regret or even think about a cloak: as weak and fevered as he was, Christopher would not last long in such weather. Pytor had to get his master back into bed. Or at least back indoors.

But Christopher had vanished among the nooks and buildings of the inner court. And now it started to snow.

Pytor called for more men and ordered a thorough search of the inner court. Stables, kennels . . . even the mews was examined, the hawks and falcons fluttering and preening nervously at the sound of heavy feet. One or two of the more slender guards stripped off their mail and shinnied up drain pipes and down into cisterns.

More snow. The temperature dropped steadily. Pytor was close to tears. He had wanted his master back, and he had been granted that wish. But his master was not his master, and though these last three weeks he had prayed earnestly for a return of Christopher's senses, now he would have been satisfied simply with his safety.

A gaunt form flitted across the rooftops. Pytor opened his mouth to cry out, but it was only the escaped monkey. And was the baron swinging across some other roof, perhaps? Pytor felt disloyal for the thought.

In the end, it was Efram, the priest, who found Christopher. Two hours later, when most of the men had given up, the old cleric came quietly, tapped Pytor and Guillaume on the shoulder, and beckoned for them to follow.

Silently, they crossed the inner court and entered the chapel through the main doors. It was a small building that had been tucked into an interior corner of the surrounding walls, but thanks to the habitual ostentation of the del-Aurvres, it made up in ornament and splendor for what it lacked in size. Even on this gloomy day, the stained glass was radiant, and the furnishings of the altar glistened with gold, embroidered silk, and gems.

Efram tottered along the side aisle and, putting his finger to his lips, led his two companions down into the crypt. They stepped slowly and silently as they went down the stairs, and Pytor heard, growing louder as they descended, the sound of dry sobbing.

The chapel was gothic. The crypt, dark and low-ceilinged, was romanesque. Eleven generations of delAurvres were

buried here, and the air was heavy with death and wealth.
Flat stones marked the resting places of the few barons who
had decided that their Creator was best met humbly, but
recumbent figures in armor and finery filled the room.

And, off in the corner, where slept Roger, a pitifully thin
figure was kneeling, embracing the cold effigy with both
arms, one cheek against the stone face. He was sobbing,
but between sobs he was speaking. Pytor drew near. The
words, muffled, took on shape.

"I'm sorry," Christopher was saying. "I'm sorry."

Pytor and Guillaume lifted him gently and took him back
to his room. And now Christopher seemed docile. He stared
at the ceiling, the tears coming still, but he drank his medicine without complaint. But Pytor, though he rejoiced inwardly at this change for the better, worried still, for
Christopher's utterances had turned into a quiet litany of
contrition.

"I'm sorry," he said, over and over. "I'm sorry."

Yvonnet a'Verne, baron of Hypprux, had taken after his
great uncle, Roger of Aurverelle. Through the inbred marital liaisons of Adria, Hypprux—along with almost every
major barony of the land—had ties with a multitude of noble
houses; and the fact that Yvonnet had acquired Roger's sheer
physical size was, perhaps, something of the luck of the
draw. Yvonnet, however, did not mind this at all, for Roger's stature had gone hand in hand with a willingness to
resort to physical violence even under the mildest of prov-
ocations, and the baron of Hypprux was quite willing to
capitalize on his ancestor's reputation.

At present, though, he was only glowering at some bad
news. "He's back?" he said.

Lengram a'Lowins, chamberlain of Hypprux, nodded.
"The reports are fairly reliable," he said. "We don't have
any . . . ah . . . informants in Aurverelle, but for this it
wasn't necessary. Christopher returned about a month ago."

"So why haven't I heard from my dear cousin?" Yvonnet
shifted a little on his bed, put his big hands behind his head.
He knew perfectly well why he had not heard. Christopher
despised him. Well, that was fine. He despised Christopher.
Silly little knightly thing! And now, added to his hatred was
the fact that, because of his cousin's return, Aurverelle was
suddenly out of his reach once again.

Lengram's eyebrow lifted. "I . . . ah . . . suppose that he has not had time."

"Is he sick?"

"Well . . . yes. Indications are that he's . . . ah . . . mad."

Aurverelle moved a little closer again. "Good," said Yvonnet. "Let him be mad. Take a message to Bishop Alphonse."

Lengram took a step away from the bed, and Yvonnet saw the look of astonishment that turned to the slow, sullen anger of insult. Lengram was a nobleman: he was not a messenger or a servant.

Yvonnet did not care. Lengram's vices paralleled his own, and sometimes, in this very bed, Lengram's body paralleled his own. Mutual vice, mutual silence . . . a silence that preserved their lives and their reputation. Lengram would do as he was told.

"Tell him to have someone look in on Christopher. A nice, friendly friar, perhaps. I want to know just how mad Christopher is. And I want it to be able to stand up before the assembled barons. Now, off with you, my little *mosca*."

Lengram hesitated.

"Something else?"

"A message from Paul delMari, baron of Furze. His fosterling, Martin Osmore, will be going home come spring. Martin will be coming this way with gifts and greetings." Lengram shrugged. "The customary progress home . . . save that, since Martin is . . . ah . . . common, it won't be much of a progress."

Yvonnet regarded Lengram ironically. The chamberlain's sense of superiority was based solely on the blood in his veins. Martin's father, Matthew, was the mayor of Saint Blaise, and could have bought Lengram and all his goods, houses, and servants several times over. Baron Paul was not so worried about class distinctions as some, and given the wealth of Saint Blaise and its mayor, Yvonnet could understand why.

But Martin . . . Yvonnet settled back, pursed his lips. He knew Martin. Very well, in fact. "Wasn't that the Martin that was at my coming of age party three years ago? Thin, dark lad? Face like a girl's? And other parts of other sorts . . . ?"

Lengram flushed. Yvonnet wondered: jealousy? Probably. Lengram would just have to learn his place.

Lengram's eyes had narrowed. "You want Martin, don't you?"

Yvonnet laughed. "Who wouldn't?"

"What about . . . ah . . . Ypris?"

"What the hell are they doing now?"

Lengram cast his eyes up at the ceiling as though choosing words, but Yvonnet knew that it was merely a ploy designed to make him wait for the news. Such was Lengram's revenge for the mention of Martin. "The embassy from Rome that you sent did not . . . ah . . . impress them at all," he said at last, "even with the soldiers. The good monsignor and his servants were beaten before they could even reach the church, and the burghers . . ." He shrugged. ". . . killed several of the soldiers. I . . . ah . . . heard it was rather the *Maillotins* all over again."

Yvonnet was on his feet. "Those *bastards*! Doing that to an anointed representative of God!"

Lengram shrugged. "If Avignon sent an embassy to us, what would you do?"

Yvonnet glowered. Lengram was showing his university snobbery again. Such things, the baron was sure, merited a place in hell even more than a few prick-to-prick encounters in a sodomitical bed. "That's different."

"Is it?"

"Boniface is for God," said Yvonnet, wondering why he was even bothering to argue. "Benedict is for Satan."

"Oh . . . indeed . . ." Lengram was nodding a bit too distinctly. "Which explains why the townspeople were . . . ah . . . calling the legate the Antichrist."

"Shut up."

Lengram's look was just as ironic as Yvonnet's had been. "Well, what do you propose to do?"

"They're putting on airs down there," Yvonnet mumbled. "They think themselves as great as Hypprux. If it weren't for Hypprux, the cloth industry wouldn't exist in Ypris."

Lengram cocked an eyebrow. "I repeat: what do you propose to do?"

Yvonnet swung his legs out of bed and stood. If he could not knock immediate sense into Ypris, he would do it to this insolent chamberlain. And when Martin came, Lengram would see just how fast his place could be filled by the slender lad from Saint Blaise. *"Shut up!"*

Roger's heritage was, once again, effective, and Lengram fell silent.

The room finally came back to him.

Lying amid featherbeds, comforters, and pillows, Christopher delAurvre, twelfth baron of Aurverelle, stared at the dark-beamed ceiling. Countless times before, he had been greeted in the morning by this same assortment of dark beams and white plaster, the trio of arched glass windows streaming with new light, the hangings, the bound chests, the heavy wardrobes flanking the fireplace; but now with years and memories intervening, his familiarity possessed no substance, held for him no more reality than a traveling miracle play—painted canvas, wings of glitter and glue, wooden swords, human entrails straight from the butchered pigs—or the fevered dreams of home and safety that had visited him as he had shivered in bracken and caves from Wallachia to Guelders. It was a familiarity reflected distantly and deeply, as from the bottom of a dark pool. He might as well have been a stranger in this place.

He passed a hand over his face and was startled to find himself clean shaven, to run his fingers across bare skin and through hair that barely reached his shoulders. Gone were the briars and the beard, and now he thought he recollected the barber hacking off the mats and tangles, his eyes moist at the sight of his master's condition.

Master?

Christopher closed his eyes and sighed, feeling still the innumerable aches, the rawness of skin burnt by sun and wind, the fevered clarity of a mind bleached as white as an old man's hair. Master. Master of what? Of Aurverelle? Of himself? Why, who was he? Who was this skeleton of a man lying in state in a bedroom of Aurverelle? The same Christopher who had set off on a May morning with fifty men and a suit of new armor to join the nobility of France on a futile and arrogant quest? No, impossible.

He started to laugh, then: a hoarse, sardonic burst of hilarity that echoed off the walls and rattled the loose panes in the windows. And if the sky fell, they would uphold it on the points of their lances! Of course they would! And Bayazet would fall down on his knees before those most

Christian knights and kiss the turds of their horses. To be sure!

As though in response to his laughter, the door opened. Pytor entered, his face concerned, and he did not look much relieved when Christopher, after taking a good look at his seneschal, burst out with second round of giggles.

"Master is pleased to be merry this morning," said Pytor.

Christopher stifled his humor. Even if it did not frighten Pytor, it racked a pair of what were obviously fluid-filled lungs. He considered coughing for a moment, but decided that if he started, he might not stop for some time. Best to save the retching and gagging for later. "What else is there to be?"

Pytor looked suddenly hopeful. "Does master know me?"

Christopher sighed. Pytor would doubtless address him in the third person on his deathbed. "Yes, yes. I know you, Pytor." He lifted his head, looked at the windows. How long? Three years? No, more. This might well be his deathbed. "Have I been raving?"

"For weeks now, master."

"Quite mad, then."

Pytor colored, looked away. "I . . ."

"Come on. Come on. Tell me. Was I out in the courtyard eating grass? Copulating with the mares, perhaps?"

The seneschal shook his head. "Master was delirious with fever."

Pytor was being polite. It was more than a fever, and Christopher knew it. There were many things that could destroy a soul, and he had been intimate with at least two of them.

Upon attempting to sit up, Christopher found that his head was splitting and, with a grimace, fell back onto the pillows. Pytor came forward, took a cup from the side table, and held it to his master's lips. Christopher gagged on the contents. "What . . . is this? It's like being clubbed over the head with an ivy bush."

"Guillaume brought it. He says that it is good for master."

Fluids, Christopher thought. Fluids and herbs. It made sense. No, he would not die. Living was worse. He would live: that was, unfortunately, the best he could expect.

He took another swallow, forced it down, gasped at the taste. "Grandfather wouldn't have put up with this. He wouldn't have needed it, either."

"Baron Roger was a . . . considerably more robust man," said Pytor, gently but insistently proffering the cup.

Pytor was being polite again. In his youth, Roger had killed boars with his bare hands, had survived, undoctored, wounds that would have killed another. His political machinations had been as grandiose as his stature, as enormous as the vices he had embraced in his youth . . . and then suddenly abjured in his prime.

The sudden change was legendary. There was even a song about it. *He had the Free Towns in his pouch and let them go again!*

Something had happened. . . .

Well, Christopher thought, something had happened at Nicopolis, too. And now Roger's descendent—the family sperm perhaps getting a little tired out after twelve generations of plotting, fighting, magnificently lecherous del-Aurvres—lay like a sick girl, lapping slimy decoctions out of a silver cup.

Christopher drank until the medicine was gone, and then he coughed for the better part of an hour. Pytor held him while he hacked up the fluid and phlegm, and when his master was finished and exhausted, laid him back down, blotted his forehead, and tucked the covers around him.

Like a sick girl. And what had happened to Roger that he had spent his last forty years puttering in his garden, planting an avenue of peach trees, and fishing in that part of the river least likely to reward him with fish?

"Did many people see me when I was mad?" said Christopher.

"None who would recognize master."

"Well, maybe I'll have to do a few capers around the town . . . just so that they'll remember me. Did I make a good bear? I'd like to believe that a delAurvre can do something right."

Pytor looked disturbed, groped for words. "Master had a hard journey home."

Christopher snorted weakly. "Journey? Ha! *Journey* implies a beginning, an end, and a goal. We *journeyed,* for example, to Nicopolis. Beginning: for the French, Dijon— for me, Aurverelle. End for everyone: disaster. Goal . . ."

"The Holy Land," Pytor prompted hopefully.

"Vainglory," said Christopher. He tried to roll over and found that he was too exhausted to manage it. Well, then, best to lie here like a log. A sweaty log. A sweaty log from a weak-loined family. "Now, coming home was no journey. It was wandering. The wandering of a madman. Capering here, capering there. Begging black bread with beans in it— it's rather good, you know, when your belly's empty—and an occasional cup of soup for the mercy of God, but not often, because the monasteries didn't want my sort of riff-raff cluttering up their hospices. . . ." Christopher fell silent for a moment, and then the delAurvre temper flared. "And where in hell's name was God's mercy when we climbed the plateau of Nicopolis?" he raged hoarsely. "Back in the monasteries with ale and fat capons and nice thick night-boots?"

He brooded on the wreck of a body he had brought back to his castle. "If you hadn't found me in the tavern, I'd have probably wandered off into the Aleser in the morning. I didn't even know where I was. Good riddance."

"My master came home," said Pytor softly, his deep voice a gentle rumble, and Christopher heard the grief that his angry words had caused. "We are all very glad to have master with us once again. There was great joy in the town when I announced his arrival, and many masses are being said for his recovery."

And there it was. Though Christopher could not keep his nose from wrinkling at the thought, Aurverelle, all of it, from Pytor down to the filthiest stable boy or the most debauched prostitute, was happy that their boyishly handsome baron was home. They cared nothing about his failure or his grandfather's failure. Their master was home: that was all that mattered.

It disturbed him that he felt so little in response. Even the sight of this room with his favorite tapestries on the walls and the sun rising swiftly over the battlements of Aurverelle brought no flicker of joy, no sense of welcome. Baron? He was no more a baron than his horse—and the Bulgarian peasants had eaten that. Noble? Nobility was a lie, a tedious deception, a bunch of men adorning themselves with metal and jewels and riding about with big words and sharp swords and wagons full of silks and cushions and pavilions and brass stoves with which to make little pies.

And Christopher had played his last part in it.

He stared up at the ceiling, uncaring, numb. Pytor was wringing his hands raw with worry. And the village was saying masses for him. Jerome, doubtless, was busy with his accounts. And—

"And where's my wife, Pytor?" he said suddenly. "Where's Anna? Is she happy I'm back?"

Pytor shifted uncomfortably. "She is dead, master. The plague took her two years ago."

Dead. Anna with her piety and her vigils and her incessant and compulsive tithes and endowments. Rosaries in the morning, vespers with the priest. . . .

It was Anna who had pressed him most earnestly to join the crusade. *A fitting gesture for a nobleman,* she had said. *A fitting deed for a delAurvre. A battle for God.* And she had kept at him, prattling on, perhaps knowing in her woman's heart—wordlessly, instinctively—that his weaknesses would eventually give her the advantage.

Easy enough for her: she had not had to face the swords and stakes at Nicopolis. And now he was home, alive, and now Anna was dead. No more rosaries. No more vespers. No more *but we can't: it's a holy day, Christopher.*

It was too perfect, too ironic, too well-balanced a fate; and suddenly Christopher was laughing again, a long, braying series of mirthless guffaws that clawed at his throat, pounded at his aching head, and sent Pytor running for Guillaume.

They gave him something to make him sleep.

CHAPTER 4

The town burned as towns burn: red flames fluttering like banners against the blue Italian sky, smoke streaming away like a young girl's scream, sudden and brittle topplings of towers and walls. Above all, like the skeleton of a bishop's miter, rose the gutted tower of the church in which the last band of citizens had held out for one or two additional hours.

But pikes and pitchforks had been no match for spears and swords, and now the former inhabitants of Montalenghe—those who were left alive—stood huddled and under guard as their town crackled and snapped itself into charcoal. Some, to be sure, had fled into the foothills of the Alps, but Berard of Onella was not one to care about what he did not have, and therefore those who had escaped had already ceased to exist for him. The town was destroyed, he and his men had its money and its food, and there were a few servants and slaves out of the bargain. Why worry about what was not in one's pocket?

What was in one's pocket, though, was a different matter, and when one of the girls of the town broke away and ran for the fields, lifting her long skirts to free her legs, Berard, laughing, shouted to his men. One of them rode after her, caught her easily, and returned, dragging her by the hair. Berard rubbed the stubble of his beard appraisingly. She was fortunate: she was not bad looking. She would find a place in the camp.

He tipped his head back, shifted his rubbing to the back of his neck where his helmet had chafed throughout a warm day. Good weather, good profit—a good day all around. The rest of the winter would be, if not luxurious, then at least comfortable. Not bad for a band of mercenaries who had so recently faced near-annihilation at the hands of the Bolognese.

It was refreshing, he decided, to work only for himself

and his men, to have told the squabbling city states of northern Italy to go to the Devil along with their schemes, their grand plans, and their intrigues. What had that Bolognese affair been about, anyway? He still was not sure. Probably Florence and Milan again, with Gian Galeazzo paying off the Pavanese to make enough trouble for Padua that Venice would have to give up its very temporary support for the Signoria and turn its attention to its closer ally; which meant, of course, in the twisted drainage pattern that was Italian politics, that Florence would have been stymied in its efforts to bring Genoa under control, since Gian Galeazzo was waiting for a commitment of men and provisions far enough away from the city to allow for a quick strike. Bologna, then, abandoned by Ferrara and Ravenna (which would, naturally, ally themselves with Venice), would fall in behind Genoa and arrange for a troublesome band of *condottieri* in the employ, or perhaps not, of Modena, which might have been supporting the Florentines, or might not (it was never wise to commit oneself), to be eradicated.

Something like that.

In the end, though, only Giovanni da Barbiano, the captain of the mercenary band, had been executed. No ransom, no chance for an exchange of prisoners, no appeal. Caught, killed. That was it.

And Berard, elected leader in a quick agreement whispered among the men in the Italian night, had led the company away into the darkness, thoroughly disgusted with the vagaries of politics. He had actually thought Giovanni to have been on Bologna's side. But, then again, maybe not.

Yes, this was better. No politics, just money. For a minute, as the prisoners were taken away to be sorted, sold, killed, or kept—the men with bowed heads, the women weeping with fear at the prospect of being used bloody that night—Berard toyed with names for his little band. *The Fellowship of Acquisition.* That sounded good. Very good. It said it all. Simple, straightforward.

He looked up to see his lieutenant, Jehan delMari, approaching on horseback, cantering across the fields with a soldier's casual ease. "Well, Messire Jehan," Berard said as the young man drew near, "what do you think of today's work?"

"Not bad at all." Jehan, blond and boyish, glanced at the prisoners, the stacked sacks of grain, the chests of valuables: Montalenghe had been small but well off. "Though I think I'd rather fight other knights. That would smack a trifle more of the noble than this . . ." He examined the peasants. An hour ago some of them had been up in the church tower heaving down stones. Now the valiant defenders shuffled through the dust, thoroughly dejected. ". . . pigsticking."

Berard laughed. "I'm sure that the rewards will flavor this pork to your liking. I imagine that we'll all eventually be quite well off. Possibly as rich as—"

"I don't want to talk about that," Jehan said quickly. "Total up your accounts and give me my share, but leave me out of commoners' work. If I'd wanted to soil my hands with money, I could have stayed in Saint Blaise and sold cheese."

"Hmm. More gold in Saint Blaise than cheese, unless things have changed a great deal since I left Adria."

"The mayor makes cheese." Jehan wrinkled his nose. "Just make sure I get my share, and I'll be satisfied."

Jehan was younger than he looked, Berard had decided long ago. Younger, and still hot with the fire of the blood that turned even commonplaces into matters of life, death, and personal reputation. To be sure, the lad could fight— for all Jehan's disdain, the burghers of Saint Blaise had obviously trained him well enough—and it was because of his temper and his rash decision to risk a skirmish at idiotic odds that only Giovanni had perished as a result of Bologna's liquid allegiances. Still, Jehan had risen about as far as Berard estimated was safe to allow.

"You did well today," was all he said.

Jehan shrugged. "Fighting is my life. It's simple, direct, straightforward. I like it that way."

Ah, the surety of the young. Berard smiled and folded his arms. "Tell me: don't you ever have any regrets about leaving Adria? After all, you could be master of Shrinerock if you went back. Baron of Furze and all that."

Jehan wrinkled his nose again. "The master of Shrinerock reads in his library, rides occasionally to the hunt, and entertains visitors elegantly."

"Visitors? Oh, yes: I've heard stories about the Elves . . ."

Jehan glared at him, unsettled and angry both. "Be serious, Berard."

It was an old tease, but Jehan reacted no better to it for that. Berard spread his hands. "Elves or not, it doesn't sound like a bad life at all," he said. "I wouldn't mind having Shrinerock for a house. I'd have silks and a golden cup, and I'd make the peasants dance for me every night. At least when I didn't have a pretty girl in my bed."

Jehan laughed. "And you'd never get near it."

Berard contemplated the provisions and money that now were his and his men's. Italy, though, was not the place to stay. Perhaps, come spring, they could cross into France and see what the other free companies had left of the place. For now, though, his men would be comfortable. "Impregnable, eh?"

"Oh, yes," said Jehan. "There are ways in, of course, that aren't normally guarded because almost no one knows about them, but the defenses are otherwise magnificent. David of Saint George designed it back in my great-great-grandfather's day, and it's actually been improved upon since then."

Shrinerock . . . and ways in. Berard found himself considering the future. He did not care about what he did not have, but he cared a good deal about what he *might* have. "Ah . . . by the way, Jehan," he said. "I think I've come up with a name for our little band. What do you think of 'The Fellowship of Acquisition'?"

Jehan looked at him with a twisted mouth. "Berard, that is evidence either of the most abominable taste or the most magnificent humor I can imagine."

Shrinerock. Interesting. What a life! "Do you like it?"

Jehan did not answer for a time. The stacked bags and chests glowed in the sunlight. "It will do."

The flames crackled and snapped. Berard heard a girl crying out somewhere.

"SCREEAARRAACH!"

Christopher opened his eyes, sat up in bed, and found his startled gaze returned by a hairy caricature of a man squatting on the windowsill. Cold winter air was pouring in through the unfastened shutters, and the caricature was waving its over-long arms about as it clutched the mushy remains of what had once been a pear. Its face, as hairy as the rest of it, writhed and contorted, alternately puckering up and opening out like a mass of dough being kneaded.

Christopher blinked. The monkey blinked back. On an impulse, Christopher bared his teeth and stuck out his tongue. The monkey did likewise.

"Very good," said the baron. "You'd make a fine nobleman."

The remains of the pear smacked into the headboard inches from his head. With a derisive wave and a lewd gesture, the monkey fled through the open window and down the outside wall of the castle.

Christopher got up and staggered to the window. The monkey was gone. "A fine nobleman, indeed," he murmured.

He closed and fastened the shutters, then turned around to face a room with which he had become much too familiar during his convalescence. Flat on his back, spoon fed sops and broth by Pytor or Raffalda or one of the maids from the kitchen, lifted bodily from bed to chamber pot and then back again, he had been given ample opportunity to count the number of chisel marks on the ceiling beams, enumerate the gilt threads in the bed hangings, learn the intricacies of tapestry stitches.

Today, though, he felt well enough to get up . . . or at least to make faces at monkeys. This was a distinct improvement. Perhaps the wretched stuff that Guillaume and Pytor had been ladling down his throat possessed some virtue after all.

Dizzy and weak now more from long inaction than from illness, he lurched to the side table, poured water from the ewer into its companion basin, and washed, still marveling at the feel of a shaved face and groomed hair. The open shutters had allowed the room to chill, and though, naked as he was, he shivered, it was a good shiver, one that told him that he was alive.

"I suppose I should be grateful," he said to himself, running his hands back through his hair. "To whom and for what, I'm not exactly sure."

He shivered again. Time for clothes. Anna's wardrobe, he discovered after opening it out of curiosity, was empty. He shrugged. Perhaps she had been buried with all her gowns. That would have been fitting.

His own, though, was well stocked, and holding tightly to the door so as not to topple, he pawed one-handed through the silks and satins and velvets. The delAurvres dressed well. So did the nobles of France, though Nevers and his company had, he recalled, preferred green. Green gowns. Green livery. Green tents. Green saddle blankets. Had it been possible to make green gold for the tableware, he was certain that it would have been done.

And then there were the lances and the tabards, the pennons and the banners and the twenty-four wagons full of delicacies and sweet wines. And that was just for the lordling of Burgundy and his immediate retinue. . . .

Christopher, spirals of light swirling through his vision, groped until he found tunic and stockings of plain black. Black, that was it. Mourning. Mourning for Aurverelle. Mourning for poor dead Christopher, who, though still alive, had seen what shabbiness underlay this glittering business of nobility.

He thought about summoning servants, but decided against it. He had gaped and capered through much of Europe without servants: he could put on his own clothes now. Odd, though, that the screech from the monkey had not brought everyone running.

Sitting on the side of the bed and resting frequently, he dressed; but when he knelt, opened a chest, and looked for shoes, he could find only a few of the pointed, curled, stuffed-toe monstrosities favored by his peers. Impatiently, he tossed them aside, and by the time he found a pair of soft boots that were as unfigured and unadorned as the rest of his somber garb, he was panting with exertion and wondering whether, now that he was dressed, he would actually be able to reach the door.

But as he had forced himself across a continent, so he drove himself across the room. Let Nevers and Boucicaut whimper about not having beds and viands of sufficient delicacy. This shambling wreck here was a delAurvre.

The door swung open on greased hinges and presented him with the sight of a serving boy sound asleep on the floor just outside the bedroom. Well, Christopher considered, it was early in the morning, and judging from the odor of wine, the lad had doubtless been carousing the night before. But that did nothing to explain the curious silence that hung about Castle Aurverelle. Where there should have been movement, shouts, the clatter of boots and spurs up and down steps, and the intermittent explosions of David's artistic temperament down in the kitchen, this morning there was nothing.

Christopher looked up and down the hall, strained his ears, heard only a faint, distant humming.

Odd. Leaving the boy asleep, he tottered down the corridor with one hand on the wall for support, following the half-felt, half-heard sound that had made itself a part of the morning. It led him to the stairwell, down, along another hallway.

Empty. All empty. Castle Aurverelle was as empty as its baron. He might well have been wandering through one of those deserted cities of African legend: food still steaming on the table, wine in the cups, merchandise left out in the marketplace . . . but no people. Just gone.

He stepped out into the courtyard. The sunlight was dazzling after his long stay indoors, and he blinked at the walls about him and at the great keep that rose up one hundred and eighty feet. Far above, the black ensign of the delAurvres—a knight standing against a lion—was fluttering in the breeze, but with the exception of one lone watchman standing guard on the lofty parapet (ah, not quite entirely deserted, then!) he was alone.

As he crossed the court towards the chapel, the humming resolved itself into voices. Plainchant. Snatches of polyphony. Still unsteady, still blinking, he climbed the steps to the heavy church door and pulled it slowly open. Incense and song rolled out to meet him. The walls were streaming with the glory of stained glass, candles glowed on the altar, and the chapel was full of worshipers kneeling in prayer.

Anna's words—wheedling, prying—came back to him: *A fitting deed for a delAurvre. A battle for God.*

For God? Nonsense. For booty, perhaps; for a chance to force one's manhood between the thighs of some struggling, conquered, and thoroughly filthy girl; for the chance to hear one's name praised in the name of chivalry or prowess—but not for God.

Yet God had sent him off to Nicopolis. Someone else— the Devil, maybe—had brought him back, but God had sent him off. And Christopher, standing in the doorway of a chapel washed in the brilliant hues of morning and the misty glory of worship, felt no sense of the holy or the mystical, only a dull ache of unfulfilled mission and quest denied.

And what did you get out of Nicopolis, Lord? What did

*my sufferings give to you? They certainly didn't give any-
thing to me.*

Shaking his head, about to turn and depart as silently as
he had come, he noticed that the choir had faltered into
silence. The priest—old Efram, was it not?—was staring
silently at him, and, one by one, those gathered for Mass
turned to look also. Christopher heard gasps and whispers,
and off to one side he saw Pytor, who had apparently compromised for once his stalwart Orthodoxy, kneeling along
with the rest, staring along with the rest.

Pytor found his voice. "Master."

Christopher looked about, still numb. "What's going on?
The whole castle is empty."

Efram, vested in white and gold, answered from the altar.
"My lord baron, it is Christmas Day."

"Oh." Another silence. Feet shuffled. Glances were exchanged. Christopher saw the unspoken question. Just how
mad was the baron?

He lifted his arm, pointed out into the courtyard. "Will
someone tell me why in God's name that monkey is roaming
about loose?"

Mad enough.

"Master," said Pytor, "it was Lady Anna's. It escaped
shortly before she died."

Christopher stifled a bitter laugh. The monkey had escaped. He had not. "Well, have someone catch it. It's
throwing fruit about."

The eyes that were turned towards him—young and old,
male and female—were wide.

"And have someone fetch me some breakfast when you're
done," he added. "I'm tired of gruel. Get me some black
bread." He turned for the door, stopped, turned back. "The
kind with beans in it."

Leaving the startled congregation behind, thwarting with
a single gesture Pytor's desire to follow him, Christopher
made his way back across the courtyard. His legs were
shaking with fatigue and his vision was blurry, but he did
not return to his room. Rather, he climbed, doggedly, step
by step, up to the top of the great keep. The startled watchman made as if to kneel to him, but Christopher told him
brusquely to stay on guard.

Turning away, the baron rested his elbows on the parapet
and stared out, first at the horizon where distant Furze and

Belroi were smears of soot and smoke, then at Malvern, gray and flecked with snow, and finally at the castle itself: towered and walled with the ponderous efficiency of the most belligerent, prideful, and arrogant family in all of Adria.

Generation upon generation of delAurvres. And then his grandfather . . .

He had the Free Towns in his pouch and let them go again!
. . . and then himself.

A flash of movement. The monkey scuttled across a roof, bounded along a gutter, and then went hand-over-hand up a drain pipe, losing itself amid the rank of buttresses along the south edge of the chapel.

Christopher watched. "Don't let them catch you," he said softly. "Don't ever let them catch you."

CHAPTER 5

Christmas at Shrinerock was splendid. Of course it was. It had to be. It was always splendid. The fireplace roared with the trunks of whole trees, singers came from as far away as Castile to sing the elaborate *villancicos* that made everyone want to get up and dance to the quickly syncopated rhythms, the tables were covered with food and wine and subtleties. Laughter. Songs. Acrobats.

Outside, where the open tables were laid in invitation to any, haughty or lowly, who would come to share in the celebration, firelight flickered on the courtyard walls late into the night, and even the dusting of snow that fell seemed no more than a layer of frosting on a particularly delightful cake. Tenants who had flouted the estate laws and guards who had clapped those same tenants into leg shackles and marched them smartly before the bailiff got gloriously drunk together, sang together, commiserated together about the cruelties of life that caused one to break the law and another to enforce it . . . and their wives gossiped and exchanged recipes for spiced wine.

Paul delMari liked that. Though a fortress, Shrinerock was a house. His house. He liked his house to be happy.

But though it seemed at times that there were smiling faces enough in Shrinerock to populate a kingdom and set it alaughing with the infectious merriment of the season, there were some faces missing, faces that had been absent at these celebrations for a long time. True, those who bore them had never come openly, and their laughter and healing and harping had always been confined to the private chambers of the castle, but Christmas was not Christmas without them, and because of their absence, Paul, as usual, found a touch of sadness in the merriment. The shadows between the candlelight and the firelight seemed darker, and the sparkles of flame that scintillated in the snowflakes held the accents of tears.

Youthful faces, faces touched with a light that was more than mortal. Some he would never see again. Others he hoped to see perhaps once or twice more, but he was afraid that he would not. The world was a darker place than it used to be, and it was growing darker.

And then, after Christmas, came a new year that, inevitably, would bring more losses, greater darkening. Jehan had left years ago and had never returned; and now, in a few months, Martin would be leaving. Living with such loss, expecting yet another, Paul did not have the heart to take in any more lads for training and nurturing: soon it would be just himself, Isabelle, and Catherine.

He wondered: what happened to humans with such memories and friendships and losses? Did they fade, too?

Still, outwardly, Paul was all smiles and cheer, going about the duties of a baron with the genial smile and bland good nature that had given him the reputation of being a trifle daft. He was not daft. His smiles were a lie—everybody lied in one way or another—that allowed him to pass off some of his stranger actions and opinions as mere eccentricities. The Inquisition had no sense of humor, but being quite mad itself, it understood madness.

But it was hard to be daft when one felt so sad, harder still to remember to keep one's tears confined to the shelter of one's bed and the arms of one's sister and wife.

Today, he was forgetting his smiles. He had the shutters in the west tower open to the cold air, and he was staring out the window at the lands that fell away beneath the steep, rocky precipice upon which his castle had been built. From below came the liquid sound of the waters of Saint Adrian's spring, as much a part of Shrinerock as the wood and stone. Off in the distance, though, was Malvern Forest, bare and gray and patched with the white of two-week-old snow. Not that far away, really. Mirya and Terrill and Natil could come for a visit if they wanted. The world was not yet that dark, and the hidden passage that led from the spring to the castle well was still open and unguarded.

He wished that he could hear Natil's harp . . . just once more. . . .

"Lord Baron."

Quick. Tears dried,
then.

"Hmmm?" he said,
Nicholas! And how are y

The steward of Shrine
Paul was bubbly. That too
many lies!

"I am quite well," said
silently acknowledged his firm
like Baron Paul had no busines
the health or circumstances of t
a visitor, my lord. Lake of Fur
me that it would please you to s

"Lake . . . hmmm." Paul p—— to be thinking
deeply, though he knew quite well who Lake was. "Lake-
lakelake . . . ah, yes. Lake. I did say that I would see him,
didn't I? Ha-ha! Where is he?"

Lake was in the lobby, but Paul instructed Nicholas to
bring him up to the library. Nicholas moved off solemnly,
an important man doing important work. Paul, for all his
forty years, bounded off in the direction of the library like
a boy with a piece of sugar waiting for him. Lies, he reflected, had their advantages. Another noble might have
steered his way through the castle like a Venetian galley and
therefore would have missed the utter joy of vaulting over
an astonished serving girl who was scrubbing the corridor
floor and sending her pelting away with a sustained shriek.

In the library, he settled himself in the big chair by the
fire and waited; and a short time later, Lake entered alone
with his cap in his hands. He gave Paul a heavyset bow, his
eyes downcast. Today the farmer, too, seemed to be wrapped
in a lie.

"Well, my man, what can I do for you?" said Paul. "Not
wanting to indenture yourself for more land, I hope. If you
work off any more contracts as quickly as you did your first,
I'm afraid I'll be calling *you* baron before too long!"

Lake looked uncomfortable. He was a hard worker. Almost inhumanly so. Always the first out in the fields, always
the last to go home. Thirty-five years ago he had come to
the estate with nothing but a bundle of clothes and a knife.
Now he owned his own land, employed his own men to
work it, and paid not fees but taxes to Shrinerock. If sweat
and labor could ennoble a man—as Abbot Wenceslas and

... that it did—Paul could indeed
...mself up to the baronage.

...ved by nature, and a bit solitary, too.
...table about people, especially important
...aul sensed that today he was uncomfortable
...easons, too. "It's na an indenture, m'lord," said
...It's my daughter, Vanessa."

...Vanessa. Ah! I remember her." Paul had, in fact, never
met her. "Lovely girl, simply lovely. Is she going to marry?
You know as well as I, Lake, that you don't need my permission for that."

"Nay," said Lake. "It's na that." He fidgeted. His gaze,
downcast until now, involuntarily rose to meet Paul's, and
for a moment, the baron wondered whether Lake's eyes were
reflecting more light than they should have.

It was possible, he supposed. After all, his own mother,
Janet Darci, had possessed a bit of elven blood. But Paul
pretended not to notice. Though the current fashion had
declared Elves to be a legend and belief in their existence
to be heretical, it was dangerous, even for a daft baron to
notice such things. "Certainly you can't be having any trouble with a suitable dowry, Lake."

"Well . . . ah . . . that is . . . me and tha wife want
sa'thing a little better for her. Vanessa is a . . . bright girl.
I think that sa'day she could . . . ah . . ."

Yes, Lake had his lies, too.

"We thought," said the farmer laboriously, "that maybe
a position would be best for her. Perhaps in a trade. She
could better herself."

Paul nodded slowly. He understood. And Jehan had
wanted to better himself, too. And Jehan was gone. "Ah,"
he said brightly, "very commendable of you, Lake."

"We thought you might be able t' help, m'lord."

"Well . . ." Paul stared at the ceiling with eyes that he
occasionally suspected showed a little too much light of
their own. "I have the personal acquaintance of some artisans in Furze—they made the new hangings in the hall,
Lake: have Nicholas show them to you on your way out—
weavers and embroideresses . . . affiliated with the Béguines, you know." Feeling Lake's increased discomfort,
he winked. "They behave themselves, don't you worry a
bit! My lord bishop doesn't worry about them. Actually, I

suspect that he worries more about the Ypris benefices he lost to Benedict than about the Béguines, ha-ha!''

Lake was not reassured. "Please, m'lord," he said. "Not Furze. We were thinking o' . . . ah . . . Saint Blaise."

"Oh, the Free Towns." Lies, lies, lies. Lake was plainly dissembling, but Paul could not help that. Lake did not pry into the delMari family and its visitors and customs, and Paul would not pry into the motives of his hard-working and talented tenant. "Very prosperous, the Free Towns."

"Aye, and Saint Blaise is friendly."

"Well, yes," said Paul. "Quite friendly, especially since my father married the mayor's daughter." Paul felt a genuine smile well up. What a couple that had been! Charles: courtly, amorous, studious; Janet: bright, practical, and intelligent, with a spark of immortal blood that made her every word and gesture a joy. Such a birthright he had received from him! With a pang, he wondered what kind of birthright he had given Jehan.

I want to play at tables, the boy had said in his last letter home, *not do accounts on them*.

Barons like Christopher delAurvre went off on crusades. Barons like Paul delMari, it appeared, stayed at home and gave parties. But Paul kept his smile. "Can't get much friendlier than that, can we?"

"Nay, m'lord."

"Hmmm . . ." Paul examined Lake's request, found nothing amiss. Lake, father of two sons and three daughters, could well afford another dowry, even if Vanessa were exceptionally ugly, which, given the light in her father's eyes, Paul knew she was not. But Vanessa's inclinations might have been towards independence, and the Towns, though their legendary tolerance had been slipping for some years, still at least understood independence. A young girl with ambitions for more than marriage or a nunnery could do much, much worse than make her way to the Free Towns.

"I think it can be managed, Lake," he said. "We can find her something in Saint Blaise. She's an intelligent girl, isn't she? Ha-ha, I knew it! She'll want something quiet, I'm sure. Can she read? Yes? Bonnerol doing his job, then? Good. How soon did you want to do this?"

"Please, m'lord: as soon a' possible."

Lake was anxious, eager. Lies. Everybody lied in one way or another. What was Lake's way?

Paul nodded slowly. "Yes, that would be for the best,
wouldn't it? But . . ." He got up and went to the window.
He knew what he could do for Vanessa. Simple, really. But
that brought him straight back to Martin. And Martin made
him think of Jehan. "But won't you miss her?"

Lake bent his head quickly.

The glass window gave a distorted and wavy view of the
landscape below. Paul could see it, and yet much remained
hidden, obscure. Just like that. Just like Paul delMari.

He had sent his son away, and now he was gone. He had
to try to tell Lake about what might be the results of his
request. "I miss my Jehan," he said. "Just about ten years
ago, he went off to Saint Blaise to be fostered with Mayor
Matthew. The mayor's son, Martin, came here." He shook
his head sadly: even the daft could be melancholic upon
occasion. "Jehan never liked people he deemed below his
status. Manly little chap." He laughed softly, but Jehan was
gone. He had no son, only a much loved fosterling and a
few memories. And Martin was leaving. "He left the household there after only a few years. Wandered off to make his
own way. He'll turn up someday, I imagine, but Isabelle
and I both miss him. He was our only child. . . ." He turned
back from the window. "Are you *sure* you want to do this,
Lake? Saint Blaise is a good distance away, and it's a big
city. Quite a change from Furze Hamlet. Are you sure you
don't want something closer and . . . smaller? Saint Brigid
is only two days' ride from here. It's a nice little town—"

But he broke off at the sight of Lake's tense, frightened
face. The farmer was shaking his head violently: short, abrupt
swings as though he were palsied. "I'm sure, m'lord. I think
it's for tha best. An' it ha' better be Saint Blaise, too."

"All right." Paul gave a last look at the window. Maybe
someday he would see Jehan riding up the road from the
lowlands, perhaps clad in armor won in some far-off battle,
a spear in his hand and the delMari griffin and silver star on
his shield. "Maybe it will indeed be for the best." He
shrugged, mustered his little grin. "After all, anything is
possible. There are only differing degrees of probability."

Lake started.

Paul watched him understandingly. Compassion. The
Elves had always spoken of compassion. It was an old way,
a good way, and he would hold to it. "I'll help you, Lake.

Martin is due to return to Saint Blaise in the spring, and Vanessa can go with him. Mayor Matthew has his pretensions, but if I send him a letter telling him to find her a good position where she can learn an honorable trade, he'll do it.''

Lake rose and bowed. ''Thankee, m'lord. We're deeply obliged to you.''

Paul offered his hand, smiled at Lake's grip. They could not acknowledge one another—Lake himself perhaps did not even know—but it was good that what bare traces of the old blood were left in the world could touch in friendship. ''You tell Vanessa that she'll be well taken care of, Lake. Ha-ha! You tell her that she has adventures—yes, adventures!—ahead of her.''

''Thankee, m'lord. I wi'.'' And bowing again, Lake went to the door. Nicholas, unctuous and official, had been waiting for him, and the steward escorted the farmer along the hall, down the stairs, and out of the castle.

Pondering, Paul examined his hand. A touch. It was not much, but it would have to do.

Lies. And it was getting to be so dark!

''*Black* bread?'' David's voice, faint with horror, echoed off the walls of the kitchen.

''With beans in it.'' Pytor nodded.

''Beans?''

''Beans.''

''Dear God.'' The chef of Aurverelle passed a hand over his face. ''But he can't *pos*sibly want to eat *that*! It's . . . it's not . . .''

''Not noble,'' Pytor prompted.

''Yes. Exactly.''

Pytor shrugged. It was Christopher who gave the orders in Aurverelle, not the seneschal, not the bailiff, nor, for that matter, the chef. ''It is now.''

''And those . . . *rags* he's wearing.''

These days, the kitchen was not a busy place, for the castle possessed less than one third of its usual population and therefore, the sound of snickering from one of the kitchen boys who was stirring a pot was loud in the silence.

But it was Baron Christopher who was being snickered at, and black bread or no, David whirled and clouted the lad on the back of the head. The boy resumed his stirring

attentively. David glared at him, then turned back to Pytor.
"Rags!"

"Raffalda would not allow the baron to go about in rags,
Master Chef," said Pytor, though he himself had unconsciously come to think of Christopher's garb as such. "His
clothes are simply of black and brown. He prefers it that
way."

"But . . . where's his *style*?"

"In black bread, at present."

David sniffed. "It's in*ed*ible."

Pytor cleared his throat: a deep rumble. "Are you telling me, Master Chef, that one who trained under the great
Taillevent himself is incapable of making a decent loaf of
black bread?"

The chef shook his head. "You have to under*stand*, Master Seneschal. This bread he wants. It's something . . . else.
It's full of . . ."

"Beans."

"Well, yes. Beans. But not just beans. It's rye and spelt
and barley and brank, the *coars*est of flours, with only
enough wheat in it to keep it from turning into a *rock*. Peasants are fit to eat it, but not anybody of any *de*cency."

Pytor, a peasant—and an escaped slave—who had eaten
black bread with beans and worse in it, said nothing. One
had to be a little tolerant of David. And, these days, of
Christopher, too.

"And peasants are . . . well . . . they're just *dif*ferent,"
David went on. "They can make a meal of thorns and acorns
if they want. Black bread is nothing to them. It's actually
good for them. But the baron . . ."

Muttering inwardly at the chef's casual bigotry, Pytor tried
to be diplomatic. "My good chef, the baron had more than
his fill of thorns and acorns during his journey home, and
he told me that a little black bread will not hurt him."
Baron Christopher, of course, had said nothing of the sort:
he gave orders, not explanations. "Besides, he fears that
the noble food you customarily prepare for him might prove
to be too rich so soon after his illness. Therefore, now that
he can finally keep down something beyond gruel, he wants
black bread. And he will, of course, look forward to eating
your delicacies as soon as he is ready."

David glared. "*Black* bread?"

The Russian sighed. "With beans."

Another voice cackled, then shouted. "Lots of beans!" Startled, Pytor and David whirled to see Christopher and Jerome standing in the doorway. Christopher's hands were balled into fists, and he raised them up above his head as he leaped down the three steps to the flagstone floor, sending the kitchen boys running in fear. "Handfuls of beans! Buckets of beans! Bushels of beans!"

"Dear God," David whispered. "He's mad."

"And a little heap under the stairs!"

Pytor's eyes narrowed at the chef. "Master is as sane as you or I," he murmured in his deep basso. "Another disloyal word like that, Master Chef, and I will have you put in irons."

"Beans!" said Christopher as he snatched a dry apple from a barrel, and for a moment, Pytor was terrified that his master was going to gnaw it down to the core and then hurl what was left at the nearest head.

But the apple, uneaten, smacked into the hands of the kitchen lad who had been snickering. "Next time," said Christopher, "laugh louder."

The boy was white. "Yes, m'lord."

"You hear me?" shouted Christopher. "Louder!" And then he whirled on David. *"Beans!"*

Faced with a direct confrontation with the master of Aurverelle, the chef wilted. "As you wish, Baron Christopher."

Christopher nodded, satisfied. "And a bowl of that lentil soup you make . . . the thick kind. The kind with the onions in it."

David nearly cried out in horror. "But I make *that* for the dogs when they're *sick*!"

Christopher was undeterred. He picked up another apple. "Such will be my supper until I inform you otherwise." The apple streaked at David's head, and the chef barely caught it in time. "Have an apple. Enjoy. And don't forget to laugh." He beckoned to Pytor. "Come, sir. Let us go and leave Master Chef to his bread and beans."

Together, Christopher, Pytor, and Jerome left the kitchen and strolled out into the courtyard. Pytor stayed close to his master's side, for though Christopher's strength had much improved, he still had to lean occasionally on a friendly arm to catch his breath. This afternoon, though, he insisted on a lengthy walk, one that took them out the castle gates, through the streets of the surrounding town, and past the inn where Pytor had discovered him.

In contrast to the wretched autumn, the weather was mild and reasonably dry for January. The majority of the towns-folk were still keeping indoors, attending to the quiet tasks of the winter, but those who were out smiled and bowed and curtsied and saluted Christopher with a cheery "God bless you, m'lord."

But when the baron lifted a black-clad arm to acknowl-edged their greetings, he did so absently. "They obviously think I've gone daft," he said to his companions. "I can see that. Poor Baron Christopher, running about in donkey skins." He looked at Pytor. "Did you and David have a nice chat about my taste in sackcloth?"

Pytor colored. "David is distressed, master."

"And what about you?"

"Master may wear what he deems most fit."

"But you don't like it, do you?"

Pytor cleared his throat, spoke cautiously. "I must admit that it is not what is considered stylish."

"Stylish! Yes . . . that's the important thing, isn't it? Per-haps I should wear green, like Jean de Nevers. After all, one can't go about looking like a friar, can one?"

"If I may say so," said Jerome, his arms still folded in his Franciscan habit, "I think that a friar is a very fine thing to look like."

Christopher laughed. "Bless you, Fra Jerome."

But Jerome shook his head. "My lord, it is not for us to question your choice of food or clothes: the holy Baptist ate locusts and honey, after all. But I might remind you of your position in Adria. Word of your ways has reached some of the other baronies of the land. It has caused some . . . dis-cussion."

Christopher stopped laughing, and Pytor, hopeful, caught a flash of the old delAurvre defiance. "Discussion? Ah, yes. I saw that letter you left on my bed. Who sent that, any-way?"

"One of your men nominally in the employ of Yvonnet of Hypprux," said Jerome. He coughed. "Nominally."

"A spy."

"If you recall, my lord, you had quite an established net-work," said Jerome. "The legacy of your grandfather. Pytor and I did our best to maintain it in your absence. We thought it prudent.''

"My grandfather . . ." Christopher mused. "Damn, but that was a man." He thought some more, but then his face turned pained. "All right, I can guess. Yvonnet is my cousin—second, third, I can't recall—and if I'm mad, I can't hold onto Aurverelle, can I?''

Jerome nodded his gray head. "One of Yvonnet's people was examining the lineage rolls in Maris about a month before you returned, my lord. Obviously, the baron of Hypprux had some designs on Aurverelle that were predicated upon its rightful master's death. Those, of course, were dashed by your return. Now, though, your—shall we call it fanciful?—behavior has raised another possibility.''

"Yvonnet is more interested in banquets and balls than in battle.''

Pytor shook his head. "If master would let me speak, I would say that I would not underestimate Yvonnet. He has ridden in his share of tournaments. But I doubt that he would himself come to attack master. There are other ways. The free companies, for instance.''

Jerome nodded his gray head. "They've been active in France since the truce with England. France has been stripped: they'll be looking for wealthier lands. And some of Yvonnet's gold might persuade them that Aurverelle is that land. The Italians have been using the companies for political purposes for decades, and in France some captains have actually been rewarded with castles and fiefdoms for their services against one nobleman or another. Common, very common. It would only take a message or two, a few bags of gold, a promise, and a wink. . . .'' The friar shrugged.

Christopher frowned. "How in heaven's name did you learn all this in a cloister? You were supposed to be praying for godless people like me.''

Jerome smiled. "I read a great deal. A clever man can learn through the eyes and ears of others who become his, so to speak, spies of the intellect.''

Christopher shook his head. "They can't take Aurverelle.''

Pytor shrugged uncomfortably. "If master would allow me to speak . . .''

"Just say it, Pytor, dammit!''

Pytor bowed. "Only an extremely large force would be interested in the castle. Even Messire Hawkwood's White Company in Italy did not concern itself with sieges. It would be the peasants who live in the town and the countryside who would suffer. The crops they tend, the small bits of money and jewelry they possess . . ." Pytor shrugged again. "It is always so."

Christopher was brooding. "Should I care about them?"

Pytor squirmed. "They support master."

The baron's mood had darkened, and he turned around and regarded the castle, its walls, the huge tower that dominated all. The sun was westering, and the shadows fell on the town, putting a chill into the air.

"It's all useless," he said. "It's all stupid: just a bunch of boys playing camping, chasing a ball about the fields and hurting everyone. Maybe I should just let Yvonnet have it all." He hung his head for a minute. Pytor and Jerome exchanged worried glances. But then Christopher lifted his head and forced an ironic smile. "But that's just what Grandfather did, isn't it? Let them have it all?"

He wavered, sagged against Pytor, passed a hand over his face. "I'm tired," he said softly. "Take me home, gentlemen. I want black bread and some soup fit for dogs."

CHAPTER 6

Spring came late that year to Aurverelle, the warm weather of January leading directly back into snow and sleet that only grudgingly yielded to the coldest of March rains. The farmers fretted about the frosty nights that nipped at the now premature barley and peas, and the dairymaids coddled their calves and piglets through the all-pervasive damp.

Christopher's strength improved. By the beginning of February, he was taking extended walks about the castle and the town, and late in the month he began once again to hold the weekly courts that Jerome and Pytor had been supervising during his absence and recuperation. His outlook, though, remained gloomy, and March and even April found him still brooding, still vacillating between manic capers and black depression.

The rumor that Christopher delAurvre was mad had, seemingly, entrenched itself in the thoughts of Adria, and far from doing anything to dispel it, Christopher actually furthered it, violating convention and custom by turning away travelers and pilgrims and refusing entrance to musicians and storytellers. This worried Pytor and Jerome greatly, for even if the insulted performers did not do their best to spread unpleasant rumors about the baron of Aurverelle, the matter of the rejected travelers was serious indeed, since hospitality was a cornerstone of existence in Europe. Barbarians, perhaps, could turn away those in need, but even a beggar was entitled to a bowl of soup and a heap of straw by the fire in the world of civilized men.

But Christopher persisted in his increasing isolation. Even a wandering friar, sick and weary, found no bed in Castle Aurverelle and had to make do with the severe hospitality of the Carthusian charterhouse at the base of the hill.

This was too much for Jerome. "My lord," he said one

day, "forgive my bluntness, but hasn't this gone on long enough?"

Christopher looked up from his loaf of black bread. Deliberately, he crunched through the half-cooked beans and spit out a bit of unhusked spelt. "Long enough?"

"That friar . . ."

"Dom Henri told me two days ago that the chapter house sent that friar packing when they caught him with a girl."

Jerome murmured an oath and crossed himself.

Christopher munched his bread noisily. "Things haven't changed much since I rode off with the crusaders, have they? Are you going to lecture me now about not going to church and taking the sacraments? You'll have to wait in line. Efram is ahead of you."

The Franciscan shook his head, folded his arms inside his sleeves. "My lord, it's the rumors. It's being said in the marketplaces of Adria that Aurverelle has no will to maintain itself. It's being said in the castles, too."

Christopher shrugged. "It's not Aurverelle's will that's lacking." He laughed without mirth. "It's mine."

"Yvonnet—"

"—is so concerned about the rebellion in Ypris that he doesn't have time to worry about Aurverelle," Christopher finished. He noted Jerome's surprised look. "Yes, I've been reading the reports as they come in. You leave them on my bed, I read them. I don't care what they say, but I read them. They're more entertaining than counting stitches in the tapestries or bubbles in the windowpanes."

Exasperated, Jerome tried once more. "Christopher, your people are *concerned*."

Christopher put down his bread, struck by the fact that Jerome had been driven to such extremes that he was willing to address his lord by name . . . and with such vehemence. "How so, Fra Jerome?"

Jerome regained his composure. "They love you, my lord, but their morale is dropping quickly. They are your people."

His people. Christopher did not want anyone to be his people, but he understood. Adria was of no concern to him, neither was the reputation of the estate. The former, as far as he was concerned, could go to hell; the latter was already soiled far beyond his power to add or to detract by his grandfather's excesses and subsequent docile reform—and

Christopher still could not say which of the two disturbed him more, or for which he had been trying to make restitution when he heeded the blandishments of his wife and set off with the crusaders of France.

But Jerome had a point. It was to people like those who worked the lands of Aurverelle that he owed his survival during his trek back from the crusade. Peasants—well-off, poor, utterly destitute—had taken him in, fed him bowls of lentil soup and black bread full of beans, given him a place to sleep when the monasteries and abbeys had turned him away.

"Thank you, Jerome," he said. "I'll think about that."

And he did. And when spring finally arrived, and when the iron-nosed plows began creeping across damp fields, the farmers and tenants of Aurverelle were surprised to find Christopher out in the fields with them. But not only did he direct the first furrow himself, holding a sword high while the plowman carved a forty-yard slice towards him as smoothly as a man might draw a paintbrush the length of a fence: as April continued and the weather turned fine, Christopher was working—ditching and hedging, pulling basketfuls of mud out of the marshes to repair the causeway and increase the farmland, inspecting the henhouse and the cowshed as diligently as some nobles examined the mews.

By day, he labored alongside his people. At night, he took walks through the town, slipping through the streets at Pytor's side as though the Russian had acquired a slender shadow. But Christopher did not see himself as a shadow: he was, rather, a ghost, a spirit who, like the shades that had once besieged Odysseus, hungered for a taste of mortal blood that would add a sense of substantiality to his spectral existence; and he listened, smelled, and watched hungrily as the estate moved through the spring.

But he was still isolated, disconnected. Yes, he worked in the fields alongside the Hobs and Jakes and Tims of the estate, but they did not need him. If Christopher delAurvre did not exist, Hob, Jake, and Tim would continue their lives without any severe deprivation. Christopher knew that, and he knew also that, as a noble, his business was merely to consume the produce rendered him by Hob, Jake, and Tim. To be sure, he was also supposed to defend them, but he had seen enough French excess and idiocy on the battlefield to recognize that equivocation for what it was. Christopher, baron of Aurverelle, was a useless appendage, and the only difference between himself and the knights who had wasted their lives and the lives of others at Nicopolis was that he happened to know it.

And so the ghost stared at the pit of blood but could not drink, for it had so lost the memory of substance that it could not remember how.

> *Greetings to the baron of Furze, Paul delMari, from Bonnerel d'Aldar, priest of Furze Hamlet: may the Lord God bless His Lordship and keep him and all his household safe.*
>
> *It is, my lord, with some misgiving that I write to you in order to acquaint you with what I consider to be a grave danger that has afflicted your prosperous and happy estate. As this matter falls more under canon law than under secular, I would, under normal circumstances, refer it directly to Bishop Wenzel of Furze, but in these days of affliction, the usual courses of action have become unclear and worrisome, and therefore I turn to you for advice and judgment.*
>
> *As I am priest of Furze Hamlet, it is my usually pleasurable duty to have the acquaintance of the thirty or forty souls in my care. Sometimes this duty, though, turns grievous, and indeed it has done so in the matter of Vanessa, daughter of the farmer, Lake.*
>
> *Vanessa did not grow up as do most children—that is, as the holy apostle said, thinking like a child, speaking like a child, and having the cares of a child— and though I tried for a long time to deny it, I have come to believe that Satan and his minions possess the girl. . . .*

Paul delMari tossed the letter aside. He could guess what the rest of it said. As he had suspected, there was more to Lake's request than the farmer had been willing to state. Fortunately for Vanessa, she had left the estate two days ago in the company of Martin Osmore. Fortunately for Lake, Paul delMari was baron of Furze.

Paul left the library, climbed the stairs, passed down the hallway. A burst of laughter from the solar told him that Catherine and Isabelle were gossiping, Isabelle doubtless showing off her embroidery while Catherine exhibited whatever new knife or sword she had acquired. Farther down the hall, though . . .

He stopped before a door, swung it open. The room beyond was empty save for a bed, a table and stool, a wardrobe, and a small writing desk with a scuffed and worn footrest. Martin's room.

And Vanessa had gone off with Martin. Yes, everything did indeed fit together, just like the Elves had always said. Like music. Like a dance. And Vanessa was doubtless playing some part in the melody and footwork that went on all the time, that included all things; and Martin . . .

What part did Martin have? Was he merely a means of conveying Vanessa from one part of Adria to another—a subordinate harmony—or did he serve some other purpose?

"Ah, my son," said Paul to the absent fosterling, "I would have knighted you, had you asked. But you didn't want that, did you? You were a peasant, you said, and you knew your place. For whatever reason, you had to hide . . . just like me."

He sighed, closed the door. He would have to think of something to say to Bonnerel, and he would have to be jolly when he said it. Good man, Bonnerel.

Etienne of Languedoc was a small, thin man who seemed to possess, despite his fine horse, his jewelry, his sword, his attendants, and the insignia of the Avignon papacy, the demeanor of a tenacious little spider; but Pytor bowed deeply to him anyway. Etienne's ways were doubtless what had allowed him to survive for so long the intricacies of Avignon politics, and in any case the monsignor's party had been waiting outside the gates of Castle Aurverelle for the better part of an hour. The churchman, accustomed as he was to proper receptions and entertainments, was angry.

But he was still outside the gates, and Pytor was about to make him even angrier.

"Master suggests," said the seneschal, "that you stay at the inn."

The small crowd of townsfolk who had gathered to stare at the Avignonese when they had first ridden up the street had stayed on to watch, and now the men were beginning to wink and nudge one another, the women to giggle. Stay at the inn! And to the face of a papal legate! Now *that* was the delAurvre style.

Etienne looked puzzled. Christopher's reply was obviously so outlandish that he was at first baffled by it. "At the . . . inn?"

A fine place for a Russian slave! thought Pytor. A May heat wave, the wind kicking up dust devils everywhere, and here he was facing an anthropomorphic spider on a big bay horse. He was glad to have Ranulf of the guard standing directly behind him: a very appropriate honor for the seneschal of a major barony . . . but also, at times like this, a very necessary precaution. "Yes, monsignor," he said with another bow, "at the inn."

Finally comprehending, Etienne flared. "Damn you, man! I'm on a mission from Pope Benedict himself! It's only common courtesy that your lord take us in!"

Pytor attempted the placid smile of a Russian peasant. "Master indicated that the inn was perfectly adequate to your needs."

A flea-infested inn for a flea-infested churchman from a flea-infested whore's knave of a pope, was what Christopher had actually said—shouted rather—but even though an embassy from Pope Boniface of Rome would have met with exactly the same reception, Pytor was unwilling to convey those precise sentiments to Etienne.

No matter: Etienne was already raging. "His Holiness has sent me personally to speak with Baron Christopher regarding the influence of that heresiarch and excommunicate, Boniface!"

The townsfolk murmured. Pytor bowed with ceremony, but he would not overrule Christopher's orders. "We of Castle Aurverelle are honored, my lord monsignor, by His Holiness' attention and estimation of our influence in Adria. But . . ." He glanced over his shoulder. Old Ranulf, veteran of a thousand battles, had lifted his deeply scarred face and was examining Etienne and his party as though picking a spot for his first thrust. "But I am afraid," Pytor continued, "that it will have to be the inn for you all."

Etienne mastered his temper only with difficulty. "And assuming for a moment that I will deign to stay in a common hostel, when will it please Baron Christopher to see me?"

"Master will not see you, my lord monsignor."

"You mean, he won't see me today?"

"Master will not see you at all."

"But he must!"

Pytor understood Etienne's bewilderment, but Christopher had kept to his isolation. It was May now, and still no one but staff, officers of the estate, and men of the Aurverelle Guard were entertained in the castle. The fortress was a dreary, empty place. Much (though the comparison pained the seneschal) like its master. "My master—"

"Your master!" shouted Etienne. "Your master this, your master that! I know all about you, Pytor of Medno: you come from Novgorod, and you're nothing but a common serf! How dare Christopher insult me by sending someone like you to speak with me?"

The men in the crowd muttered angrily, and some of them shook their fists at the legate. Pytor blushed at the esteem with which the Aurverelle folk obviously held their seneschal, but he had had enough of Etienne. Courtesy was getting him nowhere, and he lifted his head. "I beg your pardon, monsignor," he said politely. "I am not a common serf. I am a common slave."

Someone in the crowd whooped. Etienne flushed with anger. "Well, I'll show you how we treat slaves in Languedoc. . . ." And, rising in his stirrups, reaching for his sword, he urged his horse toward Pytor.

Ranulf, with a murmured "Pardon me, m'lord seneschal," strode forward and planted himself before Pytor. His hand was hovering just above the grip of his sword, and Pytor knew that the old veteran could draw the weapon and slash simultaneously, dropping all but the best protected and most determined horses even at full gallop.

Confronted now with both an angry knot of townsfolk and a mailed and armed warrior—and therefore with the reminder that more of the same were, doubtless, available to Pytor—Etienne brought his horse to a halt and considered. Pytor guessed his thoughts. True, the monsignor had attendants, and many of them were armed, but a street brawl before a major castle of Adria was risky business, and would do little for Benedict's popularity in the land.

The monsignor's sword went back into its sheath.

"Thank you, Ranulf," said Pytor.

"No mor'n your due, m'lord seneschal."

Etienne was chewing his way through courtesy as though it were a block of wood. "Would you please ask your master . . ."

Pytor was beginning to wish that the vagrant monkey that prowled Aurverelle would make an appearance with a suitably rotten piece of fruit, but then he heard movement behind him. Christopher himself was walking quietly out of the castle gate. Clad in simple garments of black and brown, without a sword or even a chain of office, he was indistinguishable from the lowliest servant; but his bearing and the sudden lifting of caps among the people of Aurverelle should have told Etienne that this was no commoner.

The churchman's temper had been aroused: he was beyond such subtleties. "You, boy," he said to Christopher. "Fetch me your master."

With a cry, the townsfolk surged forward towards Etienne and his men, obviously intending to deal with the haughty Avignonese as the Flemings had once dealt with the haughty French. But Christopher stopped their advance with a look. "I assure you, Etienne," he said in the sudden silence, "I have no master." And he pointed with his thumb at the motto carved above the main gate. Three hundred years ago, the delAurvres had taken it for their own:

> *King I am not*
> *Nor prince, nor duke, nor count.*
> *I am the Master of Aurverelle.*

"You insolent young pup!" Etienne looked ready to reach for his sword again.

Ranulf spoke. "Beggin' your pardon, m'lord monsignor, but I must ask you t'show more respect to Baron Christopher."

Etienne stared, Christopher nodded to the churchman as he might acknowledge the presence of a hound. "You don't recognize me, Etienne, but I recognize you. You were the priest who bravely blessed the brave crusaders in Vienna . . . and who then bravely stayed at home. It's amazing the way one can rise in the world by staying home, isn't it, Etienne?"

Etienne fumbled for words. "Christopher . . ."

"*Baron* Christopher," said Ranulf.

"I said that I wouldn't see you," said Christopher. "So I'll do my best to forget that I have, and that you were willing to threaten my seneschal and even more willing to give orders before my castle like the womanizing lout that

I saw you were in Vienna. *Be brave,* you said back then, *and do God's will.* That itself should have told me what kind of company I was keeping, for even if I hadn't been well schooled in whoring by then, I would have soon learned much of the subject on the way to Nicopolis.''

Etienne had gone white. ''My lord baron—''

''That's much better, Etienne,'' said Christopher. He clapped his hands sardonically and advanced until he was shoulder to shoulder with Ranulf.

''I have come on a mission of great urgency.''

''Yes. The schism. Let's see . . . which pope are you?''

This was too much for Etienne. ''You *dare!*''

''Shut up.'' Christopher's murmured command carried greater weight than Etienne's bluster, and the churchman, seething, fell silent. ''I'll tell you this. I support no one. Aurverelle is for Aurverelle, and so is Christopher del-Aurvre. He always has been, he always will be. Now take your rabble and go. Be glad I talked to you at all.''

Laughter from the townsfolk. The delAurvre style, indeed!

Etienne blinked at Christopher's bluntness. ''But, my lord,'' he stammered, ''don't you care about your soul? About the souls of the people of Adria?''

Christopher had half turned to go, but he swung back. ''My soul? Someone like you is asking about souls? You with your perfumes and your banquets and your unconscionable stiff little prick?'' His gray eyes were hot and bright. ''To answer your question, though: No, I don't care about souls, or about the popes, or about anything. I don't believe in anything. I don't go to mass, and I don't receive the sacraments, and I don't give a damn. All right? Are you *satisfied?*''

''Nothing?'' The churchman seemed as dazed by Christopher's anger as he was by his words.

''Nothing. I follow the example . . . of my grandfather.''

Pytor winced, looked away.

''He didn't believe in anything either,'' Christopher continued. ''Or if he did—'' He fell silent for a moment, shook his head. ''I'll tell you this, monsignor. There is a cask of wine in my cellar. I believe in that. Do you understand?''

Slowly, Etienne gathered his wits. ''You are an evil man, Baron Aurverelle.''

''Careful, monsignor,'' murmured Ranulf.

Christopher smiled thinly. "That's all right, Ranulf. Our dear monsignor is probably correct. I *am* an evil man. I've danced with bears, and I've rooted with pigs, and I've gone so far as to stare at the lives of common people as though they were a hot, smoking dish of venison. Indeed, I may hardly be a man at all any more." He strode up to Etienne. "Go away. The inn's good enough for you. You should be flattered: your God was born in a stable, after all."

Pytor heard the folk of Aurverelle whispering to one another. Christopher's language had been strong. Very strong.

Shaking with frustrated rage, Etienne signaled to his attendants, and they turned back down the main street of the town. The crowd parted to let them through, but Etienne stayed for a moment more. "His Holiness sent me personally, my lord."

"And I'm sending you back. Personally."

"I will stay at the inn until you see me."

"Stay as long as you want," said Christopher. "You can stay until the devils or the Elves or whoever else owns your rotten little soul comes for you. Just pay your reckoning when you leave, or I'll have you hanged as a common thief."

With a snort of contempt, Etienne turned away.

Christopher stood with a bowed head for a moment, then sighed. "Thank you, Ranulf," he said with a small bow to the captain. "I appreciate your loyalty and your fine work."

Ranulf bowed deeply in return and strode away.

Then, unexpectedly, Christopher turned to the folk of Aurverelle. "And thank you also, my friends. I'm proud to be the baron of such fine and devoted people."

A moment of silence. And then, one by one, growing from a trickle into a torrent, came the peasants' acknowledgments. *Thankee, m'lord. God bless you, Messire Christopher.* Someone began to cheer, and the sentiment rapidly became universal.

Christopher bowed, took Pytor's arm, and drew him towards the gate. "Come, my friend. And my thanks to you for your toleration of this unpleasantness." But he peered into Pytor's face as though examining it for the first time. "You are my friend, aren't you?"

Friendship was something that Pytor had never really thought about. He was Christopher's man, that was all. But he cared about the baron, and he loved him. If that was what Christopher meant by a friend, then Pytor of Medno was a friend indeed. "Master . . . I . . ." He spread his arms, his tongue constrained by his status.

Christopher nodded, clapped him on the back. "That'll do. I understand."

"Dear master," said Pytor with a gesture towards the retreating Avignonese, "was that wise?"

"To tell a buffoon that he's a buffoon?" They passed through the gate into the outer courtyard. Outbuildings dotted the lawn, and daffodils and hyacinths sparkled: yet another legacy of old Baron Roger. "I can't see why not."

But Christopher's eyes were shadowed, and Pytor caught his hand. "Do you really believe in nothing, master?"

Christopher stopped, regarded him sympathetically. "I know, Pytor. You've been separated from Orthodoxy so long that you miss your religion terribly, and so it hurts you to hear me say something like that. But I'm afraid that it's true. I once believed in Grandfather. No more. I once believed in chivalry, and that my sword could do something good, something for . . . for someone. Maybe for God. Maybe for myself. No more." He tipped his head back, gazed at the great keep. "You know, I'm not even particularly good at whoring." He dropped his eyes, shook his head. "That cask of wine sounds good to me now, but that's about all."

"Master . . ."

Christopher gripped his hand. "If you'll stay my friend, Pytor, I shall consider myself well recompensed for my continuing, miserable existence. But come now. You have your Orthodoxy, and I have my cask of wine, and . . ." He looked over his shoulder. ". . . Etienne has his inn and whatever women he can come up with to use and abuse."

CHAPTER 7

Yvonnet received the report from Bishop Alphonse's friar at about the same time as he heard of the reception that Aurverelle had accorded Etienne of Languedoc. He was nonplused. On the one hand, Christopher's rejection of the first was a serious matter, especially since the friar had been sick and weak with traveling. On the other, Christopher had done to Etienne exactly what Yvonnet had always wanted to do to an arrogant churchman, and the baron of Hypprux was doubly delighted that his cousin's insults had been directed at an emissary from Avignon.

"Remarkable man, Christopher." He propped his feet up on the heavy oak table in the council chamber. "Completely mad, of course, but really remarkable. Avignon won't like this at all."

"And what about . . . ah . . . Rome and the friar?" said Lengram, who stood with folded, disapproving arms.

"Well, I suspect that the friar was not so holy a man as he pretended to be. You know that kind."

Lengram was indignant. "He might well have had his weaknesses, Baron Yvonnet, but he was a man of God!"

Yvonnet grabbed a bowl of fruit and pawed through it until he found a pear. It must have come from far to the south, since the fruit in Adria was just now getting out of the flower stage. Expensive pears. He bit into it noisily anyway: baron's prerogative. That was what taxes were for. "Just as we all have our own weaknesses," he said. "I doubt whether either of us expects to be dealt with any better at the gates of heaven."

Lengram frowned, looked away.

Yvonnet continued with the pear, stuffing his mouth with large bites. "So it seems that that—umm, umm—cousin Christopher is not quite so mad as he was made out to be—umm, umm—or perhaps is less mad now than he was." He finished the pear and hurled the core at a servant. It struck the man square on the forehead. Well-schooled in the routines of the baron of Hypprux, the servant did not even flinch. "No matter."

"No matter?" said Lengram.

"No . . . matter. . . ." Yvonnet licked his hands clean and clasped them behind his head. "We'll just have to think of something else."

But what he was thinking of now was Martin, the lithe-loined lad from Shrinerock who was making his way home to Saint Blaise and dispensing greetings and gifts from his foster father at the same time. Yvonnet had put a close watch on the young man, and messengers in relays had been riding back and forth along the road through the dairylands of Adria with information as to his progress for the last several weeks.

Three years ago, it had been a wonderful party. Yvonnet had just come of age, he had just dismissed the troublesome and tiresome regents that had overseen him and his estate since his parents had died. He had been anticipating knighthood and, more important, money and lands and revenues enough to allow him to live as he wanted. Martin, a splendid gift on a splendid occasion, had been handsome and gay . . . and easily intimidated. In fact, Yvonnet was sure that the lad had come to enjoy their week of trysts, had come even to look forward to the occasional rough treatment to which his bedmate had subjected him.

Ah, such a fine piece of a man! And finer still, doubtless, now that he was grown up a little, was a little sturdier . . . and . . . yes, the bells of the Cathedral of Our Lady of Mercy were ringing nones. Martin would be arriving in Hypprux any time now.

"What did you . . . ah . . . have in mind?" said Lengram.

Yvonnet smiled. "Oh . . . quite a number of things. . . ."

"I mean about Aurverelle."

"Oh, that."

But a knock came to the door, and a servant brought word that Martin had arrived in the city and was even now being escorted to the baronial residence.

Yvonnet kicked the table away. The bowl of fruit clattered to the floor and unleashed a flood of tumbling apples, quinces, pears, and oranges. "I want him brought to the great hall," he said. "Bring him there immediately. I want to see him."

The servant bowed and turned to go.

"Wait," said Yvonnet. "Is he alone?"

"There are two men at arms with him along with a captain of the Shrinerock guard, my lord baron."

No problem, really. Yvonnet could easily send the soldiers off. They would relish a cup of ale and the barracks-room conversation of their peers. "Anyone else?"

"The messenger mentioned a young woman, my lord."

"A woman?" Yvonnet was vexed. Had Martin married? It would not be at all surprising. But Paul delMari had had no eligible young women in his household, save, perhaps, for his sister. And everyone knew about *her*.

Marriage, however, was no real problem. Yvonnet himself was married . . . to a woman who knew her place. But in any case, his concerns evaporated a short time later in the great hall, for Martin was obviously not at all related either by blood or by matrimony to the the woman—girl, rather—who was with him. She was but a peasant. Pretty enough, to be sure, with large brown eyes and long blond hair that she wore, according to custom, in twin braids, but a peasant nonetheless, one who was not even sophisticated enough to stand with her hips swayed forward. Martin's parents would never have approved. Yvonnet wondered why she was even in his company.

But Martin was terrified of being in the presence of the baron of Hypprux, and his dark eyes—still large, still, as Yvonnet remembered, with the look of a restless woman about them—were fixed on the floor, as though he feared that by looking into the face of his host he would ensure his submission.

Such a fine time a few years ago! Really, it was not much that Yvonnet wanted. Just a few days . . .

"Martin," he said, "so nice to see you again! And such a lovely little sparrow my brave eagle has brought with him!"

Lengram, who had followed the baron into the hall, looked away, his lips pressed together.

The dark lad's eyes were now roving about the large, tap-estried room as though seeking an escape. But there was no escape. Yvonnet a'Verne always got what he wanted, and the commoners—and yes, Martin was a commoner: he would be accommodating—were there to provide it.

With an obvious effort, Martin forced himself to stand his ground. "Vanessa of Furze Hamlet is my traveling companion, Baron Yvonnet."

"Aha!" Yvonnet kept his voice hearty and loud. "Eagles and sparrows, indeed! And is this little fledgling meat for tonight's pot? Or is she expected to provide provender for a lengthy journey?"

But when he turned his immense smile on Vanessa, he was met by eyes that stilled his voice. Dark brown eyes. Huge eyes. Eyes that seemed to see everything at once, that could take in, in a single glance, all of Hypprux, all of Adria, and then, focusing down with a piercing light, could pry into his inmost secrets and lay bare his desires and his vices.

Vanessa was lovely, but she was also alive with a feral gleam that touched her with all the crazed menace of a rabid fox. "It's a' right," she said. "I know."

Yvonnet faltered, no longer quite sure whether Martin drooped because of an imminent and forced liaison or because he had been in the company of this . . . changeling . . . for several weeks. "You . . . know . . ."

"The patterns tell me," she said, nodding. "The patterns a'ways tell me. You can't escape the patterns."

The courtiers and the servants who were in the hall, perfumed and liveried and accustomed to standing arrogantly before even the mightiest baron of Adria (with the exception, to be sure, of Yvonnet himself), had all unconsciously taken a few steps away from Vanessa. Owl-eyed, isolated in her magic circle of instinctive aversion, the peasant girl blinked and nodded.

"Ah . . ." Yvonnet groped for words. "Ah . . . excellent. Good . . . good taste, Martin." With difficulty, he dragged himself away from Vanessa's lovely, compelling, terrifying eyes. "I'm . . ." Was she looking at him? He was afraid to find out. He turned his gaze on Martin . . . and kept it there. "I'm very glad you came to visit me. It's been years now, hasn't it?"

Martin was between Vanessa and the baron. "I'm not sure I recall, Yvonnet."

"Ah! It's Yvonnet again! So nice to be . . ." The baron stole a glance at Vanessa. She was indeed watching him,

and her eyes told him that all his obscure and mazed plans
were as glass to her. She saw. She knew. ". . . ah . . . to
be known as a friend.''

Vanessa was nodding again. "Just ask him, m'lord baron.
He'll go wi'out trouble.''

Martin whirled on her. "Vanessa!''

She blinked. "In't tha' wha' you want, Martin?''

Yvonnet sat down in his big chair. Had he been a physi-
cally smaller man, he would have been trembling. As it
was, he felt weak, dizzy. "I was looking forward to . . .
seeing you again, Martin.''

"No, that's not what I want!'' Martin was close to tears
with fear.

Vanessa was still nodding. "And you still dan know wha'
you want, do you?''

She was not mad: that was the problem. Had she been
mad, she might well have been the object of laughter and
ridicule. But it was painfully apparent that she was lucid,
cogent . . . and just as apparent that she saw more than any
human being had a right to see.

Yvonnet looked up at the ceiling. "Merciful God,'' he
murmured. "How is it that something like *that* can be allowed to run about loose?''

"It's na my time yet, m'lord baron,'' said Vanessa.
"They'll cam for me when it's time, na before.''

Yvonnet was chilled. She could, he knew, have spoken
as openly and as easily about what he wanted from Martin,
about what he took from Lengram. "Damn you, woman,
be quiet!''

Vanessa nodded knowingly, blinked.

"I . . .'' Martin groped for words. "I bring greetings
from Baron Paul delMari. He sends his best wishes . . . and
hopes for your continued . . . health. . . .''

And Vanessa knew what Martin would do for Yvonnet's
continued health. She knew everything. And Martin had
brought her straight into the Château. And, at any moment . . .

Yvonnet lifted his head and glared at the assembly in the
hall. They probably knew, too, but wealth and power had
silenced them. Even the priests, even the bishops. He was
baron of Hypprux and could silence them all. But this lovely
demon in woman's form saw . . . and spoke. And, yes, she
was probably right: as was the case with madmen and

prophets and sibyls throughout the ages, if death lay ahead of her, it would, unfortunately, not come soon.

"Get out, all of you," he shouted. "Get the hell out. You damned dandies and villeins! The sight of you makes me sick! Sergeant, take care of Martin's men. Margot, give this girl a room . . . by herself. Make sure she gets supper."

Vanessa was staring at a corner of the room as though there were someone standing there. But the corner was empty.

"*Get out!*"

Martin mustered his courtesy. "Don't be afraid, Vanessa. You'll be safe."

"Safe?" said the girl. "Nay, I'm na worried abo' being safe. The patterns say it's safe, an' you can't change the patterns. No one can." With obvious repugnance, Margot took the girl's arm, and Vanessa turned those huge brown eyes on her. She smiled with a smile that seemed to go back too far, and Margot all but screamed.

The courtiers were leaving, likewise the servants. Yvonnet grabbed Martin's hand. "You're coming with me, little girl. And you'll do what I want."

Martin wilted, but Yvonnet could not help but wonder whether he wilted from apprehension or from knowledge: Vanessa might well have already told him everything that was going to happen in the baronial bed that afternoon.

Margot was leading Vanessa out of the room.

Those eyes . . .

Christopher continued to grow stronger, and as May lengthened, he began weapons practice in the courtyard. He trained doggedly, swinging a sword against bales of hay and two-inch saplings until the muscles of his arms and shoulders burned, tilting at the quintain for hours in heavy armor augmented with lead weights, clashing with Ranulf until they were both dizzy.

It was something to do. Once he had realized that, because of his ignorance regarding even the most basic agricultural theory and practice, he was actually hindering his people more than he was helping them—and worrying them considerably: what kind of baron labored in the fields like a serf?—he had courteously withdrawn from direct participation in the tillage and husbandry. But without the distraction of physical labor, he had been left with free time, time which had allowed his memories of his grandfather and Nicopolis ample opportunity to rise up and obsess him; and the severity of his depression had frightened him.

He had no taste for needless hunting or hawking, and only extended and brutal combat practice, therefore, offered Christopher a daily occupation. It was a chance to forget himself in a bath of steel and sweat, a chance to lash out vicariously at those things he had come to hate: hypocrisy, folly, perhaps even himself.

But he still kept up his nighttime walks, still made frequent rounds of the fields, looked in on the mill, examined personally the oven, the stables, the cowshed, the barracks. He was still hungry, still looking for a taste of real and immediate life. He was still a ghost. And he was still prowling, snuffling after the scent of blood.

And perhaps it was that odor that made him pause outside the door to the great hall as he came slogging in from another round of practice in the heat-drenched courtyard. Otto, the owner of the Green Man Inn, was talking to Jerome. And he was upset.

"It's the legate from Avignon, m'lord bailiff," Otto was saying. "It's not that he don't pay his reckoning—many folk don't pay till they leave. He's got expensive likes, to be sure, and it's a strain on me to have to pay for things long before I get paid for them. And like I said, he's got expensive tastes."

Jerome, arms folded in his sleeves despite the heat, listened gravely. "If it's not the bills, Otto, then what is it?"

"Well . . . it's hard to say, m'lord bailiff. I could say that it's the way of him. But that wouldn't be saying it right. And I could say it's his men, but that wouldn't be saying it right, either."

"My good man—" said Jerome.

"And then I could say—"

Christopher stumped into the room and flung himself into a chair. The flies buzzing in the hot room caught the scent of his sweat-soaked mail and made immediately for him, but he was too tired to do anything about it. "What is it, Otto? Tell me."

"He's breaking up all my furniture, m'lord," said Otto after bowing deeply and dropping to one knee before his baron. Christopher motioned for him to get up, and he did, but he looked half ready to fall to the floor in submission as he spoke. "And I particularly don't like the way he treats my folk. He knocks the stable boys about something fierce, and they've done nothing with his horses that's any different than what they do with anyone else's. And then the girls . . ." Otto looked at Jerome, blushed, looked away.

Christopher pulled off a glove of steel links and dropped it on the table with a loud chink. "The . . . girls . . ."

"Aye, m'lord . . . they're working girls, you know." Another look at Jerome. "But I wouldn't have you be thinking that I get a penny of what they get from the men they entertain. I don't run that kind of establishment, and I make sure I don't know at all what they do. It's their business, not mine, and I make sure that I don't profit at all by such unholy deeds."

Jerome cleared his throat. "Perish the thought, my son," he said, though everybody in Aurverelle knew that Otto took a little more than a tithe from the young women who plied their trade in the common room of his inn.

Christopher put an elbow on the arm of the chair and propped his chin in his hand. Etienne had not given up. Christopher could not really blame him: Avignon was far away, embassies were expensive, and even a sycophant of the most limited persistence would make at least a token effort toward gaining an audience after a journey that had doubtless lasted well over a month. "What about the girls . . . that you don't know anything about?"

"He treats them bad, m'lord," said Otto. "Knocks them about worse than the lads. Little Susanne went off with a broken crown just last night, and the day before, Dolores—you know, the one with the big, dark eyes . . ."

Jerome coughed. Christopher smiled. Spies of the intellect, perhaps, but not of the body.

". . . wound up with both of them blacked, and she thinks her nose is broke, too."

Jerome crossed himself. "I wish that Etienne were not a fellow churchman," he said, "so that I could justify wishing him as much ill as I do."

Otto shrugged apologetically. "Beggin' your pardon, m'lord bailiff. I haven't told you about the rest."

"I don't think I want to hear it," said Jerome.

"Nor do we have to," said Christopher. He was angry. This was Aurverelle. This was *his* town. If Etienne had for some reason made a practice of going swimming in Malvern

River with a feather stuck up his ass, that would have been his own business, but when he insisted upon involving the people of Aurverelle in his idiocy and excesses, he would have to deal with Christopher delAurvre.

For a moment, the baron recalled his grandfather. And had Roger not done exactly what Etienne was doing? What kind of a man was that? But what kind of a man spent the last forty years of his life planting an avenue of peach trees?

Christopher shook his head, finding that, because of his inability to decide what he disliked most about his grandfather—his excess or his reformation—he hated Etienne all the more.

"Might he be leaving soon, Otto?" he said.

"Nay, m'lord. He looks to have made himself at home. Looks to be staying for a long time."

Jerome nodded. "He's determined to see you, Baron Christopher."

Christopher laid a hand on the grip of his sword. The family sword, the one with the jewels in the hilt and the relics in the pommel, was lost now somewhere between Nicopolis and Aurverelle, vanished as completely as his faith and his belief. This was a plain sword, without any special meaning; and though Christopher no longer believed that heaven heard anything at all, relics or not, the habit of taking hold of the weapon when registering an oath persisted. "Oh, he'll see me, Jerome. He won't like it, but he'll see me."

CHAPTER 8

The company that arrived from the north was one of the strangest that Otto had ever seen. On the surface, to be sure, there was nothing particularly remarkable about a young man, a young woman, and a few guards. But while the young man was as richly dressed as a lord's son, he bore himself with the humility of one who was dressed in borrowed finery, and he sported two black eyes and numerous bruises. The guards were much like guards everywhere, but the girl was markedly a peasant. She spoke with a thick dairyland accent and gave Otto a chill every time she opened her mouth.

"Aye," she said as she and the lordling followed Otto up the stairs to look at rooms, "aye . . . this is it. This is the place."

"The place?" said Otto. He did not want to know: he asked only out of a kind of terrified fascination.

"Vanessa," said Martin softly. "Please."

"The place . . ." said Vanessa. And she nodded meaningfully, blinking enormous brown eyes that were filled with too much light. "Ah . . . I understand."

Otto licked his suddenly dry lips, as uneasy about her as he was about Etienne of Languedoc, who, after two weeks of laying diplomatic siege to Castle Aurverelle, had not yet gotten past the front gate. In accordance with custom, though, the churchman was certainly doing enough damage to the peasantry!

Even now, his voice was drifting up from the common room, shrill and impatient. "He won't? Damn him again! A pox on these delAurvres!" A muffled voice. "What? You don't like my opinion of your baron? Well . . ."

There was a crash and a cry below. Otto winced. Martin Osmore shook his head. "My father has ambitions to live like that," he said. He grinned, his blackened eyes crinkling up into dark slits. ''My mother won't let him. Who is that, anyway?''

''Etienne of Languedoc,'' said Otto as he fumbled with his ring of keys. ''Now, I'm not disagreeing with Baron Christopher at all, and I won't have you be thinking that I am, but I can't help but wonder whether it might be better if m'lord baron gave the monsignor what he wants.''

''What does he want?''

''He wants to talk to the baron. And m'lord Christopher insulted him and told him to go sleep in the kennel with the dogs! Can you believe that? Baron Christopher is certainly one like his grandfather, surely!''

Martin looked alarmed. ''His grandfather? The one who hanged travelers in Malvern?''

''Well . . . not quite like his grandfather, perhaps. . . .'' Otto found the key, opened the door. ''Now, here you are, m'lord. A sitting room with a big window, and separate bedrooms.'' Otto still could not figure it out: separate bedrooms? And a lord and a peasant traveling together?

Martin was nodding. He removed his gloves, and Otto could see rope burns on his wrists. He shuddered, made the mistake of looking at Vanessa, was transfixed by a pair of eyes that harrowed him on the spot.

''Fine, fine,'' Martin was saying.

''I'm . . . glad m'lord is pleased.''

''Don't call me lord,'' said Martin. ''I'm a commoner. I'll always be a commoner. *Master Martin* is good enough for me.''

Awash in confusion, Otto bowed. Below, Etienne was still shouting abuse, but a footstep in the hall made them all turn.

A liveried servant was approaching, his tunic figured with the papal crest. He ignored Otto, bowed dismissively to Martin, smiled at Vanessa . . . and appeared shaken when Vanessa stared back at him. ''Ah . . .''

''Speak up, my man,'' said Martin. The bruises on his face gave him the grotesque look of a jester.

The servant struggled back to composure. ''Mistress,'' he said to Vanessa, keeping his eyes averted, ''my master, Monsignor Etienne of Languedoc, could not help but note your great beauty and noble bearing. He greatly desires your acquaintance and craves your company.''

Otto shook his head, frustrated. He wished that Baron

Christopher would so something. Etienne's treatment of the servants and the girls was bad enough, but now the churchman seemed bent on the other patrons.

"Amazing," said Martin. "He's not even going to ask if she's married."

But Vanessa turned to him with those enormous eyes. "But, Martin, Yvonnet din't care if you were married either."

Martin looked away quickly. Otto suppressed a profound desire to flee.

Etienne's servant was glaring at Martin. "Well, *is* she?"

Vanessa answered . . . in her own way. "He can't ha' me," she said. "Na tonight. No one can ha' me tonight. It's na time."

"I assure you, mistress . . ."

"The patterns dan say it yet." But the girl's face turned puzzled, then agitated. "An' the patterns can't change, can they? They never change. An' . . ." She stood, shaking, for a moment, then pushed past Martin and Otto and fled into the rooms.

"We're tired," Martin said to the servant. "And you're tedious. Go away." He handed a bag of money to Otto. "We'll be leaving tomorrow morning," he said. "Please have our horses ready."

The innkeeper found the weight of the sack reassuring. It made him feel satisfied, even friendly. Good people, these. A little odd, perhaps, but good people.

And for that reason, he watched uneasily as, in the common room that evening, Etienne rose from the long table he had commandeered and swaggered over to the nook where Martin and Vanessa were eating supper. His clothing as sumptuous as that of the most excessive of the French dukes, his bearing as haughty, he stood before their table, his hand on the pommel of his sword. His pose, Otto thought, was a little too studied—rather like a monkey, save that monkeys were not supposed to wear swords. With a deeper sense of imminent disaster, Otto recalled that churchmen were not supposed to, either.

Vanessa regarded Etienne with wide, incredible eyes, but he did not seem to notice. Otto doubted that he noticed anything more than her breasts and the curve of her waist.

"Fair maiden," said Etienne softly. "Such a lovely little

butterfly has been blown into Aurverelle. What storm brought you here?''

What had Vanessa talked about? Patterns? What kind of patterns was she seeing in the papal legate? Otto started to ease around the end of the counter, though in truth he had not the faintest idea what he could do against either the legate or his score of armed guards and servants. The latter had stopped eating and drinking . . . and were now watching.

''I'm on my way t' Saint Blaise, messire,'' said Vanessa. ''I ha' employment waiting for me there.''

''Ah . . . employment,'' said Etienne. ''I might have some . . . employment . . . for you myself. May I ask your name?''

Vanessa's eyes widened, and she turned to Martin. ''Nay!''

Martin looked at her, startled, but he spoke. ''Her name is Vanessa, sir. And mine is Martin Osmore. My father is the mayor of Saint Blaise. Kindly leave us alone now.''

Etienne's expression did not change. It remained at once determined and predatory. ''You should learn your manners better, little boy.''

Vanessa was still looking at Martin. ''Martin, dan do it. They're . . .'' She blinked. ''Changing . . .'' She whirled to face Etienne just as the legate's fist lashed out and caught Martin in the throat. The lad's eye's widened for an instant, and then he toppled to the floor.

One of the Shrinerock guards was already charging across the common room, overturning tables, kicking chairs out of the way. His men were not far behind him. But as Vanessa shrank back—from whatever it was that she saw with those frightening eyes or from the legate, Otto could not be sure—Etienne signaled to his attendants, and the Shrinerockers found their way suddenly barred by a dozen men in mail.

Martin floundered on the floor. Otto glanced at Ernest, the tapster. Ernest looked at the swords that were suddenly starting from their sheaths. ''Run and fetch the guards from the castle,'' said Otto. ''I'll see what I can do.''

''Come, my maid,'' Etienne was saying as Shrinerocker steel met Avignonese. ''I always get what I want.'' He grabbed the girl by the arm and hauled her out of her seat. ''And tonight I want you. Do you understand?''

Vanessa, unaccountably bewildered, stared, her eyes filled with strange light, her lips moving soundlessly.

"Come now, girl. Much better this be pleasant, eh?"

Ernest vaulted the counter and made for the door just as Martin staggered to his feet, a dagger in his hand. With a casual gesture, the churchman drew his sword and dropped Martin with a single thrust, and Ernest was met at the door by two Avignonese who bore him backwards and over one of the tables. A heavy, mailed fist smashed into his jaw.

Vanessa began to scream: the sustained, mindless wail of an animal in a trap. One of the Shrinerockers broke free of the guards and lunged for Etienne, but, cut down from behind, fell face forward across a table full of beer mugs. Blood and froth went everywhere. People ran for the door, but Etienne's men had blocked it.

Frightened, looking for a place to hide in a room that no longer seemed to have any, Otto sidled into one of the darker corners as Etienne dragged Vanessa up against his body. "*Now!* I'll see you at the stake before I let you go!"

"You'll . . ." Vanessa was staring beyond Etienne. "You'll see me a' the stake anywa'!"

For an instant, Etienne stared at her, perplexed by her strange reply; and with a sudden jerk, Vanessa lifted a leg and kneed the churchman in the groin. His grip loosened for a moment, and she broke free and made for the stairs to the upper floors. Etienne was right behind her.

So was Otto. Fevered with worry about his inn, confused because all courses of action seemed blocked, the innkeeper scuffed up the steps as quickly as he could. From below came the sound of struggles and screams. Someone was shouting for castle guards, someone else for the bailiffs, but Otto could do nothing. He was not even sure what he could do for Vanessa.

He reached her room just in time to see the girl come up with a heavy brass candlestick and smash it into Etienne's face. The legate staggered back, bleeding badly. "You . . . *dare*! You little swine of a serf!"

"It's na time yet!" she was crying. "It's na time! I dan see wha's happened! E'erything's changed!" Vanessa swung again, putting her shoulders behind her stroke as though she were forking hay, but the effort lessened her precision, and Etienne caught her arm and twisted her wrist. Otto heard the crunch of breaking bones. Vanessa screamed and dropped the candlestick.

Not satisfied, Etienne picked it up and backhanded her across the face with it. In an instant, Vanessa's features turned into a ruin of pulped, red flesh and the stark whiteness of bone fragments. Her huge eyes still staring out from a welter of blood, she lifted an arm to ward off Etienne's return stroke, but, battered away, it dropped limply to her side, bent at a crazy angle.

More blows. Vanessa's face was unrecognizable now, and Etienne, still raging, started on her chest. Her ribs caved in first on one side, then the other. Otto could stand no more. Old and unarmed though he was, he tottered forward and seized Etienne's arm from behind.

He was immediately flattened by a fist to his face. Etienne turned back to finish with Vanessa, but the girl, scrambling with the blank urgency of a wounded bird, had used the churchman's momentary distraction to turn for the windowsill, drag herself up, and leap.

This late, the town of Aurverelle was quiet, its streets deserted. The night was warm, the stars were very, very bright, and when the Green Man Inn came into view, upper windows open and glowing with lamplight, Christopher stared at it hungrily. Here were people—not nobles, not churchmen, not anyone important—just people. People trying to get along. People trying to live as best they could. People trying to snatch some sleep. People traveling. People fornicating, gambling, blaspheming . . . or maybe praying. Christopher himself, though, a ghost, lapped futilely at the flow of life about him, craving desperately the substance that he had lost—by death or by Nicopolis, it was all the same.

He lived at arm's length. And had he not, in refusing to deal immediately and directly with Etienne, moved even farther away from connection and reconciliation? A ghost of a ghost.

He had spent the last several days raging at himself, raging at Etienne, raging at a society and a land that allowed slimy little things like barons and monsignors to prolong their existence at the expense of others. But, in the end, his oath had won out. Slimy little thing he might be, but he had Etienne to deal with. This had gone on long enough.

"It's always like this, isn't it, Pytor?" he said as they went towards the inn that shimmered in the heat waves coming off the street. "The nobles fight, but the peasants suffer. Etienne can't get back at me, so he'll take it out on my people."

Pytor was nodding. "As master has said."

But out of the glowing windows of the inn came a scream. It was a cry of fright, of pain, of utter despair.

Pytor crossed himself. "God of my fathers."

"No," said Christopher, running for the inn, "it's Etienne. Come on."

The door was barred, as were the lower windows. From within came stamps, scuffles, frightened screams and shouts:

"Let us out! *Let us out!*"

"Castle guards! Help! For the love of God!"

Swords clashed within as Pytor tried the door once more. No use. "It would be better if master perhaps called for his men."

A sudden flurry at a second floor window. A cry as if from a mouth that had lost all connection with its brain. With a rush and a thump, a body dropped, struck the roof above the inn's porch with a wet sound, and fell to the ground at Christopher's feet.

The baron bent over it, horrified. It was apparently a young woman, but her features had been pulped into shapelessness. Blond hair, blood, broken bones. She was breathing, but barely.

Pytor turned towards the castle. "Guards of Aurverelle!" he shouted. "To the Green Man Inn!"

A horn answered him. On the other side of the door, the fight continued. At his feet, the girl's breath frothed and bubbled through a smashed larynx.

Christopher's anger at Etienne had turned white-hot. There was little that he could do for the girl right now. There might be nothing that anyone could do. But he could deal with the legate. "No peasants, no guards, no soldiers," he muttered. "Just you and me."

"Master . . ."

"Take care of her, Pytor. Wait for the guards. I'll have the door open by the time they get here, one way or another." And without waiting for a reply, Christopher caught hold of the end of a projecting beam and swung up to the porch roof. His simple clothing did not hamper him, and he sprang in through the open shutters of the second floor window just as Etienne was turning to aim a kick at the head of the fallen innkeeper.

Christopher hit the churchman soundly with his shoulder, smashing him back against the wall. Etienne slid to the floor, dazed. As Christopher drew his knife, he saw a bloody candlestick lying nearby, and he noticed that Etienne was disheveled and bleeding. The girl, whoever she was, had obviously put up a fight.

The hungry ghost in him smiled. A fighter. He liked that.

But Etienne was getting to his feet. "You wanted to speak with me, dog?" said Christopher. "Well, start talking."

His face gashed from chin to cheek, Etienne shrugged. "About what?"

"You can start with that girl down in the street."

More shouts from below. Edged metal rang, and Christopher heard the distinctive sound of a mail-clad body crashing to a wooden floor. Otto, dazed, scrambled uselessly.

Etienne shrugged again. "She struck me."

"You womanizing lout!"

"What then? Did you think Frenchmen were eunuchs?"

Dagger in hand, Christopher lunged, but Etienne ducked the blow, darted out the open door, and fled down the hall. Christopher followed, angry enough for the moment to give no thought to the fact that the legate had brought numerous attendants with him, most of whom, from the sound of it, were downstairs at present, armed and fighting.

With Etienne just ahead of him, Christopher plunged down the stairs, but when he reached the common room, he stopped for a moment, bewildered by the confusion. Etienne's men were barring the doors against guests and townspeople who were milling before them, struggling to get out, screaming for bailiffs and guards who did not come. A few feet from him, two men in light mail that bore the Shrinerock arms were standing over the body of a third, battling against four more Avignonese. Tables were scattered and smashed, overturned lamps were beginning to smolder in the straw and rushes, and panic was as much an acrid presence as sweat, blood, and smoke.

Christopher debated. Some French knights, motivated by hazy but impelling thoughts of chivalry and honor, would have plunged unhesitatingly into the fray armed with no more than a bent twig. But Christopher had lost belief in chivalry and honor. Chivalry was a sham. Honor was a word exalted more in ballads and poems than in life.

But that girl out there. A fighter. That was good. Christopher could not believe in chivalry and honor, but he decided that he would believe in that girl.

One of the Shrinerock men, fighting like three, lifted a foot against an adversary and kicked him away. Etienne's man lost his balance and fell towards Christopher. The baron stepped aside and let him slam into the wall.

The man reeled. Christopher pounced, slipping his dagger beneath the mail at the man's throat and gouging deep. The soldier's scream was drowned in a gurgle. Christopher grabbed his sword and then, with a good kick, sent him directly into the big fire that blazed on the open hearth. He floundered among the flames and glowing coals.

"Aurverelle!" Christopher could not see Etienne anymore, but his shout rang through the common room, and the Avignonese, startled, hesitated for an instant. It was all Christopher needed. Slashing across the face of one who was attacking the beleaguered Shrinerockers, he whirled the blinded man about with his free hand and let Baron Paul's man finish him off. His foot skidded in the blood that had pooled on the floor, but he let his loss of balance take the point of his sword straight through the chest of another assailant.

The man went down. So, almost, did Christopher, but one of the Shrinerock men caught him. "Christopher delAurvre," Christopher shouted above the din. "Baron of Aurverelle. Pleased to meet you. Carry on!"

And leaving the astonished guard to face another of Etienne's men, he threw himself on the group that was blocking the door. Clad in nondescript garments and therefore invisible amid the crowd of peasants and guests who were scrambling futilely against the Avignonese, Christopher went undetected until his sword found its first mark.

The man fell with an astonished look. "Back!" Christopher shouted. "Give me some room!"

The people of Aurverelle, hearing the voice of their baron, obeyed without question. But though Christopher had room now, so did Etienne's men, and there were six or seven of them to Christopher's single sword.

Pytor, get those guards in here.

He recalled the door. It was still barred. The Avignonese closed on him. He still had no idea where the legate had gone.

With an inward shrug, he stooped and cut through the legs of the first guard, crouched, and let him topple across his back, thereby shielding himself from the three or four swords that came crashing down simultaneously. He straightened, threw the now lifeless body onto two of his attackers, smashed a fist into the face of a third, and managed to kick the bar free of the door.

His foot throbbed. The bar had been heavy. He would be limping for a while.

An Avignonese thrust at him, but he sideslipped the blow and let the sword bury itself in the wall. With a leap, he threw his weight on the flat of the trapped weapon and broke it. Etienne's man was astonished, but Christopher sent him reeling back onto the waiting swords of the Shrinerockers.

Another battle cry split the smoky room. *"God and Saint Adrian!"*

"That's the spirit," Christopher murmured. But the door was opening now, and he caught a glimpse of Pytor's broad face and sharp sword, and of a score of Aurverelle guards. He waved them in, but as he did he saw Etienne making for the stairs.

Etienne saw Christopher, too. He ran.

Christopher caught up with him halfway up the first flight, grabbed his ankle, and jerked him back toward the common room. The churchman fell, his face clattering against the treads like an empty bucket, but he pushed off at the last moment, tumbled the baron to the floor, then rose and made for the upper rooms again. Perhaps he would try to climb down to the street, perhaps he thought he could leap to another roof. Christopher did not intend to give him the chance.

He pounded up the stairs, but when he reached the upper corridor, Etienne had a sword in his hand.

Christopher closed in. "I thought churchmen weren't supposed to carry edged weapons."

Etienne was making a brave show, but his face, where it was not bloody, was pale. He backed down the hall. "We're not supposed to be attacked, either."

Christopher stalked the legate as though he were a boar in a thicket. "Or perhaps you'd prefer to use a brass candlestick. You seem to do fairly well with such things—"

Etienne struck skillfully, but Christopher had been hardened by training and battle, and the disregard for orthodox tactics he had acquired in the course of the crusade was matched now by his contempt for his own life. In a moment, the legate's weapon had clattered to the floor.

Etienne backed up, staring. Christopher had knocked the blade aside with only a gloved fist.

"You're dealing with a delAurvre, Etienne," Christopher said as he came on. "We're a slightly different breed. You're very lucky I'm not my grandfather. He would have served you up boiled for breakfast." He was angry enough that he did not feel the pang: his grandfather had ended his days planting peach trees and bulbs in the garden.

"I am a man of God," said Etienne suddenly. "You can't kill me. You have to allow me to be judged by an ecclesiastical court."

"You're in Aurverelle," said Christopher. "*I'm* the court here."

"You can't kill me in cold blood!"

"Why not? I'm giving you as much of a chance as you gave that girl."

"But she struck me!"

Christopher nodded. Pluck. Determination. Yes, he would believe in that girl. But she had taken the abuse that rightly should have been directed at himself. "She was obviously very discerning."

Etienne turned to run, but Christopher's sword caught him between the shoulder blades, and the legate's legs folded beneath him as though made of dried leaves. A quick backslash, and Etienne's head rolled free.

Christopher's foot was still throbbing, but that did not stop him from giving a sharp kick. The head spun down the hall, thumping hollowly, trailing a fountain of blood.

He leaned against the wall. "And that's the way it should be, you bastard," he said. "Leave the peasants out of it. Leave everyone out of it. Let them live without any parasites like you or me to bother them."

Feet were thudding up the stairs. Pytor appeared. "Master!"

"I'm all right," said Christopher, breathing heavily. He tried to put weight on his right foot, winced. "Someone take care of that girl. Call Guillaume. Call anyone. I want her alive."

CHAPTER 9

"Her name's Vanessa."

The guard from Shrinerock sat on a stool in the great hall, holding a cold compress to his bruised head. He was the picture of dejection, and Christopher could not blame him for that. His captain was dead, his master was critically wounded, and he and his surviving comrade were battered, cut, and exhausted.

Christopher, though, was not inclined to be merciful. He had fought at the Green Man Inn, but he had not fought because of duty or honor. He had fought for the girl named Vanessa, who now lay in a castle bedroom.

"What was she doing with Martin Osmore?"

"Going to Saint Blaise. Master Martin wa' her escort."

And Master Martin, too, was in a castle bed, writhing and screaming from a sword thrust to his stomach. But Martin seemed tormented by a little more than his wound. Christopher had heard him even from down the hall: *"Don't send me to hell, Yvonnet!"*

Interesting. There were rumors about Yvonnet. This confirmed them. But Christopher was more interested in Vanessa. "What was she going to do in Saint Blaise?"

"I dan know. I think Master Martin said sa'thing about her being an apprentice."

"Did you ever talk to her?"

The soldier looked up, met Christopher's eyes, and the baron saw fear in his face. "I dan't talk to her at all, m'lord."

Fear? "Why not?"

"She's . . ." The soldier dropped his eyes, clutched the cloth to his head. Trickles of water wound down his face and dripped to the flagstone floor. "I think she's possessed. I think her ma and da sent her to Saint Blaise to be rid o' her."

Possessed? Nonsense. A fighter, rather. But, like Christopher himself, a reject.

He could understand that. As much as he had turned his back on the virtues and questions of honor that impelled his society, his action had been but an echo of their rejection of him. "Thank you, sir," he said, standing. "I'll leave you now. Master Pytor will see to a room for you and your friend."

The man looked up. "An' Thomas?"

"Efram is looking after him. We can bury him here, or we can send him back to Shrinerock. I'll send messengers to Baron Paul and Mayor Matthew in the morning."

Odd. All of a sudden, Christopher was breaking his isolation. He had brought strangers into the castle—commoners at that—and now he was going to be sending messages not only to Paul delMari, whose grandfather, as he now recalled, had been murdered by old Roger himself, but also to the Free Towns, against which Roger had plotted.

Shaking his head, Christopher mounted the stairs to the upper floor of the residence, wincing slightly at the pain in his right foot.

But he forgot about the pain when he entered Vanessa's room. She lay quietly, swathed in the linen bandages that Guillaume and Jerome had applied, but Christopher had already seen the extent of the damage inflicted upon her. Broken arms, broken wrists, broken legs from the fall. Ribs caved in. A smashed skull . . . and probably damage to her brain. Her blond hair, matted with seeping blood, wicked the fluid away from her wounds and stained her pillow.

From down the hall, Christopher could hear Martin screaming: "Don't send me to hell. Yvonnet! No! Again, please . . . yesyesyes . . ."

Guillaume stood up from tying a last strip of linen in place, cocked an ear at the screams. "He'll live," he said. "Seen it before. The boy's young. Strong as a destrier. Take more than a single thrust to do him in. Hurt himself if he keeps on like that."

Christopher folded his arms. "So he'll live. Tie him up if you're worried about his wet dreams."

"Tie him up?"

"You tied *me* up. What about Vanessa?"

"The girl . . ." Guillaume shook his head, the seams of his old face growing deeper. "She's dead, I'm afraid."

This was not what Christopher wanted to hear. "She's still breathing."

"Not by much."

And, true, Vanessa's breaths were shallow, with long spaces between exhalation and intake.

"She won't last much longer," said Guillaume. "It's sad. True, though."

But though Guillaume did not know it, the girl on the bed was not simply Vanessa of Furze Hamlet. She had come to be also Baron Christopher delAurvre and whatever shreds of hope and belief might have been left to him. A fighter . . .

He would not let her go.

"Fix her," he said.

"Can't be done."

"Fix her. Do whatever you can. If you can't do it, then get help."

"My lord—"

"*Do it!*"

Christopher turned and left the room, straining to hear, as he stepped down the corridor, the sound of Vanessa's next breath.

Guillaume did what he could, and when, in spite of his art and science, Vanessa continued to sink, he shook his old head and sent for aid. At his request, Peter of Maris made the journey down from the coast; but after a cursory examination, he advised bleeding the girl—and was thrown bodily out of the castle by Christopher himself. Carl of Vienna arrived a few days later with a more cautious approach, and Jakob ben Yuzef of Belroi came with his knowledge and skill and his willingness to touch even Gentile flesh if by doing so he might bring comfort. Together with Guillaume, they labored throughout many nights, changing dressings, noting symptoms, spooning as much broth into the girl's unconscious mouth as she could be made to swallow without choking.

They tried herbs, poultices, even prayer; and once, yes, Vanessa actually seemed to rally. Her eyes flickered half open, and she peered glassily at the faces above her. Christopher, who knelt beside the bed, peered back, hoping for some sound, perhaps a word. "Vanessa," he called softly.

Her eyes focused for an instant, and the baron saw a light

in them. Not a mad light, not a sick light. It was, instead, as of someone who had seen . . . too much, and who was even now seeing. It was a frightening look, and its terror was magnified by the fact that it came from a face so broken that it was hardly recognizable as belonging to a woman.

Jerome murmured a prayer, and Guillaume sat back, shaken, but Christopher met Vanessa's eyes levelly. He, too, had seen too much. He, too, was even now seeing. "I know," he said softly. He touched her bandaged hand. "I know."

But then Vanessa's eyes closed, and she lapsed back into fevered dreams.

"Can't believe it," said Guillaume at the end of the second week. "Amazing. She's still holding on."

"Is she getting better?" said Christopher.

Guillaume dropped his eyes. "She's getting worse, my lord."

Martin, on the other hand, was improving. Though he was still in pain, his fever had left him, and he was eating. He drooped, though, and his blackened eyes and bruised wrists—emblems of an encounter, Christopher knew, that had nothing to do with the fray at the inn—were stark against a dark face that pain and fever had left the color of old ashes.

"Tell me about Vanessa," said Christopher, perching on a stool by his bed.

Martin looked frightened, and Christopher read his fear. Here was the famous baron of Aurverelle, the one who was mad. And not only was Martin a commoner, he was also a sodomite, a practitioner of a secret vice considered worse even than murder or adultery.

Christopher found himself rather unconcerned. Compared to Nicopolis—or, for that matter, Vanessa's wounds— Martin's choice of recreation seemed a paltry thing. But, yes, he was the baron of Aurverelle, and, yes, he was mad— if madness lay in seeing too much, in having no illusions.

"What . . . what do you want to know?" said Martin.

"Why did her parents send her away?"

"She's . . . different."

Christopher nearly laughed. "You're different, too . . ."

Martin turned white.

". . . and I didn't notice that Baron Paul was sending you to the stake for it."

Stripped, vulnerable, Martin scrambled for some security. "He doesn't . . . he doesn't know."

"Don't be so sure," said Christopher. "Baron Paul only pretends to be an idiot."

Martin looked worse. "You want to know about Vanessa, not about me."

Christopher planted his elbows on his knees, settled his chin in his hands. "I already know about you. If it reassures you, I don't give a damn. You can stick your prick down the throats of breeding herons if you want. I don't care. Tell me about Vanessa."

Martin shrugged. "I don't know her very well. I don't think that anyone can. Her father told Baron Paul that he wanted her to be able to better herself, but I don't believe that. I think he was afraid."

Afraid? Of Vanessa? But Christopher recalled the light in her eyes. Yes, and people were afraid of the baron of Aurverelle, too. Probably for much the same reason. "Why?"

"Has she *looked* at you?"

Christopher smiled. "Like I'm looking at you right now."

Martin shuddered. "It's nothing like it. You'll see."

"Believe me, I want to see."

Martin was silent.

"You know," said Christopher, "you've been in this castle for three weeks now, and never once have you asked about Vanessa."

Martin was silent.

"Don't you care?"

"I . . ." Martin's dark eyes flickered. "I have my own problems."

Christopher grabbed him by the front of his shirt, pulled him half up. "You don't give a *damn* about anyone else, do you? You're just like me." And then he shoved the lad back onto the bed and left the room.

Vanessa continued to worsen. By the next morning, she was hovering liminally between life and death, her breathing almost nonexistent, her heartbeat irregular, weak, fluttering. Christopher wanted to stay by her bed, but—the business of a baron once again intruding on him—Martin's parents arrived at noon. They had come up from Saint Blaise to take their son home.

Matthew Osmore was a stout man with a thick shock of dark hair that spilled luxuriantly over the silks and velvets he wore. To Christopher's annoyance, Matthew persisted in addressing him as an equal—which, from a purely economic point of view, was probably the case—and he seemed to be constantly surveying the castle as though he were calculating how much it would cost to build one just like it.

"Awfully grateful to you, Christopher," he said. "Martin's our only son—got lots of daughters, you know, but only one man in the old pecker . . ." He laughed loudly. ". . . and we were frantic, absolutely frantic about him when we heard about that little tiff with the clergyman. I imagine Martin acquitted himself well?"

Martin, as far as Christopher knew, had lunged, taken a sword thrust to the abdomen, and fallen on the floor. "I believe he did quite well, sir."

"Excellent. Excellent. We've got a real man to look forward to, then, don't we, Bonne?"

Matthew's wife was equally stout, but she wore her peasant origins proudly. Her clothes were relatively plain, with just enough ornament to show that she *could* have had much more had she wanted to . . . but she did not want to, you see.

She curtsied to Christopher, her round face touched with worry. "We're very grateful, my lord," she said softly. "Very grateful."

"What became of that churchman, anyway?" said Matthew. "I'd like to have a bit of a talk with him."

"He's dead," said Christopher. "I killed him."

Matthew quickly changed the subject.

Martin, Christopher saw, was a commodity, one to be raised like a crop of wheat, weighed and fingered to find its worth, and sold to the highest bidder. Matthew had already picked out a fine wife for him—"Ah, Martin," he said when he told him of it, "she's a good woman! She has potential . . . and money!"—and had most of the lad's life already mapped out.

Martin suffered through the reunion in silence and took his mother's anxious cooing over his wounds with comparative dignity. Christopher nodded his approval, and even graciously commented upon the lad's role in the battle—one that he made sure included ropes about the wrists and the blacking of eyes—for which Martin looked unutterably grateful.

And then the mayor and his family went off as they had

come: with pomp, and silks, and attendants, and all the little perquisites of noble blood that the wealth of Saint Blaise could buy . . . save, of course, the blood itself.

Christopher watched them go. Not once had any of them so much as mentioned Vanessa.

He was, he knew, obsessing on her. She was a peasant from Furze Hamlet, a village girl who had been burdened with some unfortunate talent that more than likely would eventually take her to the stake along with all the rest who had been rejected and abandoned and consigned to the fiery embrace of the Inquisition. Yvonnet escaped because of his position, likewise Christopher himself, but Vanessa, Martin . . . it was only a matter of time.

But Vanessa had become a good deal more than a girl to him. She had become an emblem of himself. Fighting. Fighting against the Etiennes that populated the world. Fighting against the lies and the dearth of honor. Fighting, perhaps, even against the fate that was slowly catching up with her. She could have let Etienne have his way with her. She could, he was convinced, have let herself die by now. She had not.

He ascended the stairs, entered her room. She was failing, and he could now only watch helplessly. No skill, no amount of money, no medicine could preserve any longer a body that had simply been battered into wreckage. It would take a miracle to save her, and Christopher had seen enough even before Nicopolis to know that miracles did not happen.

That afternoon, he thanked Guillaume and Pytor and Jerome and Raffalda and the physicians who had tried to help, sent them away, and settled in at her bedside.

He could not even hold her hand. Too many bandages. What little of her face showed through the layers of white cloth was raw and bloody. He did not even know what she looked like, had never heard her speak his name.

No matter. It was over now, and as the hours crawled by toward sunset, he sat beside her, waiting for the end.

The sun was touching the summits of the Aleser Mountains when Pytor knocked. "Master."

"What is it, Pytor?"

The Russian opened the door and stuck his head in. "Master, there are physicians at the gate. They say they have come to see Vanessa."

Vanessa was hardly breathing. "They're too late," said

Christopher. "Give them supper and a place for the night and send them on their way."

Pytor looked uncomfortable. "Master, they say they have come from a great distance. They wish to see what they can do."

Christopher had wanted no interruptions and no company during these last minutes with his beliefs, and the thought of disturbing Vanessa with more futile examinations and proddings revolted him. But he could not help but wonder and hope: maybe. And if maybe, then possibly. And could he deny Vanessa—or himself—that chance?

Vanessa suddenly dragged in a deep breath, held it, let it out, paused. Christopher, teeth clenched, stared at her swathed face for some time. Abruptly, Vanessa dragged in another breath, held it . . .

A fighter. "Send them up."

Pytor returned a short time later with a man and a woman. Their garments were unremarkable, and they entered quietly. But their faces and their eyes made Christopher stare and brought him to his feet to acknowledge them, for their faces were very fair—the man's as womanly as the maid's—and their eyes seemed to reflect more light than what came from the hearth and the windows.

The man regarded him dispassionately, almost coldly. "My name is Terrill, my lord baron," he said, bowing. "This is my assistant, Mirya."

Mirya was tall and straight, her hair the color of red gold and her eyes as green as emerald. Christopher could not but stare at her. "You say you've come . . ."

"From far away," she said. Her voice was a firm contralto, at once expressive and calm.

Christopher's brow furrowed. "You're physicians?"

Terrill named his credentials. They were impeccable. Montpellier. Prague. Bologna. Tolouse. Orleans. But as he spoke, he kept glancing uneasily at the bed in which Vanessa lay, and Mirya made as if to hover anxiously over her. Their faces had turned drawn at the sight of her, and their demeanor was fairly shouting: *Please, let us stop talking and start working.*

Christopher could see that their interest was as sincere as his own. He did not ask why. He looked at Vanessa, looked at himself, his hope. "Please . . . can you . . . ?"

Terrill nodded slowly. "Leave us alone with her."

Christopher hesitated. Alone? What if . . . ?

Terrill's eyes flashed. "You cannot help us by your presence." His tone was as cold—and as earnest—as his eyes. "Please, my lord."

But Christopher's doubts refused to be quashed. Others had tried. Others had failed. "Can you save her?" *Can you save me?*

Mirya looked at him as though she had heard his silent question as clearly as his utterance. Her eyes were bright, almost luminous. "We can," she said. "Please go now."

Gritting his teeth with worry and hope both, Christopher turned and left, herding an astonished Pytor out ahead of him. Shaking, he shut the door, bent his head, heard Mirya say from within the room: "Help me remove these bandages, beloved."

A minute later, Terrill spoke: *"Ai, Elthiai!"*

Mirya then—sad, grieving: "They have not forgotten."

"Nor have we."

Silence then. Christopher went down the hall hand in hand with Pytor. He was still shaking.

But if they could save Vanessa . . .

An hour went by, two hours. The light was fading from the sky and the little bell in the chapel was ringing compline before Christopher, his worry finally conquering him, climbed the stairs to the upper hall and found that the door to Vanessa's room was standing open.

Terrill and Mirya were waiting for him, but he went immediately to the bed. Vanessa had been freshly bandaged, but her breathing sounded normal—soft, regular, even—and she appeared to be sleeping rather than comatose.

Terrill spoke. "She will live." His eyes had followed Christopher to the bed, and the baron sensed that his every move was being evaluated for reasons he could not even begin to guess. "Leave her bandages on for six weeks. This is . . ." He looked at Mirya, hesitating. Then: "This is essential for her to heal properly."

Vanessa appeared to be much better. But, more than that, Christopher sensed that she *was* better. There was a feeling of health about the girl that glowed like a bowl of sunlight. "She's . . . she's well."

Terrill bowed slightly. Mirya curtsied.

Christopher sagged into a chair, passed a hand over his

face. "She's well." He felt tears starting out. "My God," he said. "I . . ."

Mirya came forward, knelt before him, touched him lightly on the shoulder. He saw grief in her eyes. "Be at peace, my lord baron. I understand." And Christopher did not doubt that she did. "Vanessa is . . . precious to us, too."

Christopher looked up. "To you?"

Mirya smiled softly. "But she is safe now, and therefore we must go. Thank you for letting us see her."

"Ah . . ." Christopher stood up. "But . . . your fee . . ."

"We have been well paid already, my lord," said Mirya. "Indeed . . ." She looked at Terrill, her eyes again sad, then turned back to Christopher. "I believe it is to you that we owe a debt."

Terrill looked away.

Pytor, who had been waiting dutifully by the door, escorted the strange visitors down the hall. Faintly, Christopher heard him offering them supper and beds, heard also their polite refusals. They had to go. They had other tasks, other healings. . . .

Wishing that he could have convinced them to stay, trembling with relief, Christopher shut the door and knelt by the bed. Vanessa was sleeping soundly, and Terrill and Mirya must have cleaned up some of the oozing blood that had covered her, for the flesh that showed between the bandages was pink, healthy, unstained.

Voices outside. Pytor was escorting the visitors to the gate, thanking them for their help over and over in his genial Russian way. Christopher bent over Vanessa, touched, with a trembling hand, her bandaged face. His hope. His hope: rescued. She was alive. He was no doctor, but he could see that. She would be well, and regardless of her strangeness, regardless of what she saw or the fear that followed her, she had given him a sign of his own possible redemption. Vanessa had lived. She might continue to live. And so, therefore, might Christopher.

Gingerly, as though parting the curtains of a temple, he lifted an edge of the bandages on her face. Healthy flesh. Not a cut, not a scrape, not even a bruise. Baffled, he went so far as to push back the dressings that covered her jaw. No blood, not a sign of a wound.

He hesitated for some time, debating, recalling Orpheus as he had once contemplated Odysseus. Then, though he was now shaking badly, he uncovered Vanessa's head.

He looked into the face of a lovely young woman. Unmarred. Healthy. Whole. And he did not doubt that the rest of her body would exhibit the same profound and complete transformation from shattered to sound.

Pytor knocked suddenly at the door, and the baron nearly cried out. "Master, they have departed."

Christopher found himself staring at the silver pendant that lay on top of the bandages about Vanessa's chest. Moon and star. It glittered at him. Another sign? Of what?

"Master?"

Quickly, Christopher replaced the bandages and tucked the pendant beneath the coverlet, feeling torn between mammoth fright and infinite thankfulness. He did not know what to think, but he settled for acceptance. Vanessa had lived. Maybe . . . maybe Christopher . . .

Pytor opened the door. "Master?"

"She's fine, Pytor," said the baron. "Terrill and Mirya did it. Absolutely amazing. We'll leave the dressings alone, as the good . . ." He looked at the door, wondering frightened, but clinging to acceptance. ". . . doctors ordered, but please tell David to prepare something nice for Vanessa. I think she'll be hungry when she wakes up."

CHAPTER 10

The next morning, Vanessa opened her eyes for the second time in Castle Aurverelle. This time, Christopher was ready.

Ready for the light. Ready for the conviction that what Vanessa saw with her brown, luminous eyes was much, much more than any one human being ought to be allowed to see, or could, in fact, stand to see. Just as it was with himself.

But this morning, mixed with that light and knowledge, the baron saw fear. Not the paltry kind that came from strange surroundings and a concern for physical safety, but a fear that could only stem from an utter demolition of belief; and though he smiled to reassure her, inwardly he saw the parallel again. Vanessa's surety had obviously perished beneath Etienne's lechery and a brass candlestick; his own beliefs had died on the sands of Nicopolis.

He talked to her, asked her questions, found that she remembered who she was and what had happened. That was good. Christopher had seen strong men reduced to idiocy by much smaller head wounds. Apparently the talents and methods of Mirya and Terrill—whoever and whatever they were, but let that pass—included the painstaking reassembly of a mind.

He told her where she was and how she had gotten there, but as Vanessa's eyes flitted about the room, taking in stolid Pytor, arid Jerome, matronly Raffalda, Christopher still sensed her fear. Deep-seated. Relentless.

"It's all right," he said. "You're safe here, and you'll be fine. You had some good doctors." Good doctors, indeed! But he squelched the thought. He was determined to keep up the charade of Vanessa's bandages for the stipulated length of time. Best, therefore, not to let her know that it was a charade at all.

"An' Martin wa' wounded," she said, her eyes, restless,

still examining the room as though it might suddenly shift into another form.

"Yes," said Christopher. "He's with his parents now."

"Aye . . . tha' I saw. Tha' I knew." She suddenly focused on Christopher. "Wi' are you doing thi' for such as me?"

Christopher smiled. "You fought Etienne of Languedoc. That means that we're on the same side. Think of it as a gesture of a comrade in arms."

Out of the corner of his eye, he saw Jerome and Pytor exchange glances. Yes, he supposed that he was sounding like a madman again, but the seneschal and the bailiff would just have to get used to that.

And Vanessa's eyes, luminous, bright, bored in at him. "You di' it because o' the battle, din't you?"

Nicopolis. She could see it. Christopher suddenly understood why Vanessa's traveling companions had been so frightened of her.

He pursed his lips. "Yes," he said. "I did."

His brutal honesty seemed to shock her a little, but she only nodded.

Though she had to remain bandaged, Christopher saw no reason to keep her confined to bed. He urged her not to exert herself too much—he had, after all, no real understanding of the intricacies of the healing that she had received—but, much to the distress of Pytor and Jerome, he gave her the freedom of the castle and, since her fingers were still clumsy with linen wrappings, insisted upon feeding her with his own hands.

He was feeding himself. He was freeing himself. He was nurturing himself. He struggled constantly to be aware of the fact that Vanessa was a peasant girl, that she had her own sorrows and her own burdens, but privately, he allowed himself to use her—in fine delAurvre style, he admitted—as a means to his own ends. If he could help Vanessa, if he could make her happy, then he himself had a chance.

But Vanessa gave him little chance to forget her individuality, for when she was not with Christopher, she wandered through the deserted corridors of Aurverelle like a restless, wide-eyed bird, trailing her sham bandages like broken feathers. No one was safe from her knowing eyes, nor from the strange, unpredictable comments she made that struck unerringly at her listener's most private and sensitive thoughts.

"It wa' the monastery, wan' it?" she said to Jerome. "You were a' fighting among yourselves about the popes?"

The Franciscan stood as though struck, crossed himself without thinking.

"It's a' right," said Vanessa. "You di' well to leave." Jerome fled.

And Pytor heard about Medno, about the money he had borrowed at a ruinous rate of interest by indenturing himself and his family, about his failure to repay it, about the sickness that had taken his wife and daughters because he could not afford a doctor. And David was confronted with wide brown eyes and reassurances about his talents and abilities. And Ranulf was told about the daughter that he had always wished that he had. And . . .

Only Christopher, who freely admitted the existence of his personal demons, was unshaken by Vanessa's words. He did not cross himself or flee: he simply nodded. He did not fear her. How could he? He *was* her.

When he found that she could read, he made sure that she saw the library and he issued orders that she be given whatever books she wanted—a relief to many, because she began to spend much time in her room with heavy volumes open on her lap. He took her for walks in the gardens that his grandfather had planted. He sang for her, taught her courtly dances, ordered several fine gowns for her. But when, on a whim, he growled for her and capered like a bear, she looked distressed and shushed him quickly. "Dan do tha'," she said. "Dan do tha' to yourself."

Christopher dropped his arms. "To myself, Vanessa?"

"It hurts you to do tha'," she said. "You di' too much o' it . . . before."

Her eyes were as strange and knowing as ever, but her voice was full of concern. Christopher considered, nodded, and taking her arm, set off once more along the avenue of peach trees. "You know," he said, "you really distress people when you go on like that."

Vanessa drooped. "I know. I see tha', too."

"Why do you do it, then?"

"I . . ." She looked up at the interlacing leaves and incipient fruit. Criss-crossing branches reflected in her eyes. She had told Christopher about the patterns that she saw:

patterns that contained everything, patterns that interlaced with greater complexity than even these pleached and twined branches, patterns that allowed her—forced her—to see into people's lives . . . and, with maddening regularity, into the future. "I can't help it," she said.

"Have you ever thought to simply remain silent?"

Vanessa hung her bandaged head, clung to his arm as though blind. "The patterns say tha' I can't. They tell me I ha' to talk. They say there's no other way. An' so I say wha' I see, an' then e'eryone hates me."

"They don't hate you, Vanessa. They're just afraid."

"People hate what they're afraid o'." The brown eyes were filling with tears now. "That's wi' my ma and da sent me awa'. That's wi' the folk i' my village din't talk to me. That's wi' your folk run awa' now."

There was a bench at the end of the avenue, and Christopher pulled her down onto it and held her while she wept. For a few minutes, she was no longer a feral little fox that had trotted into the main hall of Castle Aurverelle; she was, rather, simply a girl of fifteen summers, a girl who had seen too much pain and loss.

"It doesn't work," said Christopher, rocking her gently. "If it doesn't work, then don't do it any more. Don't even try. I learned that at Nicopolis."

"The . . ." She was seeing again. ". . . the battle."

"Yes." He smiled thinly. "You saw that right off, didn't you, my dear girl? Practically the first words out of your mouth."

She bit her lip, and the tears welled again. Christopher shook his head.

"No," he said. "No, don't cry. I didn't say that to wound. You saw it because it's become me, just like your patterns have become you. I don't play at knighthood anymore because it hurts me, and it hurts everyone around me. I gave it up. It doesn't work." He took her hands, grimaced at the intervening bandages, and, without thinking, freed her fingers from their linen swaddling.

Flesh against flesh. That was good. To his grandfather before his reform, it would have been an encouragement to strip off Vanessa's gown and put her on her back in the middle of the lawn, but Christopher, though he had possessed his share of country maidens—and, God help him, his wife, Anna—was content with the holiness of this simple touch: one abandoned soul taking the hands of another and finding in that gentle clasp a faint assurance of companionship.

And maybe, someday, healing.

"Don't try, Vanessa," he said softly. "Don't even try. Something my grandfather taught me: if you don't say anything at all, people will hear what they want to hear." And was that bit of counsel the product of the years before or after Roger's remarkable reform? He did not know. He found that at present he did not care.

"But the patterns . . ." She was shaking her head violently. "The patterns say I must. The patterns show wha' must be, an' so tha's the way it is . . . unless . . ." She drooped. ". . . unless . . ." There was a sudden flash of fear in her eyes, the same that he had seen that first morning: the look of an animal caught in a trap.

"Unless?"

Her fear was stark, uncompromising. "I saw them change," she said softly. "The patterns. I didn't think they could change, but when the legate cam up to me, I saw them change. He changed them. Everything turned about, an' then there wa' a different future. . . ."

Christopher finally understood. It was not Etienne's attack itself that had so shattered Vanessa. It was, instead, that the churchman's unexpected violence had fragmented her world of absolute predestination into an infinitude of maybes. Now, sundered from her firm, fixed, tragic universe, she was adrift in a sea of uncertainty.

"An' I dan understand it now," Vanessa was sobbing. "I dan understand anything. Wha' does it mean?"

Christopher looked back along the avenue to the castle. Straight. Unswerving. He and Vanessa had walked the length of it to the bench they now occupied. But where they went from here—whether to the arbor across the open expanse of lawn, to the fountain that spurted cool water on even the hottest of days, or to the stand of beech trees that Roger had left deliberately haphazard and unkempt so as to better resemble a little piece of deep forest—was open to choice. Anything was possible. Even God did not know everything that would happen. Or if He did, He at least had the courtesy—

No. Courtesy had nothing to do with it. It was free will.

"It means," he said, "that you're just like the rest of us, Vanessa."

She blinked at him, bewildered. "I dan understand."

"You see patterns, you say . . ." Not having Vanessa's eyes, Christopher had no real idea what he was talking about, but he was mad, and therefore perhaps his babblings—like the ravings of madmen everywhere—might, by chance, contain a particle of truth. "Maybe what you see doesn't cause the world. Maybe it only reflects it. Etienne changed the patterns because he made a choice. You can change them by making a choice, too. You can keep silent."

"So . . ." Vanessa looked at her fingers. The nails, after two weeks in bandages, were long and smooth. "So I shouldn't say anything about wha' I see?"

Christopher shook his head. "Not because you shouldn't. Because you don't have to. It's your decision."

Vanessa had obviously become accustomed to heeding the maze of images in her mind as though they were immutable decrees, had fallen into the habit of passively accepting what came as inevitable. Now Christopher was telling her something different. But he was telling himself the same thing, for he had himself accepted passively, as a redeeming standard to set up against his grandfather's vices and virtues, the tortured logic of a theory of conduct and society devised by men who had never confronted the arid plateaux of Nicopolis . . . and his world had fragmented when it had been proven false.

She was looking at him with bright eyes. "Your grandfather . . ."

He caught his breath. Unerringly, positively unerringly, she had laid her finger upon his heart.

But Vanessa started to cry again. "See? I've done it again. Now you'll send me awa'."

Christopher shook his head, still amazed. "Where . . . where on earth would I send you?"

"I'm going to Saint Blaise. I've got to go t' Saint Blaise. The patterns say I've got to go."

Christopher grappled with the wound that she had touched. He had to ignore it for now. It was important that he ignore it. "Do they . . . do they say that you *have* to? Or just that you will if you don't choose to do otherwise?"

Her tears stopped abruptly, and she stared out of her bandaged face. "But . . . where else would I go?"

"Do you have family? I mean, besides in Furze Hamlet?"

It was a foolish question, one that came from a nobleman with blood ties that caught all of Adria and much of Europe in their meshes. What family could Vanessa possibly have outside of Furze Hamlet?

But to his surprise, she nodded. "My grandma is in Saint Brigid. If she's still alive."

Saint Brigid? There was a story in that, he was sure. "Might she accept you for what you are? Patterns or not?"

"I . . . I dan know. Da said that she wa' always different, too." She stared out at the peach avenue. One of many paths. Only one of many. It was a frightening thought, but a liberating one, too. "I dan know . . . I dan know what to think."

"Give yourself a chance." Christopher pulled out a handkerchief and dried her tears. "Think about it. You can do whatever you want. Think about that."

He took her back to her bedroom and told her to rest, then went down to the kitchen and found David. "I want a feast tomorrow night," he said.

David had looked uncertain at Christopher's entrance, as though he half-expected him to seize a barrel of apples and begin pelting the kitchen boys with fruit; but at the baron's words, he broke out in smiles. "My lord, it would give me no greater *pleas*ure. May I ask whom we shall be entertaining?"

"Vanessa. Her bandages are coming off this evening." Really, though, his orders had little to do with her bandages. They had, rather, to do with her soul. Or maybe his soul. He was not sure. Or maybe it did not really matter.

At the mention of Vanessa, David's face turned uncertain again. "Ah . . . as you wish, my lord."

Lips pursed with annoyance, Christopher stalked towards the door and, on the way out, fired an apple straight at the chef. David caught it. Between the monkey and the baron, he was getting quite good at such things.

"You don't approve of her either, do you, Jerome?"

It was evening, and Christopher was readying himself for the banquet he had arranged for Vanessa. True, he had rushed the removal of her bandages by a few weeks, but she was obviously healed, and had been, in fact, since Terrill and Mirya (whoever they were) had finished their treatment (whatever that was). And so the bandages had come off, and for the first time since he had left for Nicopolis, Christopher had called for his baronial finery. Now Raffalda was lacing him into a silk undershirt and the crimson velvet tunic with the slashed sleeves and the embroidery, diamonds, and pearls; and now Jerome was standing by the door, a frowning apparition.

"My lord," said the Franciscan, "it's not for me to approve or disapprove—"

"You sound just like Pytor sometimes, Jerome. Did you know that?"

Jerome sighed. "My lord, it isn't seemly."

Christopher took the velvet cap from Raffalda and fitted it on his head. He peered into a mirror. The baron of Aurverelle. Stuffed and padded and wrapped and laced. Laughable, really. But it was a feast, and he was celebrating. Spectacle, at least, was something that he could do for Vanessa.

Christopher turned about. "Do you like this outfit, Jerome?"

"Very nice, my lord . . ." Jerome cleared his throat. "Ah . . ."

"The very picture of a baron, no?"

"Very."

"What isn't seemly?"

"Vanessa."

"Thought so."

Jerome tried again. "Baron Christopher, there are noblemen all over Europe who have acquired . . . attachments to women of lesser rank."

Christopher was deliberately preening much more than was necessary. "And occasionally to men. Right, Jerome?"

The Franciscan colored. His aversion to Martin's vice had been obvious. He had not even been willing to say hello to the lad once he had become aware of his liaison with Yvonnet. "Ah, correct, my lord."

"You should be glad it's a woman, Jerome. When I first showed up in my beard and rags, it might well have been a horse."

"My lord!"

Grinning, Christopher flopped down in a chair and stuck out his feet. Raffalda rummaged through a chest. "No, Raffalda. Not the *poulains*. I'm a baron, not a duck." But he nodded to her eventual discovery of a pair of well-made boots. "Talk, Jerome," he said as she set about squeezing his feet into them. "Tell me about Vanessa. Tell me she's a peasant. Tell me she's below my class. Tell me that—oh, dear God!—people will talk."

"They will, my lord."

"They talked about my madness. Nothing happened."

Jerome pursed his lips and did not speak.

Christopher straightened up. He knew that look. "All right. What happened?"

"One of our wool shipments on the way to Ghent was intercepted on the other side of the Aleser Mountains. Near the border with Champagne. The free companies. Brigands usually stay away from Aurverelle goods, for good reason. However . . ."

"Well, perhaps we have some stupid brigands." Christopher snorted. "Anyone daft enough to take a wool shipment . . ."

"Perhaps they are emboldened by my lord's . . . ah . . ." Jerome colored. His words had taken him a little too far.

Christopher finished the sentence. "By my lord's idiotic infatuation with a peasant girl."

Jerome stayed colored.

"Isn't that it?"

Jerome did not speak.

"Or maybe it's the fact that she's crazy, too? Or possessed? Or heretical? Or something like that?"

Jerome looked stricken. "My dear lord, I didn't say that."

"You thought it loud enough, Jerome."

Raffalda grunted and strained as she pressed the tight-fitting boots onto Christopher's feet. She was damp and flushed when she rose. "Will there be anything else, my lord?" she said with a curtsy.

Christopher stood up. He thought about wearing a sword, but he did not have any really splendid swords anymore, and the occasion demanded splendor. Better none at all, then. "Thank you, Raffalda, no. Jerome and I will continue our battle alone. You can go and help Vanessa get ready."

Raffalda curtsied again and departed, shutting the door behind her.

Jerome passed a hand across his face. "My lord, Pytor

and I are concerned. The girl is a definite liability to Aurverelle. The castle folk's morale . . .''

''What about *my* morale, Jerome? When was the last time you saw me dressed up like a properly noble idiot?''

''I admit that she has had some positive effects, my lord, but I think you can see my point.''

Yes, disagreeable though the admission was, he could see. For a while, he had allowed himself to ignore the fact that Vanessa, feral and strange, had no place in Aurverelle. For a while, he had immersed himself in her care, in his own care. But there were futures to think about, both Vanessa's and his own.

He did not love her. Even had he still been capable of love, he could sooner have loved a fox, or a beech tree, or a thunderstorm as exhibit romantic inclinations towards the strange elemental creature that he had rescued from the streets of the town. Nor could Vanessa, caught up as she was in an inner pandemonium of vision and knowledge, ever love him.

But there was more to it than love. Christopher sat down, idly examining the polished toes of his boots. He had found hope. Vanessa, perhaps could find hope, too. She would have to leave—indeed, he had himself established the nearness of her departure by removing her bandages—but maybe he could give her something before she went, something that might sustain her.

''Do you hate Vanessa for being strange, Jerome?''

''Why . . . no.''

''Is she damned, do you think?''

''I confess I don't know, my lord.''

''Could you care about someone, Jerome, even if that someone was damned?''

The friar stood, speechless.

Christopher propped his feet up on the chest. ''When I was still taking the sacraments, I heard a great deal from the priests about the Kingdom of God. About how it included everyone from the lowliest peasant to the greatest monarch. But what about Vanessa? What about all the people like her? They didn't make any choices about what they became. They didn't have any choices to make. Does the Kingdom not include them?''

Jerome's eyes were on the floor. ''I . . . am not sure that I am equipped to speak of such things, Baron Christopher.

Perhaps the learned Doctor of Aquino might have been able to answer your question.''

''But he's dead.'' Christopher stood up. ''So I'll answer it myself. *My* Kingdom includes Vanessa. *My* Kingdom includes all the Hobs and Jakes and Tims and Toms, all the madmen and all the seers . . . maybe even the bears and the horses. Because, you see, that's all we have. Each other. Those people kept me alive with their black bread and beans, and I helped them in their fields and slept in their ditches and picked them up out of the street and put them to bed in my castle. And that's what I call the Kingdom of God.''

Jerome bowed low.

''Vanessa will leave when she's healed a bit more, Jerome.'' *When I'm healed a bit more.* ''She has her life, and I have mine. But I'll tell you: as much as you condemn her, as heretical as you might think she is, she's helped me. She's given me something to believe in, and she'll always have a place in my Kingdom.''

And at dinner that night, with David's brilliantly decorated and splendidly served foods adorning the table like so many edible gems, with Pytor and Efram providing humble entertainment by singing carols throughout the evening, Christopher found that his belief was beginning to be justified; for though Vanessa was as wide-eyed and feral as ever, she spoke in measured words about . . . commonplaces. The weather. The books she had read. The flowers in the garden.

She complimented Pytor and Efram on their singing and thanked them over and over again, her dairyland speech contrasting quaintly with her glittering gown; and when Christopher offered her his hand for a dance, she accepted with tears in her eyes. Yes, there was belief. Yes, there was hope. The patterns only indicated, they did not compel. She could learn to keep silent. Maybe . . . maybe she could learn other things, too.

Not even when Christopher felt the first, queasy stirrings of nausea did she say anything. The baron's stomach, confronted with rich sauces, sugar, and fat after a six-month diet of nothing more extravagant than black bread, beans, onions, and water, was beginning to rebel, but he continued to eat and be merry. He saw that Vanessa sensed his distress and knew the inevitable outcome, but he saw also that she did not speak of it.

And so, later that night, though he was racked by alternate fits of vomiting and diarrhea, Christopher did not mind the discomfort in the least. Sitting in the privy as the chapel bells tolled lauds, holding a bowl full of half-digested grease and bile in his lap, he felt, instead, rather triumphant.

CHAPTER 11

Triumphant though it was, the banquet marked the end of the charade. Vanessa was well. She had been well, in fact, since Mirya and Terrill had healed her, but the baron, caught up in his pursuit of a vicarious and less physical healing, had been content to follow the strange physicians' instructions to as much of a letter as his inborn willfulness would allow.

But now it was over. Vanessa would be leaving. Indeed, she had to leave, for though Christopher had made inroads into her fatalism, a few weeks appeared to be too short a time for any real change, and she was still convinced that her destiny lay in Saint Blaise. He tried to console himself with the fact that she had begun to get control over her tongue, but the fact remained that Vanessa was not free. And therefore Christopher was not free. As tied as she was to the inner visions that forced her into patterns of cause and effect created by others, so he himself was still constrained by his past, his heritage . . .

. . . his grandfather.

"There was nothing subtle about grandfather," Christopher told her as they took their last walk together along the peach avenue. "At least not at first. He brawled and raped and taxed and plotted through forty years of his life. And then, just as he was about to succeed beyond even his own expectations, he gave it all up. Overnight. As if by mag—"

His voice caught. He recalled Vanessa's sudden, miraculous healing. And what powers, really, were there in Adria or anywhere else in Europe that could accomplish such a thing? Legends and stories that no one really believed anymore told of some of them, and Roger had maundered on about them toward the end, but Elves and the miraculous transformations they wreaked were the stuff of children's meals and the repasts of senile old man. They had no place at Christopher's table.

Nonetheless, without question, Vanessa had been healed, and so he had been willing to accept the dish. But now the spell was breaking. Vanessa's belongings, with the addition of suitable gifts of money and clothes, were packed: the bundles were waiting up in her room. Ranulf was readying the horses. When the morning mists burned off just a little, she would be leaving for Saint Blaise. And now Christopher was wondering.

"As if by magic," he said. "Suddenly he was entirely different."

Compared with her former, wide-eyed owlishness, Vanessa seemed almost self-possessed this morning. "It wa' the Free Towns he wanted."

He glanced at her, but she shook her head. "I din't look to know, m'lord. I've heard talk o' the Free Towns."

"Yes, it was the Free Towns," said Christopher. Magic. It had to be magic. But he pushed the thoughts away lest she should see. "Suddenly, he was actually *protecting* them. He thwarted several spurious annexation attempts, and even led a hundred lances against the men of Bishop Clarence a'Freux. Entirely different."

"Maybe that wa' for the good in the end," said Vanessa. "I'm going to the Free Towns." She blushed. "I'm being selfish. It's good for me . . . I guess."

Christopher offered her his arm. She took it. Self-possessed. Almost.

"You're not selfish," he said. "You're frightened. There's nothing wrong with being frightened, is there?"

She shrugged. "I suppose na."

"I could . . ." It was an absurd request, but he had to make it. His grandfather had let the Free Towns go without a whimper. He could not let Vanessa go without trying to force the futures in another direction. "I could ask you to stay."

She shook her head. "I can't stay, m'lord. E'en wi'out the patterns I know tha'. I'm a country girl, an' I belong among my kind. Wha' place would I ha' in Aurverelle? I've . . ." She even laughed a little. "I've already frightened e'eryone."

He bent his head. "Did I help, Vanessa?" he said. "Or did I merely prolong the pain?"

"I dan know." There was warmth in her smile, but it was human warmth. "But, m'lord, you've been good to me, an'—"

He lifted his head, laid a finger on her lips. "Call me Christopher."

She blinked at the familiarity, and again he saw the fear in her eyes. He had made a sudden, impulsive decision, and he had acted upon it immediately. The patterns had not, could not have forewarned her.

"You see," he said. "We make the choices."

Slowly, thoughtfully, owlishly, Vanessa nodded.

"I hope I helped a little, Vanessa," said Christopher. "I just wish I could do more." The thought of her making her way down to Saint Blaise and entrusting herself to the care of Matthew Osmore and his mercenary disinterest panged him. She was defenseless, and there was nothing he could do about it.

But he stopped, pulled off his signet, and put it on her index finger. His hands were small, hers were strong: the ring fitted her tolerably. "Take this. If you ever need anything, if you ever need someone, I'm there. It isn't a chain to bind you. It's a talisman of protection. Everyone in Europe knows not to stir up the delAurvres . . ."

He suddenly recalled the free companies and their attack on the wool shipment. Perhaps not everyone. He would have to do something about that. For Vanessa's sake.

". . . but even if you never need it to keep you from harm, whenever you feel that you're all alone and haven't a friend in the world, you look at that ring and remember Christopher delAurvre, your friend. And believe in that."

She believed it. He knew she believed it. She smiled, and his eyes misted at the sight. If he had done nothing else right in his life, he had helped Vanessa. This, indeed, was his Kingdom.

"Thankee, Christopher," she said. "But you need sa'-thing, too." She put up her hands and unfastened a chain from her neck. "My da gave it to me before I left. I dan know wha' it means, but it's cam to remind me too much o' him . . . too much o' a' the bad times. So I dan think I wan' to keep it. But maybe it wi' remind you o' me."

Vanessa had her family and the patterns, Christopher had his grandfather and Nicopolis. He took the pendant from her and held it up. Moon and rayed star conjoined, it glit-

tered in the soft morning air. The workmanship was exqui-
site, the style unlike anything he had ever seen. How
Vanessa's father had come by it was beyond reckoning, but
the baron of Aurverelle bent his proud head to let her fasten
it about his neck.

And then she left him. The horse that Baron Paul had
given her for the trip was frisky and alert after two months
of running free in a rich paddock, and Vanessa, in the fine
traveling clothes that Christopher had bought for her, looked
far away but rather genteel. The delAurvre signet glittered
on her hand.

Ranulf would be her escort for the short trip down to
Saint Blaise, but Christopher rode with her as far as the
edge of the village. There, the road passed through a gate
and turned down toward the lowlands. He could see Saint
Blaise in the hazy distance, and Malvern Forest was close
enough that, given the drop, a man with a strong arm might
have pitched a stone into it.

At the head of the road, he reached out to her, took her
hand. He had never offered or asked for a kiss, but she must
have seen that he needed one, and so she leaned out and
touched her lips lightly to his. "G'bye, Christopher," she
said.

"Farewell, my dear lady."

That was all. She went down the road with Ranulf. By
mid-afternoon, she would be in Saint Blaise, starting a new
life. And perhaps she would now have a few tools with
which to make it a happy one.

Christopher rode back toward the castle. He acknowledged the bows and curtsies of the townsfolk, but he hardly
saw any of them. Vanessa still was not free, and so neither
was he. Only that dratted monkey was free, and it did nothing with its liberty save pelt people with fruit.

Was he any different? Since he had risen from his bed on
Christmas morning, he had acted the part of the ape, grinning and mocking, tossing fruit at all the customs and mo-
res and sacraments of his society. Only since Vanessa had
arrived had he really taken on, once again, the attributes of
a civilized man.

A civilized man. At the gate of the castle, he dismounted
and handed his horse over to a stable boy. He looked down
at himself. Silks and velvets again. Even a sword. The baron
of Aurverelle.

He laughed, suddenly. Howled. He could not stop. By the time Jerome and Pytor—summoned by the panicked gate guards—came running to see what was the matter, he was so weak with his sobbing mirth that he was leaning against the whitewashed wall, tears streaming down his face.

"Dear God, my lord," said Jerome. "What's the matter?"

With an effort, Christopher managed to stop laughing, but his tears still flowed. "I'm the baron of Aurverelle," he said. He took Vanessa's pendant in his hand, held it up before his eyes. The moon and star flashed. "That's what's the matter."

No. He would never forget her.

Townsfolk were staring at him, frightened, and he realized that, as he had moderated his excesses for Vanessa's sake, he would have to do so for his people, her peers. He straightened, composed himself as best he could. "I'll talk with you about those free companies now, Jerome," he said, tucking the pendant into his tunic. "If we let them get away with this, they'll be eating off our plates by next spring, whether Yvonnet pays them or not." He wiped at his eyes. Vanessa was gone. And he was the baron of Aurverelle. He would rather have been the monkey.

Pytor and Jerome exchanged glances. It was quite obvious to Christopher that they were wondering whether he was going to begin once more to caper like a bear.

"Master should rest," said Pytor. "Master's harper has said that she would be willing to play for him at any time. Would he care for a song?"

Christopher blinked. "Harper?" What idiot had decided to see if the baron was really mad? And a woman at that?

"She arrived late last night," Pytor explained. "I did not wish to disturb master. I gave her a room—it was not seemly to ask her to sleep with the men in the hall."

"Yes, yes. But why do you call her *my* harper?"

Pytor squirmed. "She played for me, master. She's very good. I . . . I thought . . . I . . . ah . . . offered her a position."

Pytor was trying to help, Christopher realized. The good-hearted seneschal had not wanted him to be lonely or un-occupied, and so he had allowed a wandering harper—they were all glib ones, those harpers—to talk him into a permanent post.

"Fine, Pytor. Thank you. But I don't want her to play. Not now."

Pytor shuffled his feet. "Some other time, then, my master?"

Christopher turned toward the gate. Pytor was trying to help, and doubtless the harper was good. But there were free companies to deal with, and there was also a cask of wine in the castle. He was not sure how he felt about the free companies, but with Vanessa gone, he had nothing left to believe in save the monkey and the cask. And he could not drink the monkey. "Yes, yes," he said absently. "Some other time. Maybe."

"Thankee, Ranulf."

Patterns pressed close about Vanessa, and she saw them all as she and Ranulf halted that afternoon before the gates of Saint Blaise. There was a part of the pattern for Saint Blaise—a sea of housetops bright with money, blue slate glowing in the yellow sun—and there was a part for each house, and there were individual lines and mazes for all the people within. The gate guards in their fine livery participated, as did those who came and went before them. All a part of the multitude of patterns that wove through her mind, that always wove through her mind.

And all the patterns indicated that she would enter Saint Blaise and deliver herself and her letters to Matthew Osmore, the mayor. The end was death, of course. Vanessa had been living with that knowledge for years now, ever since she had, for the first time, gropingly deciphered the maze of images, faces, and voices in her head. Whether it came at the stake or by hanging or in any one of a thousand violent ways, it was still death that faced her, and it was still inevitable, and everything about her—Saint Blaise, the farmlands, the guards, the people—contributed to the patterns that enfolded her and drew her on toward that inevitable fate.

Ranulf was nodding gravely. "Baron Christopher told me t'ask if you had your letters, Mistress Vanessa."

She wanted to cry. Christopher had treated her kindly, but even he had eventually bowed to the patterns. For a moment, she cleared as much mental space as she ever could amid the whirl of patterns and allowed herself to remember him. He was handsome and he was sad, and he had fought for her. It was like something out of an old tale. Save that, in the tale, she would have stayed in Aurverelle . . . with Christopher.

Impossible. She reached to the pouch on her belt, opened it, showed Ranulf the letters of introduction that Baron Paul had written to the mayor. "I ha' them."

"Shall we go in, then?" said the captain. "I know the mayor's house. I can take you to his door."

He wondered at her. That was in the patterns, too. Vaguely, she blinked at the sky, but she saw little save images, scenes, fragments of faces, and snatches of conversation that lay in the future. Far off lay death. Closer were Ranulf's doubts. She was tempted to say something to him about them, but she was silent. That much she had learned. She did not have to speak.

And then something else struck her. Choice. She did not have to speak. And that meant . . .

With Ranulf waiting patiently for her reply—he had, like everyone else who had ever had any dealings with her, grown used to her sudden lapses of attention—she sat, stunned, on her horse, transfixed by the sudden motion among the patterns. A moment ago she had seen only her entrance into the city, her first interview with the mayor. But now, mixed with those images of exile, were others. A long ride. The face of an old woman, her lake blue eyes bright with knowledge and love. A little town.

Somewhere else.

She started to tremble, but she suppressed it. She did not want Ranulf to see her fright and so become determined to accompany her straight to the mayor's door. She wanted . . .

The patterns blurred. More images. Other deaths, to be sure, but less violent. Impossibly, Christopher was there, too, almost lost in the blinding, visual cacophony of interweaving and contradictory patterns.

. . . freedom.

"Nay, Ranulf," she said. "Thankee for your company, but I think I'll go i' the town alone. If I get lost, I can ask for help." Her hands were clenched. Christopher's signet was a reassuring presence on her finger.

Ranulf frowned. Vanessa saw his doubt, but she also saw—and the patterns were shifting more and more quickly—that the captain would accede to her wishes. "Well, all right,

Mistress Vanessa,'' he said after a moment. "I'll leave you here, then. God be with you.''

"An' wi' you.''

He hesitated, still frowning. Vanessa did her best to banish his doubts by digging into her purse and holding up a coin to demonstrate that, yes, she had the penny gate toll. She saw another future forming. She wanted it. She fought for it.

Still obviously worried, Ranulf nodded to her, wished her good day and good luck, and turned his horse back towards Aurverelle.

Choice. She had a choice, just like Christopher had said.

"Do you need help, mistress?''

A woman stood beside her horse. Her gown was plain, but even through the patterns of future action and being that were now toppling rapidly into probability, Vanessa saw her red gold hair and her green eyes. Straight and tall, a basket on her arm, she might well have been an ordinary towns-woman on an errand, but she was a part of the patterns, too. A large part.

"I can take you in, if you are frightened of the city,'' she said.

Vanessa shook her head. She did not want to go in. She had chosen not to go in. She pointed south. "Is thi' the main road through the Free Towns?''

The green eyes were kind. "It is.''

"Does it lead to . . .'' Shifting. The patterns were shifting, the alternate future expanding, growing larger, unfolding like the petals of some immense flower. ". . . to Saint Brigid?''

"It does.''

"Then, thankee, but I'll be fine.''

The patterns wavered, then suddenly blurred and re-formed. The choice—her choice—had been made. She had created her own pattern. And if that was possible, then . . .

"I'm going to Saint Brigid,'' said Vanessa. She was smiling. "I'm . . . I'm going to find my grandma.''

Brother Jerome approached the duties of chief bailiff with the same finicky sense of detail with which he had once supervised a monastery library, and when Christopher entered his office that afternoon, he found a large map of Adria and eastern France already spread out on the big table.

Markers showed the positions of reported free company attacks. Jerome had also tallied up the exact amounts of the losses resulting from the missing wool shipment, and was prepared with an admittedly tentative projection of future movement on the part of the mercenaries.

"It's hard to estimate anything exactly," he said in his old, dry voice. "But since most of the fertile valleys of France have been stripped, it's logical to assume that they'll be moving into the passes of the Aleser fairly soon, and then into Adria proper."

Christopher, though, was having difficulty keeping his mind on the free companies. Much as he tried to look at the markers that lay scattered across Burgundy and Alsace and Auvergne, his eyes kept tracking back across the Aleser, searching out Aurverelle, and then the road south, and then Saint Blaise. Vanessa would be there by now. How was she being treated? If those fat burghers dared to give her so much as a moment's tears, he would—

Would what? Raze Saint Blaise? Even his grandfather had never contemplated such a thing. Trumping up charges of heresy against the fiercely independent Free Towns and thereby providing an excuse for political conquest was one thing, out-and-out siege and destruction was entirely another.

"My lord?"

Christopher blinked. His grandfather again. And Vanessa. "I'm sorry, Jerome. What were you saying?"

Jerome frowned in a manner that made him look every inch a monastery librarian confronted with a pack of unruly novices. He had obviously guessed what was on Christopher's mind.

But Vanessa was gone from Aurverelle, and Jerome more than likely assumed that she would soon depart from Christopher's thoughts, also. And so he went back to his facts and his projections . . . without comment.

There were many free companies, all independent, all deriving their income from their own form of pillage and extortion. In size and composition they ranged all the way from bands of ten or twenty destitute soldiers who sacked isolated steadings and an occasional unprotected village to virtual armies of knights, men-at-arms, and archers who wore fine armor, sold their booty through long-established agents, lent their service to emperor and king, and could make even the pope tremble and offer them large sums of money if they would only go away.

And they all moved and milled and scattered like flies on a dung heap. A troop might winter in a given area, might even spend an entire year in a captured castle, but spring would find it on the move again. Christopher could see a certain wisdom in hunting down the company that had attacked the wool shipment, but even had he still possessed a taste for battle, the brigands in question were probably pillaging somewhere else by now, the Aurverelle pack train just one conquest out of many. A regrettable one, too, for wool wains were a notoriously clumsy prize to dispose of. It would, doubtless, not happen again.

He said as much. Jerome was nodding. Pytor agreed, too, but he spread his hands. "But if master does not show them that he can protect his property . . ."

"I know," said Christopher. "They'll think they can help themselves." And they would indeed help themselves. The century had been born in war, had sustained itself by war, was ending in war. War was profitable, war was easy. Christopher could hardly blame out-of-work soldiers for falling back on the skills that they knew best. "But that's where we'll have them. Once they enter Adria, then they'll be on our lands. We can track them, pick our place to fight, and win."

"But if they enter Adria, my lord," said Jerome, "it will not be in twos and threes, but in hordes. Aurverelle alone cannot protect the entire land."

In hordes. Yes, the good brother was right. And though Baron Roger had been unwilling to use overt force against the Free Towns, companies of robbers who had no homes, marital relations, or political appearances to keep up, would have no qualms about leveling a town or two.

Christopher was suddenly very worried. Baron Roger had wanted the Free Towns because they were wealthy. The companies, doubtless, would feel exactly the same way. And Vanessa . . .

Had he been his grandfather, Vanessa would have still been in Aurverelle. She might well have been chained to a bed in some upper room, but she would have nonetheless been in Aurverelle. But the old steel and thoughtlessness, it seemed, had gone out of the family with Roger, and his descendants had lost their resolution. Christopher's father had done nothing except add to the castle library until the plague had claimed him and his wife shortly after the birth of his heir; and now Yvonnet dallied with sweets and silks and sodomized handsome little boys like Martin Osmore, while Christopher spent his days obsessing on attractive peasant girls and trying to free himself from his defeat.

A shadow flickered at the window, and a grotesque face peered in. The monkey. Pytor cursed aloud. Christopher laughed. The monkey disappeared.

"Let him go," said the baron. "He's not bothering us. And if we can let the free companies make off with an entire shipment of wool, we can stand to lose a few pieces of fruit.

"It's not the fruit, master," said Pytor. "It's the fact that he throws it."

Christopher shrugged. "He's a lot like me, I suppose." Pytor and Jerome stared. "But as for the free companies . . ."

His voice trailed off. He cared little for anything outside of Aurverelle, and for a time he had not been sure just how much he cared about Aurverelle. But now that Vanessa was involved . . .

He studied the map, examining Adria in earnest. Mountains, rivers, forest. Pale lines delineated the boundaries of political and economic influence, and light washes of color demarcated regions loyal to the rival popes.

A disjointed assortment of baronies, large and small, that were always at a quiet but constant political simmer, Adria was much like France. And France, thanks to the free companies, now lay as gutted as an unbraced mallard. The same thing could happen to Adria, and, true, Aurverelle could not protect everyone.

The silver pendant—moon and rayed star—slipped out of his tunic and swung free, glittering, above the Free Towns.

CHAPTER 12

The harper's name was Natil. She was deliberately vague about where she had come from, but Christopher was used to that: harpers were a rather scruffy lot, and perhaps this Natil had some legal fracas in her past—thievery, prostitution, or the like—that made her unwilling to be specific about her origins.

In truth, though, this seemed unlikely, for Natil stood without a trace of a slouch or self-deprecation when presented to the baron in the great hall of his castle. Nor did her demeanor seem prompted by an unjustified or overweening pride: no, she was perfectly comfortable with herself, perfectly at ease. Her dark hair unbound and shot with streaks of silver, her eyes blue, her face tranquil, she appeared ready to confront everything from a mad baron to a forest fire with equal equanimity.

This disturbed Christopher. Even when his madness had not vested him with an aura of latent and irrational violence, he had been used to deference, and deference was obviously not what Natil was offering. "You've entered a household where your talents might not be required," he told her.

"I understand that," she said calmly. "As my lord baron wishes." She curtsied, but her slender hands held her small harp as though she would like nothing better than to begin playing immediately.

"You'd probably do better in Hypprux," Christopher snapped. "It's more courtly there. Yvonnet likes the little niceties. Harps, food, silks . . . ah . . ." He recalled Martin. Toothsome little morsel. The thought of the vices to which his line had sunk made him queasy. ". . . other things . . ."

"But I am here," said Natil.

Christopher glowered. He had spent a sleepless night

worrying about Vanessa and the free companies, slipping, at most, into brief dozes filled with images of small villages encircled by troops of men and horses, the gleam of armor alternating with the dull glow of greedy fires. He did not have any heart for the antic or the mad this morning, and though Natil's perfect composure rankled him, he could not but feel a little afraid of this woman whose sense of self and dignity was obviously far more deeply rooted than his.

He slumped in his chair. "Play something," he said brusquely. "Anything. I want to make sure you're not a fraud."

A servant brought a stool, and Natil seated herself with a soft swish of her blue gown. She set her harp on her lap, tried two strings to see if they were true, then smiled graciously. "A dance, my lord?"

"Whatever."

Natil played, and she had not finished the first phrase before Christopher understood why Pytor had hired her even though his master had expressed no interest whatsoever in harpers. The music was splendid. Passages of dazzling intricacy and rapid-fire ornaments fell from Natil's hands as effortlessly as the daylight fell from the windows, and the melody moved through the room, a presence at once gay and holy, mysterious and immediate.

When she finished, Pytor was beaming, and Christopher had to fight to suppress an admiring smile. Yes, he could see how the Russian had been won. "All right," he said. "You can stay. You have the freedom of the castle, but don't expect that I'll be wanting your services very often. And if I hear you playing in the garden or something and I don't want to hear it, I'll tell you to shut up, and that will be that. Do you understand?"

Natil remained unruffled. "I do."

She was unnerving, as discomfiting as that Mirya and Terrill. Christopher tried to find some reason to send her out of the room that would not give away his true feelings, but could think of nothing. He gave up. This was his day for open court in the hall. He would simply ignore her.

He spent the next two hours listening to men and women from the town and countryside, sorting through matters of estate justice and grievance: taxes in arrears, trespassing, theft, assault, occasional rape. Jerome usually heard most of these, but an insistent defendant, if dissatisfied with the chief bailiff's decision, could, by right, appeal directly to the baron; and even Roger in his rake-hell days had never abrogated that privilege.

All the while that Christopher listened and judged, though, he was conscious of Natil's presence. The harper stood quietly off to the side, her harp in her arms, but her eyes, though downcast, flashed more brightly than Christopher had ever seen in anyone before, and for some reason he kept thinking of Mirya and Terrill.

Toward the end of the afternoon, he suddenly realized both that he was staring openly at her and that silence had fallen in the hall. With an effort, he shook himself out of his fascination. "All right, then. Who's next?"

At Jerome's signal, the men-at-arms brought in a young peasant man. This, the Franciscan explained, was Walter, one of Christopher's lowland tenants. Walter looked terrified, and appeared not to expect much more than an instant hanging. Probably at the baron's own hands.

"What's he done?" said Christopher.

"He's been stealing fish from your ponds," said Jerome. "Quite a lot of fish, in fact."

Christopher shrugged. "Well, the monkey steals fruit."

"I thought the matter rather straightforward," continued Jerome with a touch of annoyance, "as he even admits his guilt."

"I daresay the monkey would admit it, too."

Now Jerome was frowning openly. If Christopher would not defend his baronial rights, he could expect as little regard from his people as he was apparently receiving from the free companies. The estate folk were willing to accept strange clothes and occasionally antic behavior, but some appearances had to be kept up.

Christopher glared at the unfortunate Walter. "Explain yourself, man."

Walter shuffled forward. "It's my wife, m'lord. She's with child, and she seems to be able to keep down only fish these days. God knows why she couldn't have fixed on something readier, but I can't afford any more fish from the market, and so I . . ." He wrung his cap in his hands.

"So you admit stealing my fish?"

"Yes, m'lord. I done it."

Christopher's head ached. His grandfather would have made short work of Walter. At least during his first thirty

years. But his grandfather would have kept Vanessa in Aurverelle, too. At least during his first thirty years.

Planting peach trees. To such a fine end had the del-
Aurvres come!

"This story about your wife: is it the truth, Walter?"

Walter looked too frightened to say anything but the truth.
"Yes, m'lord."

Jerome was right. Very straightforward. And the poor
wretch had somehow scraped together enough temerity to
appeal his case to the baron. But on an impulse, Christopher
turned suddenly to Natil, hoping to catch her off guard.
"What do you think, harper?"

Her blue eyes flicked to him. "Of what, my lord?"

Perfectly composed.

"Of Walter. Should I cut off his hands?"

Natil was unshaken. "If you cut off his hands, my lord,
he will be unable to steal, to be sure. But he will at the
same time be prevented from doing honest work."

And how much honest work, he wondered, had ever come
from the hands of Christopher delAurvre? The nobles lived
on the backs of the peasants, made war on the backs of the
peasants, sometimes (and he thought again of his grandfather) took their sport on the backs of the peasants . . . or
rather on their fronts. This Walter paid taxes and tithes, and
had contributed his fair share to the clothes that Christopher
was wearing, to the chair he sat in, to the food—black bread
or gilded haslet, it did not matter—he ate.

And Vanessa, too, was a peasant. And Vanessa . . .

Such was his Kingdom.

"Jerome," said Christopher, "send a provost out to check
on Walter's wife. If she's having difficulty eating, see that
she gets what she needs. I'll have no sickly whelps on this
estate." He fixed Walter with a glance. "Walter . . ."

Walter quailed.

"You're lucky I'm not my grandfather." No, he certainly
was not. And, in fact, towards the end of his life, his grandfather had not been his grandfather, either. Was that good?
Bad? The Free Towns, intact, were a place for Vanessa to
go. She had said so herself. That was good. But . . .

The puzzle made his head hurt all the more. "I'll take
you at your word. But you know how this estate is run. The
next time, say something to the provosts or come and see

Pytor or Jerome *before* you start stealing fish. Then we'll all be happier, won't we?''

Walter bobbed his head, tugged at his forelock, seemed ready to drop to his knees in gratitude. Christopher waved him away and stood up. "I'm done. I'm sick of this. I'm going to go sit in the garden like a daft fool. Natil . . .''

She was already looking at him as though she had anticipated his utterance of her name. "My lord.''

Damnably unnerving. "Go and play your harp . . . someplace else. I don't want to hear it. Are you educated?''

"I have not studied at a university, my lord, but I know several languages in addition to Greek and Latin, and I am well conversant with the classics . . . as well as with music, of course.''

Of course she had not studied at a university: she was a woman. But if she were even half as knowledgeable as she said, then there was other work for her in Aurverelle. "Go and talk to Efram, the priest. Maybe you can help him teach some of the village lads.''

Natil curtsied deeply. "And the girls also, my lord?''

Unnerving. And cheeky, too. And he was letting her get away with it. His grandfather . . .

But he was not his grandfather. He had proved that over and over again. But what sort of a man would break men's necks for imagined slights, or rape peasant maids in the forest for recreation? How different, really, was Roger from Yvonnet? Or, for that matter, from the men of the free companies who took whole towns for all they were worth?

Natil was still looking at him, calmly waiting for an answer. "The girls?'' he blurted. "If you can find any whose mothers can spare them.''

And Vanessa's mother and father had put her out of the house.

Feeling sick, wanting to hide, Christopher turned and stalked out of the hall.

Natil found him late that night in the stables.

Christopher had given up hiding in his chambers. Even after so many months, they still reeked of Anna's presence; and, now that Vanessa was gone, his still-healing mind had doggedly reverted to reestablishing old associations and outworn memories: there seemed that night to be nothing in his bedroom that did not remind him in some way of his dead wife, and therefore of the Crusade, Nicopolis, and his grandfather.

As he had many times before, then, he prowled the corridors and corners of Castle Aurverelle, slouching down the deserted halls, peering into vacant rooms with fevered urgency, surprising kitchen boys and scullery maids. He was not sure what he was looking for. He was not even sure he would recognize it if he found it. Eventually, though, he found the wine casks, decided that they were good enough for now, and drank himself nearly insensible. Then, strictly ordering the servants in the cellar not to tell anyone of his destination—actually, he did not know himself—he crawled up the stairs, vomited his way across the dark courtyard to the stables, and finally collapsed beside the earthy presence of a mule.

Straw. Turds. The big brown eyes of the beast glinted at him in the darkness.

Christopher laid his cheek against the animal and wept. Aurverelle seemed a shadow. His life was a waste . . . and not even a particularly glittering waste. He himself was still half mad, and there did not seem to be much of a cure in sight. His only hope lay in a peasant girl who, far from loving him, regarded him only with a sense of frightened pity.

Much better he curl up with this beast, then. A mule was but a mule, a monkey but a monkey, and Christopher delAurvre but a lowly fool who, though he had temporarily given up his capering and his bellows, deserved no more than a stable.

The church bell was tolling matins when he became aware of a faint shimmer out of the corner of his eye. There was a rustle of a gown in the darkness, the sound of a knee settling to the earth and straw beside him. The mule stirred.

"My lord?" Natil. Quiet, calm, tranquil. She might have been sitting down with her harp instead of kneeling in a stinking stable.

"Leave me alone."

"That I will not, my lord," she said softly. "I agreed only to cease playing at your order. I said nothing about leaving you alone and friendless."

"I'm not friendless," he said dully. He thumped the mule. "This is my friend, Brunellus. He comes from as ancient a lineage as I. And considerably more honorable.

One of his people bore the Savior on his back. The del-Aurvres just climb up on everyone else's. Natil, Brunellus. Brunellus, Natil.''

To his surprise, the mule and the harper seemed to acknowledge one another's presence with a look and a brief nod. But when Natil spoke, she spoke to Christopher. ''You need to go to bed, my lord. Mules have straw, and foxes have dens, but men have sheets and blankets.''

He laid his head back down on the mule's rough coat. ''I don't care.''

Natil took him by the shoulders. She was surprisingly strong for a woman, and in a moment, she had dragged him to his feet. ''Christopher,'' she said gently. ''You are acting like an ass.''

She had called him by name, had spoken to him in terms to which his grandfather would have instantly responded with a lethal blow. But, indeed, he no longer cared. ''Of course I'm acting like an ass. All the delAurvres have acted like asses. Me, my father, my grand—'' He broke off, sobbed. It was too close. He was only wounding himself. He wanted to stop, but he could not.

Natil sighed softly. ''Dear Lady, what have we done?''

More pity. He did not want pity. He wanted—what? Expiation? Death? Wandering? He still did not know.

But the harper put her head to his, and he smelled green leaves and wildflowers: a forest after a rain. The whirl of his thoughts slowed, and though the tears still ran down his face, his soul ached a little less.

''Come, my lord,'' she said, ''come to bed. I will sit with you, if you wish, and keep your tormentors away, but you must rest.''

''Vanessa . . .''

''She is safe, my lord.''

''But for how long?''

Natil, he judged, knew the answer to that question no better than he, but slowly, calmly, seemingly breathing her own tranquillity into him, she guided him across the courtyard. Pytor, searching frantically for his master, stumbled upon them at the door to the baronial residence, and together the harper and the seneschal bore Christopher up the stairs and down the corridor to his room.

Natil called for basin and cloth and herself cleaned the tears and dirt from his face. She would have sung for him,

but he told her not to. "I'm too drunk to listen," he said,
but what he did not say was that he was still afraid of
her, afraid of her self-possession, afraid that she would do
. . . something. . . .

Something like what? Like magic? But was that not really
what he wanted? Vanessa had been healed in the space of
an hour. Christopher did not dare expect anything so dra-
matic, but he could at least hope that, as some kind of
intervention—human, deific, or diabolical, he did not care—
had raised Vanessa from what surely would have been her
deathbed, he, who had taken the girl as a symbol of himself,
might be similarly favored. Mirya and Terrill had touched
Vanessa; perhaps Natil . . .

"Tomorrow," he said. "I want you to sing and play tomorrow."

A cool hand on his forehead. Natil's eyes were blue and
shining. There was pity in them. But maybe there was understanding, too. "And what would my lord wish to hear?"

The magic. He wanted magic. He wanted healing.
"Something . . ." he mumbled. "Something to bring it all
back. You know . . . something."

"Wool."

For what must have been the fiftieth time in two weeks,
Berard of Onella prodded the large, heavy sack with his toe
and shook his head in disgust.

"There are fifteen more just like it in the wain," said
Jehan delMari. "And ten wains. That makes one hundred
and fifty sacks, and at three hundred and eighty pounds per
sack that makes . . ." He frowned as he calculated mentally.

"More wool than we know what to do with," said Berard
sourly.

He prodded again at the sack. There was not much one
could do with wool wains. The sacks, packed tightly with
rolled fleeces, were too heavy to move easily, and if cut
open, their contents would burst out like pus from a lanced
boil. The only fit place for a full woolsack was in the market
place of a weaving town—like Ghent, for instance—and
Ghent was exactly where this particular pack train had been
headed . . . until the Fellowship of Acquisition had stepped
in.

Now Berard was stuck. His men were grumbling—not

loudly, but grumbling nonetheless—about the lack of pay and plunder, and all that he had managed to come up with in this clean-picked wasteland of southern France was a pack train full of wool. And, of all things, Aurverelle wool at that. Everyone knew about the delAurvres.

"I suppose we could try to sell it off in Picardy," he said. "There are a few weavers there."

Jehan glared at him. "Or how about Paris?" he said with ice in his tone. "We could haul it right up the Rue Saint Denis, and I'm sure that all the townsfolk would come out to wave their banners at the brave knights."

"Now, Jehan . . ."

"I tell you, I'm sick of this! I won my spurs in battle, good solid battle. Sword against sword and men falling at my feet. And what are we doing now? In France, the capital of chivalry, we're stealing wool!"

Berard ran a hand over his face. It was July, and it was hot. He was rather glad that Jehan's obsession with chivalry and knightly battle had not born any recent fruit, for he was sure that, in armor, they would all have wound up boiled like crabs. The king of France had lost his wits, it was said, because of armor and heat, and Berard did not want to try the experiment himself: he was too close to going mad over one hundred and fifty sacks of wool.

"I admit this wasn't what I had in mind," he said.

"I'd rather be back in Italy," said Jehan. "There was gold there, and people who respected us. Not these illiterate peasants who go and hole up in caves at the first sign of our approach."

"Can you blame them?"

"They're peasants," said Jehan. "They're there for us to use. It's very simple: they get in our way, we ride them down."

Berard himself had been away from his peasant origins long enough that he did not feel as much rancor at Jehan's statements as he might have once. "Well, maybe we can use a few of them to unload this wool."

"Commerce? Pah!"

"Well," said Berard, "you can *pah*! your way on over to the men and explain to them why we can't do anything with their hard-earned plunder."

He pointed to the camp. Tents, horses, idle and irritated men. As much as Jehan had not counted on the commercial aspects of brigandage, so the men had not foreseen the lean periods.

And what was worse, most of France was a lean period. The Fellowship of Acquisition, for all its dignified and mercenary background, was but a gleaner left with a field that had been thoroughly picked over by wave after wave of free companies out to support themselves in the only way they knew: war and plunder.

That night, though, a company from Avignon rode into the camp, and its leader was Eustache de Cormeign, a representative of Bardi and Peruzzi. The firm, having failed as a banking house in Italy, had reestablished itself as a brokerage in France and, as a matter of course, had contacts with a wide assortment of clients. Bardi and Peruzzi dealt in everything. Arms, armor, jewels, clothing, grain . . .

"Wool?" said Berard.

Eustache blinked. "Wool?"

"Fifty-seven thousand pounds of wool," said Jehan. He glanced at Berard. The captain read his eyes: *The fruits of chivalry. Pah!*

But Eustache had recovered from his surprise. He cleared his throat. "We can handle it. We can handle anything."

Berard, already interested because of the wool, was suddenly more interested. "Anything?"

Eustache seemed affronted by the tacit doubt. "Anything."

Anything, indeed. Eustache traveled with a secretary, a group of well-armed guards he jokingly called his *kataphraktoi*, and enough money for a down payment. They struck the bargain that night. The Fellowship of Acquisition had but to guard the wool for another week, and then, after tendering the rest of the gold, Bardi and Peruzzi would take possession of the troublesome cargo.

But a few days later, another man arrived, and not only did his words brighten the prospects of the Fellowship even more, but they also fired Berard's imagination far beyond that, for the messenger was from Adria, and he brought greetings and a tentative offer of employment from Yvonnet a'Verne of Hypprux.

CHAPTER 13

An ass.

Precisely, Christopher thought, what he was. Having acted the proper fool in Aurverelle for months now, thereby sending Pytor and Jerome into fits and piquing Yvonnet's hopes of an eventual claim to the estate, he had compounded the idiocy by revealing his weakness to a female harper about whom he knew absolutely nothing.

Now it was evening, and Natil would play for him. Wearing the fashionable clothing that Vanessa's presence had encouraged him to take up, he sat in the great hall of the castle, occupying his official chair with the fringed canopy as though he were the perfect baron. In truth, he felt the perfect idiot, but as Natil entered, he saw not a shred of patronization or contempt in her demeanor. She stepped into the room as though she were royalty, true, but as she stood before him in her deep blue gown and her gray cloak, her eyes met his with a gaze as of a sympathetic equal.

"My lord," she said softly, "you asked me to play this night. I am here."

Christopher's hand was clasped about Vanessa's pendant, his only link to anything approaching hope. Here was the pendant, and there, somewhere else, was Vanessa. Yes, he would remember her, he would always remember her. He hoped that, among the maze of patterns that twined about her life, she would remember him.

He opened his hand and the pendant thumped down against his chest. Natil was suddenly looking at it, her flashing eyes intent. But she smiled warmly, as though she had just seen the best thing in the world.

"What would you have me play?" she said.

What indeed! What could counter Nicopolis? What his grandfather? "Anything, Natil," he said, the bitterness a sharp edge among his words. "I'm sorry now that I asked. But I asked. So play."

Natil was unruffled. Her eyes were still sympathetic. "Anything?"

"Anything."

She curtsied and went to the stool that was waiting for her near the hearth. As she sat down and arranged her gown and cloak, Pytor, standing across the hall, shifted his feet. His head was lowered in discouragement. He had hoped that Natil would bring his master some cheer, but Christopher read in his posture that he was accepting his mistake and the disappointment that came with it.

Jerome, too, was here, and he was attentive, as were Ranulf, some of the senior men of the castle guard, and one or two ranking bailiffs and provosts. Raffalda was off in the corner, spinning, David was waiting expectantly. Whether or not the baron found what he was looking for, it was nice to have music in the castle again.

Natil's hands went to the strings, and a chord rang out— root, fifth, octave—a spare flash of crystalline brilliance that seemed to light the hall as brightly as the torches and the blaze on the hearth. For a few minutes, she played an intricate arrangement of a simple but vaguely familiar melody, weaving it in and out, now allowing it to shine forth majestically, now almost burying it in countermelody. Her eyes were lowered as though in thought, but her playing was such that when she lifted her head and took a breath, the baron found himself leaning forward in his chair, his hands clenched apprehensively about Vanessa's pendant.

And Natil sang, her voice pure, sweet, touched with an inflection that Christopher could not place:

> *"Carles li reis nostre emperere magnes*
> *Set anz tuz pleins ad estet in Espaigne*
> *Cunquist la tere tresque en la mer altaigne*
> *Ni ad castel ki devant lui remaigne*
> *Murs ne citez ni est remes a fraindre . . ."*

Christopher caught his breath. *The Song of Roland.* Natil had chosen the most glittering of the old *chansons de geste*, the one most weighted with mystique, most fraught with luminous image and valorous act. In quaint, limpid French

that was at once two and a half centuries out of date and all
the more compelling for exactly that reason, Natil began the
account of the betrayal of Charlemagne and the death of
Roland and the peers of France. It was a martial tale, a
man's tale, but somehow, even the harper's maidenly voice
contributed a fitting energy and a passionate drive to her
song.

Christopher could have stopped her with a gesture, but he
sat, rigid, listening. An hour went by, two hours, *laisse*
after *laisse* chanted and plucked masterfully by the slender
woman who was as much an actor as a harper, for with her
voice and a hand she freed occasionally and momentarily
from the strings, she added interpretation and gesture to the
music and the words; and he did not ask her to stop.

If music was magic, this was it. If a maid's voice could
touch with splendor a world that had fallen into leaden dull-
ness, this was it. The Saracen plot. The glitter of the French
battalions. Lives of valor, the breaths of which were edged
in bright color. Listening to Natil, Christopher saw it all as
though it blazed forth in the stained glass of a cathedral.

And yet, through the splendor, he saw the charade, too.
It was not Roland's piety that distinguished him, but rather
his single-minded, belligerent pursuit of an abstraction that
he himself had created. The lives were valorous, true, but
only because the men who lived them ignored everything
else. Natil made no effort to disguise either, and yet she
sang on, telling of the charge, the fighting, her voice now
grating with frantic determination as Oliver and Roland and
Turpin battled desperately, now turning soft and sweet as
Oliver and Roland met for the last time and took hands in
the midst of the slaughter.

But even though they had died for nothing, they had died
believing in themselves. That, Christopher considered, was
something, at least. It was a small something, to be sure,
when weighed against all the needless death, but it gave
back to the tawdry little tale of pigheadedness something of
a sense of grace. Roland might have been an idiot, but unlike the current baron of Aurverelle, he was at least a con-
sistent idiot.

> " 'Sire cumpainz, faites le vus de gred?
> Ja est ço Rollanz ki tant vus soelt amer.' "

The sentiment was curt, monosyllabic, and Christopher, filled with the memories of the absurdity that had taken place on the plateaus of Bulgaria, could well imagine the feelings behind Roland's words. Men about him, dead and dying, more Saracens closing in, Oliver—or maybe it was Coucy or Philippe de Bar or Odard de Chasseron: the memories pressed about Christopher, and for an instant, he did not know where he was—blind with blood and wounds and lashing out at anything that came within reach. And yet, with despair hovering over him like a dark angel, still Roland—or Christopher, perhaps?—had spoken with affection: *Sir Friend, did you strike me on purpose?*

And that look from Coucy as Bayazet had swept in. . . .

Despite Nicopolis, despite madness, despite a bitterness that had driven a stake of wormwood through his heart, Christopher found that he was weeping. Yes, they had believed in themselves and in their actions. And how much did he himself believe in Christopher delAurvre?

I am the Master of Aurverelle.

Master of what?

The *Chanson* was a long tale, and no harper regardless of skill or endurance could hope to finish it in a single night. The custom had always been to end the first evening with the death of Roland, and to take up Charlemagne's revenge, the Moors' defeat, and Ganelon's execution on the second. So Natil appeared to be intending, for her music and her voice soared up plaintively as she sang of Roland's care of the dying Oliver, and then finally of the count's own death.

> *"Devers Espaigne gist en un pui agut*
> *A l'une main si ad sun piz batut . . ."*

And perhaps that was for the best, after all. Roland had played his part, and he would never have wanted to finish out his days in France, an old man in his dotage, planting peach trees in the garden. No, he would die a conqueror, his face toward Spain, his arrogance and his pigheadedness undiminished. Smaller, lesser men would come after, pick up the pieces, fit together some sort of an accommodation that would hobble along until another Roland rose up and ground it into the earth.

Christopher wept. But it was late, and Natil was drawing her song to a close.

> *"Sun destre guant en ad vers deu tendut*
> *Angle del ciel i descendent a lui.*
> *Aoi."*

Christopher lifted his head. Natil sang on:

> *"Sun destre guant a deu en puroffrit*
> *E de sa main seinz Gabriel lad pris;*
> *Desur sun braz teneit le chief enclin*
> *Juintes ses mains est alez a sa fin.*
> *Deus li tramist sun angle cerubin*
> *E Seint Michiel de la mer del peril*
> *Ensemble od els Seinze Gabriels i vint*
> *L'anme del cunte portent en pareis.*
> *Aoi."*

Natil's final cry rose up, filled the space beneath the vaulting of the hall and, with a shimmer of harpstrings, faded to silence.

No one in the hall moved. Christopher was prepared to believe that no one, including himself, was even breathing, and he saw that he was not the only one with tears on his face. Old Jerome, dried up and pragmatic, had covered his face with his hands and was sobbing, and Pytor had fallen to his knees. Raffalda had left off her spinning and was crying openly, and even Ranulf, veteran of a thousand battles, noble and ignoble, was wiping his eyes.

But as Natil, as though exhausted by her performance, sat with bowed head, a single line of her song was still ringing in Christopher's memory, shining out like a star from all the death and the futility. He had wanted the magic, and he was suddenly wondering if he might have been given a little piece of it, just enough so that he could, perhaps, find his way back to the rest on his own.

Sun destre guant en ad vers deu tendut . . .

Roland's last act was something that, though sparkling with the same chivalric glitter that had dusted the rest of his gleaming life with diamonds, had a touch of the humble to it, an ackowledgment of his limitations.

His right glove he lifted up to God.

And what delAurvre had ever lifted up his right glove to anyone? What delAurvre had ever done anything that was motivated in the least bit by humility? Even Christopher's journey to Nicopolis had, at bottom, been an attempt to burnish up what he had seen as the tarnished honor left behind by his grandfather.

Sun destre guant en ad vers deu tendut . . .

If he could do that: offer his glove to . . . to someone. Not to God. That would not work. He did not want to pledge himself to any transcendent being whose existence had been used alternately as a lure and a club for the last fourteen centuries. If he, a delAurvre (and there it was again, that overweening pride) was to offer service, it had to be to something untainted by exploitation or profit. It had to be humble, without reward, and it had to smack of common humanity, of that Kingdom that included all the Hobs and Tims and Toms—and Vanessas—of the world.

He stood up. The hall seemed to breathe again. "My thanks, dear harper, for your song."

Natil lifted her head, stood, and curtsied. "Have I pleased you, my lord?" Her eyes were luminous, as though gleaming with starlight. "Did I give you what you desired?"

Christopher nodded. Humility. Common humanity. And he knew what he could do. "You did indeed. Thank you."

Paul delMari, baron of Furze, read the letter a second time. When he finished, he was just as puzzled as he had been the first time. He sat back in his chair and contemplated trying the letter a third time, but he knew that he had understood it perfectly well the first time. Reading it twice had been superfluous. Thrice would be the mark of an idiot.

"What do you make of this, Isabelle?" he asked his wife as he rose and offered her the parchment.

Isabelle set aside her embroidery and took it. She knew how to read better than most educated men, and for an instant, her eyebrows lifted at the salutation, but then she skimmed rapidly over the words, her lips barely moving.

She finished, dropped the letter onto her lap. "Christopher delAurvre?"

Paul nodded. "Christopher, indeed. He appears to have recovered from his trip home from Nicopolis, although whether also from his madness remains to be seen."

"Asking for help?"

Paul shrugged. At times like this, without any clear-cut problem or solution at hand, possessed only of a sense of bewilderment, he was inclined to be at a loss. Perhaps that was why Jehan had left him: the boy had recognized his father as something of a ditherer. "It's for a worthy cause."

Isabelle shook her head, pondering. "Didn't his grandfather kill your grandfather?"

Paul shrugged again, uncomfortably. "That was fifty years ago," he said, "and a case of misunderstanding, I believe. Roger was always a bit hasty. Except toward the end."

Isabelle usually kept her feelings to herself, but a bubble of incredulity rose to her normally tranquil surface, broke, and spread openly across her face. She held up the letter. "Husband . . . I'm not sure at all about this."

"Well, it's very simple," said Paul. He rose and took a turn about the bedroom, hands behind his back. "He's worried about the free companies destroying Adria—as though we need much help these days—and he wants an alliance. He's certainly not being underhanded about it."

Isabelle snorted delicately. "The delAurvres have always been underhanded."

"Not since Roger reformed. They've actually been rather exemplary since then."

Isabelle set the parchment aside and resumed her embroidery: an ornate chasuble for Abbot Wenceslas of the Benedictine monastery across the valley. "What do you want to do?"

"Well," said Paul, "initially, I want your opinion of getting entangled with Aurverelle." Politics. He did not like them, but his position occasionally forced him to roll up his sleeves and plunge his hands into the stink. "I think I have it, though."

"The delAurvres are too unpredictable," said Isabelle as she tied off a thread. "Look at Roger: one day he's about to destroy the Free Towns, and the next he's turned completely around. Everyone knows that story. He came back from Beldon Forest a changed man. Some minstrel even went and composed a song about Roger of Tarsus."

"And was promptly flattened by Roger for his temerity, as I recall."

Isabelle went back to her embroidery. "You must admit that it was a sudden conversion."

"I suspect there were . . . reasons for that." Paul went to the window. If he craned his neck, he could peek around the corner of the tower to the left and catch a glimpse of

Malvern Forest. So few these days. And fading fast. Isabelle had not known about the Elves when she had married him, but she had reconciled herself to their existence and visits as befitted the dutiful and honorable wife that she was. She did not like to talk about them, true, but she had accommodated them.

Very few now, though, were willing to accommodate them. Very few, in fact, believed in them at all, nor, indeed, had any cause to. Perhaps for that very reason, it had been a long time since anyone from Malvern had come to Shrinerock. Times were changing. Getting darker. Much darker. Autumn had taken hold of the world.

"Reasons?"

"Ah . . . reasons."

Isabelle looked at him, inquiring, and he was afraid that he was going to have to talk about the whole messy incident when the door opened and his sister Catherine strode in, tall, blond, and strong. She was clad in simple garments of green and gray: a tunic, and breeches that bloused just above soft, knee-high boots. "Look at this," she said. "I've been looking for these for years, and I finally found them. They weren't with Mother's things at all: they were up in a chest in the third storeroom. They fit, too!" Hands out from her sides, she modeled the garments. "Well, what do you think?"

Paul had sat down hard when she had entered, and now he caught his breath. "Dear Lady, Catherine, you gave me a turn. I thought one of the Elves had come."

Catherine beamed at the compliment, but Isabelle was shaking her head fondly. "Perhaps you'll be moving to the forest full-time now, sweet?"

Catherine smiled at her. "Only when you and Paul move with me, dear sister."

Smiling affectionately, Isabelle plunged her needle into the embroidery once again.

But Catherine's sudden appearance had started Paul thinking. Roger had changed. And now Christopher, after remaining cloistered for months, had suddenly offered his hand in friendship to all of Adria. Transformation, reconciliation. But why should the few remaining Elves turn their attention toward a family that had in the past been so cruel to them? Roger's fate had been, perhaps, appropriate. But Christopher . . .

Christopher had taken care of Martin after the incident with the papal legate, but who was Martin Osmore to the Elves? No, there was something else.

Then he recalled Lake's daughter, Vanessa. And Vanessa . . .

Catherine was reading the letter now, plodding through it laboriously, mannishly. She had always preferred horses, weapons, and forestry to learning and huswifery, and at thirty, she was still a spinster. Hugo of Belroi had tried to tame her, but faced with his demand that she obey him, she had thrown him out of his own bedroom and had gotten a good night's sleep before returning home. With her dowry. No one in the city had even considered trying to stop her.

"Dear Lady," she said when she finished. "What's gotten into Christopher?"

"I wonder . . ." said Paul.

CHAPTER 14

Christopher was fighting a battle. To be sure, it had nothing
to do with swords and armor, but it was a battle nonetheless, for he was fighting complacency, habit, and the deep
rift of schismatic alignment. The first skirmish, however,
was discouraging. Of the fifty odd barons, great and small,
to whom he wrote, only Paul delMari expressed a willingness to cooperate. The others, for the most part, replied
evasively, expressing a vague interest that had nothing to do
with actual commitment. The smaller barons, as Christopher expected, were looking to Hypprux and Maris, the
centers of economic and military power in Adria, for guidance.

But Yvonnet's answer came almost by return messenger,
and it was abrupt and unequivocal: he had simply scrawled
NO! at the bottom of Christopher's letter and sent it back.
And though Ruprecht a'Lowins of Maris sent a long, official
document—in Latin—full of erudite turns of phrase and frequent untranslated quotations from the Greek philosophers,
it proved, when Jerome and Natil had plowed through its
intricacies and ornaments, to say the same thing. Ruprecht
simply did not take the threat seriously. He, after all, occupied the multiple-walled fortress that had been built up
four hundred years ago by Alfonse-Dylan IV, the ill-fated
king of Adria who had been concerned about the very kind
of baronial uprisings that had eventually deposed him and
ended Adria's days as a kingdom. Ruprecht, taking a lesson
from the king's downfall, was not about to be lured out of
his stronghold for frivolous reasons.

"*And so . . .*" Natil was reading the letter out loud once
more. She really did know Greek and Latin extremely well,
and translated on the fly. Even Jerome, who considered
woman to be very much the weaker vessel, was impressed
enough by her learning that he had not objected to her in-

clusion in Christopher's councils. "*. . . as the great Aristotle says—*"

"Kill them all," Christopher finished sourly. "Let God sort them out."

"No, my lord," said Jerome, "that was Robert of Geneva."

"Right now it's Ruprecht of Maris." Christopher plopped his feet on Jerome's desk as the Franciscan scurried to move his maps and papers out of the way. "Well, he obviously doesn't give a damn, and neither does Yvonnet."

Natil looked up from the document. "Did you wish me to continue, my lord?" she said politely.

"No, Natil. Thank you very much. If I hear one more elegant turn of phrase from Ruprecht's secretary, I'm sure I'll throw up." Though the reactions of Yvonnet and Ruprecht were absurd, they were, he admitted, neither unexpected nor without precedent. The same thing had happened in France. The nobles of that country had simply not been able to believe that bands of unemployed soldiers could destroy their lands and their prosperity and then move on. Perhaps someone else's lands and prosperity, but surely not theirs.

But it had happened, and in some cases, the nobles themselves had hired the free companies to carry out vendettas against other nobles.

"Well," said Christopher, "they thought I was mad before, and so I suppose they think I'm raving now." Paul delMari's letter lay nearby. Christopher grabbed it and glanced over it for relief. Good old Baron Paul! No dissembling, no fancy obfuscation. Just wholehearted acceptance. And Paul was apparently even willing to put aside the unfortunate matter of his grandfather's murder.

"Paul has adequate forces," said Jerome efficiently when he saw Christopher pick up the letter. "I took the trouble to tabulate his last reported strength. It's twenty-five years out of date, but it gives us some idea."

"We don't have a spy in Shrinerock?"

"Ah . . . no," said Jerome, holding up the tabulation. "Somehow, we've never managed to keep one there."

Natil put aside Ruprecht's letter, extended her hand to Jerome. "May I?"

With a shrug, Jerome handed her the document. She glanced over it quickly, not even moving her lips. "This is indeed out of date," she said. "These are pre-plague levels. Baron Paul's forces have been substantially reduced."

"Well," said Jerome, "the entire population of Adria has been substantially reduced since the plague hit back in Baron Ingram's days."

Natil shook her head sadly, as though the plague were some kind of personal failing. "It is unfortunate that it could not be forestalled any longer."

Christopher lifted his head at her tone. Natil was, for the moment, abstracted, pensive. But she indicated Jerome's tabulation. "Paul's forces have fallen to approximately one third of this."

Christopher frowned at the news. "I daresay the same applies to the other baronies."

"More than likely," said Natil. "Though Ruprecht might well have made an effort toward keeping his forces at maximum levels."

"He is a keen one for battle," said Jerome. "As long as the odds are in his favor."

Christopher laughed bitterly. "Then maybe *he* should have gone to Nicopolis. But then he might have gotten his precious armor all dusty, eh?"

The anger and defeat were still there, still lurking, still waiting for a chance to fasten their teeth into him once more. He had been given a glimpse of the magic, but he had to find the rest himself.

He glanced at Natil. The harper met his eyes levelly, their tranquillity a reminder of the task, inner and outer, that he had set for himself, just as the harp at her feet was a reminder of the method he had chosen.

Sun destre guant en ad vers deu tendut . . .

He had offered his glove, but Yvonnet and Ruprecht had rejected it. And the smaller baronies, linked with the capital cities of Adria by blood and intricate alliance, would follow their lead. Somehow, he had to win over the barons of Hypprux and Maris.

"You were right, Jerome," he said. "You and Pytor both. I went about mad, and proud of my madness, and that's going to make this task that much harder. I suppose I need to start acting like a baron again."

"My lord, you've taken great strides toward that end since—" Jerome caught himself, blushed.

Christopher grinned. "Since Vanessa showed up? Quite right, Jerome."

Natil was watching him. She was smiling fondly, and the expression made Christopher feel warm inside.

"I think I'm going to pay a visit to my . . . uh . . . dear cousin, Yvonnet," he said. "I'll have to try to convince him in person that he needs to help. Ruprecht . . ." He drummed his fingers on his knee, shrugged. "Ruprecht I'll figure out later. For all I know he's expecting the Hanse to protect him. If that's the case, we'll have to pressure some contacts in Bruges. For now, it's Yvonnet." He stood up, opened the door to the hallway, bellowed: "Raffalda!"

He turned around to Jerome's questioning face. "I'll be going to Hypprux," he explained. "But I'll be going in state. Official business. I'll need silks and velvets sewn up and fitted—God help me, no *poulaines:* I'm not that far gone!—and I'll need a dozen soldiers properly equipped to attend me."

He smiled at Natil.

"And . . . some things for my personal harper."

Natil nodded graciously. Jerome looked incredulous. "But . . ."

Christopher silenced him with a glance in the grand old delAurvre style. "William of Normandy had Taillefer," he said. "Christopher delAurvre has Natil." He heard Raffalda approaching with quick steps. "William took all of England. Let's see what I can do about Adria."

The proposed visit of Christopher, baron of Aurverelle, occasioned a great deal of talk in Hypprux. It was well known that the baron was mad, that he dressed in sackcloth and ate raw meat, and that, like his grandfather, he had a weakness for peasant girls—but whether that meant in bed or on a spit was open to conjecture.

So when Christopher, Natil, Ranulf, and a dozen men of the Aurverelle guard rode in through the main gate of the city and made their way along the Street of Saint Lazarus, the crowds were thick, and the windows and balconies above the street were filled with curious faces.

If the people of Hypprux had expected overt madness, though, they were disappointed. Christopher, boyish and slender, smiling, waving, and occasionally tossing out a few gold coins, seemed the perfect picture of a baron. His silks and velvets, embroidered and decorated with jewels, were cut in the latest fashion, and a gold-hilted sword gleamed at his side. His men-at-arms wore the very brightest mail covered by perfectly matching surcoats, and his personal harper, clad in a gown of sky blue and a gray cloak and carrying her small instrument before her, smiled with tranquil and unnerving warmth upon all.

They turned left at the Street Gran Pont and proceeded towards the Château. Christopher still waved and tossed coins, but he sidled close to Natil's side. "I daresay they still think I'm mad," he said.

"Really, my lord?"

He grinned. "And I might be, Natil. Imagine the madness required for visiting a baron who has well-known designs upon Aurverelle."

Natil's brow furrowed. "Are you concerned, my lord?"

"About Yvonnet? Not really. The delAurvres have a reputation. No one crosses us."

But the memory of the missing wool shipment came back to him. Someone had crossed the delAurvres and had gotten away with it. How far had the general reputation of Aurverelle fallen? In his own way, he had been as detrimental to the family name as his grandfather.

"Fear not, Baron Christopher," said Natil. "There is no danger." Her sight seemed to turn inward. "So far . . ."

The Château of Hypprux had been built to rival the fortifications of Maris. Its walls were thick and high, and its gates were masterpieces of the art of the castlebuilder: double, offset, triple-barred, and murder-holed. Along the top of the walls, merlons stood up like teeth, and arrow-loupes stared down at the visitors.

Christopher could understand why Yvonnet was not worried about the free companies, and since Maris' fortifications were superior even to these, Ruprecht's sentiments were equally comprehensible. But it was not for the nobles of Adria that Christopher was proposing this alliance. It was (though he dared not speak of such a thing before his peers) solely for the peasants: those whose lands and lives would be wasted while their overlords held quaint dances to beguile the tedious hours of a siege.

For the peasants. For Vanessa.

Yvonnet was waiting for him just inside the main gate. Behind him, the formal gardens were in late-summer bloom, the flowers brilliant, the hedges and trees sparkling in the sunlight.

"Well, cousin! How nice to see you!" The baron of Hypprux always spoke at full volume in public. Christopher theorized that the custom had something to do with intimidation. He was not intimidated. Looking at Yvonnet, though, he was reminded in a disturbing way of his grandfather.

"Hello, Yvonnet." Steeling himself, he dismounted, embraced Yvonnet, and even managed to kiss him without gagging. Upon what lips—or other bodily part—had his cousin's mouth been most recently planted? Christopher suppressed an inward shudder. "I'm very glad to be here." It was a lie, and everyone knew it, but this was an official visit, and so Christopher assumed that insincere kisses and outright lies were in order.

"Ah, so you are!" said Yvonnet, his basso reverberating off the walls. "But not as glad as I am!"

Christopher noticed that Natil looked worried, but the harper curtsied deeply to Yvonnet when presented to him, and even offered to play that evening. Something in the new style from the courts of Italy and France?

Yvonnet was faintly interested. "Perhaps," he said, dismissing Natil with a glance. "Perhaps after our dear Cousin Christopher . . ."

Son of a bitch Cousin Christopher, Christopher translated, *who didn't have the decency to stay missing or dead.*

". . . and I have a chance to talk of . . . the matters that have brought him here." Yvonnet turned to Lengram, the chamberlain of the city, and lifted an eyebrow. "Whatever they are."

"I think my dear Cousin Yvonnet knows," said Christopher quietly.

"Yes . . . well . . . we'll have to talk about that, won't we? Later."

"Whenever you wish, Yvonnet."

"But first, we have hospitality! Yes! Hospitality! We can't go on letting our dear cousin stand out here in the hot sun after such a long journey, can we? Hospitality is the mark of a . . ." He eyed Christopher. ". . . civilized man, isn't it? Girls! Get out here!"

And the young women of the castle, well-schooled by Yvonnet's wife, whose name Christopher could never remember, took the visitors in hand. Natil was escorted to a room of her own, and Ranulf and the men were taken to the barracks, but Christopher was bathed, fed, and given clean clothes—more embroidery, more gems—and made to feel like an honored guest.

This, too, was a sham, and he made sure that he kept a knife at hand even when in a tub full of scented water. Yet, though it probably was indeed the action of a madman to come to Hypprux, he decided that he would rather be mad and offer his glove than be sane and stay huddled up in Aurverelle while the entire country went to hell.

Nonetheless, he was relieved when Natil and Ranulf appeared a few hours later, the harper with her harp, the soldier with his sword. Lengram brought them and also delivered a message that Yvonnet was expecting to meet with Christopher in his private chambers to discuss the matter of his visit. There would be a feast that night, of course.

"Will that be with or without poison, Lengram?" Christopher inquired with a smile.

Lengram stared, swallowed. "Ah . . ."

"Don't worry, Chamberlain. I was . . . just joking."

"Yes . . . ah . . . of course. . . ."

Was it Natil's tense expression earlier that day, or was Christopher detecting a sense of unease in the Château? He shrugged. He was here for a purpose. Best to get on with it.

But though, delivered in person, Yvonnet's reply to Christopher's plan was less terse than before, it was substantially the same. "I'm not interested in sending my men into battle for anyone except myself and my own," he boomed from his gilt-canopied chair. The bedroom echoed with his words, and the old cleric with a deformed nose who was acting as secretary was nodding unconsciously in agreement. "If the free companies want to come to Hypprux, let them come. They can batter themselves against the walls as much as they'd like." Sitting in an equally ornate chair—a symbol of his rank, or, more likely, of Yvonnet's ability to afford such things—Christopher sighed. Complacency. Idiocy. As the crusade, so Adria.

"Really, dear cousin," said Yvonnet. "I can't see what's gotten into you. Aurverelle is as ably fortified as Hypprux. Perhaps . . ." And he nodded to Ranulf, who was standing with Natil near the secretary's desk. ". . . even more ably."

Ranulf did not appear to be aware of the flattery.

"It's not a matter of Aurverelle or Hypprux being attacked," said Christopher. "Or even Ypris." He noticed Yvonnet's eyes narrow at the mention of the rebellious town. "It's the land itself. Who pays for all this finery and these castles? The commoners. Where would we be without their taxes and tithes? Penniless."

"You know as well as I that we can borrow from the Jews."

"And the Jews themselves are commoners, too. It's the same thing. I can't put this ornately, Yvonnet, because it's not an ornate subject; but if we want to continue to live as we do, then we have to safeguard the foundation upon which we live. The commoners."

Yvonnet snorted. "They breed like pigs. There will always be more commoners. And if there are commoners, then there will be taxes and tithes."

And so it went for an hour. Yvonnet was proof against argument or coercion if only because he had obviously made up his mind that he would not be swayed. No words, gifts, or reason would move him.

Christopher was tired. Tired of lying. Tired of arguing. Tired of false and artificial flummery. Despairingly, he looked to Natil, but she shook her head. It was hopeless.

A thought struck him. "What about the Free Towns? Will there always be more Free Towns?"

Yvonnet was suddenly cautious. "Why do you mention the Free Towns?"

"Oh . . ." Christopher was cautious himself. "I had a visitor from the Free Towns a few months ago. Martin Osmore."

Yvonnet stared at the unshuttered window, his expression that of a man who had just had a handful of ants dumped into his tunic. "I . . . don't believe I could care less about the Free Towns," he said. "I certainly haven't heard of them paying any taxes to *me*!"

He laughed. Behind him, Lengram covered a smile with his hand. The old cleric giggled.

Christopher was undeterred. "But you have to admit that they're quite valuable to Adria as a whole. The best artisans work there, and a substantial amount of taxes and fees from the Free Towns do wind up in your coffers, Yvonnet. Your yearly market fairs for example."

"Well, yes."

"And what would Adria do if we lost the Free Towns?"

Yvonnet's mouth was set. "Well, I'm sure we could find another baron mad enough to let himself be overthrown by his own towns. Wasn't David a'Freux related to the delAurvre line somewhere?"

Lengram snickered audibly.

"We're *all* related to one another," Christopher snapped. It had been a direct insult, but anger would do no good, and he struggled to soften his voice. "Well . . . then what about the people of the Free Towns? People like . . . Martin Osmore . . ."

Yvonnet stiffened. "You're a fine one to talk about the Free Towns, Christopher. Your grandfather tried to overthrow them."

"That was my grandfather. This is me." Christopher felt relieved at his own words. Yes, this was Christopher delAurvre, defending the Free Towns, bonding with Shrinerock, attempting to unite the barons of Adria against an outside threat. He was decidedly not his grandfather.

But he saw the flicker in Yvonnet's eyes. The baron of Hypprux was frightened, and therefore dangerous. Christopher had pushed too hard.

"I don't think that I'm at all concerned about commoners," said Yvonnet. "Not concerned at all. I might as well be concerned with . . ." He groped for something unlikely enough. ". . . with Elves, for example."

He laughed loudly at his own joke, and the old scribe looked up from his tablets with a toothless smile. "Old Roger believed in Elves, my lord," he said. He fingered his deformed nose. "And in beating his clerks!"

"Well said, Amos!" Yvonnet continued to laugh. "And it looks to me like his fist was the more substantial of the two!" Still chortling, he turned to Christopher. "You know, I've always thought the delAurvres prey to occasional fits of . . . ah . . ."

"Whimsy," suggested Lengram from his place behind Yvonnet's chair.

"Whimsy, yes! I hope, cousin, that when you leave Hypprux you won't be telling everyone that Elves sabotaged your efforts here." Yvonnet giggled.

Elves. Children's stories and the tales of doddering old men. It was another insult.

But Christopher was staring at the scribe. Roger had been chamberlain of Hypprux at the time of his sudden reformation, and despite his love of forestry and hunting—deer, boar, and peasants, too—had spent most of his time in the city with his co-conspirator, Bishop Aloysius Cranby. If Roger had struck Amos, then the scribe had surely known the baron before his change. And, more important, it was quite possible that Amos had known Roger *during* it.

Something had happened to Roger. Christopher found himself seemingly possessed of an opportunity to find out what.

''We're done here,'' Yvonnet was saying. ''It's time for a feast.'' He grabbed Christopher's hand and stood up. ''And pledges of friendship between Hypprux and Aurverelle! God and Rome know, we've had our differences, but we'll settle them tonight in the Château!''

Christopher caught a hint of dissemblance in Yvonnet's voice, but while he recalled that there were many ways of settling differences, he was still staring at the old man. Feast or no, settlements or no, he was going to talk with Amos.

CHAPTER 15

Christopher suffered through the banquet, picking at the dainties and richly sauced dishes that were put before him. Good God, he had actually made a habit of eating this way? Black bread had a wholesome way about it, and watered wine was a good enough drink for any meal. He had actually grown to like both of them, and he found it difficult to reconcile his stomach to the task with which it was now confronted.

But he smiled and joked and improvised rhymes with the best of Yvonnet's courtiers and councilors. He laughed at the right times, applauded at the right times—how quickly the properly noble idiot came back!—and, as far as he could tell, gave the lie to the rumors of his madness and deranged behavior. Even Yvonnet's wife, a mousy little woman with prematurely graying hair, perked up at his flattery, and when Christopher danced with her, though he still could not remember her name, he actually managed to bring a smile to her face.

Her husband, though, seemed worried, and Christopher was reminded of nothing so much as a caged cat. Something was afoot, and he wished repeatedly that Natil were at his elbow, but the Château staff had classified the harper as a servant, and she had been given a plate at the table in the kitchen and a place toward the end of the night's entertainments. At present, she was probably off somewhere in the maze of corridors that made up the Château complex, tuning her instrument or combing her hair and arranging her costume.

Christopher looked in vain for Amos, too. The old scribe was obviously not needed at the festivities, and in fact, Christopher suspected that his presence at the meeting that afternoon had been solely for appearance's sake: Yvonnet no more wanted a written record of Christopher's proposal than he wanted his liaison with Martin Osmore carved on the west tympanum of the Cathedral of Our Lady of Mercy.

It was late when the feast quieted down enough for Natil to play. She was, as always, radiant, her blue eyes flashing and her long hair unbound and cascading down her back like a river of jet and silver. Clad simply—she needed no ornament to draw every eye—she settled herself just far enough away from the hearth so that the heat would not throw her strings out of tune, and after a quick, introductory arpeggio, began the story of Blondel's search for Richard of the Lion's Heart.

Christopher listened appreciatively as the harper's sweet voice rose up, and he wondered if any of the jaded courtiers in this hall could feel even a tenth of what she offered through her music. No, probably not. And Yvonnet himself continued to look like a caged cat, alternately eager and close to tears. Lengram, the chamberlain, leaned frequently over his shoulder and whispered to him, but whatever he said seemed not to help.

And, in Natil's song, Blondel continued his search.

Christopher was proud of his musician, proud of Pytor for hiring her. And then he noticed that Natil's eyes—gleaming, earnest, as worried as he had ever seen them—were fastened upon him.

And Blondel continued his . . . search.

After a moment, Christopher understood, nodded, and rose. Yvonnet grabbed his arm. "Dear cousin," he said, "away so soon?"

"I have to piss," said Christopher with a smile, "and I'm not going to do it in my wine cup. I'll be back."

Laughing at his cousin's roguish humor, Yvonnet let him go. But Christopher did not go to the privy. With Natil's voice fading slowly in the distance, he followed one corridor, then another, got turned around first, then hopelessly lost, and finally was directed by a serving girl to the wing of the Château where Amos, who turned out to be the master of the scribes and secretaries, had a small bedroom to himself.

Christopher's first knock brought no response, but his second elicited a muffled reply, and the old man appeared at the door a minute later, wrapped in a thin robe. His pale eyes widened at the sight of his noble visitor, but he swung the door fully open and bowed Christopher in.

Christopher sat down and came directly to the point. Amos knew his grandfather, did he not? Was there anything to tell about Roger's sudden . . . change?

Amos was a genial man, and was obviously flattered that anyone of Christopher's rank found it necessary to ask him anything. "Oh, it was a few days after he broke my nose," he said. "Did a right good job of it, too. You can still see that it isn't what it used to be!" He flicked the end of his lopsided nose with a finger and laughed when it wiggled like a dead fish.

"Why did he strike you?"

"Oh, he was angry. Baron Roger was chamberlain of the city then, just like Lengram is now . . ."

Christopher winced. Not just like Lengram, he hoped.

". . . and he'd just gotten word that Paul delMari—that's the present Baron Paul's grandfather—was milk brother of the mayor of the Free Towns. Now your grandfather—saving your grace, my lord—had just killed Paul, and a few days before he'd lost his friend Aloysius Cranby and found out that Clarence a'Freux had his own plots . . . and somewhere in there—I don't quite recall anymore, it's been so long—someone managed to break into the Château and free a prisoner who was a witch, so Baron Roger was in a terrible fierce mood, and I was the one unlucky enough to have read him Paul's will." Amos laughed again and waggled what was left of his nose.

Christopher had followed the account with some difficulty, but that did not matter: Amos had not yet touched upon the real question. "When did Roger change?"

"A few days after that, my lord."

"How did it happen?"

"No one knows, really, my lord. He went off with a girl and two servants—went off hunting, you know—up in Beldon Forest."

Christopher knew about Beldon Forest, but if a girl had been involved, hunting would not have been on Roger's mind at the time.

"And when he came back," Amos continued, "he was as different a man as you could have seen. Oh, he still had a terrible fierce temper, and he was the very devil in a battle, but he was . . . like . . . well . . . courteous."

"Courteous?"

"Something like you, my lord. You talk to people as though you really see them, you know."

"Yes . . . yes . . ." Christopher was not sure that he appreciated the compliment, but Roger's change was still a mystery. "Did he ever say anything about what happened in the forest?"

"Oh . . . well, you know . . ." Amos shrugged uncomfortably. "Men say odd things sometimes when they've had a little too much to drink."

"Odd?" Christopher felt a chill. Of course it was odd. It had to be odd. What was odder than the sudden renunciation of a life's habits? "Tell me."

Amos squirmed some more. "Oh, my lord, it's embarrassing."

Christopher summoned up the delAurvre glare and hoped that it would work on one of Yvonnet's people.

It did. Amos squirmed again, then bobbed his nearly hairless head. "Well, I think it had to do with the plan that Bishop Cranby and Roger had put together about the Free Towns. It was heresy they wanted to prove. Heresy . . . and Elves."

Christopher's chill deepened. He had heard about the plot. Everyone had. But the reasons and foundation for it had grown hazy over the years. Heresy was an obvious ploy. But why Elves? It did not make sense.

"Now, whether folk believed in Elves back then, I don't know," Amos continued. His toothless mouth was drooling, and he murmured an apology and dabbed at his moist lips with a cloth. "I never did, though. And I don't know if Roger did, either. But toward the end, he was certainly going on about them. He even claimed that the people who broke into the Château and freed the witch were Elves! Think of that! And then when he came back from his hunting . . ."

The old man hesitated, coughed, shrugged with embarrassment. Christopher glared again, and he went on.

"Well, he said once that Elves sometimes knew a little more than humans." Amos was deeply embarrassed. "His very words, my lord. Please excuse me."

It was something Christopher had learned to live with. Roger had believed in Elves, and had once claimed to have actually met one. Even Pytor, loyal though he was, had blushed at that, but Roger had been old, and that was, perhaps, some excuse. But Roger had not been old when he had talked to Amos, and hearing someone like the scribe go on about his grandfather's weakness (was it just simple insanity, then?) with such embarrassed familiarity gave Christopher a queasiness that had nothing to do with the indigestible meal he had eaten that night. "Excused," he said with difficulty.

"I'm sorry, my lord."

Christopher forced a smile. "No need to be sorry, my man. My deepest thanks to you for your help."

"May I say, my lord . . ." Amos mumbled another apology, dabbed again at his mouth. ". . . that Aurverelle has had no finer master in my memory than yourself. Roger went home a few weeks later, and he was a credit to his lineage. And you're certainly a worthy, worthy grandson."

Christopher acknowledged the clumsy compliment with a short nod, for he had spent altogether too many years attempting to live down both halves of his grandfather's life. But he shook the old man's hand, handed him a bag of coins for his trouble, and left the room as he had come: unannounced, worried.

Had Amos told him that Roger had experienced a religious vision in Beldon Forest, it perhaps would have been more acceptable to Christopher, but to be confronted with reasonless, irrational conversion when what he had wanted was . . . was . . .

Retracing his steps, pausing and frowning at the numerous crossings of hallways and corridors, he realized that he had not known what he had wanted. A reason, perhaps. An explanation.

Well, perhaps he had it, unpalatable though it was. And maybe his own madness—capering and fruit throwing—was yet another piece of delAurvre tradition that had been passed down to him courtesy of Roger. Unpalatable indeed!

He heard the cathedral bell tolling and realized that he had spent more time than he had thought trying to find Amos. The banquet would be over by now, and he would be missed. Well, he could always tell them that he had gotten lost. Given the complexity of the Château's hallways, it would be a believable story.

But when he found his way at last to the empty hall, he heard the tread of numerous thick boots and the clink of mail. Lengram's voice echoed faintly down the stairwell:

"He's not? Then find him! The baron wants him confined before dawn."

Yvonnet's agitation, Natil's worry. Everything was becoming clear to Christopher. The baron of Hypprux had indeed been a cat in a cage, but now the cat was loose.

"Ever hear of mice with fangs, cousin?" muttered Christopher. But he knew he was in trouble. He was separated from his guards, unfamiliar with the layout of the Château, and he did not even have a sword.

He turned and started back toward the servant's wing, but more footsteps were approaching from that direction. Hesitating only for an instant, he ducked behind a hanging just as a group of servants came in, picked up a load of dishes, and left. The sound of boots and mail grew louder.

Christopher stuck his head out from behind the hanging and was about to run when he heard someone else coming. He pulled his head back in as another servant entered the room . . . on tiptoe. As Christopher watched, unseen, the man looked about carefully, seized an uncut loaf of bread, and thrust it into his tunic. Suddenly aware of the approaching soldiers, he started, looked for some escape, and finding none, darted behind the same hanging that concealed the baron of Aurverelle.

He was unconscious in a moment. Christopher held him and kept him from crashing to the floor as the soldiers arrived.

Lengram was complaining. "Well, damn you, *look* for him."

And to Christopher's horror, the soldiers broke up into twos and threes and spread out for a thorough search. One pair began to poke about the banquet room, their efforts obviously half-hearted. Christopher here? Nonsense.

And then one lifted the tapestry and found himself confronted with the unexpected sight of an unconscious man flying straight at him.

The servant was a clumsy projectile, but the soldier went down. Loudly. As his companions stared, then shouted for help, Christopher made for the stairwell, darted up a floor, then suddenly cursed himself when he realized that he was heading straight for the rooms that Yvonnet had given him. Of *course* they were going to be looking there.

Only one flight up, then, not two, and he darted into the corridor that presented itself. In the distance, he heard more footsteps, the clang of a sword against the wall. But he had been followed up the stairs by the second soldier, and the man was just sucking in a breath to call for help when Christopher spun, set his feet, and smashed his gloved fist into the mail at the man's throat. A muffled crunch of breaking cartilage, and the man fell, but the distant footsteps suddenly were not so distant. And now there was movement on the stairwell. A great deal of movement.

He grabbed the dying man's sword, shoved him into the shadows, and scurried for the marginal shelter of a window embrasure. He had been an idiot to come to Hypprux, but perhaps if he made an entirely glorious fight of it, people would tend to forget the idiocy.

"My lord," came a soft voice from outside the window.

Christopher looked over his shoulder and saw a fair face framed by dark hair shot with silver. Blue eyes flashed.

Natil.

"What—?"

"Hurry, my lord." And with a slender hand, she helped him out the window and onto a narrow ledge. Sixty feet away was the inner curtain wall. Forty feet down was the ground. Christopher tried hard not to look at the ground, but Natil, perched on the ledge, looked quite comfortable.

"What are you doing here, Natil?"

A smile. "Helping you, my lord."

"How did you know where I was?"

The smile again: gracious, kind, but, inexplicably, a little sad. "I knew."

And then he saw that she was clad in garments of green and gray—tunic and breeches and soft boots—that blended softly with the color of stone and night. She had tied back her hair and tucked it down the back of her collar, but her beloved harp was slung over her shoulder.

He shook his head, bewildered—only Natil would go climbing about on the outside of a castle with a harp—and was speculating about her probable life as a burglar when the two groups of Yvonnet's soldiers met in the corridor.

"Seen him?"

"No. Didn't he come this way?"

"Didn't see him."

"Well, keep looking. And—"

The man Christopher had struck wheezed out his last breath with a rattling gurgle, and the soldiers gathered around him with oaths and ineffective help. "Run fetch the leech," someone said at last.

"But he's dead."

"Run fetch the leech anyway."

"He'll just want to bleed him. And he's dead. It can't help."

"Dammit, it can't hurt. Do what I say."

Eventually, the physician showed up to recommend bleeding, and the body was hauled away. The soldiers turned once again to the task of hunting down the baron of Aurverelle. "Where's he gone?"

"If I knew that, I wouldn't be here now, would I?"

The corridor finally cleared, and Natil rose. "We have a few minutes before they search this hall again."

"We have to get out of here," said Christopher. "Yvonnet wants Aurverelle, and he'd be very pleased if I suddenly disappeared. Or died. An accident, you know."

"Of course." Natil looked into the corridor, nodded. "We will have to escape." With unnerving grace and silence, she swung into the corridor, then reached back and helped Christopher in. "And we have Ranulf and the men to think of, too." She paused, considered, looked up and down the corridor. "Did you want to worry about the horses?"

Christopher gaped at her. The horses? "I'll be satisfied with our skins. Preferably intact."

Natil nodded. "Then let us go."

She moved with an uncanny surety, slipping along corridors, waiting for search parties to pass by stairwells and corridors as though she anticipated their movements, occasionally beckoning Christopher out onto a ledge to wait while servants and soldiers argued and exchanged reports a few feet away.

Somehow Natil was guiding him through the Château with complete impunity, as though she read the future movements of the soldiers even as those movements were being planned. Given her behavior at times, he wondered, too, whether she could also see in the dark.

Quite a thief. He shuddered. She probably could have carted away all of Aurverelle between compline and lauds without anyone noticing.

A short time later, she pulled him into a cul-de-sac. "My lord, you must choose. We can either escape, you and I,

and leave Ranulf and the men—I doubt that Yvonnet would
be harsh with them—or we can attempt to take them with
us.''

Her eyes flashed even in the dark. Christopher heard, distantly, muffled voices, slamming doors. It was late, and the
searchers were baffled and angry. He was not as sure as
Natil that Ranulf and the men would be spared. But escape
for fifteen was more of a distinct problem than escape for
two, not to mention the fact that the Aurverelle men were
more than likely sleeping in the barracks with Yvonnet's
soldiers. ''I don't know how on earth we'd get them out.
Unless . . .''

It was an insane thought. But he was, after all, mad. And
he was angry enough to consider further madness.

''. . . we had Yvonnet with us.''

Natil nodded. ''I believe that would be the only way.''

Christopher eyed her. Quite a thief. And, as far as he
could tell, absolutely loyal to him. William of Normandy
had conquered England with Taillefer at his side. What
might he have done with Natil! ''You can take me to him,
can't you?''

''I can.''

Of course she could. For a moment, Christopher wished
that his grandfather had had someone like Natil. Maybe
things would have been better. Maybe Roger would not have
been mad.

Inwardly, he shook his head. Madness was not only unpalatable, it was indigestible. He simply could not accept
it. ''Lead the way, harper,'' he said. ''I think it's about time
I had a little chat with my dear cousin.''

Out a window then, and up the wall. Natil climbed like
a monkey, her garb invisible in the moon shadow, the strings
of her harp glinting a soft gold in the starlight. Christopher
followed more slowly, his shoulders and arms aching as he
felt for patches of old and crumbly mortar that would offer
a finger-hold.

Across a roof, down a drain. A stone gargoyle stared into
Christopher's face as he locked his legs around the pipe. ''I
imagine you're one of my relations, too,'' he said.

''Shhh,'' said Natil from below.

And a few minutes later, they were crouching to either
side of a wide window. It was early September, but the

weather was still warm, and the shutters and casements were open.

Natil nodded. Yvonnet's bedroom.

Christopher waved his thanks and stood up slowly, steadying himself with a hand on the shutters. He gestured at the room within, raised an eyebrow. Natil nodded again. Yvonnet was there. Christopher did not know how she knew, but he accepted that she did, just as he accepted that she had known about Yvonnet's plot and his own decision to look for Amos.

He wondered what else she knew. Probably too much. Damn, but she reminded him of Vanessa sometimes.

But now he was hearing a deep voice from the room. It was Yvonnet. At first, Christopher could not understand it, but then he realized that his cousin was crying: deep, mannish sobs, half muffled as though with cloth.

Startled, he glanced at Natil. She shook her head, sadness gleaming in her eyes. Natil, it seemed, could feel pity for anyone.

Christopher strained his ears, began to make out whispered words.

"I've done it now, Lengram," Yvonnet was saying. "I've done it. There's no going back. I can't help it. And what will God say to me when I die?"

Lengram's tone was that of a mother shushing a fretful child. "He'll say that you did well to preserve the Church of Rome. That will . . . ah . . . count for a great deal."

"You and I are bad enough, Lengram. But a fratricide? What will He say to that?"

"Christopher's not your brother."

"He's close enough."

Christopher wrinkled his nose. At present, even *cousin* was too close for him.

Yvonnet continued to sob, genuinely frightened. Sword in hand, with Natil behind him, Christopher eased into the bedroom. The spill of moonlight was faint, but it was enough for him to be able to see the tangle of sheets and lovers' limbs on the bed.

"And I can't stop it, Lengram," said Yvonnet. "I can't. I couldn't stop with Martin, no matter how he pleaded—he wanted it anyway, I know—and I can't stop this with Christopher now."

Natil was already slipping across the room to the door.

Her pale hands went to the latch, made sure it was locked. She looked to Christopher, nodded.

"But you want Aurverelle, don't you, Yvonnet?" said Lengram.

"Of course I want it. But I don't want to do such a thing as . . . as . . ."

Christopher said it for him. "As kill your dear cousin, Yvonnet?"

Silence. Hoarse, labored breathing.

"Get up." The contempt was loud in Christopher's voice. "Get up, you *damned* coward."

Slowly, Yvonnet disentangled himself from Lengram and staggered to his feet. Strong but heavy, hirsute to the point of ursine shagginess, he held his big arms clutched against his chest like a woman caught in adultery. "Christopher," he managed.

"*Dear Cousin* Christopher. As you so often reminded me."

Lengram was sitting up, the sheet wrapped about him. "I will . . . ah . . . shout. You'll never get out of the Château alive."

Unnoticed, Natil had slid behind him, and the chamberlain's eyes widened when he felt her hand on his hair and the touch of a knife at his throat. "Say nothing," whispered the harper. "Do nothing." Her voice was calm, with just a touch of pity.

Yvonnet, trembling, hung his head. "What are you going to do?"

Christopher shook his head. "The question would be better put, dear cousin, as: 'What are *we* going to do?' And the answer is that *we* are going to take a little trip." Yvonnet lifted his head. "Yes," said Christopher. "A little hunting trip. We have to start early. Very early. And we're taking Ranulf and my men with us."

Yvonnet started to speak.

"Shut up," said Christopher. "You won't need any of those dandies you call attendants. Ranulf and the men will suffice. And . . ." He glanced at Natil, grinned without mirth. "And our horses, too."

Yvonnet stared.

"Call off the search, dear cousin," said Christopher. "And send word to my men that we're leaving immediately."

Yvonnet was weeping.

Christopher stepped forward and laid the point of his sword against Yvonnet's naked chest. "Call," he said, "or I swear that I'll put you on the floor with a hole in your heart."

Shaking, with Christopher's sword at his back, Yvonnet went to the door and called.

CHAPTER 16

Christopher returned to Aurverelle just ahead of an autumn storm that pelted the fields first with rain, then with hail, then with sleet, and quickly churned the just-sown earth into a sea of cold mud. Standing as they did on a high outcropping of rock, the castle and the town were relatively unaffected, but the bad weather continued for several weeks, and the lowlands—and the tenants and crofters who lived in them—were soon flooded.

Another baron might have holed up in his fortress and waited for sunshine, but not Christopher. He gathered castle folk and townsfolk and took them down to help; and together with the peasant farmers they labored in the pouring rain, dredging out canals, repairing dikes and hedges, scrambling through the mud with loads of reeds for the thatchers. It was brutal, cold work that demanded no skill, only endurance and will, but the baron of Aurverelle, mindful of his Kingdom, labored in the water and filth beside his people, as did his soldiers, his officers . . . and even his harper.

Despite bad weather and hard labor, Christopher felt rather good. He had evaded Yvonnet's clumsy attempt to seize Aurverelle, and he had done it in a manner so devastating to the baron of Hypprux that, before Christopher had released him some miles from his city, Yvonnet had, with frightened and shamefaced tears, pledged his support for the alliance.

Christopher knew that Yvonnet was a dubious ally. Fighting with his own cities over schismatic alignment, embroiled in his fears of divine retribution, the baron of Hypprux could hardly be depended upon to keep his word. But he was a start, and since word of his pledge had already begun to spread throughout Adria, the lesser baronies that

were aligned with him—Friex, Kirtel, Bomar, and others—
had followed.

Which left Baron Ruprecht of Maris and his allies.

But the storms lasted through September, and by the time
Christopher and his people had salvaged the fields, winter
had closed in with the October snows. Roads disappeared
beneath a blanket of white, Malvern settled into a muffled
sleep, and travel was out of the question.

Christopher chafed at the forced inactivity, and since the
idle time gave him the opportunity to reflect on the words
of Amos the scribe, he chafed all the more.

Madness. It was simply not acceptable. Attributing Roger's reformation and subsequent behavior to madness was
something like saying the sky was blue because it pleased
God for it to be that way. While God's pleasure might be
acceptable to the theologians and the doctors of the Church,
it did not satisfy Christopher delAurvre any more than did
madness.

But who believed in Elves? Was that not madness? And
now Christopher had discovered not only that Roger's belief
in the legendary immortals had begun well before his sudden change but also that the old man had, in effect, blamed
the collapse of his plots against the Free Towns on them.

Worse and worse.

Christopher wished frequently that he had been able to
examine some of the old records kept in Yvonnet's library.
Roger had been chamberlain of Hypprux: surely something
had been documented—letters, transcripts, maybe even
something about that escaped witch—that might reveal the
genesis of his change. But Christopher had not had time to
look, and now he was very sure that he did not want to
sample any more of Yvonnet's hospitality. Dear cousin, indeed!

And the question nagged at him. And he chafed.

"Roger was a good man, Natil. I can't ignore that fact."
A December storm was throwing snow against the shuttered
windows of Castle Aurverelle, and the cold drafts were only
marginally damped by the hangings and the tapestries.
Christopher was sitting in an arm chair in his bedroom, his
bare feet stretched out toward the hearth, warming himself
after a trek through the town. Nothing special, really. Just
making sure that everyone was all right. "He was a bit of

a bear, even when I knew him, but he was a good-hearted bear. If you know what I mean.''

"I do.'' The harper smiled. She was sitting on a pillow on the floor, tailor-fashion, her harp on her lap and her gown tucked neatly in about her toes. She seemed much as she always had: sweet and kind, always willing to play and sing, helpful . . . and tranquil in her helpfulness.

And yet Christopher knew her also as someone who was perfectly willing to climb about on the outside of a fortified castle and hold a knife to the throat of the chamberlain of Hypprux, or to ditch and dredge in the fields alongside the men. A strong, fearless woman, as loyal as he had ever seen. And so, though some of her comments and actions seemed to be as cryptic as her past, he liked her, trusted her, and eventually had been moved to confide in her about his grandfather.

"I always liked him when I was a boy,'' he said. "He took me fishing. And he taught me how to hunt, and how to fight. Manly things. He didn't seem mad at all. He seemed . . .'' He fell silent. The storm battered at the shutters. "He seemed considerably more sane than I.''

Natil's eyes were on him, seemingly reflecting more light than came from the fire.

"I mean, he didn't go about throwing fruit at people. Or climbing up drainpipes. Or acting like a bear.'' He felt himself grow warm, but not from the fire.

The harper sighed softly, regretfully. "You bear your grandfather . . . like a burden, my lord.''

The old wounds twinged. "What am I supposed to do, Natil? Roger was first a failure at being a human being, and then he was a failure at being a delAurvre. He started it all, my father thrashed about like a fop until the plague got him, and then I—damn my eyes—continued the fine old tradition. Roger failed with the Free Towns. I failed at Nicopolis. Roger acted like a fool. I act like a madman. And now every rag-tag bunch of robbers thinks that they can just ride off with a sack of Aurverelle wool. And they're right, too.''

"What . . .'' Natil seemed to be choosing her words carefully, her eyes flickering with firelight . . . and something else. Again, she reminded Christopher of Vanessa. But if Natil saw too much, she did not blench. "What did you hope to accomplish at Nicopolis, my lord?''

He glared at the fire. "Redemption.''

"For yourself?"

Christopher kept his eyes on the fire. "For myself, for being a delAurvre. And for my grandfather, for being a . . ."

Natil's eyes were luminous, compassionate. Christopher felt their gaze, tried not to look at them.

". . . a coward." He struggled with his bitterness. Natil's questions had lanced a festering boil, and the pus came eagerly. "For my entire family, for being a bunch of mean-spirited, single-minded brutes without a shred of compassion or decency."

Natil was looking at him, he thought, in much the same way as he had looked at Vanessa. "And yet you condemn your grandfather for showing compassion and decency."

"I didn't say that it would make any sense." Christopher picked up the poker, prodded at a burning log. Fire. This was what they used to burn witches. And, if the old stories held any truth, Elves, too.

Elves. The word kept surfacing. Christopher would have preferred madness.

"Let me tell you about something," he said, giving the log another shove. Sparks flew up like stars and mounted into the chimney. "Years ago, I went to Paris with my grandfather. Mother and Father were dead by then, and Roger took me everywhere with him. He more or less raised me." He grinned at the heat from the flames. "Fitting, eh?"

Natil said nothing.

"The reason for the Paris trip was the coronation of Queen Isabeau. Roger was only distantly related to King Charles, but Charles was determined to have a fine show, and so he invited everyone. Roger went, so I went. I was already having doubts about the old man, though. I'd grown up worshiping him. Roger could do anything. Roger was God. But then I'd started hearing stories—people talk, and all that—about what he was like . . . before. The people he'd hanged. The girl he'd chained to his bed and left to die. And then I heard about the Free Towns . . ."

And Vanessa was in the Free Towns, safe, because Roger had failed. Christopher fought the thought away, for it made his throat ache with her absence.

". . . and suddenly I didn't worship him any more. All his gardening and all his quiet little ways just seemed to me then to be the marks of a man who was a failure. So I tried to ignore the fact that I was with him. Roger of Aurverelle: the man who had lost the Free Towns . . . and his nerve. As far as I was concerned, I was there on my own.''

Natil nodded but did not speak. Her harp was on her lap, and she had folded her hands on it and rested her chin on her interlaced fingers. Her eyes were gleaming, and for a moment, Christopher wondered whether he saw a hint of radiance about her.

''The festivities were wonderful, of course,'' he said. ''There were plays and pageants and processions . . . even a fountain that spurted white and red wine. People dressed up like angels and all that. Ostentation, you know, but I was impressed by that sort of thing back then. But what really struck me was something that happened that evening. You see, they'd strung a rope from the tower of Notre Dame Cathedral all the way across to the top of the highest house on Pont Saint Michel, and an acrobat walked that rope in the darkness. He held a lit candle in each hand. He was singing. It was . . . beautiful.''

Natil smiled.

''I wanted then . . .'' Christopher's jaw trembled. ''I wanted to be like that. Here was this man, walking a tight-rope high above the earth, carrying lights in his hands . . . and singing.'' Christopher sighed. ''And I wanted to carry light into the darkness, too. I wanted to be valiant. I wanted to be brave. I wanted to accomplish something. Instead . . .'' He shook his head, stretched his feet a little closer to the fire, snatched them back when a log crackled and sent a spark flying toward his toes. ''Instead, I turned out much like my grandfather.''

Natil's face mirrored only compassion, and she was silent for a time. Then: ''And do you not carry light?''

Christopher blinked.

''You saved Vanessa's life. She was a peasant girl, but you saved her. And now you offer aid to all the people of Adria. Something that the barons of Aurverelle . . .'' And there was a sudden flicker of pain in Natil's eyes, deep pain. ''. . . have never done before. You chose that course of action, and you chose it freely, just as Vanessa freely chose not to speak of what the patterns said to her . . . and it was you who first showed her how to keep silent. Do you not call that the bearing of light? Is that not valor?''

Though he wondered how the harper knew so much about Vanessa, he could not argue with her. But he still had questions. "But . . . but what happened to grandfather?"

"Does it so matter?"

"Yes, it does." Christopher got up and paced about the room, his bare feet padding across thick bearskins and oriental carpets. "There was a reason for it all. There had to be. I'm not him. All right. Fine. But until I know what happened to him, whether it was a harper playing for him, or an acrobat holding candles, or . . . or Elves or witches or God knows what else, I won't be satisfied. And I won't be free."

Natil nodded slowly. "I . . . understand. . . ."

Christopher turned around abruptly. "You're a harper, Natil. You know all the legends."

Natil was suddenly cautious. "I know . . . some of them, my lord."

"What do you know about Elves? Roger talked about Elves. He was obsessed with them before his change, and he talked about them after. He'd say . . . odd things . . . when I knew him—nothing ever definite—and he even mentioned them on his deathbed." He felt a little ashamed: confessing Roger's obsession with fantasies was much the same as revealing that a cousin was a sodomite, or a grandfather a habitual rapist.

Natil had been caught off guard. "I know a little."

"Are they real?"

It was a rhetorical question only, something by which he hoped to satisfy himself once and for all that fantasies and delusions would remain fantasies and delusions. But Natil looked away quickly, and Christopher realized that his sudden, impulsive question had actually disconcerted her.

Her reply, though, disconcerted him just as much, if not more. "They are."

He stared. He did not doubt her. If Natil said it, it must be true. But if it were true . . .

What had happened to his grandfather? Elves? But that *was* madness!

There was a sudden scrambling at the windows, a frantic clawing and scratching and hammering. Startled, Christopher at first blinked in astonishment, then, his hand on his dagger, cautiously approached and unfastened one of the shutters.

It was pulled open from the outside, and a grotesque head was thrust into the room. Beetle-browed and pop-eyed, it was rimed with frost and snow, and it gaped and gibbered at Christopher for a moment before the baron realized that it was the renegade, fruit-throwing monkey.

A muffled shout from the hallway. "This way! We've got him now!"

His eyes stinging from the blast of driving snow, Christopher stared at the frightened, half-starved, half-frozen creature that clung to the slippery shutter, its eyes pleading for warmth and protection. *Poor thing,* he thought, for he himself was just as desperately looking for an escape from another kind of cold.

Elves? Was that supposed to be an escape?

"Master! Master!" cried Pytor from outside the door. "The monkey! Is it there?"

"Yes . . ." said Christopher, not really sure whether he was referring to the monkey or to himself. "It's here." And, not knowing what else to do, he allowed the beast to force its way into the room. Screeching and gesticulating, it bounded through the window, up the bedpost, and along the hangings as Christopher grappled with the shutter and managed to fasten it shut against the wind.

He turned around, dripping, to find that Pytor and a number of castle guards had entered the room. One man slammed the door, and the rest spread out to surround the monkey.

Christopher watched. In just such a manner had Yvonnet and his men closed in upon the baron of Aurverelle.

The monkey was weaponless, friendless, trapped, and its eyes were wide with the knowledge of its imminent death. Pytor and the men were unmoved. All of them had taken too many pieces of fruit in the face. "Ranulf," said the seneschal.

"Aye, m'lord. It's time we made an end of this pest."

But Natil laid aside her harp, unfolded her long legs, and rose. "A moment, please."

Turning, she stretched out her arms to the monkey. The beast stared as though seeing her for the first time, and then, with a bound, it threw itself into her arms, at once shivering with cold and quaking with fear.

Pytor and the men stepped forward. Natil turned around, her eyes flashing. Pytor and the men stopped short.

"Leave them alone," said Christopher.

"But, master . . ."

"Leave them alone." But he was himself staring. The monkey was huddled in Natil's protecting arms. Just as . . . in the Château . . .

Natil peered into the monkey's face. "You have been throwing fruit and making a nuisance of yourself, have you not?"

The animal covered its eyes, tried to hide its face. Christopher thought of all the apples he himself had flung.

"Will you promise not to do that anymore?" The harper's voice was kind.

Christopher could not be sure, but he thought he saw the monkey nod. With a growing sense of horror, he found that he was nodding also.

"Will you be a friend to those in this castle?"

Again, a nod. Christopher was shaking.

"Then the hand of the Lady be on you, child," Natil said as she touched the monkey's forehead. "Be healed, and be at peace." She looked at Pytor. "My lord seneschal: some food for this prodigal?"

Pytor stared.

The monkey fumbled at Natil's hair, reached beneath the black and silver tresses, and tugged at her ears. "Now, now," she said, laughing. "Not that!"

Pytor found his voice. "Mistress Harper," he said, "that monkey . . ."

"Will give us no further trouble, Pytor," said Natil. Smiling, she handed the creature to Christopher. It crawled up on his shoulder, reached into his tunic, and with delighted shrieks, extracted Vanessa's pendant.

Absently, Christopher reached up and patted the beast. Another baron of Aurverelle, it seemed, had found refuge in the arms of the mysterious harper. He half wondered whether he should be afraid.

Berard of Onella was not at all overawed by the display that Yvonnet a'Verne provided. He had seen much the same, if not better, in Italy. Florence was always trying to outdo Milan, and Milan was out-pomping Rome, and Rome tricked itself out in gutter finery in an attempt to upstage Naples, and nobody liked Venice. But when, at the great council of the free company captains invited to Hypprux,

Yvonnet named the terms and Lengram named the rates, even the most sophisticated mercenaries raised their eyebrows. Truly, the baron of Hypprux was a wealthy man!

Jehan, Berard knew, would not be interested in the matter of payment, for the poor boy still thought of valorous meathacking as payment enough. That Yvonnet was on the same side of the schism as Furze was an excellent coincidence, but even had that not been the case, Jehan could be counted on to cooperate, for the matter of the Aurverelle wool wains had left him with a bad taste of commerce in his mouth that would require some bloodletting to wash away.

And bloodletting was indeed in the future, for Yvonnet was not offering terms and rates in exchange for the taking of a village or a single castle, but for the entire city of Ypris.

"I want it razed to the ground," the baron fairly shouted. "Those apostates have defied God long enough. It's time that they learned the rewards of heresy."

Berard, who long ago had lapsed into cheerful and atheistic hedonism, was unmoved by the baron's religious sentiments, but the money, fortunately, was enough, and he cheered Yvonnet's words as loudly as anyone present. Yvonnet worshiped God. Berard worshiped gold and wine and the struggling mystery of women's loins. Each to his own.

In a few days, the documents had been drawn up, argued over, signed, and sealed; and, more important, the initial fees had been paid. Berard had no doubt that the gold that he and his escort would be bringing back to the Fellowship would ensure more than enough enthusiasm for the spring maneuvers. And though he himself had only been assigned a subordinate post in the combined mercenary army, he did not mind in the slightest, for the pay was good, likewise the leadership.

And, in any case, provided that all went well, Berard himself would eventually become the commander of a substantial army, and Adria would be his. Even—and he examined the vaulted ceiling of Yvonnet's great hall while, about him, wine flowed, food was masticated and swallowed, and the captains celebrated their contract—even Hypprux might be his.

But first things first. There was Ypris, and then . . .
. . . and then Jehan.

Berard felt better and better. The true pope? Who cared?

Yvonnet rose, lifting his golden cup, and his voice resonated among the ribbed nervures and rattled the frost-covered windows. "Hail to you, my brothers in arms . . ."

Or in banditry. Berard found it hard to tell sometimes. *If God Himself were a soldier, He would be a robber.* What an excellent sentiment! He wished that he had said it first.

". . . comrades of my heart . . ."

Berard winced. Not at all to his liking.

". . . bearers of the sword of Christ!"

Really. This was too much. But gold, Berard reflected, had a way of making people keep their mouths shut. Just as wine had a way of making them open them up. And there was wine in the future.

"A toast! To . . ." Yvonnet threw back his head and laughed. "To Ypris!"

The captains, twenty-four of the most experienced and successful commanders of the free companies, lured through the hideous winter storms by the promise of gold and loot, rose as one, lifting cups. Silks shone, gems sparkled, swords were bright in the light of innumerable torches. The captains' voices were loud in reply: gold had bought their loyalty, food and drink their enthusiasm. "To Ypris!"

And Berard was on his feet, too—just as loyal, just as enthusiastic—though as he drank, he murmured deep in his throat, so deeply that no one but himself heard or understood: "And to Shrinerock!"

CHAPTER 17

Spring in Adria was warm and dry, and above Maris, the sky was blue and cloudless: the perfect weather for an Easter celebration. The fortress complex that dominated the entire northern half of the city was decorated this Sunday with fresh flowers, and ribbons and pennants floated from its every spire and window. The rest of the city was aflutter with hangings that ranged from bedsheets in the poor sections to, in the rich, elaborate tapestries commissioned especially for the day; and in the streets, the crowds were fierce, surging, a sea of eyes and faces that lapped about the players, pageants, musicians, and acrobats that Ruprecht, baron of Maris, had summoned to help celebrate the central and most profound mystery of Christendom.

But Ruprecht did not allow the secular entertainments to reign alone, for as he was a pious man, he was profoundly conscious of the deeper significance of the day. He had risen early to sing lauds with his chaplain (he prided himself on knowing by heart the entire year of psalmodic devotions), had attended mass twice (once in his private chapel, once in the cathedral), and had spent the rest of the morning in meditation before the figure of the Crucified One that dominated his bedroom.

He prayed for guidance, for Maris was the light of true religion in a land that was, with few exceptions, plunged into heretical night. The pernicious advance of the Roman papacy in England and in the Holy Roman Empire had turned Adria into a dark world of corruption in which even a papal legate could be hunted down and killed with complete and arrogant impunity. Ruprecht thanked God that France at least still rejected the simoniacal impostor who slouched so bestially upon a counterfeit Throne of Peter!

Justified, encouraged, Ruprecht rose from his devotions then, and descended from his tower bedroom. Though his inner prayers continued, he had business to attend to, for he could think of no better way to discomfit the forces of Satan than to show them with what pomp the true servants of God could celebrate the risen Christ.

He spent the morning inspecting the great kitchens, edifying the servants with solemn words about the significance of the day, speaking personally to the officers of his household, and more importantly, instructing his wife on the importance of her appearance and deportment at the festivities. A baron, after all, was judged by the company he kept: peasant girls in homespun might be good enough for a nest of savages and madmen such as Aurverelle, and little drabs for Hypprux, but the lady of Maris had to display nobility in every point of her bearing.

Just before lunch, though, he paused in his study and picked up a sheet of parchment. ''What's this?''

''Another letter from Christopher of Aurverelle, messire,'' said his chancellor, William. ''It came yesterday.''

''Just like a devil-worshiper to shove business beneath my nose on a day like today!'' Ruprecht examined the salutation, tugging thoughtfully on his beard. In the vernacular, of course. Mules and village girls, a mendicant friar for a bailiff and an escaped slave for a seneschal: there was probably no one left in Aurverelle who could turn even half a phrase in Latin.

He tossed the letter aside after a moment. ''What does he want?''

''The same thing, messire.''

''Oh . . .'' Ruprecht allowed the sarcasm to well up. ''Wants to speak with me, does he? Wants to be allowed in my house, at my table, in my chambers, does he? And what did he say to Etienne of Languedoc?''

''Messire pointed that out to him in the fall.''

''Yes . . . I did.'' Christopher's temerity was infuriating. Not only had he actually proposed that the forces of the alliance be used to protect the land as a whole—peasants, serfs, Free Towns, and all—but he had also indicated that such protection should be provided without regard to papal loyalty. Absurd. And all this after he had killed an official envoy from the true pope, Benedict. In cold blood!

Biting back his anger, Ruprecht grabbed the letter, flung it into the fire, watched it crisp and curl. His chancellor, however, was thoughtful. ''I would be remiss, my lord, if

I did not say that I believe Christopher makes some cogent points.''

Ruprecht smiled. "Such as, Messire William?"

"Such as the threat of the free companies to all. Allowed to congregate in Adria, they might well prove a potent force. They could conceivably menace your lordship in his own house."

Ruprecht roared with laughter. "Maris? Really, William!"

"It is . . . conceivable. They could . . ." William considered. "They could, for instance, ally themselves with factions of malcontents, and so foment rebellion."

Ruprecht's voice turned cold. "Very funny, William."

"Yes, my lord."

Angry that the day was being spoiled with such thoughts, Ruprecht folded his arms. "Christopher is a fool."

"He's mad, my lord."

"Yes, William. Quite mad." Frowning, Ruprecht watched the last of the parchment curl up and flicker into ash, the wax from the delAurvre seal running down and flaring as it was consumed. "And damned." He shook his head, waved away the thought. "But we can ignore Christopher, can't we, William? On this day of all days? It's time for celebration. And what have we planned for tonight?"

William recounted the entertainments scheduled for the feast, and Ruprecht's enthusiasm, kindling, banished any remaining cares about Aurverelle. By the end of William's list, the baron was nodding approvingly.

"Very good. Very good."

"And . . ." William smiled. "A special treat for the end. We thought that the players from Castile would be acknowledged as those who had traveled farthest, but some new arrivals have put them in second place."

"And who are these?"

"A tumbler and a harper. Ah . . ." William thought for a moment. "The tumbler is but fair, but the harper—I heard her this morning—is of rare quality indeed. I believe they call themselves Christy and Nattie. They come from Bulgaria."

Ruprecht pursed his lips. "Bulgaria. Well, that's quite a journey. And they came all that way for my feast?"

"They said that they had made the trip especially for the sake of the honored Baron Ruprecht of Maris."

Ruprecht was smiling. Let Christopher delAurvre gibber in his dank castle. The fortress of Maris would shine! "Excellent, William. Give them a place to sleep in the hall tonight, and make sure they're well fed." He folded his arms, eyed the charred parchment. "If they have any skill at all, it will be quite a night!"

Moving under cover of darkness, avoiding the main roads, remaining scattered and unobtrusive until they simultaneously wheeled and gathered, the free companies surrounded Ypris.

Despite their precautions, though—precautions for which Yvonnet had paid handsomely—it appeared that Ypris had discovered them at the last minute, for when the sun rose on Easter morning, the gates of the town were shut and the parapets were manned with archers and soldiers. A thousand trails of smoke indicated that vats of oil and pitch were being brought to a boil, to be hauled up and emptied upon anyone foolish enough to attempt to scale the walls.

Berard had seen worse. Examining Ypris with an eye schooled by the brutal necessities of years of battle, he was already picking out weaknesses. The fortifications, for example, were old, the product of slow evolution rather than masterful planning, and the lines of sight from the towers and arrow loupes left uncovered numerous angles in which a determined band of men could conceal themselves while readying ladders. Uncut brush and trees came right up to the walls in some places: adequate cover for mines and saps. The main source of the city water supply was a canal from the Bergren River, and as such was easily interrupted.

Berard did not doubt that the commander of the assembled companies, a former lieutenant of the great Muzio Attendolo Sforza himself, had discovered even more. With any luck at all, though, the walls could be penetrated by subterfuge rather than by attrition. Berard hoped so. Ypris was a wealthy city, and he wanted to make up for the wool wain debacle with as little fuss as possible.

At his side, Jehan fidgeted like a full-blooded destrier. "Why doesn't Gonzago give the word?" he said.

"Probably because Gonzago is still making his final plans." Armed and armored, Berard settled himself in his saddle. He hoped that the commander would have the wisdom to order a general dismount before the attack. In Berard's personal experience, masonry walls were extremely unimpressed by cavalry charges.

"I want to fight."

"*I* want to start getting paid," said Berard. He gestured at the city. "Inside those walls is my pay chest. I intend to get it. I don't care how. Robert of Geneva took Cesena with hardly a struggle—"

Jehan was indignant. "That butcher? That was out-and-out lies and deception!"

Berard smiled. "Lies and deception are good enough."

"Really, Berard!"

The morning mists were burning off rapidly, and the sun was warming up armor and, therefore, the men inside it. Berard heard murmurs about the heat from the members of the Fellowship, turned, and looked over his shoulder. Horsed and ready—and doubtless sweating—his company was gathered up behind him, pennants flying and armor glinting. Not quite so impressive as the carefully polished mail of Hawkwood's White Company—it was said that the mere sight of that glittering horde could induce surrender— but impressive enough.

He stole a glance at Jehan. And, with luck, quite adequate.

"Well," he said, "how would you handle it?"

"A frontal assault," said Jehan promptly. "Straight up the middle . . ."

Berard listened blandly. *And the horses can bounce off the walls.*

". . . and then a battering ram to break down the city walls . . ."

While molten lead drips down on everyone.

". . . we could shatter it in a trice . . ."

Given say, several hours, since the gates are reinforced with iron.

". . . and then we could ride right up the main street to the aldermen's hall."

While the townspeople wave and smile at us. Berard rubbed the back of his neck. It was indeed getting hot. "I must compliment you, Jehan: very forthright."

Jehan tossed his head. "That's the way to do it. That's the only way to do it. Fie on Robert of Geneva."

Berard sighed inwardly. Had Jehan not been such a devil of a fighter when it actually came to hand-to-hand combat, he would have quietly gotten rid of him sometime in the last few months. As it was, though, Jehan was convenient, and Berard hoped that, in the near future, he would become even more convenient.

It was as good a time to start as any, he supposed. First move, then. A pawn. "I can't help but wonder if there might be another way in," he said idly.

"There's no other way in. Or if there is, only a coward would take it."

This was brutally unfair, Berard realized. After all, Jehan did not even know what game he was playing. But he continued. Another pawn. "The canal, for example. It must go through the wall somewhere."

"Are you saying that we should slog our way through the water and come up in the middle of a sewer?"

"It would simplify matters."

"I—"

"Besides," Berard yawned, "Gonzago is in charge. We follow his orders." He glanced sidelong at Jehan, who was now peering anxiously at Gonzago's plumed helmet. "There's always a way in. A good attacker exploits whatever opening comes his way. A good defender does his best to stop him . . . or at least keeps the openings from being discovered in the first place."

Jehan's temper, always faintly simmering, was rising to full boil.

"Like your father," said Berard, moving a bishop. "A very wise man."

"What do you mean?"

"Well, he entrusted the secret of the hidden access to Shrinerock only to you."

"I'm his only son! Of course he'd tell me!"

"It must be quite a burden . . ."

Jehan was forthright. As usual. "None whatsoever."

". . . to know something like that." Berard reached up to scratch his head. His fingers were interrupted by his helmet. He shrugged philosophically: a soldier's lot. "Why did he construct such a thing in the first place?"

Jehan was hot and angry. "He didn't construct it. It's a part of the mountain. You'd spend ten years and several fortunes trying to fill up all those caves."

Berard nodded, edged a pawn forward another square. "That wouldn't do at all."

"Shrinerock is safe enough. Who but a coward or a thief would come up from the spring, anyway?"

The second bishop now. "The spring?"

"Saint Adrian's spring. You know, that holy place that all the pilgrims are always visiting. Surely you remember Saint Adrian, Berard. He's the patron of this whole country."

Gonzago's plume was in motion now, the commander dispatching a flock of messengers to bear his decision to the captains of the individual companies. Stealth? Berard wondered. No. Probably a fight. But not—please God!—a frontal assault. Gonzago was a better man than that.

Loot, and a few women, and wine. It would be a hard day, a good night. But Berard had a few moments left to pursue his game. "Yes," he said, idly reaching for a knight, "I remember Saint Adrian." He chuckled. "How ironic that his spring should contain the greatest weakness of the castle that guards it!"

"Yes . . ." said Jehan, watching the messengers apprehensively. "Ironic."

Berard positioned the knight and turned to hear what the messengers had to say. Mate in two, if he were lucky.

The April afternoon was cool, with just a trace of a breeze from the sea, and the streets of Maris were crowded with townsfolk and visitors come for the celebration. Mimes and acrobats worked and busked the plazas. Servants in Ruprecht's livery rode along the main thoroughfares, scattering coins and flowers. Everyone was to be happy, everyone was to participate.

And Christopher delAurvre, not one to spoil the mood, leaped and tumbled in the middle of the great common that lay before the fortress of Maris. His hair and beard, left to grow for the last two months, were shaggy, unkempt, and deliberately spattered with mud; and his clothing was ragged and fantastic with tatters and scarves. He looked like an itinerant savage, and, indeed, he played the part well, growling like a bear at the children, scattering them amid feigned and sincere squeals of fright, propositioning a donkey so sincerely—and graphically—that the bystanders howled. And when Natil, laughing as hard as the rest, at last swallowed her mirth and struck a chord on her harp, he grinned brightly, turned his cap upside-down, and broke into an expansive dance.

Everyone clapped. Christopher was a good dancer, and an even better madman. The perfect oddity to compliment such a pretty harper whose modesty was such that she actually blushed at the applause given her. But Natil, regardless of her origins or her reasons for serving Christopher so steadfastly, seemed to be almost innately modest, whether about her skills as a harper . . . or her knowledge of the Elves.

Natil actually knew a great deal about them, and listening to her stories that winter, Christopher had begun for the first time to understand something of the maze of patterns that surrounded his family.

No one—perhaps deliberately, perhaps because those who had firsthand knowledge were dead—had ever told Christopher that his ancestors had all been obsessed with the Elves, seeing in their effortless, sylvan existence a challenge to the delAurvre dominion over man, field, and forest. Some had actually made a practice of hunting them, and that ferocity had gone so far as to infect the people of the estate in general. Nearly four hundred years before, went one tale (and Natil, overcome by her own skill, had wept when she had told it), two Elves, male and female, had been captured alive by Aurverelle men. The female had been raped and tortured to death, but the male had escaped, only to return some time later to slaughter the captors and their families.

It was a horrible little story of witless violence, anger, and revenge, perfectly in keeping with delAurvre excess. Roger, it seemed, had been but the last and most bestial of his family, pursuing his vices in open defiance of any kind of decency and justice.

Elves. Christopher did not doubt that within the flamboyant conventions of the storyteller's art lay the grain of truth for which he had been searching. They existed. They had power. Roger himself had mentioned them. It had not been madness, then, that had caused the old man's sudden shift in allegiance and behavior: it had been magic.

But though Christopher had been elated by the revelation that lay within Natil's stories and tears, still it chilled him that an ancestor, someone he had known, had been so struck by such inhuman powers, and that those same energies had, indirectly, touched his own life. It was because of Roger's inexplicable change that Christopher had been moved to try to make up for his grandfather's dichotomous failure of character, to finally journey to Nicopolis and have his last particle of belief dashed almost irrevocably.

Almost irrevocably, but not quite. Vanessa had come, and she had awakened his compassion. And then Natil had arrived . . . and she had brought her own kind of magic. And now Christopher was dancing in the streets of Maris, offering his glove to all of Adria.

He was not yet free. But he had gotten his bindings loose.

Christopher and Natil finished up, and the baron, his tongue lolling out the side of his mouth, rolled on his back, received a scritch on his belly from the pretty harper, then rose and padded off after her, now and again sticking his tongue out at the laughing townsfolk. If he recalled that the monkey had behaved in just such a fashion before its encounter with Natil had turned it into a model citizen of Aurverelle, he also kept in mind that the parallel had been first drawn by himself.

They ducked into the portal of a small chapel, and Christopher counted the coins they had collected. "Thirty pennies," he cried gleefully. "Just enough for dinner . . . or . . ." He glanced at the crucifix on the wall, waggled his eyebrows roguishly. ". . . or to buy Jesus."

As charming in motley and tatters as she was in furs and fine cloth, Natil shook her head and sighed at his poor taste. "Baron Ruprecht will be providing dinner," she reminded him. "You should rest before we have to perform."

"Yes . . . you're probably right." The cathedral bell began to toll. "My God, is it that late?"

"It is."

"I've been having too much fun." Christopher stretched out his arms and laughed. "I haven't acted like a madman for some time now. I rather miss it."

"You are not mad, my lord."

He laughed again. "Really, Natil: you say the most absurd things sometimes. Who but a madman would do this?"

Her eyes were knowing, almost unnervingly so. But, nonetheless, Christopher liked her and trusted her. In fact, the particularly audacious entertainment that they had planned for Baron Ruprecht tonight—late tonight—would have been impossible without her.

It would be difficult, dangerous work. Pytor had wrung

his hands at the idea, and Jerome had crossed himself, but Christopher was actually enjoying it all. "Come on," he said. "I'll race you to the fortress. Last one there is . . . umm . . ."

Natil lifted an eyebrow.

". . . is an Elf! How about that?"

She laughed, and Christopher bounded out of the alley at a run. He beat her to the gates easily.

CHAPTER 18

"Now," whispered Natil.

Silently, undetected by the slumbering acrobats and entertainers who had been granted the shelter of the great hall of Maris after the Easter feast, Christopher and his harper rose. Deep as they were within the high, multiple walls of the fortress, there was not even a faint glimmer of moonlight at the windows to relieve the absolute darkness; and Christopher wondered how they could ever find their way across the hall and into the corridors without causing an uproar. But Natil took his hand and led him unerringly toward the doorway, speaking in the faintest of murmurs to tell him to step over one of the sprawled sleepers or avoid a table or a chair that had been left out.

If there were guards nearby, their attention had apparently wavered for an instant. Christopher and Natil, unnoticed, crept out of the hall, followed a corridor towards the deserted kitchen, and finally stood in a cul-de-sac just off the pantry.

Christopher could see nothing. He had been forced to take Natil at her word when she told him to rise, step, or turn. The harper's perceptions, on the other hand, seemed undiminished. She knew where she was. Judging by her movements, the castle might well have been fully lit by the sun. It was incredible that she could find her way through the darkness, and yet Christopher was somehow not surprised.

Working sightlessly, he stripped off his tatters and motley to reveal tunic and stockings of simple, dark cloth. Soft shoes, a long knife at his side—a sword, he knew, would have been too clumsy—and a coil of rope over his shoulder completed his arrangements. Save for Natil's beloved harp, they left everything else in the cul-de-sac. If they were successful tonight, they could retrieve it at will. If not, it would not matter.

"I'm ready," he said.

"The hand of the Lady be on you, my lord," said Natil. And again, she took him by the hand and led him through the darkness.

She had said much the same thing to the errant monkey, but whose hand? What Lady? He was sure that she had not been referring to the Virgin. But Christopher supposed that the harper's blessing, whatever it meant, was as good as any, for ladies' hands had been on him throughout his life, and it was from soft arms and softer faces that he had learned much, whether sterility, compassion, or rebirth.

The windows of the upper floors looked out above the encircling walls, and the light of the moon and stars poured into the corridor. Outside, the fortress and the sleeping city lay silver in the heavenly light, and beyond them, the sea glittered, sparkling.

He was still holding Natil's hand, and he saw that she was clad in the same tunic, breeches, and boots that he had seen before. She slung her harp over her shoulder. "Do you wish to continue?" she asked formally.

He grinned. "You know I do. This is the best thing I've done since I rode off to Nicopolis. Better in fact."

Natil's eyes twinkled. "Indeed."

She bowed, touching her hands to her head and opening them wide, then turned and put a foot out the window. Unlike the Château, the fortress of Maris was without ledges, almost without any sort of handhold whatsoever, and she spent a minute or two examining the wall before, feet on the sill and fingers hooked under the lintel, she stretched up and found a hold. Christopher stared as she lifted herself with the strength of one arm.

He leaned out and peered upward. The harper's garments blended with the wall even in moonlight, but he saw that she had ascended to an upper window, and that she was stretching down a hand to him.

"Isn't there another way?" he said.

"There are guards on the stairs," replied Natil. "Ruprecht is a cautious man. He worries about plots, and frequently fears for his safety. Hence, his tower bedroom."

With a shrug then, he took her hand and strained himself

up until he was perched beside her. He tried to ignore the drop beneath his feet. "What now?"

Natil's eyes flickered inwardly. They were in shadow at present, but further climbing would inevitably expose them to the light of a moon only a few days past full. "Up to the roof. Then across and down. The guards on the parapet can be avoided."

"Is that what the . . ." He decided to risk it. He was already thinking it, for it was becoming uncomfortably obvious. ". . . patterns say, harper?"

Her eyes were on him. The breeze from the sea was cool, moist. "Patterns can change, my lord."

"So Vanessa found. You see them, too, then."

"I do."

He forced a nervous laugh. "I don't see you going about terrifying everyone—except maybe for me. There's hope for Vanessa, then?"

"There is always hope."

"What about . . ." He glanced down, wished that he had not. "What about for us?"

Natil shrugged. "Anything can happen. There are but differing degrees of probability."

"You could be burned for saying things like that, you know."

Natil looked away. "We have."

Christopher regretted his words. Natil's past and her people were her own business. She was helping him. That was enough. "I'm sorry."

"Be at peace." Natil rose, took the coil of rope from Christopher, and went clambering up the wall. In a few minutes, the end of the rope came whispering down, and Christopher knotted it about himself and, thus supported, fumbled his way up.

When he at last crawled over the edge of the roof, he collapsed, gasping. "How much farther?"

"Across, then down to a subsidiary wall, across to another, then we double back and climb again." Christopher shut his eyes and groaned softly. "The only staircase is guarded," Natil explained, "and the guards are awake."

Christopher rubbed his face. "Yes . . . of course . . . that's what you said before, wasn't it?" It was going to be a hard night, but it was precisely the presumed impregnability of the fortress that would give strength to Christopher's arguments.

Nothing was safe. Not Hypprux. Not Maris. Not even Aurverelle. And . . .

With a pang, he looked southward as though he could see a city there: a wealthy city with tiled roofs and a conceited fool for a mayor.

. . . certainly not Saint Blaise.

At times, it occurred to him that, somehow, he might have eventually made Vanessa happy. It was not pity that moved him now, nor was it the yearning of a starving ghost for the blood of mortality: it was to her humanity that he had at last responded.

He smiled softly. *Yes, Vanessa, I think I've come far enough to love you.*

He looked up into Natil's eyes. "I'm ready," he said.

"Then let us go."

Chimneys, flèches, eaves . . . Christopher and Natil ducked and wove among them. Natil's footfalls were silent, and her eyes peered, Christopher assumed, into the patterns of action and inaction that made up the fortress. Padding as quietly as he could, seeing but what was before him, he followed her.

She brought him to the edge of the roof, and he looked down on a stony sea of walls and towers. The bright moonlight turned all into a maze of light and profound darkness, but the darkness, he knew well, was not impenetrable: it was, rather, merely obscure. Profundity or impenetrability stemmed solely from his point of view. And in much the same way, his own guilt and despair had stemmed from his ignorance and limited perceptions. They also were a maze built solely of moonlight.

He was beginning to understand that. He was not his grandfather. He had his own choices. He could be free. He wanted to be free.

Natil stood at his side, watching him. "Are you ready?"

"Probably about as ready as my grandfather was when . . ." He shrugged. Whatever the final confrontation, Roger had obviously lost.

Natil looked away as though in shame, and Christopher was surprised by her reaction: she appeared to take some kind of personal responsibility for Roger.

"One of us obsessing on my grandfather is quite sufficient, Natil," he said. "Let's go see Ruprecht."

Painstakingly, they worked their way along the route that Natil had . . . what? Felt? Saw? Foretold? Christopher did not know. But though the path—or the pattern—that the harper took was an intricate blend of backtracking and stealthy approach, they drew steadily closer to the tower that contained Ruprecht's bedchamber until, just as a distant bell was ringing lauds, they stood on top of the peninsular wall that joined the tower with the rest of the fortress.

Natil was examining the climb. "Very difficult," she said.

"Impossible?"

"Nothing is impossible."

Christopher met her eyes, saw a distinct gleam. "There are only differing degrees of probability." Natil nodded. "I learn fast," he said. "They'll have to burn me, too. How do we get up?"

"I will go first," said the harper. "Then—" She suddenly froze. "O dear Lady . . ."

"What is it?"

Her sight was inward. Patterns again. "Something is happening in the castle. I see men and swords . . ."

"We've been discovered?"

She shook her head. "It is—sweet Lady!—the chancellor. He is going to try to murder the baron."

Christopher leaned against the tower and passed a hand over his face. "Of all the damned luck. Adria's being threatened by a horde of human locusts, and William's grabbing for power."

Natil was still staring into empty space. "He has a number of men in his employ, including the tower watch and several captains of the guard."

"And with enough money, the rest will shift allegiance without complaint."

She looked sad. "That is indeed what he is hoping."

Patterns. Shifting patterns. Anything could indeed happen. "If we climb, will we arrive before William?"

"Unless something else changes."

He chose. "Then let's go. We climb."

As though impelled by the sudden urgency, Natil swarmed up the side of the tower, her fingers finding invisible handholds, her boots clinging to what seemed to be nonexistent edges. She climbed directly, no longer attempting to stay within the concealment of moon shadow. Perhaps the patterns told her that caution was unnecessary.

Bracing herself in a window slit, she dropped the rope, and Christopher hauled himself up. His heart pounded at every accidental scrape of his feet, for though the attention of the tower guards might well have been taken up by the imminent coup, it might also have been sharpened by nerves.

Slip. Haul. Slip again. A foothold turned traitor and left him dangling by his hands one hundred and thirty feet above a cobbled courtyard that shone frostily in the near-vertical moonlight. For an instant, he shut his eyes, but then, angered by his fear, he pulled himself up the last twenty feet with nothing more than the strength of his arms.

When he arrived at the window, he heard snoring from within. Natil touched a finger to her lips, eased her feet in through the open window. Christopher followed. It was dark in the bedchamber, but enough moonlight seeped in to allow him to see that the baron and his obedient wife slept in separate beds.

What is this? A monastery? Yvonnet at least shared his sheets with his lover.

But the unorthodox sleeping arrangements simplified Christopher's task considerably, and a minute later, Ruprecht awoke to find Christopher sitting on his chest and a needle-sharp dagger pricking his throat.

"Not a word, messire," said Christopher. "Not a sound save it be soft and sweet."

"What is the—?" The baron's demand stopped short at a light jab from Christopher's blade. He dropped his voice. "Who are you? What do you want?"

A stirring from the other bed. Ruprecht's wife sat up, cried out.

"Tell her to be quiet," said Christopher, applying a little more pressure to the knife. His face ashen in the faint light, Ruprecht did as he was told. His wife settled down with a shudder.

"Now," said Christopher, "to answer your questions. I'm Christopher delAurvre, baron of Aurverelle, the horrible apostate that you refused to see."

Ruprecht's anger was plain, even in the semi-darkness. "And the murderer of a papal legate."

"Papal legates shouldn't go about beating up girls," said

Christopher, "but we can talk about that later because I
have to answer your other question. Originally, I would have
said that this little visit . . ." And he prodded Ruprecht's
throat again with the dagger. ". . . was to show you that
your fortress isn't as secure as you think. If I can do this,
then someone else surely can. The free companies, for instance. I was going to plead with you—yes, God help me,
plead—to reconsider your reply to my offer of an alliance."

"Hmmph! An alliance of heretics and apostates."

"An alliance of the nobility of Adria," said Christopher
smoothly. "An alliance that will allow us all to save our
own miserable skins. But never mind that. I'm not going to
plead with you."

"That's very good," said Ruprecht. "Pleading will get
you nowhere. I don't believe you anyway. Who but a madman would go climbing about a fortress in the middle—"
He broke off, the thought obviously occurring to him that
the madman in question was sitting on his chest with an
unsheathed dagger.

"Quite right," said Christopher. "A madman. Who else?
But enough of that. I'm not here to plead. I must instead
tell you that . . ." He looked up. "Natil?"

She was by the door. "They are on the stairs now, my
lord."

Ruprecht started at her voice. "What—?" Another prick
silenced him.

"Your chancellor, William, has some ambitions," said
Christopher. "He's tired of being a chancellor. He wants to
be a baron. He's on his way up here with a squad of soldiers."

Ruprecht grappled unsuccessfully with the obvious.
"What does he want?"

"Your life, your title, and your lands."

"That's absurd." Ruprecht nearly laughed. "Doubtless
he's coming to arrest you and put you to the death that you
so richly deserve. And I assure you, you'll get no more
mercy from me than you gave to poor Etienne."

"Poor Etienne. Who beat up young women." Christopher shrugged. "I'm afraid you'll just have to take my word
for it."

Footsteps. A sudden pounding on the door. "My lord
baron!" cried William. "A matter of extreme urgency has
arisen!"

Despite the dagger, Ruprecht smirked. "Do you want to surrender peacefully, Christopher? Or shall we fight it out? Or maybe you want to try to use me as a hostage?"

Christopher lifted the blade away from Ruprecht's neck. "Why don't you ask him what he wants?"

Ruprecht glared at him. Then: "What is it, William?"

"There is rebellion among the people of the southern parts of the city . . ."

Rebellion, thought Christopher. *Just the thing to bring Ruprecht to the door in an instant.* He smiled down at Ruprecht. "Intruders, Ruprecht?"

". . . and we need your leadership."

Ruprecht was plainly puzzled. "But . . . that's not right. . . ."

Christopher leaned down towards him, his face a hand's breadth from Ruprecht's. He could smell the baron's dinner on his breath. "Will you do me the favor of disproving me to my face? Go ahead and open the door. I'll wait."

"Your . . . companion . . ."

"She'll wait, too. Just say nothing about us until you determine who's right. If I'm lying, kill us. If not, join my alliance."

Ruprecht hesitated.

"As a favor," said Christopher with a smile, though his heart was pounding with the thought of what was on the other side of the door, "to a mad apostate about to meet his just desserts."

Ruprecht grunted his assent, and Christopher helped him out of bed and into a robe. At the door, the baron of Maris paused, his hand on the bar. "You'll keep your word?"

Christopher and Natil had vanished into the shadows between two huge wardrobes. "If you'll keep yours."

With a mirthless laugh, Ruprecht unbarred the door and threw it wide. William stood there, surrounded by torchlight and men in mail. "Come in, William," said the baron. "Tell me more about—"

But his words were cut short, for the chancellor lunged at him. Instinctively, Ruprecht ducked and rolled, and William's sword stroke ended with nothing more than a clang on the flagstone floor. But the soldiers were already surging into the room.

Christopher's voice was loud. "Was I right?"

"Dear God," cried Ruprecht. "You were!"

Perplexed by the strange voices in the bedroom, William and his men hesitated, thereby giving Ruprecht just enough of an opportunity to smash his shoulder into the stomach of a guard. The man stumbled and fell, Ruprecht seized a stool and knocked a second to the floor, but one of his fellows was stepping in with lifted weapon.

"Swords, Christopher!" Ruprecht shouted. "On the wall behind you!"

Natil was already pressing a blade into Christopher's hand. She was there, and then she was gone, and a moment later, the attacking guard dropped with a glazed expression.

William was lunging again for Ruprecht. Christopher, though, slid in between the two men and caught the thrust on the crosspiece of his sword. He stared into the chancellor's face as though memorizing it. "Ever hear of treason, William?"

William looked a little hysterical as he struggled to free his weapon. Christopher kicked him away, and Ruprecht's wife started to scream as the baron's sword flashed. William sprawled on the floor.

The soldiers, thoroughly demoralized by the sudden shift in fortune, gave up. Natil and Christopher disarmed and bound them face down on the floor while the baron of Maris went to his wife's bed and held her until her panic subsided into fitful sobs.

"O God, O God," she murmured, "I thought we were safe."

"As did I, Clarissa," said her husband.

Christopher tied a last knot, stood up. Ruprecht looked at him somberly. "Is anyone in this castle still loyal to me?"

Natil answered. "The men in the barracks are loyal. William arranged the guard schedules so that he would have complete control by morning."

Ruprecht blinked at the slender woman's dispassionate statement. "How . . . how do you know all this?"

How did Natil know everything? The patterns. The same patterns that had overwhelmed Vanessa. But Vanessa had learned to control herself, and the fact that Natil moved through the world with ease and assurance was a lightness in Christopher's heart. He wished that the two could meet. "Natil makes a point of knowing a great deal," he said.

"Can I get word to them?"

"I will bring them," said Natil. "Fear not."

Ruprecht handed her his signet. "This will answer any of their questions," he said. She nodded and slipped soundlessly out of the window.

Still holding his wife, Ruprecht offered his hand to Christopher. "And as for your question, Messire Christopher, my answer . . ." He smiled wryly. ". . . is yes."

Christopher took Ruprecht's hand. He had offered his glove, and it had been accepted. The selfish, conceited legacy of the delAurvres was crumbling. The future—his own, Adria's—was looking brighter.

I wish you were with me, Vanessa.

But the next evening, word came from Ypris: the city had fallen to an assembly of free companies in the pay of Yvonnet a'Verne.

CHAPTER 19

"That traitorous bastard!"

Ruprecht's black beard contrasted markedly with his livid face and made his outrage seem all the more passionate. He struck his fist on the polished table in time with his words, and the impacts echoed off the walls of the study despite the thick hangings that covered the bare stone.

Ypris, according to the sketchy report, had been thoroughly destroyed and looted. Several thousand men had been involved, perhaps more, and the effectiveness of the operation was attested to by the distant column of black smoke that Christopher and Ruprecht themselves had seen from the topmost tower of the fortress of Maris.

Gutted. Completely gutted. Such was the city's reward for allegiance to the wrong pontiff.

"I should have seen this coming," said Christopher. "Yvonnet had designs on Aurverelle, and since I put an end to that . . . with a certain amount of help . . ." He smiled thinly at Natil, who was perched on a stool by the fire. ". . . he turned his plots elsewhere. Or maybe he just used some other plots. God knows how many he's got."

"He's a viper," Ruprecht agreed. "Just when we're trying to protect Adria, he goes and drags in the very mercenary bands we've been trying to keep out."

Up until a few hours ago, Ruprecht had not cared in the slightest about Adria. But Christopher let that pass. "He's obviously trying to use piety and zeal for Rome to make up for . . . ah . . ." But he had already said too much. Mentioning Rome in Ruprecht's presence was unwise, and even more so was revealing Yvonnet's sexual appetites. "For certain . . . uh . . . indiscretions of his."

Ruprecht rumbled. "Sizable indiscretions, if you ask me."

"Well . . . yes. I imagine so."

Ruprecht eyed Christopher. "Well, what do we do about it? We can't very well attack a fellow member of the alliance, much as I'd like to." He plunked his elbows on the table, interlaced his fingers as though Yvonnet's throat lay between his hands. "That Roman bastard."

Christopher, too, wanted to lay ungentle hands on his cousin . . . though not because of schismatic alignment.

"Of course, it may not be an alliance at all," said Ruprecht. "Quite possibly, this is but the first step in a larger campaign against the other baronies. Perhaps . . ." Suspicion suddenly wrapped about him like a dark cloak, and he glowered at Christopher from above his black beard. ". . . a campaign in the name of Rome."

Rome. Avignon. The conflict was inescapable, a blight on the newborn century. *I wish there were a few Elves about who would do something about Yvonnet,* Christopher thought, *and about the Church in general.* He realized that Natil was watching him carefully and wondered whether the harper's grasp of the patterns allowed her to read his mind. It was an unsettling thought.

"I don't think so," he said. "Yvonnet is too concerned with immediate gain. Besides, the free companies are involved now. Regardless of what Yvonnet intends, it'll soon be a matter of what the companies themselves want." His stomach turned tight at his own words: having struck at Ypris, the massed free companies were only about a three days' march from Saint Blaise.

"Might I suggest diplomacy?" said Natil softly.

Ruprecht glared at her. He was unused to the presence of women at his councils. "We're dealing with an apostate villain here, woman," he said. "Yvonnet serves Rome. That alone indicates what kind of fellow he is." He glanced at Christopher as though considering once again the matter of Etienne of Languedoc.

Natil was unflinchingly polite. "That may be true, honored lord, but at present he is our only non-belligerent link with the mercenary captains. With appropriate inducements, the baron of Hypprux might convince them to leave Adria peacefully."

Ruprecht's beard twitched. So did his dark eyebrows. "But then they'll have learned too much of Adria and its wealth. They'll be back."

"I respectfully submit," said Natil, "that they were already aware of Adria's wealth. Yvonnet only hastened the inevitable. If they can be persuaded to leave, though, we are merely back at the point at which we began: any incursions will doubtless be made by single, independent companies, and can be dealt with as such. The very task for which the alliance was proposed.''

Ruprecht chewed over her advice. ''Wise words, madam,'' he finally admitted. ''I can see that my . . . ah . . . friend Christopher is a very fortunate man to have you among his councilors.''

Natil rose and curtsied. ''Thank you, messire.''

''A letter, then?''

''No,'' said Christopher. ''Letters have a habit of . . . not being answered.''

Ruprecht met his gaze. Christopher maintained an expression of studied innocence. He had obviously been referring to . . . somebody else.

Ruprecht suddenly laughed. ''Well said. What do you have in mind?''

''We don't have much time,'' said Christopher. ''We have to move while the companies are still assembled in one place. If they break up and start raiding independently, we're lost. So I'll be paying Yvonnet another visit. More formal, less stupid.'' He considered, weighing wishful thinking against practicality. ''I suppose I'll have to do it outside the city walls.''

Natil blinked. ''Bernabò Visconti?''

Christopher winced. She could indeed read his mind. This was not good. The harper was an attractive woman, and . . . how many times had he idly fantasized about bedding her? He winced again. Well, at least she was still loyal. Natil was obviously a tolerant one.

''Bernabò's fate would be appropriate, wouldn't it?'' he said. ''But no, I'm not going to do anything that extreme.'' He sighed. He was not sure that he liked his own plan. ''I'll settle for blackmail.''

''Blackmail?'' said Ruprecht.

Worse and worse. The alliance was teetering precariously and now Christopher was about to try to shore it up with rotten wood. ''Blackmail,'' he said. ''How the hell else does anything ever get done?''

* * *

Ypris had been taken. Its walls lay shattered and burnt, breached in a hundred places. The gates had been ripped from their hinges. Within, the last few houses and shops were still burning, but everything of value had already been carried off to be sorted, distributed, and sold. What people were left were sold, too: slavery was not a particularly nice fate, nor was it an honorable business, but money was money.

The Fellowship of Acquisition received another visit from Eustache de Cormeign and his *kataphraktoi,* and even the experienced dealer from Bardi and Peruzzi was astonished at the piles of cloth and clothing, jewelry and gold, tools, equipment, arms and armor, crossbows, candlesticks, leather bottles, wine casks, and a multitude of other things with which he was presented.

"My word . . . my word," he said over and over as he examined the take, dictating furiously between exclamations while his secretary, padding behind him with stylus and wax tablet, exhibited a marvelous command of tachygraphy.

"Much better than wool, eh?" said Berard. He was feeling jolly today. His men were happy, the brigand's life was looking good, the wool wain was far in the past, and there were larger prizes in the future.

"Much better," said Eustache. "Much." He nearly stumbled over a girl who was picking through a pile of jewels heaped on a sheet of canvas. She was dressed scantily, like one of the *bonnes amies* of the amorous robbers of Languedoc. She did not rise, but she turned large, dark eyes up at the broker as she tried to eke a few extra shreds of modesty out of the revealing frock she had been given.

"That's Joanna," said Berard with a wink. "She's not for sale." Joanna looked away, scrabbled through the jewels. "Well, did you find it yet, my little sweet?"

Silently, Joanna shook her head. If she wept, she wept silently.

"Well, keep looking," said Berard. "It's there." He shrugged. "Unless it's not." Eustache was puzzled. "It's a necklace her mother gave her," explained Berard. "Her favorite. I promised her she could have it back if she didn't scream last night." He smiled at the girl again. "She didn't."

"Very commendable," said Eustache, but he tugged at his mustaches and frowned.

"Indeed." Berard regarded Joanna amiably. Young and lithe, she had moved under him like a frisking horse. He rather believed that she had enjoyed the experience in spite of herself. Not that he cared.

He wondered what the women of Shrinerock were like.

"But tell me, Messire Eustache . . ." He linked arms with the broker and took him for a stroll past the piles of armor and swords that lay carefully stacked by themselves, glinting in the sun. With satisfaction, he noticed that the broker's eyes widened. ". . . what can Bardi and Peruzzi do for my little band?"

Eustache could not answer immediately, but by evening he had a rough estimate, and with the men of the Fellowship gathered around the big open square in the center of the encampment—Berard preferred it that way: no one could ever accuse him of holding anything back—he announced it loudly.

The men cheered and applauded and whooped. Off to one side, though, Jehan stood with folded arms, scowling. This was precisely the side of the Fellowship's enterprise that he hated the most. He would rather play at tables than do accounts on them, and if he had wanted to sell cheese, or anything else, he could have stayed in Saint Blaise.

But Jehan was here tonight, and that told Berard that he had at least some interest in the proceedings. Well, that was to be expected. Knightly behavior and knightly equipment were expensive, and as Jehan was passionately devoted to both, he had to make sure that his share of Ypris was sufficient to float his beliefs for another few weeks.

Another few weeks. Though Jehan did not know it, he probably did not have to worry about any more of a future than that. Berard had already made a few private inquiries as to the willingness of some of the other companies to follow him into a certain venture that, though he could not at present reveal any particulars to them, was likely to offer substantial rewards, and he had been elated by their enthusiasm. Now, just a little more information from Jehan, and Berard could dispense with the chivalric little nitwit.

The men were still cheering as Eustache turned to Berard. A handshake, a nod, and that was that. At least as far as Bardi and Peruzzi was concerned. Berard, though, had other plans, other matters to which to attend. He had started a game of chess with Jehan, and now it was time to finish it.

Business being over, it was time for celebration. But as the men gathered around the fire with wine and food and women, Berard called Jehan into his tent to talk about . . . well . . . business. Leadership. Not much of anything really. No need to spare the wine.

Jehan had always been of two minds about brigandage, and he inevitably became maudlin when he was drunk. "I remember my father," he said, staring at the torchlight that flickered on the walls of Berard's tent. "He always wanted me to be something. He sent me to Saint Blaise because . . . because . . ."

He drank. Berard refilled. He had appointed himself Jehan's personal cup-bearer tonight.

"I don't know why. There was something in Saint Blaise he wanted me to learn."

"Well," said Berard, "I think you learned something there." He glanced at his bed. Joanna was huddled in the sheets, waiting. Those eyes! And that figure! But right now he had Jehan to deal with. "You learned that you didn't want to make cheese."

"Or sell it."

"Yes. Yes."

"But I suppose I was supposed to be something more than a robber." Jehan fell to staring at the torchlight again. "I wonder if he hates me."

"Oh, I don't think he hates you."

"He must."

"No, not at all."

Jehan snorted.

"Come now," said Berard pleasantly, refilling Jehan's cup again. "What makes you think he hates you?"

"I didn't do anything noble." Jehan was lapsing into a sizable depression. "Look at Christopher delAurvre: he went off on a crusade and killed people for God."

"But he's mad now," said Berard.

Jehan was undeterred. "And what have I done? Sacked towns, gotten drunk, fornicated . . ."

Off in the bed, Joanna shuddered, balled herself a little tighter in the sheets. Berard was annoyed. He had not hurt her. At least not badly. But he returned to Jehan. "You don't know what your father thinks," he said smoothly. "For all you know he might well be proud of you. You've never found out."

"How am I supposed to find out?"

"Well . . ." Berard pretended to think. "You could pay him a visit. We're in Adria, Shrinerock is in Adria . . . it's not that big a country."

Jehan blinked blearily at the light. From outside came the sound of music: a musette and a drum. A whoop and a shout of *higher!* told Berard that Petro was dancing.

Girlish laughter. Well, at least some of the women of Ypris were making the most of their new occupation.

"Visit my father?" said Jehan.

Berard glanced at Joanna. She could *try* to enjoy it a little. "Of course," he said. "You could ride down to Shrinerock and be back here before we had to move out."

The lad shook his head. "There'd just be a big fuss. I don't want a fuss. It might not be the kind of fuss I want."

"Well . . ." Again, Berard pretended to think. "Maybe you could pay your visit in private."

"How?"

"You've got that . . . ah . . . secret entrance to the castle. You could go in at night, climb up the wall—"

"It's not a wall. It's a spring."

"Of course," Berard agreed. "How stupid of me. Well, you could dive under the spring—"

"You don't dive under it, Berard." Jehan drank deep, drops of wine escaping the rim of his cup and running down his beardless throat. "You just go behind the little waterfall above the pool. It's dark there. No one ever goes back there, and so no one ever sees it."

"Oh . . . I see. . . ." Berard nodded as he refilled Jehan's cup. "But you see what I mean. You go behind the waterfall, climb the ladder . . ." Jehan was looking at him with an impatient expression. "But . . . I'm getting it all wrong, aren't I?"

"There's no ladder involved." Jehan's voice was slurring, his eyes drooping. "The cave comes out at the well in the courtyard."

"Ah, yes."

"The Elves used it all the time."

Berard was suddenly speechless. Elves?

"They'd come late at night," Jehan continued. "It was amazing: you couldn't even see them in the moonlight. Their clothes, you know. Green and gray. Blended in with the stones. Father and Aunt Catherine liked them. Mother didn't, but she went along with it.''

Berard was staring. If Jehan was raving like this, then how much of what he had said about the secret passage could be correct? "They . . . ah . . . used the tunnel?''

Jehan chuckled. "All the time.''

"And the tunnel . . .''

"Goes up from the spring. They were nice people, really. Natil could certainly play the harp. . . .'' He stared gloomily at the torchlight as cheering broke out among the men gathered outside. "*They* probably don't approve of me, either.''

Berard groped. "I'm sure that . . . their feelings are in keeping with . . . ah . . . their feelings . . .''

"I suppose so.'' Jehan finished the wine in his cup. Berard did not offer a refill. The lad had obviously had too much already. Elves, of all things!

"Why don't you go to bed, Jehan?'' he said. "I think sleep will do you a world of good.''

"Yes . . . bed . . .'' Jehan eyed Joanna. The girl gave him an anxious look and curled up even more tightly.

He left the tent, staggering. Berard watched as he wandered drunkenly away, threw up several times, and finally crawled into his own tent. Did he have a girl in there? Maybe. But if he did, she would be cleaning up after him for a while.

Joanna uncurled at a word and a slap, and Berard smiled as he nestled between her thighs. "Ah, my little sweet,'' he said, sliding his hands beneath her smooth shoulders, "you shouldn't be so frightened. It turns out that you've come to be among religious men.'' He listened to the singing and the clapping that came from the roistering men of the Fellowship. "Pilgrims, in fact.''

Ruprecht insisted that Christopher take a sizable escort when he went to see Yvonnet. Christopher countered that anything that looked remotely like a threat would ensure that Yvonnet would stay safe within the Château. They compromised: a small party, but large enough to befit Christopher's status as a leading baron of Adria.

Christopher needed clothes, too, as did Natil. And though the baron of Aurverelle fretted over the resulting delay, he saw the wisdom in Ruprecht's counsel. As much as Yvonnet would be terrified by a show of force, he would be equally unimpressed by a ragged beggar of a nobleman and an equally bedraggled harper—though Christopher doubted that Natil could ever look bedraggled, even in sackcloth.

It was after a week had passed, therefore, that the party left Maris, and four more days before they took over an inn two miles from the north gate of Hypprux and sent the frightened host to the Château to request the honor of entertaining baron Yvonnet a'Verne. Christopher made sure the invitation was polite, but he also made sure to include enough of a veiled reference to the status of Lengram a'Lowins vis-à-vis the baronial bed to ensure that Yvonnet lost no time granting such a . . . polite request.

The business was delicate and of extreme urgency. Alone with Yvonnet in an upper chamber, then, without secretaries or witnesses of any kind, Christopher first casually made sure that the door was barred, then turned and smashed a jeweled dagger into the tabletop directly in front of Yvonnet's face. *"You damned idiot!"*

His unexpected action, coupled with his reputation for madness, produced the desired effect. Yvonnet was terrified. Mutely, he stared at the dagger as the jeweled hilt quivered in the afternoon light.

"What have I done?" he said, his basso dwindling of a sudden to a whisper.

Christopher kept his rage firmly in place, gesturing widely, stomping up and down the room. "I was asking myself the same question! Just when I think I'm dragging your little promiscuous prick into some semblance of family honor, you have to go and stick it somewhere else!" Weighing his actions carefully, Christopher decided to kick a chair across the room. It tumbled and cracked in two quite satisfactorily when it hit the opposite wall.

"I . . . have soldiers . . . downstairs . . ." Yvonnet's basso dwindled even more.

Christopher leaned across the table, flicked the dagger with his finger. It quivered again. "So do I."

"What . . . do you want me to do?"

Christopher told him. The companies of mercenaries were to be gotten out of Adria as quickly as possible, regardless of costs, promises, or humiliation. Maris and Aurverelle would help. Shrinerock, doubtless, could also be counted on.

"You'll have to work fast," said Christopher. "They're not going to be satisfied with Ypris for long. They'll start to splinter, and then we'll have different companies going off in different directions . . ." *Saint Blaise! Dear Lady, Vanessa is in Saint Blaise!* ". . . raping and pillaging and leveling towns. Did you know that they sometimes break up mills and ovens and tools just for the pleasure of destroying them? What in heaven's name were you thinking of when you dragged twenty-four companies right up to your doorstep?"

Yvonnet suddenly glared at him. "I was thinking of my soul, Christopher. Perhaps you ought to think of yours."

"And what's that supposed to mean?"

"I saw the Maris livery on your men. You've been dealing with Ruprecht."

Christopher sighed, passed a hand over his face. "Yes, yes . . . the Antichrist. Excuse me, I forgot."

Yvonnet's fear was rapidly giving way to anger. "*I* don't forget," he said. "The schism is the greatest challenge to the Church of Christ in all of recorded time. The Devil is triumphing while people like you go about . . ." He pulled the dagger out of the table, sneered, tossed it away. ". . . playing with knives."

Christopher's initiative was slipping. He let it go, dropping one weapon for another. "I imagine you don't forget something else, too," he said. "Like who sleeps in your bed."

Yvonnet turned white, then red. "You wouldn't dare!"

Christopher let the silence grow, let it lengthen painfully. Yvonnet began to look uncomfortable. Christopher said nothing. Finally: "I'm mad. Remember?"

Yvonnet groped for a suitable counter. "No one would believe you."

"Do you really depend on that, dear cousin?"

"I—"

"Your immortal *soul,* dear cousin?"

"I—"

"Rome might not be overly enthused at being supported by someone who is a—"

"Stop it."

"Let's see. What shall we call it?"

"Stop, please."

"Something delicate?"

"Not so loud . . . please . . ."

"Delicate and flowery?" Christopher leaned across the table. "Or something gross and putrescent, like the smell you get when you've been sticking your—"

"Stop it!"

Christopher stopped.

Yvonnet was pale, shaking, breathing heavily. He collapsed back in his chair, fanning himself. "It's bloody hot in here."

"Yes," said Christopher quietly. "It's unseasonably warm."

"You're an evil man, Christopher."

Christopher folded his arms. Evil? Compared to what? Given the inanities he was seeing from Ruprecht and Yvonnet, Natil's heterodoxy, whatever it was, was looking more and more attractive. *Lady,* he thought, *would you entertain devotion from a madman who's lost his faith?*

Yvonnet, thoroughly broken, was still fanning himself. "But it's too late. Most of the companies have already dispersed. I don't know where they've gone."

The battle had been against time, and time had won. Christopher thought of what could happen, of what was now almost inevitable. His temper snapped. "And you didn't even think to find out, did you? You didn't care at all, did you?" He grabbed Yvonnet by the front of his tunic, hauled him, large though he was, half out of his chair, shook him until his eyes glazed. "You were just worried about your soul. That's what's important, isn't it? No one and nothing else, just your *filthy . . . little . . . goddam . . . soul!*"

He flung the big man back into the chair, turned, and stalked towards the door. Yvonnet struggled with his wits. "What . . . what are you going to do?" he said.

Christopher flung the bar out of its holders and threw the door open. "The Lady help me," he said, "I'm going to try to clean up your mess. And when I do, I'm going to make sure that you never forget what it means to be a delAurvre."

Yvonnet goggled. "But I'm not a delAurvre."

Christopher was already stomping down the stairs. "That's all right," he shouted over his shoulder. "*I* am."

CHAPTER 20

Christopher reached out with a booted foot and prodded a charred beam—all that was recognizably left of the north gate of Ypris. "They were thorough," he said. "I'll grant them that."

The morning air was still. Crows called harshly from somewhere nearby. Natil stood mutely, her harp in her hands. On her face was a mixture of tragedy and sorrow. "It is the work of men."

It was an odd choice of words, but Christopher agreed with her. Beyond the beam lay a motionless sea of blackened ruins, crumbling walls, rubble-choked streets; and the clinging odor of charred and smoldering wood hung in the warm air . . . along with the sweet stench of death and decay. The free companies did not appear to have been overly concerned with such things as Christian burial.

Christopher was reminded of Nicopolis: the same futility, the same wanton destruction. But the plateaux to the south of the Danube had been strewn with the bodies of men who—whether their reasons had been foolish or altruistic—had come to fight willingly. Here it was different.

Angry, Christopher kicked the beam. It turned over once and then lay still. "They didn't have to level it," he said.

Natil's voice was hollow. "The companies doubtless acted under orders."

"From Yvonnet." If the baron of Hypprux had not counted for nearly a third of the alliance, Christopher would have simply killed him at the inn. "Cesena had Robert of Geneva, and now Ypris has Yvonnet a'Verne."

There was not much to examine in the city. There was not much of the city left. A few shacks that had managed to survive the flames, one or two plazas that were not completely filled with tumbled plaster and stone . . . that was all. The festering bodies that lay everywhere—picked at by crows and ravens—soon, though individually horrific, blended *en masse* into a numbing sense of general devastation.

Christopher gave up on the town and turned to the trampled fields that surrounded it. Here lay the marks of the free company encampments, and together with Natil and Ruprecht's soldiers, he examined tracks, fire pits, dropping-covered patches that had obviously been used for stabling horses, a few scattered pegs and discarded ropes left from tents and pavilions.

At least one rope appeared to be made of silk. Yvonnet had hired the best.

The tracks, however, were mostly too muddled and trampled to give any indication whether they had been made coming or going. One sizable group, though, had clearly headed to the south.

"Belroi?" said Christopher.

"It is likely, messire," said the captain of the guards. "Belroi is a wealthy city."

"Too wealthy," said Christopher. "If I recall aright, it has quite a wall about it, and good men to defend it."

"That is true, messire."

"We should probably notify them in any case. Though I don't doubt that they've already noticed this little affair."

"I can send some of my men, messire."

"Yes. Do that." Christopher watched Natil as she touched, sadly, a felled willow tree. Well away from both the fighting and the encampment, it had apparently been hewn down simply because it was living and because it was there.

The harper's calm face was troubled. *It is the work of men.*

"I'll send word to Baron Paul delMari when I get back to Aurverelle," said Christopher.

"As you wish, messire."

In a few minutes, two of the men galloped off to the south. Christopher hoped that they would reach Belroi without incident, but with the countryside now harboring the scattered free companies, hope was about all he could do.

He sent the remaining guards back to Maris with a message to Ruprecht to prepare for sudden action, and he and Natil struck off to the southwest, cutting across the trampled flax fields. Aurverelle was comparatively close, and

Christopher wanted to reach it as soon as possible. He had his own preparations to make.

Time was the enemy. The free companies had no plans other than looting, no objective beyond profit. They could strike anywhere, at any time, and then be gone within days. Holding a counterforce in constant readiness under such circumstances was useless: the normal period of feudal service for vassals and tenants was only forty days per year. Hence, the alliance had to identify a stricken region quickly, call up its forces, and strike before the companies could disperse. Not an easy task at all, even without the problem of Yvonnet's instability.

But while Yvonnet was unstable, Ruprecht was suspicious, and the papal schism lay waiting like a flock of crows at the edge of a battlefield. Christopher was doing his best, but he could not shake the feeling that his best was not even remotely enough. He had, after all, done his best at Nicopolis, too.

Night was falling as he and Natil skirted the north edge of Malvern Forest. "We'll have to stop for the night," said Christopher. "I think there's a village ahead, but it won't be very large. We have a choice: vermin, or ditches."

Natil's face was shadowed by the dusk and by what she had seen that day. "Vermin live as they live," she said, "just like people. And I have no objection to sleeping in ditches. But piles of bracken and sheltering trees are far better."

"You want to sleep in the forest?"

"Why not?" Natil smiled. "Fear not. We shall be safer in the forest than in ditches or towns."

"But . . ." Roger's fate was a lead weight in Christopher's mind. "What about the Elves? Don't they live in the forest?"

"They do." She sighed. "But there are too few left in the world to pose any threat to humans. Besides . . ." The trees were gleaming softly in the twilight: shades of green and gray, a shimmer of leaves. She looked at them longingly. "Elves want only to help and heal. They are no threat. They have never been a threat."

Christopher was still unsure. "Then why are people so afraid of them?"

"In the beginning," said Natil, "I think that people needed Elves to help them. Later on, much later, they needed Elves to believe in. Then they needed something to fear. And now they need something to hate. The Elves have not changed: they remain as they are—healing and helping—in a world that no longer wants them to do either.''

''Healing and helping.'' Christopher eyed the trees. ''Unless they're attacked.''

''Or unless those whom they love are attacked.'' Natil dismounted, looked at him sidelong. ''Had you any such plans?''

Hesitating only for a moment, Christopher swung down from his horse. ''None.'' He looked into the dark forest as though it were a deep pond containing an elusive fish. ''I'd like to ask them a few questions, though. About my grandfather.''

''Perhaps you will have your chance someday.'' Natil set aside her harp and began to gather branches of dry bracken.

They reached Aurverelle the next morning, galloping up the main street accompanied by salutations from the townsfolk and the screams of children delighted with the opportunity to race the horses. The tower watch had seen them climbing the switchback road up the hill, and Pytor and Jerome were both waiting at the castle gate.

''Did master hear?'' said the seneschal. ''Ypris . . .''

''Never mind Ypris,'' said Jerome crossly. ''The baron's alive. That's more than we dared hope for when he rode off.''

''We did it,'' said Christopher, ''thanks to Natil.'' He swung down and offered his hand to her. She took it and dismounted gracefully. ''Ruprecht is on our side. Yvonnet is on our side . . .'' He shot a glance at Natil. ''. . . more or less.''

Pytor was nodding. ''But Ypris . . .''

''That's why I said *more or less*. Yvonnet brought the free companies into Adria to take Ypris. They're all over by now.''

Jerome crossed himself. ''By Our Lady.''

Natil bowed. ''Indeed.''

A chittering from above. The monkey swung down the outside of the gate, bounded up to Christopher, and leaped into his arms. Christopher made a face at it. It made a face back and scrambled to his shoulder. ''But that means we'll have to move quickly,'' said the baron. ''Everyone who owes any kind of service to me will have to stay ready. We'll wait until the companies strike, and then, the Lady willing, we'll have them.''

Jerome looked suspiciously at Natil, who appeared blithely unaware of Christopher's possibly less than orthodox allusion.

Not even pausing to bathe or eat, Christopher called Pytor and Jerome to the bailiff's office in the castle and began dictating letters to the steadings, manors, and monasteries that owed him service. He would allow no scutage: contributions had to be in the form of actual warm bodies. Fighting warm bodies.

"This will be a hardship for many," said Jerome as the clerks scribbled furiously.

"It'll be more of a hardship to have their homes razed," said Christopher as David arrived bearing a basket of hot pasties. Christopher snatched one, bit off a huge quantity, and sprayed crumbs on the table as he continued. "Tha'll jus' hapf to adjufth."

Natil nibbled delicately. "Lovely, Master Chef," she said. "Thank you."

David bowed. "My *pleas*ure, Mistress Harper."

"Wine!" shouted Christopher. "*Now!*"

David backed away hastily, and a shrill chitter from the monkey sent him down the hall at a run.

Over the next month, replies from Christopher's vassals trickled in. Many were distressed at his demands, but all admitted that Christopher, as a good lord and an honest man, was certainly worth some inconvenience, and therefore they would be happy to cooperate.

"They really don't understand, do they?" said Christopher, glancing over several of the letters one afternoon. "It has nothing to do with *my* convenience. It's *their* convenience that's the question." He plunked himself down on his bed, swung his feet up. "And they still think I'm mad."

The monkey, perched in the window, chittered and scratched itself in the warm sun. The weather had remained hot and rainless, and now dry winds were sweeping up from the southeast. Already the vegetation that had been spurred into enthusiastic growth by the arrival of spring was beginning to wilt, shrivel, and brown. People were talking about drought again, but the monkey did not seem to care: it liked the sun.

It looked up at the baron of Aurverelle and stuck out its tongue. "The monkey agrees," said Christopher.

Natil was sitting on the floor, tuning her harp. "I daresay, my lord," she said, "that the monkey is no expert on madness."

"On the contrary," said Christopher. "He's quite knowledgeable. For instance, he's taught me that what most people call madness should actually be referred to as sanity."

Natil lifted her head, smiled. "The monkey is wise, my lord."

Christopher put his hands behind his head and stretched out. "I wish my vassals were as wise. But Paul delMari . . ." He shook his head. "I'd hoped for better. His was the first letter I sent off. That was a month ago. I even sent it with my best messenger. But I've heard nothing from Shrinerock. I can't understand why he's delaying. It's just a good thing that the companies haven't done anything yet: without Shrinerock to cover the southern part of the country, we'd be in trouble."

Natil nodded, eased two strings into consonance.

"What . . ." Struck by a thought, Christopher sat up. "What do the patterns say, harper?"

Natil lifted her head, and for a moment he wondered if he had, in some way, offended her. "There are many things fading in the world," she said slowly, "and the vision of the patterns is among them. In the Château and in Ruprecht's fortress, I saw what was nearby and imminent. Shrinerock is distant. I cannot see as far as I used. None of us can."

None of us. Did that include Vanessa? But Christopher saw the grief in Natil, for what had been for Vanessa a source of torment was apparently for the harper a talent and a gift, one to be shared, one with which she could help and heal. But it was fading. Natil was amazing and, in her own way, terrifyingly powerful, but she was fragile, too; and as Christopher had responded to Vanessa's fundamental humanity, so did he now to that same quality in Natil.

From the courtyard below came the rapid sound of a horse's hoofs clattering on cobblestones, the shouts of the servants. Hoping that the commotion marked a reply at last from the master of Shrinerock, Christopher rose from his bed and went to the window. But it was not a messenger from the baron of Furze. The rider was a slim, dark young man whose demeanor, even at a distance, held a touch of nervousness. Christopher wondered why Martin Osmore would pay a visit to a madman who knew too much about his shameful relationship with Yvonnet; but hoping that, whatever Martin's reasons, he might be induced to share some news of Vanessa, he pulled on his boots and went downstairs with Natil following and the monkey on his shoulder.

Unlike his father, Martin was exceedingly conscious of the social gulf that separated him from Christopher. At the baron's approach, he dismounted and bowed deeply, and upon straightening, he searched Christopher's face as though for some indication of what kind of reception he might receive today.

The monkey chuckled and pulled on Christopher's ear. "Yes, little friend," he said, "I've been tamed a bit also." He offered his hand to Martin. "Don't be afraid. I won't eat you."

"God bless you, Baron Christopher."

Christopher called for the grooms to take away Martin's horse, waved the servants away, and personally led him towards the door. "Did you want to make this a formal visit, Martin?" he said, wondering how it was that he had become so gracious a host. "Shall I tell Raffalda to draw a bath and set out clothes?"

Martin blushed, at once overwhelmed and a little frightened. "If it please you, my lord, I think I'd just as soon speak now."

Christopher stopped on the porch. "All right, then. What is it? Has your father finally decided that Aurverelle might be a worthwhile ally?"

"It's not that at all." Martin looked extremely worried. "It's Baron Paul. I've written to him fairly regularly, and he's written back. About once a week. We were very close, almost like . . . uh . . . father and son . . ." Martin looked uneasily at Christopher. ". . . but lately, I haven't heard a word from him. No letters, nothing. I wrote again after a fortnight, but the messenger didn't come back, and there's still no word from Shrinerock."

And Christopher had written a month ago. No reply. And the messenger had not returned, either.

A shout from the watchman at the top of the great keep,

but Christopher was too intent upon Martin's words to make out what he was saying.

"I'm worried," continued Martin. "I've talked to Father, but he isn't bothered by anything: he just wants me to get married. But lately, I've heard some rumors. Nothing definite, you know, but they all say that something's happened down by Furze."

And the free companies had disappeared. Nearly four thousand men . . .

The guard at the top of the keep was still shouting, and he had become insistent enough that Christopher finally listened to him:

"*Smoke! Smoke to the southeast!*"

The realization struck Christopher like a leaden fist, and, pulling Martin after him until the lad understood and followed on his own, Christopher ran across the court to the stairway that led to the top of the keep. Cursing, taking the large steps two at a time, while the monkey clung to his neck and shrieked with fear, Christopher bounded upwards.

When, panting, he burst out into the open, he looked off to the southeast. It was as the watchman had said: beyond Malvern, beyond the wide dairylands that stretched from the far edge of the forest to the Bergren River, a pillar of smoke, black and gray, was rising into the cloudless sky.

Martin was at his side. "What . . . what is it?" he said when he found his voice.

Christopher planted his elbows atop the parapet, covered his face with his hands. "It's Furze. Dammit, it's Furze."

CHAPTER 21

The smoke rose and spread into the air as Christopher watched. It could only be Furze. Yes, the free companies were in Adria, and yes, their movements were erratic. Indeed, they had completely bypassed Belroi and had instead, knowingly or not, struck directly at the alliance.

A puffing from the direction of the stairs told Christopher that Pytor had arrived. "Get some messengers off, Pytor," he said without turning around. "Tell Ruprecht we'll need immediate aid at Furze. And tell Yvonnet . . ." He wished indeed that he had strangled his cousin. "Tell that son of a bitch that . . ."

He noticed that Martin looked away quickly.

"I'm sorry, Martin," said Christopher. "I know you didn't have anything to do with this. He turned back to Pytor. "Tell him the same thing you tell Ruprecht: that we'll gather the forces at Furze as quickly as possible. Make whatever arrangements you think best."

Pytor spread his hands. "What about master?"

"I'm going ahead of you all."

Martin lifted his head, wiped his eyes. "I'm coming, too."

"Can you fight?"

"Of course I can fight."

"But not against churchmen."

Martin colored. "I was stupid. Etienne surprised me. I learned."

Pytor was wringing his hands again. "Is master sure of this?"

"Of course I'm sure," said Christopher. "You have the word of a madman."

Pytor did not look reassured, but before an hour had passed, Christopher, Martin, and Natil were cantering down the switchback road to the lowlands. The men were both armed and wearing light mail. Natil, though, had dispensed immediately with her customary gown and reverted openly to her garments of green and gray.

Christopher performed introductions on the fly. "Natil, Martin Osmore," he called above the dusty clatter of hooves. "Martin, this is my harper, Natil."

"God bless you," said Martin, but Natil, peering out across the miles of dark trees with a stricken look in her blue eyes, acknowledged him but distantly.

When they reached the base of the hill, Malvern Forest lay squarely in their path. There was no road through it— there never had been—and Christopher gestured to right and to left. "It won't make much difference whether we go north or south," he said. "It's going to be a long ride either way."

"The south road will take us through the Free Towns," Martin pointed out.

"Would your father have any available men we could snatch up?"

The lad shook his head, embarrassed. "Father's never taken any of your concerns very seriously, Messire Christopher. I believe he thinks he can buy the safety of his city if the companies approach."

Christopher wished that he were indeed as mad as he claimed: then he could scream and throw things with perfect justification. "What in the Lady's name happened to the Free Towns? You people fought like devils when you threw out old David a'Freux."

Martin shrugged. "That was many years ago. Times have changed . . . people are more comfortable . . ."

"And complacent, yes," Christopher snapped, though when he saw Martin's hurt look, he regretted his words.

Natil spoke. "Some of the Towns have preserved their old ways," she said. "But times have indeed changed." She pointed at the forest. "I can take you straight through Malvern," she said. "We can be at Furze in two days."

"But there's no road," said Christopher.

Natil's face was set, and when she looked at Christopher, there was a grimness about her eyes that he had not seen before. "None . . . none of which humans know," she said. "But our need is great, and so I am willing to reveal what has previously been hidden."

Martin was suddenly staring at the harper. Christopher

saw suspicion in the lad, suspicion rooted in both fear and
wonder.

"Will you trust me?" she said.

Christopher did not hesitate. "With my life."

"Then come."

Christopher had never been fostered out to a distant baron's household: old Roger had raised him. As a result,
Christopher knew Aurverelle and portions of Malvern as
well as he knew the halls of his castle. But Natil led him
towards the thick trees and overhanging branches, and he
found himself riding into an opening large enough for a
horse and rider.

An opening he had never seen before.

Natil led her companions onto a path carpeted with leaves
and soft moss. It led straight ahead and into the green distance.

Christopher was staring. "Where did this come from?"

"It has always been here," Natil replied calmly.

"That's absurd. I've been in this forest a thousand times.
How could I have missed it?"

Natil glanced back at him. "Well . . . perhaps you were
not looking for it, my lord."

They rode, and the shadows of the afternoon slipped towards dusk. But, occupied as his thoughts were with Furze
and what might have happened to Paul delMari, Christopher
could not help but think of Vanessa and wonder why Martin
had said nothing about her. It had been almost a year since
she had taken the road to Saint Blaise: surely there would
be some news of her.

Conscious that the already delicate balance of the alliance
was steadily becoming even more delicate, Christopher was
unwilling to confess his obsession to a practicing sodomite,
but as the miles passed, he began to become annoyed. Dammit, Martin's family had as much as been given ownership
of the girl. Surely, after all that had happened, the lad would
have something to say about her.

But no, nothing.

Selfish bastard.

A chitter from his saddlebag answered his thought, and
he started with a gasp. Natil turned, staring, then laughed
as Christopher unfastened the bag and extracted the monkey. It grinned at him and clambered up to his shoulder.

Christopher sighed. "Two riders . . . and two monkeys," he said. "Thank you for reminding me."

Late in the afternoon of the second day, Christopher, Natil, and Martin rode out of the trees and onto the pastureland that stretched eastward from the edge of the forest. But even in the shadows that the Aleser Mountains flung far to the east—a premature dusk—Christopher could see that the normally lush grass was brown and withered, the gullies dry, the streams sluggish. Spring had brought a drought, and it was a bad one.

"It's about five leagues to Furze," he said.

"Five leagues," said Martin. He looked at the sky, plainly worried. "There's a little light for now, and there'll be a moon tonight. We could ride."

Christopher wished that Martin would demonstrate as much concern for Vanessa, but he looked to Natil for advice. She nodded to the horses. "We should not ride fast, my lord. The animals are weary."

"I have no intention of riding fast." The monkey on his shoulder looked relieved. "But I do want to find out what happened at Furze. And if the free companies are about, I don't think I want to do that in full daylight. Can you read the patterns, harper?"

Martin started, then suddenly stared at Natil.

"They are clearer, my lord," said the harper. "But they do not look at all reassuring."

There were no roads here—none were needed—and they rode straight across the rolling fields and into a falling darkness in which herds of thirsty cattle were a rustling, stirring shadow, and herders' huts and dugouts gleamed now and again with the faint yellow of rushlights and hearth fires. A moon barely touched with gibbous waning lit their way, but the shadow that was Furze was not pierced by its light. Growing larger as they approached, it remained dark, black, impenetrable, lit only occasionally by sparks of red that arose, flared, then subsided like a failing heart.

Near midnight, they left the horses and the monkey in the shelter of a dry canal and approached on foot. Keeping to the shadows, they crept about the perimeter of the city until they came to a gatehouse. The gates, though, were gone: the massive, bronze-bound doors were lying on the ground ten yards from the wall, shattered and broken.

Christopher pointed at the city. "Can you see?" he whispered to Natil.

"I can," she whispered back. "There are a few survivors. The gate is guarded. Those who did this are . . . elsewhere."

"Where?"

"I am not sure." She closed her eyes, her brow furrowed. "It will take time."

"Then let me be mad a little longer," said Christopher. He drew his knife. "There's a guard, you say?"

"One." Natil's eyes were sad, their light troubled. *The work of men.*

Alone, Christopher worked his way slowly up to the opening in the wall. A shape in the darkness just within the gate showed the rough outlines of a man, and in another minute, the baron had slipped behind him and laid a blade against his throat. "Not a sound unless I say, or you're dead."

The man nodded mutely. He was clad in rough leather armor, but he did not have the manner of a seasoned warrior. A townsman, then, Christopher guessed: conscripted by disaster, guarding against another invasion . . . and feeling hopeless about it.

"What happened here?"

"Who . . ."

"Who am I?" Christopher grinned. "I'm Christopher, baron of Aurverelle. The one who's mad."

"You'd ha' to be, to cam here."

"What happened?"

"Robbers. Thousands. They cam up from the south. We wan't expecting anything, an' as most o' them wore the Shrinerock arms, we ha' no reason to."

Shrinerock arms? That meant . . .

Shrinerock? *How?*

But Christopher betrayed nothing of his dismay. "And then, once they were inside, they started looting and burning."

The man nodded. "Orders o' Baron Paul, they said."

"You believe that?"

"Nay."

"Good. Don't."

"An' then, once they'd taken e'erything, they left."

"Which way did they go?"

"To the south."

"All right." Christopher removed the blade from the man's throat. The guard shuddered with relief, looked close to tears. He had seen his town looted and burned, had probably watched his friends or his family die. Christopher was moved to give him a pat on the shoulder. "Carry on, friend. Just remember: you didn't see me. You never saw or heard anything tonight. I wasn't here. Understand?"

"Aye, master."

"Good man. I'm doing what I can, remember that." Christopher slipped back into the darkness. Shrinerock. Dear Lady!

They returned to the horses and put several miles between them and the city before Christopher called a halt. The horses were exhausted, as were—with the exception of Natil—their riders. The monkey was cross and petulant, and it squished up its face and rubbed its eyes as Christopher waggled a finger at it. "Don't you wish you'd stayed in Aurverelle?" he said. "You could be throwing fruit at David."

The monkey looked sad. Christopher gave it some bread and dried meat, plunked a cup of water down beside it. The monkey squatted down and ate.

Christopher himself was almost too tired to put food in his mouth, but in the contest between hunger and sleep, hunger was winning for now. Nevertheless, he ate mechanically, his thoughts on Furze . . . and on Shrinerock.

Natil, too, was abstracted. Sitting cross-legged on the ground, she was staring off into space, eyes closed, mouth set. Abruptly, she came to herself and sighed. "Shrinerock has been taken," she said.

She had only confirmed what Christopher already suspected. With an effort, he swallowed a bit of bread. "What about Paul and his people?"

"They are . . ." She stood up, peered to the southeast. Ten miles away rose the mountain that gave the castle its name. "They are somewhere near the castle."

"Dead?"

Her voice was hoarse. Grief? Fatigue? "Many."

They spent the rest of the night and most of the next day in the shelter of a series of low, tree-covered hills. The sun glared down, parching an already parched land. Christopher fretted, Natil looked strained, Martin fidgeted. Even the monkey seemed more serious then usual, and when Natil offered to play with it, it shook its head somberly.

When dusk came on, they mounted and rode towards Paul's castle, staying off the roads, keeping to valleys and depressions. The outlines of Shrinerock grew. This was Vanessa's country: dairyland accents, pastures, cows, the silhouette of the loveliest castle of Adria rising against the sky. Somewhere nearby was the hamlet where she had been born, the little cluster of houses and huts that had first nurtured, then rejected her. Christopher wondered whether her parents were alive or dead. He was not sure that he cared. They had sent their youngest daughter off into the care of strangers and therefore had, in his opinion, renounced all claim to her.

The sound of Saint Adrian's spring was loud in the cricket-sown darkness as they rode into a stand of trees and dismounted. Above them, the mountain was dark, the fortress that surmounted it a collection of white walls and towers and spires that turned silver as the moon rose. Lights gleamed from a few windows.

"Baron Paul and his people are nearby," said Natil. Her voice was pitched economically: just loud enough to carry above the water, no more.

Martin seemed awe-struck by her certainty. "Can . . . can you find them?"

"I believe I can."

Still carrying her harp, Natil led them deeper into the trees. Christopher tried to leave the monkey with the horses, but the three had not gone twenty paces before the little creature came scampering after them. It clung to Christopher's neck and refused to be dislodged. It was not an encouraging sign.

The forest was thick, dense, but this was not Malvern. Once, perhaps, this place might have been wild and forbidding, but the years it had spent in the good-natured hands of the barons of Furze had gentled it. Nonetheless, it was a dark place, and the moonlight only patched the forest floor with isolated puddles of silver.

After a time, Natil halted. "The patterns are confused, my lord," she said. "They have faded so much . . ." She bent her head.

Christopher put an arm about her shoulders. She seemed terribly thin and frail tonight. His demands had been draining her for weeks, months perhaps, but for some reason she was willing to give, to keep giving, to heal and to help so long as there was strength left in her. It seemed at times to be her only reason for existence.

To heal and to help? Natil had once said something about that. Christopher could not recall exactly what.

"Patterns?" said Martin.

"She sees the way the world works," said Christopher. He was suddenly defensive, unwilling to expose a trusted friend to the judgment of someone like Martin.

But Martin's eyes widened. "Fair One!" he said softly.

Natil shook her head, then led them onward. Slowly, they worked their way around to the side of the mountain opposite the road to the castle. Here, the ground was steep, overgrown, the trees close together as though shouldering and jostling one another. Not quite Malvern now, but close.

The monkey murmured. Christopher shushed it. "I learned from you," he said softly, "now you learn from me. Be quiet."

A gruff voice suddenly, heavy with threat. "Halt i' the name of the baron o' Furze."

Natil stopped. The monkey snuffled. Christopher suddenly sensed men ahead, to both sides, and behind. They had been surrounded.

"Who comes?" said the voice. A ring of a sword sliding from its sheath. "Speak or die."

Natil answered, her voice clear. "Natil of Malvern Forest and her friends," she said, bowing. "Be at peace, and blessings upon you this day."

A torch suddenly appeared, its light revealing a number of armored men who wore the gryphon and silver star of the delMari family. Their faces were gaunt and grim both, and their eyes were wary. "Messire Paul ha' upon occasion mentioned sa'one by the name o' Natil," said a man who seemed to be their captain. "An' he gave us also a test. Who wa' your father?"

Natil stood, unarmored, slender, her harp slung from her shoulder. Christopher did not dare put his hands anywhere near his sword, but he decided that if one of the guards even touched her, he would draw it regardless of the consequences.

Her answer, though, startled him. "I have no father," she said. "My Mother brought me forth, and I am She."

The guard nodded and sheathed his weapon. "We're honored, Fair One."

"Natil?" came a voice from deeper among the trees, and Paul delMari was suddenly striding into the circle of light. His face was careworn and etched with grief, but it brightened with pleasure when he saw the harper. "Natil! It *is* you! Oh, dear Lady, beyond all hope!" Paul seemed close to tears as he and the harper embraced. "*Alanae a Elthia yai oulisi, marithea.*"

Christopher stared, as bewildered by Paul's greeting as by Natil's words.

"*Manea,*" said Natil. "I grieve that it took so long to find you."

"It wasn't supposed to be easy," said Paul. He shook his head as though infinitely weary. "It's what's kept us alive these last days." But then he caught sight of Martin. "Martin! Come back to us! Is everything turning around?" He caught the boy about the neck. "Oh, in the name of the Lady, welcome and welcome again!"

"Lord baron," said Natil. "There is a third among us." She nodded to Christopher. "Christopher delAurvre, lord of Aurverelle."

"Messire Christopher!" Paul bowed deeply. "A pleasure, sir."

Christopher took his hand, still confused. "You . . . you know Natil?"

"Of course," said Paul. "Natil and the other Fair Folk used to come to Shrinerock quite often. We haven't seen any of them in years, but ever since I got that letter from you, my good baron, I had a feeling that the Elves were involved!"

Elves? Christopher looked at Natil, his stomach suddenly clenching. Elves?

Natil looked away, biting her lip.

Paul suddenly became aware of her consternation. "Oh . . ." His hand to his mouth, he looked up at the dark canopy of leaves and branches. "Oh, dear. I . . . imagine I wasn't supposed to say anything about that, was I?"

CHAPTER 22

The forest that lapped about the lower slopes of Shrinerock Mountain was thick with the growth of ancient trees and riven by a multitude of ravines and crevasses. It was the perfect place to hide, and Baron Paul, familiar with his estate as his conquerors certainly were not, had concealed beneath its shadowed canopy of leaves and branches nearly three hundred survivors of the sudden and incredibly effective assault on his Shrinerock estate.

With him were his wife Isabelle, a few servants, and about a hundred and fifty men of the castle guard. Villagers and freeholders filled out the group, along with the abbot of the looted Benedictine abbey and a few of his monks. But though, as Paul explained to Christopher, the forest was providing concealment, its safety could at best be termed relative. The baron and his people had little food, no blankets, no horses, and a number of wounded. They could not even make a fire, for the free companies were looking for them.

"It was unbelievable," said Paul. He was sitting dejectedly on a stone, away from the shelters of sticks and leaves that his men had put together for those most critically hurt. "Absolutely unbelievable." He bent his head with emotion, ran a hand through his thinning hair.

Isabelle, beside him, took his hand. The plight of the estate had overcome her customary shyness as it had extinguished Paul's daft humor. "They came as pilgrims to Saint Adrian's spring, Messire Christopher. They came in the night, and of a sudden."

Wenceslas, the abbot, shook his bullet head. "Pilgrims. God's curse on 'em." The half dozen monks with him crossed themselves at the oath, but appeared to agree with it.

"They entered the cave late in the day, when few were

about,'' said Paul, ''and then they climbed the passage that leads up from behind the spring all the way to the castle well. They opened the gates to the others. How they knew the way, I don't know. Besides myself, Catherine was the only one who knew the secret, and she . . .'' He put his hands to his face and sobbed. ''She held the door against what looked like fifty while we escaped.''

Isabelle put her arms about him. ''She was a valiant woman, husband.''

''The heart of a man in the body of a maid.''

''No,'' said Isabelle. She smiled softly, as though remembering past times. Good times. ''The soul of a Fair One wrapped in fair flesh. She was wearing green and gray when she died.''

Paul was nodding. ''It's true. She was.''

Fair One. Clothes of green and gray. Faintly, Christopher heard the sound of Natil's harp. She was away with the wounded and the frightened, doing what she could for them, and he sensed with the surety of instinct that there was more to her music now than vibrating strings.

An Elf. All this time, all his trust, and she was an Elf. And what was she doing for the wounded? Healing them? Probably. Now there was no need for her to hide her abilities. So she could heal openly, just like that . . .

He stared. Mirya and Terrill. Miraculous healing. Elves again. And they had—dear Lady!—healed Vanessa!

He had been shaken by Paul's inadvertent revelation, but now he felt distinctly ill. What did Vanessa have to do with this? It was a good thing Natil was out of sight, or he would have . . . would have . . .

The monkey climbed up on his shoulder, pulled his hair, nibbled at his ear. Christopher patted it absently, feeling something collapse within himself. Tamed and taken, just like the monkey. And when would he start finding himself possessed by an irresistible urge to plant peach trees?

But Paul was still shaking his head at the utter defeat he had suffered, and Christopher forced himself to thrust aside his thoughts about the harper. Time enough for that later. ''Are you sure no one else knew?''

''No one in Adria.''

That did not answer the question. Or, rather, it raised another. ''Who else?''

Paul shrugged. ''Well, my son Jehan. But he's . . .'' Paul

suddenly lifted his head. "Oh, dear Lady. Oh, no. *Ai, ea sareni, Elthiai!*"

Abbot Wenceslas frowned at the elvish words, but Isabelle clung to her husband. "Paul . . . Paul . . . it couldn't be Jehan. It just couldn't be. Why would he do such a thing?"

"I failed him, Isabelle," said Paul. "I failed him from the start. He was high-chested and fiery, like a spring colt, and I sent him off to be nurtured by . . . by marmosets."

Martin had been standing off by himself, arms folded, head down, almost lost in the darkness; but at Paul's words, he turned and started to walk away.

Paul was on his feet instantly. "No, Martin," he said, stretching out his arms to the lad. "Forgive me. I didn't mean that."

Martin stopped, shook his head. "You did, Messire Paul. But that's what I always tried to tell you. I know my place. I've always known it. I'm a marmoset, like my father, like his father. It's our lot. We make cheese."

"You're not like that."

Martin's smile was bitter. "I'm much worse, actually."

Christopher, though still annoyed with Martin about Vanessa, could not but admire his honesty: he had revealed as much as he could without committing himself irretrievably to the stake. But Paul was shaking his head furiously. He was a man who had lost everything, even, so he believed, his son, and he was now trying frantically to cobble together some fragments of faith.

Christopher did not know what to say to him: his own faith had been abruptly shattered once again.

But now Natil was approaching, her harp in her hand, her steps silent—as much a part of the forest as the trees about her—and Christopher felt like a fool for not having seen it long before. Every motion of her body, every gesture of her hands, every glint of immortal starlight in her eyes screamed out at him that this was no human woman. This was something else, something other, something alien: a wild thing that had walked out of the forest and into his castle, bringing . . .

He stared at the Elf. She returned his gaze tranquilly, a little sadly.

. . . what? Healing? Comfort? Was that not what she had

given him? And yet, at the hands of her kind, his grandfather had—

Shaking, he turned away from her, forced his eyes and his attention onto Paul, Isabelle, the abbot and the black huddle of his monks, Martin's darkling presence at the edge of the clearing. People: ripe with the odor of good, human sweat, pungent with the aroma of defeat.

"We can't stay here," said Christopher. "We've got to get all of you away."

Wenceslas' broad face was shrewd with the knowledge of one who had once been a soldier. "I doubt we have enough weapons to go around, even if we all could use them. And with no horses, 'twill be a long way across the pastures. We'd be seen afore we reach cover."

"I doubt we could fight our way out in any case, Abo," said Paul, "but Messire Christopher is right. Fields or not, we'll have to get away. The companies are already looking for us."

"Haven't they done enough?" said the abbot. "They've taken the castle, they've done their killing." He looked discouraged. He had obviously entered the monastery to escape the very thing that had found him. "They've got what they want."

"Not all of it," said Christopher. He was too conscious of Natil's presence. She might well have been a star, blindingly incandescent to his inner sight. "That's a nice gold cross you have, lord abbot. And those rings of yours . . . I'll bet they'd fetch a fine price." He paused meaningfully. "As would you."

To Christopher's surprise, the churchman removed his rings and his pectoral and tossed them on the ground. "So much are they worth to me, Baron Christopher. I'd give 'em all—including my life—for the safety of those who are here. Or even for the healing of a single scratch of one of the wounded."

Natil spoke. "Payment," she said, "is not required. What I have, I give freely. Those who were hurt are healed."

The monks looked plainly frightened, but the abbot shook his head resignedly. "I knew you had some strange friends, Messire Paul. You and your father both."

"Friends, indeed," murmured the baron. He reached out,

and Natil took his hand. "You can trust Natil with your life, Abo."

Christopher remembered his own words. He also had trusted Natil with his life, and he had said so. And she had never given him any reason to regret that trust.

Could he still trust her? She had not indicated otherwise. Indeed, any distrust he felt was apparently of his own making, for Natil, to all outward appearance, was still Natil. She harped, and she healed. That she had suddenly been revealed as an Elf and a worker of magic had not changed her. And Christopher recalled that, though she apparently held immense potencies in her hands, her attentions toward him had been only of the most mundane sort: a touch, a smile, good counsel, and sweet music.

But what the hell did she want?

He could have asked, but he was unwilling to parade his fears and his grandfather before everyone. Yet, at the same time, he was not at all sure that, even had he and Natil been alone, he would have had the nerve to utter the question. Feeling helpless, feeling frightened, he let it be. There were more immediate problems at hand.

He told Paul and the others that he had already sent word to the members of the alliance . . . though he omitted certain pertinent facts about Yvonnet's involvement with the free companies. But he estimated, and Paul and Wenceslas concurred, that it would be another week at least before the forces of Hypprux and Maris were gathered and equipped. It was almost a certainty that the companies that had taken Shrinerock would find the refugees hiding in the forest by then.

They had to get away, but fifteen or sixteen miles of open pasture lay between them and Malvern Forest, the nearest cover. On foot, the refugees had no hope of crossing it undetected. The companies would see them . . . and ride them down.

The stars hovered about midnight like a flock of white geese. Christopher eyed them. Bad days and worse news. "Everybody go to bed," he said brusquely. "We're just going to give ourselves headaches if we keep on this way, and I'm sure that's exactly what the companies want. We'll . . ." He glanced at Natil. As tranquil as she was, she almost seemed embarrassed, like a girl caught stealing fruit. "We'll figure out what to do tomorrow."

Paul was silent for a time, then, at last, he nodded as though relieved that someone else was willing to give orders for a few hours. He rose slowly, offered his arm to Isabelle, and took her away to a bower of bracken that his men had prepared. Wenceslas and his monks retired to bare dirt. The soldiers arranged watches.

Natil eyed Christopher as the camp rustled into a silence broken only by the call of night birds and the faint clink of mailed and vigilant guards. Christopher ignored her and climbed a tall oak tree. The monkey ascended leisurely beside him, but Christopher grunted his way up, smiling inwardly with a bitter irony. Taken and tamed, perhaps, but not quite a monkey.

From the upper branches, he could see the castle standing upon the mountaintop, shimmering in the moonlight like some impenetrable fortress out of an old poem. Pinnacle upon pinnacle, tower upon tower, whitewashed and filigreed and chimneyed and spired, Shrinerock seemed hardly to belong to the world of men and women and their constant and humiliating depravity.

Tired, discouraged, Christopher wedged himself into a fork, wrapped his arms about the trunk, and dozed, his mind still slogging through the problem: one of the capital fortresses of Adria, taken without a struggle, its calamity brought on by the idiocy of the very barons whose help Christopher had enlisted. And now it was supposed to be saved by that same help.

Oh, this was as stupid as Nicopolis! As stupid as his ancestors' constant preoccupation with the fool's question of elven dominance. As stupid as his own obsession with a simple peasant girl who saw too much in the world.

And Vanessa indeed saw too much for a human. Just like Natil, by her own admission, saw too little for an Elf.

He remembered Mirya and Terrill, knew now what they were. But why Vanessa? Why a peasant girl? It did not make sense. Nothing did, unless Vanessa herself, in some way, were—

Gritting his teeth, horrified by the logic of his thoughts, he pressed his forehead against the bark. "Please," he whispered. "Please not that. I just love her for what she is. I don't want her to be . . . to be like that."

Beside him, the monkey chittered restlessly and then curled up against him and went to sleep.

''Not that.''

He slipped into uneasy dreams, and it seemed to him that he was wandering in forests of moon-spattered darkness, searching for something. His task was an urgent one, and his eyes proving useless, he had to feel his way along the twisting paths with outstretched arms, groping and staggering without even brute instinct to guide him. And then, searching as he was for unknowns in this wilderness of dark trees and twining roots, of sound and odor and half-glimpsed things that flashed in the moon's bright beams and then flitted away as soft as owls, he realized that he was lost. Lost forever. Even God could not find him here, for God belonged to towns and castles and cities, to the vaults of cathedrals and the jeweled hands of moneyed prelates. God had no more business in this forest than did Christopher delAurvre.

Ahead, shining like a star: light.

And now the inescapable question: having cast away jewels and prelates and towns and cathedrals, having cast away even God, did he want light? Or was he, in fact, groping about in the wilderness by his own choice? Was it not comforting to be lost, to have given up, to be sure at least that the goal was absurd, the maze all encompassing, the patterns inhumanly intricate, beyond even the vaguest comprehension by mortal beings?

The light beckoned.

It would be easy to give up. It might even be comforting. He could stay in his castle while the country went to hell, and he could eat himself alive with the acrid bitterness of hope denied. But he was a delAurvre, and, proud, imperious, pig-headed, he had made his decision long ago.

Of course he wanted the light. He had wanted the light from the moment he had heard about his grandfather's loss of nerve. He had craved it since he had witnessed it borne aloft by a singing acrobat. He had followed it all the way across Germany and Hungary until he had drawn up with the French and German knights on the plains of Nicopolis. He had groped in the darkness for so long afterward precisely because he felt that it was there—it had to be there—*somewhere.*

Hands out before him to feel his way, eyes fixed on the radiance that sent the shadows of the forest fleeing before it, he pushed through the trees. Yes, he had made up his mind already. He had, as always, chosen the light.

And Christopher opened his eyes to find himself staring into a dawn of pink and gold fire, a dawn that limned the trees of the forest with ephemeral flame and sparkled on the many windows of Shrinerock Castle.

Tall, straight, its walls thick and its defenses manifold, it was quite capable of holding out almost indefinitely against any power that he could bring against it. But had Roger not seemed equally invulnerable? And he had fallen.

And Christopher himself, with Natil, had successfully breached even stronger and more impenetrable fortresses, even when they were bent not upon keeping him out, but upon keeping him in.

He suddenly found himself examining the castle from a different perspective. In.

Fifteen or sixteen miles of open fields, and Baron Paul and his people on foot. Even if they started out in the darkness, daylight would still find them far away from shelter. In.

And Roger had thought himself indomitable. In.

It came to him, then. In. And an elven hand had felled his grandfather.

Christopher stretched. The monkey yawned. He gave it a scritch and climbed down to the ground. As he expected, Natil was waiting at the base of the tree.

He looked into her face, and he tried not to be shaken by what he saw there. "What do you want, Natil?"

She did not flinch. "I want what my lord wants."

"Don't give me that *my lord* crap. I'm no more your lord than this monkey is."

Natil did not falter. "I took service with you, Christopher delAurvre. An Elf's word is binding throughout all the Worlds."

"Even though you're fading."

"Even more because of that, my lord."

He thought of Shrinerock, locked and bolted and barred, thought of how it resembled a very large, very tightly made stone box. And boxes could contain as well as protect. "And what do you see among the patterns, harper? What do you see that your lord wants?"

"I . . ."

"You're close enough to me to see what I want, aren't you? You can see that much."

"I see, my lord."

"Can you do it?"

Natil hefted her harp in both hands. "I am a healer, lord."

His mouth clenched, and he stifled an insane urge to grab her by the front of her tunic and shake her. *"Can you do it?"*

She looked over her shoulder in the direction of the castle, and Christopher did not doubt that she was examining in earnest what few comprehensible shreds of the labyrinthine patterns were left to her. Poor Natil! She was as limited as the humans she was trying to help!

But after a time, she nodded. "I can."

Berard of Onella entered the great hall of Shrinerock to the accompaniment of shouts and the clash of weapons. It was one of the luxuries he was beginning to permit himself. Nothing really ostentatious as of yet: just the slow examination of a new existence. It was a bath of money, so to speak, and he wanted to be sure of the temperature before he settled in.

He seated himself in the canopied chair at the high table, and at a wave of his hand, the captains who had transferred their allegiance from Hypprux to the Fellowship sat down. Servants began cutting up loaves of bread and filling wine cups, and platters of meat appeared, announced by trumpets.

Berard was reflective. Once, he had been but a subcommander, one faceless man among the many brought to Adria by the Christian zeal of Yvonnet a'Verne. Now he had everything. Joanna was waiting for him up in his chamber (she had no choice: she was shackled to his bed), there were servants and entertainers and camp followers aplenty, Eustache de Cormeign provided a convenient and on-site liquidator for the loot, and Shrinerock was an impenetrable base of operations from which the vastly augmented Fellowship—unshakably loyal to him so long as the success was easy and the money plentiful—could reach out and shake ripe apples from the heavily laden tree that was Adria.

He reached for the fruit bowl and picked up an apple. Shaking apples from Adria. Apples of silver, apples of gold, apples (he thought of Joanna—surely she was starting to like him, was she not?) of flesh and blood. They were all apples, they all came to him easily. They could not but come.

Adria was much like France. But where France was a worn-out whore of a country, her face lined and seamed with the use of many men, Adria was something like Joanna: soft and pretty, made to be enjoyed. And, like Joanna, Adria seemed to respond fairly well to a slap.

The same, though, could not be said for Jehan. He had, in fact, not responded at all well to the news that Shrinerock was to be the first object of Berard's affections. Informed of the plan just before the attack, the young man had actually caused such an unpleasant scene that Berard had been forced to order him bound.

Berard could understand. Paul was, after all, Jehan's father, and Jehan had always thought a great deal of his father. Poor lad: his father had probably not cared a fig for him.

Nevertheless, sometime during the night, Jehan had managed to slip his bonds and had run off. The lad had been well liked by most of the men of the Fellowship, and doubtless the guards had not made it too difficult for him. Berard could understand that, too. But with Jehan now missing, the task of eliminating all the possible heirs to Shrinerock was going to be that much more difficult. And Jehan was one to nurse grudges: that could possibly mean trouble.

Berard stuffed his face philosophically. This was the good life, come to him as though it had dropped out of the sky, and the rest would fall soon enough. It did not really matter that Paul and many of his castle folk were hiding in the forests below the castle. They would be found soon enough . . . or they would die of starvation. Either was fine with Berard. It did not even really matter about Jehan. A technicality, that was all. Berard was not overly worried. If he could weather the meandering politics of the Italian city states, he could find his way through the much simpler maze of Adria and the delMaris.

Baron Berard. It had a nice sound. Too bad about Jehan.

CHAPTER 23

The roar of Saint Adrian's spring was a torrent of sound that spilled out of the holy cave and cascaded down the slopes beneath Shrinerock. The old man, so went the tale, had caused the spring to appear out of the dry stones of the mountain, turning the lands all about from desert to forest, from waste to rich pasture; and the spring gushed out of the cave as though quite prepared to beat the unbeliever to the ground rather than suffer the slightest doubt as to the verity of the miracle.

Christopher believed. At present, creeping as he was towards the entrance of the shrine, he was willing to believe in almost anything. He was even willing—with the pigheaded audacity so characteristic of the delAurvres—to believe that tonight, in the absolute darkness that preceded the rising of the moon, yet another miracle would take place at Shrinerock Mountain, one conjured forth not by any saint of the Church, but rather through the power of one whose beginnings were lost in the dim and terrifying mysteries of the First Creation.

With him were Paul, Wenceslas, and the strongest men he had been able to find among the guards and the refugees. The roar of water muffled their footsteps and drowned the clink and thump of the heavy tools that they carried—hammers and picks and mauls salvaged from the ashes of town and village—as, with moonrise still two hours away, they groped their way along the upward path, eyes wide, hands reaching, working more by feel and smell and hearing than by sight.

And somewhere else, Christopher knew, Natil was sitting down with her harp, her hands to the strings and her eyes on Shrinerock, preparing to work magic. Elven magic.

His hands turned damp and sweaty. Peach trees. Any urge yet? No? So far so good.

Dark as it was, it was even darker within the cave. The roar of the spring buffeted the men, and Christopher caught Paul by the arm. "You don't happen to have any night vision in that elven blood of yours, do you, Messire Paul?"

"The Lady knows I wish I did, my friend," Paul replied over the sound of the water. "But the blood came into my family a long time ago, and I am as are many others: immortal blood in my veins, but too little to make much of a difference."

Yes, Natil had talked about that, too, months ago, when she had told him about Elves, about what the old stories said. Old stories! Christopher was still cursing himself for his gullibility—and for his cursing. Without Natil, the alliance would have been still-born. Without elven help, he himself might even now be locked in a cell beneath the Château. Or dead.

The turbulence of the spring churned moisture into the air. Christopher's face was damp, his hair lank. "You know the way to the passage?"

Paul squeezed his hand. "In my sleep."

Christopher passed the orders back down the file. One hand on the shoulder of the man in front. Follow. Watch your step.

The men moved slowly along the edge of the rushing water, toward the mouth of the passage that led up to the castle above. This was no martial advance: attack by such an ill-equipped few would have been brave but foolish, and Christopher had given up such idiocy. He was, instead, intent upon the much more practical goal of getting Paul and his people to safety—to Malvern, at least, perhaps as far as Aurverelle.

He suddenly stopped short, his hand tight on Paul's shoulder. Ahead, broken into a faint cascade of glittering sparks by the cataract that fell from the rocky wall and plunged into the pool below, was a flickering light.

Guards.

He felt Paul nod. "They can't have heard us," said the baron of Furze. "I can hardly hear myself. But you've good eyes, my friend."

"Fear does that."

Paul led the party up the invisible path by feel and then ducked behind what seemed to the touch to be a massive wall of boulders. The waterfall was off to the right now, jetting out with such force that it contacted the receiving pool some distance behind the party.

"The drought hasn't done anything to this, has it?" Christopher said in Paul's ear.

"It's a miracle."

"Whose?"

But their advance had brought them within sight of the passage, for Christopher saw a flickering glow that outlined the shape of an opening among the rocks behind the falls. Yes, there were guards. He murmured a prayer of thanks, realized a moment later that he had addressed it to the Lady whom Natil so frequently invoked. He had asked Her for help before, and his request had obviously been granted.

So much attention he was getting these days! "I'm going in," he said with a dry mouth, but a massive hand descended upon his shoulder, and the abbot's deep voice rumbled close by:

"And I also, my good lord baron of Aurverelle."

"You're a churchman."

"Aye, but once I was a knight. And I have a right hand. And as long as I have a right hand I can pick up a club. And as long as I can pick up a club, I can revenge the deaths of some monks who died praying for the souls of such men as killed them."

Together, the two went toward the light, inching along a foot-wide ledge with the water jetting out above them; and when they reached the passage, Christopher bettered his grip on his sword and peered cautiously around the corner. The light was spilling from the far side of a turn. The guards had taken up their positions away from the wet.

"Too bad for them," he whispered to the abbot.

Wenceslas hefted his club. "God be praised."

The baron grinned wickedly. "She certainly deserves it, doesn't She?"

Wenceslas crossed himself. Christopher clapped him on the shoulder and winced a little at the feel of rock hard muscles. Without waiting, though, he made for the turning; and the two guards who were occupying the dank chamber beyond were caught unawares by the sudden, murderous attack from the downside of the passage. Wenceslas' cudgel smashed one to the ground with a solid crunch as Christopher's sword tore through the throat of the other before he could even gasp in surprise.

The water masked the sound of the fight and the fall of the bodies. In a few minutes, though, it would have to mask even more.

Wenceslas dragged the dead guards out of the way as Christopher took one of the torches, went back down the passage, and waved the rest of the party forward. Paul led them up, climbing spryly, and when he reached Christopher, he shook his hand. "My thanks, Messire Christopher."

Christopher grinned. It was time to drop the formalities. "My pleasure, Paul."

Paul smiled, took the torch, and led them forward, first through the chamber in which the guards had been slain, then beyond. The air was damp and stagnant, the ground stony, the passage narrow and steep. Abbot Wenceslas, a big man, now and again had to force himself through a constriction as though he were shoving a grape through a finger ring.

But a short distance upwards, the passage opened out into a large room that was loud with dripping water and irregular with pits, depressions, and outcroppings of a thousand shapes and sizes. On the far side, another aperture led further up, but immediately above it, the roof dipped down in a cluster of rough boulders that seemed thrust into the room like a finger.

Without comment, Paul pointed at the cluster, and with dour nods, the men set to work. Hammers, picks, clubs: anything heavy that might persuade a stone to break smashed rhythmically against the overhang with the regularity of swiples falling on a floor of wheat. And, as though the men were indeed threshing, Wenceslas himself called the changes in a low voice that reverberated throughout the room, carrying even over the still tumultuous roar of water.

Christopher worked, too, raising a sledge and smacking it home, showing his companions that even the baron of Aurverelle knew how to keep time to a caller's chant. But as he worked, he wondered what Natil was doing. Was she keeping her word? How would he know?

Minutes passed, lengthened. The work went on. The temperature in the chamber rose. The air was sodden with humidity. Dirty, sweaty men strained aching muscles against the impassive stone.

An Elf's word is binding throughout all the Worlds, Natil had said. And, true to her word, she had raised him from a stable floor, harped him back to some sense of honor, preserved him from captivity and death. But had he now asked too much? He did not even know why she had come to help him. An Elf? Helping a delAurvre? Dear Lady!

A fragment of stone wavered and fell, but only a fragment. The rest of the mass was proving obstinate.

But it must have been at about that time that Natil began harping, for there was a sudden change in the atmosphere, and the pervasive, liquid roar was joined by a sound that was not a sound, a vibration in the air that, though faint and almost without substance, nonetheless cut the ear as though with knives and razors.

At its appearance, Wenceslas staggered back as though he had been struck in the face, and the assault on the overhang lost momentum. Paul nodded and touched his forehead. *"Elthia Calasiuove."*

The sound continued, building into a thrumming shriek of ephemeral energy. Magic. Elven magic. Christopher's thoughts fled to his grandfather, and he could not help but wonder what Roger had seen and felt during those last moments before his old, brutal life had been ripped from him. Shaking, he fought to keep himself from plunging away down the tunnel to the spring.

But Paul was unfazed. "Honor your God in your house, Abo. Honor my Lady in Shrinerock!"

He grabbed the heavy maul that the abbot had dropped and, with a cry in Elvish, smashed it into the outcropping. The stone suddenly vibrated, and an urgent groan came from above.

"That's done it!" he shouted. "Everyone out! Hurry!"

They ran, Christopher and Paul standing on either side of the downside aperture and thrusting the members of the party through as they counted heads. When everyone was out, and as rocks started dropping to the floor of the cave, Christopher pointed to Paul and jerked his thumb down the passage.

Without comment, Paul seized Christopher and shoved him out of the cavern ahead of himself just as the entire, ponderous mass of the ceiling shook itself loose and fell, sealing the room and pelting the two men with dust, gravel, and cobble-sized stones as they ran down the passage to the spring.

A stream of loose stones and gravel skittered along the slope after them, then abruptly rustled to a stop. The whine of Natil's energies hung in the otherwise silent air like a taut harpstring, and Christopher discovered that he had a clear view of the moonlit mouth of the cavern. The cataract was gone. The pool was emptying.

"Sacrilege?" whispered the abbot. His voice echoed in the hush.

Faint grindings, growing louder. Paul snatched a torch, held it up, examined the mouth of the spring. "No," he said. "It's stopped up. Run, you idiots!"

And now even the ubiquitous tremolo of Natil's magic was suddenly threatened with eclipse, for the groan of tortured rock built, mounted, crescendoed in lithic apocalypse. A loud crack, and a stream of muddy water exploded out of the passage, doubling and redoubling, growing in the space of a few heartbeats into a torrent that quickly overflowed the pool and went raging down towards the entrance to the shrine.

The men dropped their tools and fled. Christopher and Paul, following right behind them, sprinted down the path and threw themselves out and to the side of the entrance an instant before the flood filled the entire cavern and screamed and frothed its way down the slope.

Still, though, the air was caught in a noose of magic that seemed to be one with the very substance of the mountain. Lying on the moist earth beside the flood, Christopher looked up at the castle. It was glowing softly, its towers and roofs limned in pale blue. He swallowed and looked away quickly.

But the energies abruptly peaked, faded, dwindled into a murmur, vanished; and when Christopher looked again, the glow was gone. But though Shrinerock still lifted white towers toward the stars with a beauty and strength that many might well have deemed imperial, something was different about it now. Christopher, searching, straining his eyes in the moonlight, realized finally that the glint of its many glass windows was absent, as was the glow of lamplight and torchlight that had previously seeped from its closed shutters. In fact, when he looked more carefully, he discovered that, as far as he could see, windows, doors, and gates alike had been replaced by hard, unyielding surfaces of fused stone.

The word of an Elf was indeed binding: the free companies were trapped within Shrinerock.

Paul delMari was approaching middle age, but he bounded down the road like a youngster. Christopher's plan and Natil's magic had bought the refugees in the forest several additional hours in which to cross the pastures unmolested, but not until he was well out of earshot of the castle did Paul risk even a muffled call: "Isabelle! Martin! It's done!"

At his words, those who had gathered in the shadows just within the edge of the trees stepped clear and started off towards Malvern Forest. They were burdened lightly—they had little to begin with—and Natil had healed the wounded. They would make good time.

But Natil herself was not with them. Christopher was almost relieved. Perhaps she had decided that her work was finished, that it was time for her to depart. But she had admitted that the magic for which Christopher had asked would be taxing, and he was unnerved to find himself deeply worried that something had happened to her.

He ran, caught up with Paul. "Where did Natil say she was going to be?"

Paul paused in his merry jog down to the forest. "Up on the higher ground, my friend."

Christopher frowned: he did not know the way. Paul, however, guessed his thoughts.

"I don't see her, either," he said. "Let's go look."

Together, they struck off along the moonlit paths of Shrinerock Forest. Paul knew the way of the woods, and he led Christopher through the trees, up slopes and across deep ravines.

The ground rose and turned stony and unfit for trees. Bits of scrub and weeds did little to soften a barren landscape. The two men puffed their way up, their boots clattering on loose shale and gravel. "They say that this is what all of Shrinerock looked like before Adrian worked his miracle," said Paul. He laughed quietly. "I wonder, though, if Adrian had anything to do with it."

"Elves?"

Paul nodded. "They've been here from the beginning, Christopher. I wouldn't be surprised at all to hear that they magicked up a spring and turned a little patch of Adria into a garden.''

Garden. And how about some peach trees? Christopher winced. "Do they . . . always do things like that?''

"Once.'' Paul's boots sent a rattle of gravel down the slope. "It's different now, of course. They've faded, and it's harder for those who are left. Natil . . .'' He shook his head, suddenly tight-lipped.

Christopher struggled after him. "What about her?''

Paul extended a hand, dragged Christopher up the last few feet. "She may have given everything, Christopher.''

Christopher stared. Everything?

"They're like that,'' said Paul. The moonlight glinted in his blond hair. "That's all they seem to want to do. Give. Just as human beings always seem to want to . . .'' He shrugged, shook his head. ". . . take.''

And Roger, a human being, had certainly taken. Gold, people, lives: it had all been the same to Roger of Aurverelle. Christopher, himself preoccupied with what life offered—or could be made to offer—found himself struggling with the idea of an entire race whose bent seemed so utterly opposite to anything he had known before.

Giving. Helping. Healing. Natil might well have killed herself to aid the survivors of the delMari estate after selflessly entering the service of a man whose ancestors had waged a genocidal war upon her people. Before that, Terrill and Mirya had braved Castle Aurverelle in order to bring healing to a dying peasant girl.

Christopher suspected that he knew why, but it was a grievous knowledge. "Paul . . .''

Paul had started off up another slope, but he stopped, turned.

"Did you know Vanessa, Paul?''

"I never met her. I knew her father, though.''

"What . . .''

"Charming girl, Christopher?''

Christopher blushed. "Very nice,'' he said. "And very hurt.''

Paul strode up the slope. "Yes,'' he said, "I heard that you took her in. And Martin, too. My deepest thanks. How is she now?''

Christopher followed him to the crest of the rise, laid a hand on his arm. "How should I know?''

Paul swung around, perplexed. "Isn't she with you? Martin said she'd stayed in Aurverelle."

"She did. But then she went down to Saint Blaise."

Paul shook his head. "She never reached Saint Blaise."

"But Ranulf—" Christopher's voice caught, for, a short distance away, Natil lay stretched out on the rocky ground, unmoving. Her harp lay at her side as though it had been dropped, and someone was kneeling beside her, holding her hands.

Shocked by Paul's words, frightened for Natil's welfare, Christopher ran to help, his hand reaching for the grip of his sword. Natil did not stir, but the stranger with her rose gracefully. Like Natil, he was clad in green and gray, but his hair was as pale as frost. His gray eyes examined the baron piercingly, and then he touched his forehead and bowed.

Christopher recognized him, recognized his garb, recognized the immortal light. Terrill. An Elf. But he had guessed that already. Dizzy with confusion and worry, he knelt beside Natil, took her hand. "Dear harper . . ."

She did not appear to see him. Her eyes reflected the moon and the stars, and her gaze seemed to go through him, stretching upwards or inwards into regions that he knew he could never comprehend. But her lips finally moved. "Fear not."

Fear not? "Natil! What the hell happened to you?"

Terrill spoke. "The spell was a difficult one, Baron Christopher. Natil took what she needed from the stars . . . and from herself."

Giving. Giving and giving and giving. Christopher put his hands to his face. "Dear Lady . . . please . . ."

"She will recover," said Terrill. Christopher noticed that he wore a sword, and that his hand looked ready to go to the grip in an instant. But the Elf nodded with as much reassurance as he seemed able to muster. "Be at peace. It is difficult to kill one of my people."

Weakly, Christopher sat down on the ground. Paul hurried up, cried out at the sight of the harper.

"She will rise by morning," said Terrill. "It would be best for you to follow your people, Paul."

But Paul embraced Terrill, then knelt and kissed Natil's hands. "There is more valor in your fingers, sweet lady," he whispered to her, "than in all the armies of Europe."

Natil murmured a reassurance, but Christopher could only mumble, "But . . . where the hell is Vanessa?"

Paul looked up. "I don't know, my friend."

Terrill spoke again. "Vanessa is in Saint Brigid. Two days' ride from here."

CHAPTER 24

Berard had finally cuffed Joanna out of her incessant sobbing and into something resembling acceptance of the fact that she was chained to his bed, that she would remain chained to his bed, and that no amount of tears and hysterical weeping was going to change the fact that she was chained to his bed. He was just slipping into sleep when the pounding came to his door. "My lord!"

Heart racing, sweating from the oppressive heat, Berard was on his feet in an instant. "What's the matter?"

The voice was muffled. "The doors and windows of the castle, messire. They're . . . funny."

Funny? Startled and sleepless, Berard wondered who had been idiot enough to disturb him against his express orders. "I'm not impressed by your sense of humor, soldier."

Joanna was crying again, but he silenced her with a kick, then pulled on a robe and went to the door. But the latch did not yield to his hand. It did not even rattle. In fact, the iron itself appeared to have been replaced with . . . something else.

Funny . . .

"Joanna, open those windows." Joanna, though, was shackled to the bed, and his words only sent her off into a fresh bout of sobbing.

Groping, Berard went to the window himself. It was pitch dark in the room, without even a shred of starlight or moonlight to light his way—something which struck him as damnably odd—and he stumbled over a footstool and barked his shins on a chair before he reached the casement. He fumbled for the latch, but its touch and lack of cooperation informed him that it had acquired the same mysterious affliction as the doorknob.

Funny . . .

"Damnation!" He smashed a fist against the panes and was rewarded with a set of bruised knuckles.

The man in the hall was alarmed. "My lord!"

Joanna sobbed.

"Shut up, all of you!" Berard's fatigue was rapidly giving way to bewilderment, and thence to outright rage; but he groped about until he came up against a wall sconce. He removed a candle and thrust it into the embers of the banked fire. It caught in a moment, and he carried the light to the window.

But, instead of glass, he found only an unyielding surface of smooth, gray . . .

Stone?

"What the hell's going on?"

It was granite. It had to be granite. And as his shaking fingers now discovered, the formerly wooden rails and stiles were also granite, as was the window frame itself.

He stood, stunned, but was roused by another worried cry from the corridor. Heart sinking, he went to the door. Granite. Hard, impenetrable granite.

He crossed himself. "Mother of God." But Joanna was sobbing hysterically again, and he recalled that God's mother probably cared for him little more than his own.

He threw a boot at the girl, then rapped on the door, carefully, with the pommel of his sword. "Get some men up here with hammers and picks."

"Ah . . ." The man on the far side seemed to hesitate. Berard pursed his lips. A mutiny? That would explain a great deal. The expanded Fellowship was held together only by the promise of loot and the fact that Berard seemed to promise more of it than anyone else. It was always possible that some other captain . . . "I'm afraid that will take time, Messire Berard."

Berard wanted to scream, but he forced himself into calculation. Panic would do him no good. Panic was what had cost poor Giovanni so dearly outside Bologna. "What do you mean?"

"All the other doors and windows in the castle have been turned to stone, too. We're breaking the men out of the barracks now, and then we'll have to break into the storage rooms for the tools."

Berard stared at the blank expanse of stone that had once

been a door. The whole castle? But that . . . that meant . . . that meant that . . .

He did not know what it meant.

He stared at the granite. The granite stared back. "Then *do* it!" he shouted.

"As soon as possible, my lord!"

"Faster than that, you idiot!"

He heard the man run off. With the candle still burning in his hand, he leaned against the wall. Every door and window in the castle. Who on earth could do such a thing? And what powers would they have to be wielding in order to do it?

He recalled Jehan's drunken babbling about the Elves, felt a shiver in spite of the stifling heat. Elves? No, ridiculous. Just a legend.

But Jehan had seemed so sure, so matter of fact. But then again he had been drunk. But then again . . .

Berard's head was suddenly hurting, and an ache gnawed at his stomach. An obstacle—an exceedingly clever and definitely preternatural obstacle—had appeared in the road that he was traveling toward the free conquest of Adria. And Berard knew from experience that such obstacles did not just happen. Which meant that someone—equally clever, perhaps (and the ache in his stomach increased) equally preternatural—was behind it all.

"I'll find you," he murmured. "I'll find you. And then we'll see who you are, and what I'll do about you."

Two hours later, the tramp of heavy feet outside his door gave way to the crack of hammers and mauls and battering rams; but the door fell only with a half-hour's concerted work, for as the wood had been thick, so was the stone it had become. Long before Berard could escape his prison, though, he heard more shouts from outside. Muffled though they were, they obviously proceeded from the castle walls.

The door finally caved in. Berard grabbed the first man that came to hand. "What's going on outside?"

"There are people on horseback down on the slopes."

Attack. He thought so. "How many?"

"Two, messire."

"Two?" Berard stared for an instant; then, with a curse, he ran down the corridor, skidding and slipping on the fragments of stone that littered the floor.

The sun had risen during his confinement, and when he

gained the top of the curtain wall, he could see clearly that the man had been absolutely truthful. Below, about a hundred yards away, were two figures on horseback: a man and a woman. The man appeared to have a monkey on his shoulder.

"Who goes there?" Berard shouted. "Damn you, what do you want?"

The shout came back. "I'm Christopher delAurvre, baron of Aurverelle, and I want you and your scum *out of my country*!"

Berard eyed him. Christopher of Aurverelle? The one who was mad? He suddenly felt better. Christopher was but a man—in this case, a man with a monkey on his back—and therefore the uncanniness of Shrinerock's transformation began to give way to the simple humanity of an adversary.

Doors and windows could be battered open, humanity could be attended to. Berard beckoned to one of the guards. "Get a crossbowman up here, quickly."

The man took off at a run. Berard turned once again to Christopher. "And is sorcery among your talents, my good Baron Aurverelle? That could prove interesting to the Church."

"I've got a lot of talents, mush-head," came the reply. "And I don't give a damn about the Church. Who the hell are you?"

"Berard of Onella." Berard could not see anything wrong with admitting it. He was, after all, rather proud of his rise.

"You're from Adria? You're doing this to your own country?"

Berard did not feel obligated to inform Christopher that money was his country; but now the archer was arriving with a clatter of boots and tackle, and without saying a word, Berard pointed at Christopher and drew his finger across his throat. The bowman nodded, put his foot in the stirrup of his weapon, and began to crank it up.

"You've got two days to take your men and get them out of Adria," Christopher was shouting.

The crossbow's string creaked into position. A *snick* as the trigger caught.

"Otherwise, I'll see you hanged like a common thief."

Berard was offended. Common thief? Ridiculous. Uncommon thief if anything, but robber first and foremost.

"And how," he inquired, trying to put irony into his shout, "do you intend to manage that?"

"I have . . . friends," replied Christopher, and Berard sensed a deep threat in his words and tone that reminded him of the mysterious transformation of the castle. If Christopher had friends who could turn wood and glass and metal to fused stone, then what if. . . ?

But the crossbow was ready. The archer positioned himself in an arrow loupe, braced himself, took aim . . .

"Friends?" Berard taunted. "You have only a monkey and a woman, as far as I can tell. You'll have to do better than that, Christopher."

But the woman, who had until now been slumped, motionless, on her horse, suddenly leaned towards Christopher as though speaking to him. Christopher nodded and, just as the archer released his bolt, calmly sidled his horse two feet to the right. The bolt whizzed between Christopher and the woman and buried itself in the ground.

Berard stared. But for the baron's sudden change of position, he would have been dead. How had he known. . . ?

Friends.

Berard's mouth went dry. The archer looked up. "Sorry, messire."

"You'll have to do better than that, Berard," Christopher shouted. He was a fairly good mimic: he had duplicated Berard's taunt perfectly. "You've got two days. After that, we'll hunt you down like rabbits! Remember that: two days!" And then he and his companion both wheeled their horses and set off to the south.

Berard whirled, shouting orders. "Fetch the horses! Gather the men! I want that bastard out there dead!" But when he turned back, he saw not only the dwindling forms of Christopher and his strange companions, but also a distant flutter of movement out to the west. It looked like . . . no, it was indeed a group of people. On foot. It could only be Baron Paul and the survivors of the castle and the towns heading for Malvern Forest.

Berard cursed, kicked the parapet, bruised his foot, cursed louder. "Get those horses out there, and get your unholy asses in their saddles, damn you all!"

Within minutes, the horses were gathered, and a good portion of the men of the company were assembled, armed, and ready to ride. At their head, Berard lifted his sword.

"Five thousand pieces of gold to whoever brings me a dead Christopher delAurvre!" He signaled to the gate guards to open the thick doors and raise the portcullis.

The men leaped to the ropes, seized the arms of the windlass, pulled on the chains. But the twelve-inch thick gates would not budge. Like all the other doors and windows in the castle, they had been replaced by a smooth, seamless, immovable expanse of solid granite.

Despite the cocky arrogance he had displayed, Christopher was worried as he rode southward with Natil. Though Berard was, for the time, trapped within Shrinerock, he would be able to smash his way out within a day or so, and the free company captain obviously possessed a large, well-trained force that included archers.

But at least Paul and his people were safely away, making now for the shelter of Malvern Forest under the guidance of icy-eyed Terrill, who had promised to guide them as far as Aurverelle. But if Christopher regretted that someone as level-headed and forthright as Baron Paul would by necessity be missing from the gathering of the allied forces, he regretted even more that he possessed none of Paul's equanimity regarding the immortals who had involved themselves so intimately in his life and his plans.

He stole a glance at Natil. She was still pale from her efforts the previous night, and she clung to her horse as though her weakness must inevitably topple her to the ground. Nonetheless, she was otherwise as calm and tranquil as ever, and with perfect equanimity and flawless courtesy she had brushed aside Christopher's opinion that she was too weak to travel and had remained at his side, even though the road he had chosen would lead her far away from security and rest.

This was the road to Saint Brigid. As the southernmost of the Free Towns, it lay well within striking range of Berard and his company. Worse yet—much worse—Vanessa was in Saint Brigid.

The monkey clung to Christopher's shoulder with the set face of an old man as the miles fell beneath the hooves of their mounts; and the road looped well out to the south before it turned west, skirting the edge of Malvern Forest as it crossed the otherwise open grasslands.

It was a human trail—open, prosaic—and therefore reassuring to a man struggling with revelations of immortal influence. Christopher embraced it, enjoyed it, relished even the hot east wind and the hotter sun that were parching and browning the countryside.

But Christopher said little to Natil, even when they stopped for the night. He did not know what to say. His confusion was absolute, his fears profound. Not until the sun had risen well into the sky on the second day did he summon up enough courage to break his silence. "Why?" he said suddenly. "Why are you doing all this?"

Natil answered as though she had expected his question. "One defends what is precious, my lord. You defend Adria. I defend you for that reason."

"You didn't know I'd be doing any of this when you took service with me."

"I did not. But at that time, we owed you a great favor in return for the favor that you bestowed on Vanessa."

Christopher did not need patterns or telepathy to tell him that Natil's words held a touch of dissemblance. "You're trying to make up to me for what you did to my grandfather, aren't you?"

Natil nodded slowly, eyes downcast. "We are. We seek to mend what we once marred."

Christopher stared straight ahead, jaw clenched. As he had suspected. Then: "That makes two of us." He almost tried to hate her. How could anyone, immortal or not, ever make up for the absolute violation of a human soul? Berard of Onelia and his free companies had taken Shrinerock, and the Elves had taken his grandfather. Shrinerock, though, could be rebuilt. Roger was gone forever.

The monkey on his shoulder was becoming agitated, and when Christopher glanced at it, it stuck its tongue out at him.

He wanted to swear: even the monkey seemed to know more than he. "And Vanessa?" he said. "What about her? Or do you make a habit of reassembling peasant girls?"

Natil did not speak for some time. Then: "Vanessa is a kinswoman. Her grandmother Roxanne took an Elf for a lover, and by him she conceived Vanessa's father, Lake." She bent her head. "Who is now dead," she said softly.

"So Vanessa's part Elf." Christopher was torn between frustrated rage and disappointed tears.

"She is," said Natil. "There are many in the world who

are so. In times past, Elves were loved without fear or shame, and therefore we loved in return. Only since the rise of the Church have our two peoples been sundered. Many of your race now bear within them a trace of the elven blood. It slumbers. In some it sleeps only fitfully, in others it awakens.''

But Christopher was not thinking of faceless multitudes: he was thinking of Vanessa. Elven she was, perhaps, but he had seen the fragile humanity in her. Warm, womanly, yet tortured with an affliction over which she had no control, she had leaned on his arm, looked to him for guidance, departed from him—he flattered himself—only with reluctance.

He turned to the Elf, tears stinging his eyes. ''What the hell are you doing to us?''

Natil shifted the harp on her shoulder. She looked sad. ''We try, my lord. We try to heal and to help. But we are fading as a people, and we do not see the patterns as we used. Perhaps for those very reasons we have become even more frantic in our efforts, for we know that we do not have much time or ability left to us.'' She rode in silence for a time. Then: ''We are old, my lord. Very old. But years do not always bring wisdom, and in any case, it appears that wisdom is not always useful.''

There was grief in her voice. Fading. And limited and fallible in that fading. But Christopher was angry. ''You're just like us, then, aren't you?'' he snapped, and he spurred his horse towards Saint Brigid.

He was tired and dusty, but he rode on, following the westering sun towards the southern borders of the Free Towns; and by late afternoon, Saint Brigid appeared out of the long shadows cast by the Aleser. Despite its walls, its palisade, and its ditch, the village seemed quaint and unassuming in its rustic simplicity; and Christopher wondered whether it had folded Vanessa, feral eyes and all, into its little bustle of life and living, whether she had found a secure place among its patterns.

They rode directly to the gate, and the stout man on duty stared at Natil, but not, Christopher noticed, out of shock or fear. ''Fair One?''

''I am Natil,'' said the Elf. ''This is Baron Christopher of Aurverelle.''

The man goggled at Christopher. ''But . . .''

"You're all in danger, my man," said Christopher. "There's a massing of free companies at Shrinerock, and I can guarantee that they're going to be spreading out to strike at the Free Towns before the summer's over. You'd better get your council together and start pike practice for the lads."

But a cry went up from the street beyond the gate— "Christopher! Christopher!"—and the baron looked up to see a young woman running towards him, leaping and shouting. Her hair was blond and curling and unconstrained by braid or fastening, and she was dressed in homespun; but she had tucked up her skirts to free her legs, and when she saw that he had noticed her, she redoubled her speed.

He stared. It was Vanessa.

He swung down from his horse, and leaving Natil to make explanations, ran to meet her, drew her to him, wrapped her in his arms. "Dear Lady, Vanessa, you're safe."

But when she looked up at him, smiling, it was not with strange eyes that held a mixture of forbidden knowledge and fear. Her face was clear, her eyes brown and calm, and within her he felt a wellspring of humanity and peace that nearly dropped him to his knees.

"Vanessa?"

Her smile was genuine, open. As though to reassure him, she put an arm about his neck and kissed him. "It's me, Christopher. It's really me. See . . ." She held up her hand. "I've kept your ring. It's ne'er awa' fro' me."

"But . . ." He stared at her. She was just a girl. Human. Wonderfully human. "But . . . what happened?"

"I cam to Saint Brigid because I thought I'd ha' a better chance here tha' i' Saint Blaise," she said. "I wa' right. My grandma wa' dead, but a friend o' hers took me in. An' she helped me, an' the Elves helped me, too . . . and . . . and . . ." She smiled through tears. "You were right. I dan have to see the patterns. I dan have to look, an' if I look, I dan have to let them tell me wha' to do. I can just be me."

Christopher clung to her, filling his arms with her common, warm humanity. "The Elves?"

"The Elves, Christopher." She was crying. "The Elves showed me." She tried to laugh, but managed only a fresh burst of joyful tears. "They helped me, Christopher. They're good people, an' they helped me."

Helping and healing, Natil had said. They tried. Sometimes it all went awry, but at least they tried.

Christopher held her tightly. "They helped me, too," he murmured into her hair. Despite his grandfather, despite Nicopolis, despite his confused and shamefaced vacillation between anger and gratitude, he wanted to believe it. "Dear Lady, Vanessa, they helped me, too."

CHAPTER 25

Terrill led the way through Malvern Forest with silent, elven footsteps, but the secret path existed for twos and threes, not for hundreds, and the men and women and children of the Shrinerock estate spread out in a long straggling line that plodded forward towards Aurverelle.

By the end of the second day, they had covered only about a third of the distance through the woods. Exhausted women gathered hungry children together as the shadows fell. The men collected bracken and dry leaves for beds and shelters. Paul's guards took the watch. Abbot Wenceslas and his monks chanted vespers and compline from memory, then helped with the sharing of a meager ration of food. On Terrill's advice, they lit no fires, for the drought had turned the forest tinder dry, and in any case the smoke would give away their position.

Paul sat down, his legs aching. "Are you actually expecting them to be looking for us?"

Terrill's eyes glittered in the falling darkness. "I do not know," he said. "Once, I might have seen. But everything is obscure now." He sighed, passed a hand over his face. "I see only your people, and great sadness."

The figures of the refugees were a shadowed mélange of lights and darks: clumps and hummocks of human beings settling down amid the roots of oaks and beeches and rowans, trying to snatch what little sleep they could in the middle of a forest of trees and fears both. Paul knew their questions. He was asking many of them himself. Would they live? Would they return? What would they return to?

It was easy to see sadness. Shrinerock taken, the free companies in Adria, and the Elves fading. And . . .

He thought again of Jehan and the surprise attack, bent his head. It was inescapable. It had to have been Jehan. Terrill saw great sadness. Paul, too, saw great sadness.

"My lord." It was Martin. Dark and lithe, the lad slid through the forest, stepping over sleeping figures and sliding through bushes and leaves as quietly as Terrill. And yet the unobtrusiveness of his comings and goings did not seem to Paul to derive so much from skill and inner harmony as from a desire for invisibility.

A stranger would not have noticed it, but Paul noticed. He could not help but notice. Martin was fearful, even ashamed, of something.

"Everyone's resting," said the lad. "Prunella is having difficulty, though."

Paul sighed heavily. "It's hard on the women that last month."

Martin looked to Terrill. "I have heard, Fair One, that Elves can heal."

Terrill's gray eyes were dispassionate. "That is true."

"Can you help Prunella?"

The Elf was silent. "I am no healer," he said at last, "but I will do what I can, young master."

For an instant, almost wavering, and still with that sense of shame, Martin looked at Terrill as though he were going to ask something else, something that had nothing to do with Prunella. But then his gaze flicked to Paul, and he faltered. "I'll take you to her."

And the two slipped away into the falling dusk.

Paul received bread and nuts and a fragment of cheese from the hand of one of the monks—*"Benedicamus Domino."* *"Deo gratias.* And thank you also, Brother."—and settled down to take what comfort he could from his dinner . . . alone. True, he was surrounded by the men and women of his estate, and Isabelle came from helping with the children to cuddle and hold hands with him for a short time before sleep, but Paul was nonetheless alone. He was the baron, and these were his people. They looked to him for help and for protection.

He felt his impotence. He did not have a castle, he did not have a sword, he did not even have a son. Jehan was gone. In fact, Jehan . . . Jehan might be a traitor.

Isabelle slumped against his leg, asleep. Paul signaled to a guard, and they stretched her out on a bed of bracken and covered her with her cloak, but Paul did not sleep. He was still thinking of Jehan, and of Martin.

Jehan, prideful and demanding, had turned his back on

his father and his family because he had not been given immediately what he wanted. Martin, though, had never asked for anything. Ever conscious, it seemed, of his social position, he had not thought to be so forward. Paul had hinted about knighthood, but Martin had shied away almost with a kind of fear, as though he wanted nothing more out of life than to fade into faceless and unremarkable obscurity.

And now, Jehan had betrayed Shrinerock, and Martin was apologizing for his existence with every word he uttered, every gesture he made, every expression of his dark face.

Ashamed? Of what? Paul did not know. He had never seen Martin like this save . . .

His back to a tree, he lifted his head and regarded the darkening sky through a screen of heat-gilt leaves. Never . . . save once.

It had been a few years ago, at Yvonnet a'Verne's coming of age party. Martin had disappeared in the course of the evening. With Yvonnet. And when he had turned up after an absence that had lasted several days, he had been touched with the same aura of shame that now clung to him. For a long time after, he had not been able to look Paul—or anyone else—in the eye. There had been a sense of damage about him.

Yvonnet . . .

Paul considered. Martin had visited Yvonnet again in the course of his journey home with Vanessa. Odd. And now the shame again.

My son. My son: what happened to you?

He must have fallen asleep then, for when he opened his eyes, it was quite dark, and only the faint glint of a waning moon filtered down through the trees. He heard voices nearby, recognized Martin's tenor and Terrill's firm, factual intonation.

"My thanks, Fair One, for your help."

"We do all that we can, Master Martin. While we have strength, we will continue to labor."

The camp—if such a straggling line of refugees could be called a camp—slept. Snores. Mumbles. The voices of Terrill and Martin were hushed, but Paul sensed that Martin was struggling with something. The night was tense with it.

"Fair One . . ."

Terrill's form was lithe and taut in the moonlight, and

Paul, his elven blood stirring into uneasy wakefulness, saw the soft, pervasive shimmer that surrounded him. "What would you, Master Martin?"

Martin still struggled. "You helped Prunella," he said. "Can you . . ." Paul felt the lad's tension. "Can you help me?"

"What do you mean?"

"You know what I mean. You know about me and . . ."

Paul's hands clenched on his knees. He was beginning to guess. Martin's shame . . . and Yvonnet. There were rumors about the baron of Hypprux. Yvonnet's position kept him safe from inquiry, but Martin could find safety only in absolute obscurity.

My son.

He wanted a son. He had been dispossessed of sister and castle and lands, but he would settle for a wife and a son. But Martin and Yvonnet . . .

"Do not tell me unless you wish me to know," Terrill was saying.

"I'm a sodomite."

Terrill was silent.

Martin's voice was hoarse. "Elves can heal, Fair One. Will you heal me?"

Paul was weeping. Silently, soundlessly, the tears streaked his face, dampened his beard. He shut his eyes to the swirls of light that were all that was left of the stars.

Terrill's silence continued. In his mind's eye, Paul could see the Elf searching, examining, evaluating Martin. What did Terrill think? Was he disgusted with the depravity of the vices to which humans clung like drunkards hanging on their flasks? Was he sick with the knowledge that it was to such as these that the Elves had been forced by time and circumstance to yield their world?

And still he wept. *My son.*

"I cannot heal you," Terrill said at last.

"I . . . understand."

"You do not understand," said the Elf. Neither reproof nor repugnance touched his voice. "I say that I cannot heal you, for that which is not sick cannot be cured."

Terrill had said it. It had to be true. But still Paul wept. *My son.*

"Then I'm lost," said Martin bitterly. "I'm surely lost."

But, abruptly, Terrill had turned toward the east, back towards Shrinerock. "Something is wrong."

And Paul suddenly noticed a tang in the air, a piquant scent of wood smoke and burning leaves. The east wind, which had slackened this last day, now returned, freshening, roaring through the treetops in whirling song. The odor increased.

"Ai, Elthiai."

"What is it?"

Paul knew before Terrill answered. Malvern was burning. Angry, vengeful, desperate to kill the refugees and the baron who led them, the free companies had fired the forest.

Christopher wanted to be angry. He wanted to rage, to shout, to vent a frustration that mingled so inextricably with fright that he could not even begin to say where one left off and the other began.

The Elves had struck his grandfather, sending him into a mild little life of peach trees and gardens, sending Christopher himself on a fool's journey to Nicopolis and disaster. It was a terrible power they had, one that could alter the very substance and soul of a man. And yet their regret at what they had done—an immortal regret, continuing undiminished throughout the years—had caused them to work for Christopher's healing, to save his life, to undo, as much as was within their power, what they had done.

And now Christopher held Vanessa in his arms again, and had found that the patterns that had battered her life into a hell of borderline madness had been quelled. Again, by an elven hand.

"It wa' Mirya who helped me," Vanessa told him. "She wa' the one who healed me in your castle. She can heal minds as well as bodies . . ."

Christopher thought of his grandfather, tried to fill himself with Vanessa's calm brown eyes. Healing? Was that healing?

". . . but she would na do it wi'out my permission and help. An' so we went out among the patterns together, an' we danced wi' them, and she helped me to reweave them. They can be woven, you know, like a piece o' cloth. An' together we wove them, and now I only see patterns whan I want to."

Changed, like his grandfather. Struck by magic . . . and

happy in being so stricken. What, he wondered, had Roger felt? Relief? Had his grandfather's rage and arrogant disregard for anything resembling common humanity been a burden for him, one to be put off with the same rejoicing that Vanessa now exhibited for her own newfound clarity?

Peach trees. Christopher wanted to throw some fruit.

Natil—wisely—vanished for the rest of the day, and Christopher had a chance to hold Vanessa, meet and thank those who had taken her in and befriended her, learn something of her life in the village. But when, after dinner, the harper reappeared to ask permission to return to the forest to recuperate from her efforts at Shrinerock, he gave it to her curtly, trying to make up in appearance for anger that smacked of the illegitimate. "Go. Go on. Go find someone else to meddle with."

His words disappeared into Natil's calm like a stone thrown into a lake: a plash, a ripple, and then . . . nothing. "I will come at need," she said, and then she bowed deeply, touching her hands to her forehead, picked up her harp, and departed soundlessly into the darkness.

Christopher looked after her. "It's mad," he whispered to the deserted streets. "It's all mad." The monkey perched on his shoulder mumbled reproachfully, and Christopher glared at it. "You're forgetting who's the monkey around here, sir," he snapped, and then, out of an irony that had become habitual, he forced a wan grin. "You run Aurverelle. I'll throw the fruit."

But Christopher had not come to greet Vanessa's friends: he had come to warn them. That night, the town council gathered in the house of Abel, the smith, who, though dark and hairy as a savage out of an old tale, formally and courteously introduced Christopher to a room crowded with the descendants of those whom old Roger had once thought to conquer.

They were not entirely unprepared for his news about Shrinerock. Rumors of the catastrophe had been filtering through the southern part of Adria for the last two weeks, and the council had ordered the defenses of the town strengthened. The gates, long in disrepair, Abel had mended himself, and he and the other men had also reinforced the walls, deepened the surrounding ditch, and had installed the encircling palisade of fire-hardened saplings. Saint Brigid was no Maris, to be sure, but neither was it a helpless, undefended village.

Christopher, though, suspected that the preparations would prove useless. Berard had several thousand men with him, and judging from what was left of Ypris and Furze, they possessed, in addition to armor and weapons, siege machinery and several heavy guns.

"I'd recommend that you all evacuate," he told them. "I'm sorry to have to put it so bluntly . . ." Would his grandfather have apologized for bluntless? Never! But Christopher went on without hesitating. ". . . but I think you've lost from the beginning."

But an older woman near the front of the room shook her head and stood up. This was Charity, Abel's mother, the weaver and midwife to whom Vanessa had apprenticed herself. She was respected and loved in the village, and though Christopher suspected that her religious beliefs were no more orthodox than Natil's, even Dom Gregorie, the priest, seemed on friendly terms with her.

She was over a decade past her half century, but her face was essentially unlined, and her voice was as clear as a girl's when she spoke. "If we leave," she said, "I think that they will not be satisfied. If we go to Alm, they will come to Alm. If we go all the way to Saint Blaise, then they will eventually come all the way to Saint Blaise. Once, long ago, I told Mirya . . ." And she looked around as though to ask whether any in the room remembered another threat now fifty years past. ". . . that we faced a battle that had to unite all of us. I will say it again. But this time we embrace the grandson of our former enemy." She smiled at Christopher: it was a warm smile, and along with forgiveness, he caught a trace of light in her lake blue eyes that reminded him of Vanessa . . . and of Natil and Terrill and Mirya. "And I for one bid him welcome to Saint Brigid, and hope he will not think us too stubborn because of our determination."

Charity sat down. A fighter. They were all fighters. Vanessa's father, Christopher recalled, had come from Saint Brigid. "You're all sure of this?"

He saw the men and women of the council exchange glances as the shadows from the hearth fire flickered across the walls. Glances, nods, murmurs. Yes, they were sure.

"You're all mad, you know."

Abel scratched his bald head. "And would you leave Aurverelle to the brigands, m'lord baron?"

Christopher was indignant. "Of course not."

Abel smiled, his mouth a dark line in a face patched with the scars of old burns. "Well, then . . ."

The monkey seemed to agree, for it bounded in through the open window, clambered to Christopher's head, and stared at him, upside-down, from inches away. Charity clapped her hands appreciatively, and Vanessa, present because Christopher was present, laughed.

But Christopher turned to Vanessa. "What about you?"

Vanessa shook her head. "These people tak me in. They've been good t' me. I wan leave them."

It was suicide. "Vanessa . . ."

"Nay, m'lord. I've found my home a' long last, an' I wan leave it willingly." She stood up, held out her hands to the monkey, and with a yip, it leaped into her arms. She stroked it for a moment, then lifted her brown eyes once more. "I mean it."

A fighter. She had fought Etienne, fought herself. She had struggled against the fate mapped out for her by her parents, and she had, it seemed, triumphed; for as she stood before Christopher and pledged her loyalty to what had once been a village of strangers, she seemed to have nothing at all in common with the helpless, frightened child who had opened her eyes in a bedroom at Aurverelle. Vanessa was a woman now, a human woman, and a strong one; and Christopher, despite his fears for her safety, knew that he would not have loved her otherwise.

But her refusal meant that her continuing survival would be based not upon Christopher, but upon the alliance. Looking at her now, looking at the faces—old and young, worried and determined—that were turned toward him in this little house in a little village, Christopher was shaken. Into the hands of such as Ruprecht and Yvonnet he was commending these?

He calculated. Another few days remained before the alliance forces would begin to gather at Shrinerock. And he knew—he had no illusions or false humility about it—that, without his presence, the gathering would eventually fragment. He would, therefore, have to leave Saint Brigid. He would have to leave Vanessa. And he would have to leave soon.

"All right," he said. "You hold out. I'll try to make sure that the free companies never make it this far."

Abel stuck out an almost black hand. "We trust you, Baron Aurverelle." He grinned. It was an unlikely thing for a man of Saint Brigid to say.

Christopher took his hand. "Could anyone have imagined this happening fifty years ago?"

Abel laughed. "Times change. Some things fade, others come to take their place. But I'll tell you, m'lord: the baron of Aurverelle will always have friends here in Saint Brigid."

The time of the Elves was over. It was up to human beings now. Sickness, and death, and what dull embers of loyalty and friendship could be fanned into flame. Memories that knew no more than a few decades, hearts that were anything but steadfast, hands that knew murder as well as comfort: these were all they had. The legacy of elven blood and elven heritage was sleeping—perhaps it would sleep its way into death—and those who bore it called themselves but men and women, saw nothing but what was before their eyes, and worked to carve their lives out of unseen patterns and shadowy mazes of moonlight.

He said good-bye to Vanessa the next morning, and as he held hands with her just inside the village gate, and as the hot wind from the east blew dust and straw about their feet and the sun threw light against the tower of the church, he recalled another parting. "I . . . could ask you to stay," he said.

She understood. "I ha' no place in Aurverelle, m'lord."

He put his finger to her lips. "Christopher."

He dropped his hand, and she smiled. "Christopher."

"You see, Vanessa," he said. "You say my name like one born to the gentry. I couldn't ask for more."

She blushed. "You're making fun o' me."

"No, not at all. How could I make fun of someone I love?"

She looked ready to cry. "Oh, dear Lady, Christopher . . ."

He took her by the shoulders. Symbol she had once been, symbol and guiding light—but now she was a woman, and a determined, courageous one at that. A fitting mate for a delAurvre, regardless of her parentage. "Don't you feel it? Don't you feel anything for me?"

She made a face through misting eyes, forced a laugh. "It's like out of an old tale."

"Things like elven blood and magic are out of an old tale, too," he said. "And—who knows?—someday, you and I will be a part of an old tale ourselves, and our names will live on in chimney corners and children's bedrooms long after our . . ." He grimaced at his wayward tongue. ". . . peach trees are all planted."

She blushed again, dropped her eyes, then, impulsively, threw herself against him and held him. "I do love you, Christopher," she whispered. "You helped me. You tak me in whan e'eryone else turned me out. An' you were e'erything to me that e'eryone else wan't. But . . . but I . . ."

He shushed her. "No. No decisions now. You've told me enough. That's all I need for now." And he held up her hand: his signet glittered on her finger. "You bear my token. And I . . ." He drew the moon and star pendant from his tunic. "I bear yours. Whatever happens, we're together."

Vanessa touched the pendant. "Tha's an elvish symbol," she said. "It's the moon and star o' the Lady. I know tha' now." She colored, dropped her eyes. "I know about my grandda, too, and about my da. They—"

"I know," said Christopher. Elvish meddling. But Roger had meddled, and now Christopher was meddling. There were all sorts of meddling, he supposed, some more comely than others. "I don't care, Vanessa. You're human. That's all that matters. That's the Vanessa I love."

He kissed her, and then she stepped away as he sprang into his saddle. Her hands were clasped, her face earnest. A wife watching her husband go off to war? He wondered. He hoped.

Hope. The Elves had given him that, too. Should he curse them for that? Should he hate them?

"G'bye, Christopher," said Vanessa.

He thrust the thoughts of immortals from him, smiled down at her. Hope. The Elves had none, men and women— blind though they were—had all. "The French have a better word," he said. "And since, my beloved lady, they're supposed to know all about such things as love and chivalry, maybe I'll take a lesson from them." He wrinkled his nose. "For once." He bent, caught her hand, pressed it to his lips. "Adieu."

CHAPTER 26

For four hours, the men of the Fellowship of Acquisition had pounded at the lithified gates of the castle with an improvised battering ram, and the granite had finally cracked, shivered, and crumbled . . . but just enough to allow one rider to squeeze through at a time. Berard had given orders for the aperture to be enlarged for the wagons and guns, but he and a dozen of his men who possessed the fastest horses had threaded their way out and prepared to set off along the south road.

"What about the baron of Furze and his people?" his new lieutenant had asked.

"Burn them."

"What?"

"Fire the forest. It's tinder dry. And I want the men ready to ride by afternoon. And when they are, Jaques, bring them after us. Bring everything: cannon, supply wagons, everything."

His mind had burned with thoughts of Christopher delAurvre, and now, two days along the south road, it was still burning. All had been going along as planned, and then the baron of Aurverelle had appeared, skipping lightly through the intricacies of his plots like a monkey scampering among the roofs and towers of Shrinerock. Somehow, Christopher had sealed up the castle. Somehow, he had known about that crossbow bolt. And Berard feared that somehow, if he were not killed quickly, he would bring the Fellowship's glorious and profitable future to dust.

He and his men camped that night to the south of the threatening shadows of Malvern, and he noted with approval that the stars to the northeast were hazy with rising smoke. Jaques had done as he was told. Now, if the rest of the expanded Fellowship proved to be as dependable, he might speedily be rid of Christopher, and Adria would fall into his hand like a piece of ripe fruit.

On the third day, the smoke was rising fiercely, the drought-scorched trees and litter igniting quickly and, driven by an east wind, carrying the flames further into the forest. Berard gave a moment's thought to the possibility that all of Malvern might eventually be consumed, but then he shrugged philosophically: if Paul delMari and his people died, that was enough. Forests always grew back.

The horses clattered along the sunbaked surface of the road. Berard could not be absolutely certain that Christopher and his companion were still ahead—they might well have turned off into the pastures and the fields—but he had expert trackers among his party, and nothing that they had seen indicated anything but that they had stayed on the road.

And then, in the early morning, as the road swung in to skirt closely the ranks of trees, they saw Christopher trotting towards them on a gray horse. Unarmored, unaccompanied, his thoughts apparently turned within, he looked very much the foppish noble out for a morning's recreation. He had a sword at his side, true, but what was one sword against a dozen?

Christopher looked up, saw them, stared. Berard rose in his stirrups. "Get him!"

The horses leaped forward. By the time Christopher had realized the threat and wheeled, the gap between him and his enemies had closed by half.

Christopher fled, the road smoking behind him. Berard spurred his horse bloody. To the right was the forest, the trees thickset and impenetrable, to the left was open grassland: the baron was trapped between too much cover and none at all. It was only a matter of time.

Christopher increased his speed. Berard shouted encouragement to his men. "Ten thousand pieces of gold! Red sealed! I want his head!"

In response, Christopher turned his head and stuck out his tongue at his pursuers.

Berard dug the goads on his heels deeper into his horse. "Scum, little cock-a-whoop?" he muttered. "We'll see. I'll cut your throat and have you stuffed and mounted like the miserable monkey you are."

Movement suddenly. To the right.

Berard tore his eyes from Christopher just in time to see

two riders—women, both of them—charging out of the trees. Clad in green and gray, riding without saddle or bridle, they wove effortlessly through the scattered trunks at the edge of Malvern and bore directly down on Berard.

Berard stared. They had to be crazy. They were *attacking*.

But, regardless of their mental state, they were closing quickly, and one of them had a sword; and so Berard pointed at them with a shout. Immediately, three of his men swerved to intercept them. Women they might be, but Berard was not taking any chances, and Christopher was still loose.

Christopher, as though heartened by the women's appearance, had abruptly turned about to drive straight at Berard, sword in hand. Berard stared, aghast. "My God . . . he *is* mad."

Mad or not, Christopher's first stroke caught Berard's parry soundly, and the captain was almost unhorsed. "I told you to get your scum out of Adria," cried the baron. "It's been two days now. You're a dead man, Berard."

"The hell I am." Berard shoved Christopher back and waved his men forward. Surrounding and disarming a single man by sheer force of numbers was not a particularly chivalrous act, but Berard had given up on chivalry years before.

But as he wheeled to give himself room, he was shocked to see that the three men who had set off to intercept the women were now lying on the ground. And the woman with the sword, carrying herself with frightening grace, was again bearing down on him. Her red-gold hair floated free, and her face was both eerily lovely and terrifyingly determined.

Christopher's sword feinted, doubled back, swept in. Berard barely blocked in time, but he was nonetheless confident: the rest of his men were now encircling Christopher, spreading out to surround him, drawing weapons. Ten to one. Only a matter of time.

Before they could complete their envelopment, though, the second woman, dark haired and bearing no weapon save a harp, cut in among them and . . .

She must have done something. Berard had no idea what it was, but abruptly, all the horses save those ridden by Christopher and his allies were rearing, beating the air with frantic forelegs, whinnying shrilly. Berard managed to save himself from being dumped into the road, but a number of his men wound up in the dust.

Angry, Berard threw his weight forward, pounded his horse into obedience, and lashed out with his sword at the dark-haired woman. He landed only a glancing blow, but her arm opened at the shoulder, and her blood was as red as any man's.

"Natil!" Christopher was screaming, and before Berard could get in a killing strike, he was again face-to-face with the baron of Aurverelle.

Christopher's gray eyes were hot, his sword quick, and Berard was suddenly parrying frantically, fighting off a raging flood of blows and thrusts. He looked for help, but his men were still struggling with their horses, and the other woman, the one with the sword, had already plunged in among them and wounded several. Berard's previously favorable odds were suddenly tipping in distressing directions.

But the woman with the sword swept past Christopher. "My lord of Aurverelle," she said with strange courtesy, "I would advise you to flee."

The baron smashed another stroke into Berard's parry. "I should have known it was going to be you, Mirya." He sounded almost irritated. "What about Natil?"

The wounded woman's face was pale. "I will follow. Go, my lord!"

Christopher backed. Berard saw his opportunity and lunged, but a stinging blow from Mirya's sword toppled him from his saddle. Christopher and his rescuers turned their horses and pelted down the road, vanishing around a distant turn as Berard, the wind knocked out of him, struggled to rise, gasping out calls for his men to regroup and follow as soon as they could.

Grimly, he dragged himself to his mount, climbed into the saddle, prodded it into motion. Christopher was ahead. Christopher was going to die.

His horse was weak with a morning's fill of running, but he kept its head pointing to the west. The east wind was a hand at his back, and the telltale dust from the passage of three sets of hooves encouraged him. The signs were obvious. Berard did not need trackers to tell him where the baron and his friends had gone.

And, indeed, it was not long before he saw a village ahead. Its walls were stout and ringed by a ditch and a palisade, but it was still just a village. A small village. A small village that had only men with pikes and a few weedy boys to defend its walls.

He stopped a good distance away and examined it. Just a village. But Christopher was in that village. And Christopher was going to die.

A clatter of hooves behind him. One of his men approached. "Captain!"

"Go fetch the rest of the troops, Raoul," said Berard without turning around. "They shouldn't be any more than a day behind us. I want this village surrounded. I want it taken. I want it destroyed. And I want everybody inside it killed." At last he swung around. "Do you understand?"

Raoul regarded him from dark eyes, and Berard saw his puzzlement. A little village? Throw four thousand men against a little village? For what? Sacks of beans?

"Do it," he said. "Just do it."

Still plainly confused, Raoul nodded, turned his horse, and set off at a trot.

Berard turned his eyes back to the village. "Miserable little monkey."

Christopher and Abel lost no time in preparing Saint Brigid for imminent siege. Within hours, sweating groups of men armed with shovels and baskets had deepened the trench that surrounded the walls and had studded it with pits and traps, and the women had gone out into the fields and gathered in anything that was even vaguely ripe. As the massed body of the free companies approached, raising clouds of dust that echoed the smoke streaming into the distant sky, the gates of the town were shut, fastened, barred, and the gatehouse was rammed full of earth.

Christopher handled shovel and basket along with the rest and supervised the sealing of the gate. "I daresay it's all right," he remarked to Abel. "I don't think we'll be wanting to leave any time soon."

He tried to sound casual and optimistic, but he was dismayed. He was trapped in Saint Brigid along with the villagers, and though the fact that the free companies had now left Shrinerock had made it even more imperative that he get word to the alliance, there was now no way that he could do so.

All day long, the companies poured into the fields that surrounded Saint Brigid and examined with ironic faces the little village that had arrayed itself against them. But at the end of the long columns came the siege guns: great squat things with huge bores. They could batter down walls much thicker than Saint Brigid's in a matter of hours. Tipping and bucking on their tumbrels, they rumbled down the road, and Berard had them brought forward and aimed directly at the gate.

"Now you see why I wanted the dirt in the gate," said Christopher as he and Abel watched from the wall. Beside them, the monkey looked worried. That was all right, though: Christopher was worried, too.

Abel rose, squinted at the guns. "You're a shrewd man, Baron Aurverelle."

"No, I'm mad. Ah . . . stay down, Abel: Berard has a way with crossbows."

Abel nodded and crouched behind the parapet, but the monkey capered in the open, making lewd gestures at the companies. Christopher, laughing without mirth, dragged it into cover. "I wish we could do away with them that easily, little friend," he said. But then he thought of the monkey as he had seen it once, cradled like an infant in the arms of an Elf, and, shuddering, he let it go to resume its dance and its gestures.

He sighed. Christopher and the monkey: still identical twins.

Below, in the village, the people were boarding up their windows. Abel's apprentice was directing the men who were putting up chains across the streets in case Berard's men managed to break through, and Vanessa and Charity were helping Dom Gregorie, the village priest, herd the younger children and the pregnant women into the church, which, thick-walled and at the center of town, offered distance and protection from the fighting.

Christopher settled himself on the inner edge of the wall, dangling his feet, watching. Pikes, swords, farm tools, stones, buckets of molten pitch and seething oil. Poles. Hatchets . . .

Ypris had fallen, and Furze had fallen. How could Saint Brigid—and Vanessa—hope to survive?

A flash of red-gold hair. Mirya, elven and silent, was ascending the steps to the top of the walls. Aside from her garb and her sword, she was much as Christopher remembered her from her visit to Aurverelle. Invariably polite and gracious, even in the middle of a battle, she regarded everything from out of emerald-green eyes that mirrored a deep tranquillity, and yet when she addressed Christopher it was always with a sense of deference.

She too, seemed to be well known in Saint Brigid, and the villagers, though dismayed by Natil's wound, had welcomed Mirya cordially when she had entered the gate with Christopher. They had stood aside respectfully, even admiringly, as she had healed Natil's arm, and they seemed glad and relieved when she had told them that she would be staying in the village to help in the fight against the mercenaries. Now she climbed to the parapet and examined the siege guns. Christopher did not bother to warn her about the crossbows. She was an Elf. She saw the patterns. And sometimes, he recalled, she changed them.

The thought was an ache in his stomach.

"An hour, perhaps, before they are fired," she said.

"So soon? Christopher got to his feet. Yes, Berard was ordering them set up immediately, even before his camp was finished. "That's odd."

"They have no respect for a small village," said the Elf. "They expect an easy conquest."

Abel struck fist into palm. "Well, they'll be dard surprised when they dan get it."

The smith was tense, and Christopher heard the dairyland accent coming out strongly in his speech. He smiled, remembering Vanessa's quaint way with words. "You're from Furze?"

"Nay, m'lord. But my grandda came from tha' part of the country. Francis. The man who made the gates."

Another grandfather. Christopher seemed to move along the shadows of grandfathers. "Well," he said, "we'll soon see how they hold up against guns."

Mirya spoke. "They will not hold."

Christopher turned on her, annoyed. "Thank you, Mirya, for your kind encouragement."

She turned calm eyes on him. "My people see a little more than yours, Baron Christopher. Pray make use of what we have to offer while we are still able to offer it."

"You don't think I've been doing exactly that? How's Natil?"

"She is well."

Just another change of the patterns for Mirya. Effortless. Just like . . .

He grinned to cover the twinge. "See? I use you like I use everyone else."

Mirya smiled. "You are merry, Baron Christopher."

"No," he said, "I'm crazy, remember?" But she knew, he suspected, his thoughts, and he turned back to the guns.

At Nicopolis, siege equipment had been considered dishonorable and unsporting. Real knights, Jean de Nevers had declared, could take the strongest city with only a few ladders and their belief in God. Well, whether Berard possessed belief in God or not, he certainly possessed guns.

"I wonder how long they can keep firing," he said.

"Long enough, I'm afraid," said Abel.

Mirya suddenly lifted her head. "It is unfortunate for them that they have stacked the casks of powder so close to the guns."

Christopher was puzzled. "What do you mean?"

Mirya shook her head, bowed to them in the elven manner, and descended the stairs.

"They're a strange people," said Abel. "But I can't blame her: Malvern's burning like a tallow dip, and Terrill's out there in't."

"Baron Paul, too," said Christopher. "And Mirya and Natil are trapped in here."

"I wouldn't ever say that an Elf was trapped, Baron Christopher."

"Well, what would you call it?"

The monkey suddenly determined that it was going to sit directly on top of Christopher's head. Christopher attempted to dissuade it, and it shrieked and squawked alarmingly.

Abel pointed: the men of the companies were loading the guns. "We'd better go."

"A moment please," said Christopher, and mindful still of crossbow bolts, he stood up on the top of the parapet. "Is that bitch's whelp Berard out there?" he called

"I'm here," came the answer.

The monkey crawled determinedly to his head. Christopher folded his arms and pretended not to take any notice of his new hat. Let them wonder. He actually wished that he had a few pieces of fruit. "How does it feel to be the loser, Berard?"

But on a hunch, he suddenly leaped down and ducked

just as a crossbow bolt whizzed by. "He's quick," he said to Abel. "I'll grant you that."

Berard was shouting orders as Abel dragged Christopher away from the vicinity of the gate, but the baron insisted upon staying on the wall to watch. "Remember," he said. "I'm crazy."

"Yer as sane as me."

"Yes, and you're up here on the wall, too, aren't you?"

Abel growled, but the two men and the monkey peered out from behind a crenel as the guns were loaded and aimed at the mass of iron and earth that blocked the gate. One of Berard's men applied a smoldering fuse to a touchhole. In a moment, a flash of light.

Abel clamped his hand on Christopher's shoulder and shoved him down as the roar of igniting powder combined with the crash of rending metal from the gate. The wall shook, and Christopher knew that only a few more such projectiles would level it.

But, a moment later, another detonation thundered through the air, and then another, and another: a long, sustained series of rumbles and booms that made Christopher, in spite of the danger, rise up to take a cautious look.

The mercenary camp was filled with smoke and more smoke. The casks of powder, stacked in haste much too close to the cannon, had obviously caught a stray spark, ignited, and exploded in an incendiary blast that had destroyed the guns, toppled the wagons, overthrown tents, dismembered men, and leveled everything within twenty yards.

Another cask blew up. Smoke, fire, and splinters rolled out. Berard's men were running, and not a few were dying.

Christopher stared, recalling Mirya's words. Powder, peach trees: it was all the same to the Elves.

CHAPTER 27

An east wind was gusting through the canopy of leaves and branches that formed the roof of Malvern Forest, but though its force among the trunks was muted, smoke was nonetheless filtering along the elven path, first as tendrils that groped deep into the wood, then as a haze that stung the throats of Paul delMari and his people, then as a gray cloud that burned in their lungs and threatened to choke them.

Terrill still led the way, waiting patiently for his human charges to stagger along as fast as they could, but always encouraging them and urging them onward. As the smoke thickened and the humans' pace consequently slowed, though, his eyes narrowed and his mouth acquired a determined set. At present, he told Paul, it was not the flames that were the danger: it was the smoke. Another day or more lay between the refugees and the western edge of the forest, and by then . . .

Despair was growing on the baron. He watched his people grope their way through the acrid clouds. "Maybe you should just go on without us," he said heavily.

The Elf looked offended. "I said that I would lead you through Malvern."

"But . . . the smoke. Even Elves have limits, Terrill."

"I believe that the Inquisition has proven that, my good lord." Terrill's gray eyes lost none of their dispassionate calm, but he shrugged as though willing a painful thought to pass. "I will just have to lead you more quickly."

And so, it seemed, he did, for he redoubled his efforts, and Paul began to suspect that the Elf was giving aid of a non-physical sort to those who were weakening under the strain of what had become a forced march through a poisonous atmosphere. Beneath his hands, those who were nearly strangling with the smoke rose to walk again, and even Prunella, whose eight-and-a-half-month belly appeared bent on putting her on the ground, managed a wan smile and staggered on.

All through the day and into the night they struggled, measuring out their rests by minutes, their meals by mouthfuls. But the smoke continued to thicken. Paul guessed that the fire was raging hellishly by now, eating its way through a dry forest, urged on by the continuing east wind. And that, too, he was sure, was a strain on Terrill, for the forest was as much of a home as the Elves had ever known. With what emotions did the Elf confront this final insult to his fading kind? Paul, fresh from having lost his castle, could only guess. He had lived in Shrinerock for forty years, but the Elves had been one with Malvern since the time of the first saplings.

The path shimmered in his sight as much from the pervasive toxins in the air as from the magic that sustained it. Paul stumbled, stumbled again. He wanted to breathe, he had to breathe, but he could find nothing to fill his lungs save smoke, and his heart was empty.

He struck the ground, lay still. "I've failed," he murmured. "I tried, dear Lady, but it wasn't enough."

Birds called wildly from the branches far above, exploding into frantic and blind flight as the thickening smoke overpowered their nocturnal reluctance. In the distance, Paul heard the frantic rushings and collisions and bellows and cries of panicked animals as they fled towards the west, warned by the smoke and their instincts that their home was lost.

Lost. Paul was lost, his people were lost, the Elves were lost. Everything was . . .

He looked up to find Martin standing over him. The lad had stripped off his tunic and hat, and had been laboring barechested alongside Terrill and the men of the estate, coaxing, ordering, cajoling, dragging the people towards the dwindling hope of safety. Lithe and strong, Martin was dripping with sweat, his face was gray, and his arms and chest were smeared with dirt and dust, but he knelt beside Paul, took his arm. "Come, my lord. You can't lie here."

Paul rested his forehead on the ground, his eyes clenched. "I should lie here and die." Where were his smiles now? His little daft witticisms? His boyish boundings along the halls of Shrinerock? Those, it seemed, belonged to another life, another century, another age. Much better that old dod-

dering men like Paul delMari should just die—along with
their friends and their sons—and get it over with.

Martin was not satisfied. He pulled Paul's arm about his
neck and stood up, dragging the baron to his feet. "Would
you have let me say something like that when you were
teaching me how to use a sword?"

Paul turned hollow eyes on him. "What good is it, Martin? You just wanted to hide. You wouldn't even let me
knight you, and now you're going to die in the middle of
Malvern along with the rest of us."

"Don't talk like that, my lord."

Paul hung his head. It had all come to naught.

Gently, with his free hand, Martin touched Paul's cheek.
When the baron looked up, the lad was crying. "Don't talk
like that.." He sobbed. ". . . Father."

Paul shut his eyes, rested his head against Martin's.

Martin dragged him forward. "Come on, Father," he
said, stumbling over the words. "We have to get to Aurverelle."

The clouds of smoke were almost opaque now, a sustained chorus of coughing was coming from his people, and
Aurverelle was still miles away. It seemed hopeless.

But Paul gripped Martin's hand. "We'll make it, my
son."

The loss of the siege guns and of well over a hundred
men only delayed Berard's plans. Throughout the remainder
of the day, the men of the companies buried their dead,
tended their wounded, and established camp, but with the
next morning came a shout from Berard and a rushing of
armed men at the walls of Saint Brigid.

The villagers were ready. The palisade took the brunt of
the charge and forced the attackers to either climb over it
or break it down in the face of a pelting hail of slingstones,
arrows, and sacks of dung. But even if they succeeded in
penetrating it, there was no longer a bridge over the deep
ditch that lay between them and the village walls, and
weighted with armor and weapons as they were, they were
forced to stumble down one side and clamber laboriously
up the other, now and again catching an ankle or a leg in
the pits and traps that pocked the bottom. And while they
struggled across, there were, to be sure, more rocks, more
arrows . . . and more dung.

It was Christopher who had proposed this last, odoriferous defense, for he knew from personal experience that armor weighing anywhere from one hundred to two hundred pounds was very nearly intolerable to wear even under the best conditions. Given the stifling heat and dust, Berard's men were doubtless anything but happy, and Christopher was eager to add to their misery.

He himself flung a sackful that, trailing a spray of droplets, arced through the air and smacked solidly into Berard's visor. A moment of stunned shock on Berard's part, and then the captain fumbled frantically for the fastenings of his helmet, stripped off the clumsy thing, bent, and threw up.

Christopher was gratified. And his satisfaction increased even more when, a moment later, a cobble-sized stone caught Berard on the head and sent him sprawling onto the ground with a loud clank.

His men saw him fall, hesitated. But as two of his companions hauled him to his feet, he was already shouting at them to continue. They turned and went on, slogging through obstacles and disgust to reach the walls, only to find themselves then flooded with boiling oil and flaming pitch and pounded with rocks the size of boulders.

Berard lost men. Inevitably, so did the villagers. Berard's crossbowmen were staying out of range of dung and missiles, but their weapons, windlassed up to two hundred and fifty pounds of tension, easily cast twelve-inch bolts as far as the walls. At such an extreme distance, their aim was not good, so they clustered their attacks; and after a few bracketing shots, heavy rains of pointed steel periodically dropped into the village.

Behind the walls, the village women took charge of the wounded, and what they could not cure with bandages and water was attended to by elven hands, for Natil harped and healed, and Mirya left her sword in its sheath as her magic closed wounds and stanched of blood. Starlight and music mingled with the dust and din of battle as the Elves did their work.

Christopher raged and catcalled at Berard, scampering from one side of the ramparts to the other as fast as if he had indeed been a monkey. He threw stones and dung, helped hoist boulders into position, even grabbed a bow and sent off a few arrows himself.

"Surrender!" Berard was shouting, but he had drifted too

close, and one of Christopher's bodkin-point missiles caught him in the chest. The steel plate turned the head, but Berard looked shaken, then enraged. "Damn you! Yield!"

"No!" Christopher shouted back with a foppish lilt to his voice. "You'll hurt us!" And another arrow clanked against Berard's cuirass.

Berard had several thousand men, and eventually, simply as the result of pressure and momentum, they reached the walls. Scaling ladders went up, clattering into place against the stones of the parapet. The hands of the villagers went out with pikes and staves and forked sticks. The scaling ladders went back down.

But they went up once more, and then again, rising like reeds from a turbulent lake. The crossbowmen cranked, loaded, released; and shouting encouragement to one another, Berard's men swarmed upwards.

A group of nearly fifty mounted a thicket of ladders near Christopher, and he signaled frantically to the men who were hoisting a cauldron of pitch into place. A nod from them, and brimming with boiling and smoking liquid, the cauldron pivoted at the end of its crossbeam, swinging towards him, missing the heads of the defenders by only a hand's breadth.

Christopher grabbed the lip of the hot vessel with his gloved hands and muscled it into place directly above the mass of climbing brigands. "Give up?" he called down to them.

He heard curses from below. With a shrug, he let the pitch go.

It flooded down, burning, scalding. Berard's men fell back, some plainly on fire, some suffocating in their layers of plate and mail, some simply but obviously demoralized. Another rain of stones and shit, and they started away from the walls. They slid and stumbled back down into the ditch and began struggling up towards the confining palisade. But, black and vengeful, Abel rose up with a huge sledgehammer, took aim, and hurled the tool at the props that were supporting an improvised dam in the stream that ran hard by the town.

The drought had reduced the stream to a trickle, but over time, the dam had built a sizable reservoir behind it. Abel's hammer smashed directly into the props, and the waters leaped forward with a roar, rushed down the canal, and inundated the ditch.

Christopher watched Berard's men flail and drown as he wiped the sticky pitch from his gloves. "Thank you, Abel. And they'll have a devil of a time mining under that now, too," he said.

"Aye," said Abel, "but they're not going to give up that easily."

"No. I daresay it'll be siege engines next."

"They'll have to get 'em over the ditch."

"They've got the time." Christopher looked out at the retreating men, could not resist another catcall. But a crossbow bolt smacked into the ramparts inches from him and cut it short.

Indeed, Berard had plenty of time. Saint Brigid was besieged, and its people, including Christopher and the Elves, were trapped. The free companies could amuse themselves, hunt, and wait for the food supplies of the village, already scant because of the drought and the time of year, to give out.

Berard, though, did not appear to be overly interested in starving the village into submission. He had attacked actively, and since he was now shouting orders that had to do with battering rams and assault towers, he obviously was going to continue along similar lines. Christopher had no idea why. Perhaps, he considered, Berard was as crazy as a certain Christopher delAurvre.

He put his hands to his head in frustration. "I've got to get to Furze. Everything Berard's got is right here at Saint Brigid. It's too good to let go. Dammit . . ."

He looked up to see the monkey perched on the parapet before him. It stuck out its tongue, and viciously, Christopher returned the gesture, then repeated it at Berard who, though still giving orders regarding further assault, appeared to be completely bewildered by his opponent.

But, a moment later, Christopher was also bewildered, for above the sound of the rushing water in the ditch, the cries from the men who still floundered in it, and the clatter of staves and shouts of triumph from the so-far successful defenders of Saint Brigid's walls, he heard Natil screaming to him:

"Christopher! Vanessa! The church!"

The two Elves had their hands full of bleeding men, but

their faces told Christopher everything. Without bothering to shove his way to steps or ladder, he leaped from the wall, caught the end of the rope that had held the cauldron, and used his momentum to carry him out over the street and down to the ground. He was already running when his feet touched down, and when he exploded into the church, he found that Vanessa, Charity, Dom Gregorie, and several of the pregnant women, armed with heavy candlesticks and staves, were attempting to hold a dozen armed and mailed men away from the other women and children who had taken shelter within the thick walls.

Christopher understood. Taking advantage of the battle at the main gate, a group of free company men had obviously scaled the wall on the other side of the village with the intent of doing as much damage as they could.

A pool of blood and a scattering of soft corpses about the nave told of the men's success, but Vanessa and her companions were fighting on. Vanessa herself, with only a stick in her hand, was confronting a man easily three times her size. "Christopher!"

The baron did not wait. Leaping forward, he slashed the man's legs out from under him, then followed through with a chop to his face. The man's features were abruptly buried in blood, and as his companions turned to face this new threat, one fell beneath Gregorie's candlestick. Overweight, pop-eyed, and unspeakably angry, the priest waded towards another, and the soldier seemed torn for a moment between terror and laughter.

He went down a moment later beneath several of the pregnant women. Their faces white with rage and streaked with the blood of their sisters and their children, they toppled him to the floor with staves and held him down with their weight of their own bodies. Someone produced a hammer, and the man was battered into lifelessness in an instant.

The other men were counterattacking, but the women, unarmored and quick, scattered from them. Christopher struck again, killed one, and kicked another into the arms of the women. The hammer fell once more.

Gregorie attempted to repeat his success, but he was backhanded across the room. The priest stumbled, fell. One of the soldiers pointed at Christopher, who was already closing on him. "That's ten thousand florins right there, mates. Seal the doors."

The man was skilled, but—strike, parry, riposte, back-slash—he dropped with a clatter that echoed off the high ceiling of the church. The interchange, though, had given the others a chance to surround Christopher, and when he felt a mailed fist grab his hair, he knew that a sword through his neck was imminent.

The hand in his hair wavered, and a high, determined cry told him that Vanessa had thrown herself on the back of his assailant and was beating on his helmeted head with her fists, looking for eye slits, openings, something . . .

Cursing, the soldier reached back for her, groping. Christopher got his hair loose, kicked two attackers away, and turned around, slashing. But the man was already down, for an unexpected ally had joined the baron. Tall, slender, deadly, Mirya had appeared, and her sword was no longer sheathed.

"Elthia!"

She drove into the free company men, her movements as hypnotic as they were lethal. Sidestepping and weaving, she simultaneously blocked counterstrokes from two opponents, backflipped behind them, spun, and killed them both with the same strike, her sword slicing through leather and iron as though through dry leaves.

Berard's men gave up on the doors and closed on Christopher and the Elf. One grabbed Vanessa and dragged her away. He started to put his sword to her belly, but Charity appeared and smashed a pewter candle holder down onto his head. He reeled, dropped Vanessa. The girl seized the candlestick from her teacher and began beating his helmet into a piece of bent metal.

Christopher was attempting to fight his way to her side, but while one of his opponents went down, another planted a heavy boot in his stomach. He staggered back, caught his feet on the altar steps, and crashed into the statue of the Virgin that stood at the edge of the sanctuary.

He sat down hard on the stone floor, staring stupidly at the two soldiers who were approaching with lifted swords. But the life-sized statue, jarred loose from its pedestal, was toppling forward, and not only did it catch and block the swords, it also knocked one man senseless and fell across

Christopher in such a way that it sheltered him from the other.

Christopher's wits returned in a moment, and he found himself looking into the face of the statue. It was of plain, unadorned wood, but the baron did not need paint or ornament to tell him that Her hair was dark, Her eyes gray, Her robes of blue and silver. . . .

He stared. He knew. *"Elthia."*

A fleeting glimpse of Divinity. He tore his eyes from Her as his second opponent kicked the statue away and slashed. The vision fled, and Christopher struggled to block, but the man abruptly lurched backward as a shrieking caricature of a human being swung down from the ceiling beams and smacked into his face, biting and clawing.

He recovered in a moment, grabbed the valiant monkey in a mailed fist. Throwing it to the ground so hard that it split open like a ripe grape, he trampled it into a smear of blood and viscera; but its bestial sacrifice had given Christopher a chance to rise, set his feet, and deliver a blow that revenged it instantly.

A few feet away, Mirya's sword went through the ribs of one opponent, then another, then a third. She moved effortlessly, killed with surgical precision. Berard's men died, their blood pooling on the stone floor, joining with that of their comrades and the women and children they had slaughtered.

One left. He was rushing in from the main door where he had been standing guard, and he had almost reached the crossing of the church when it apparently dawned on him that he was alone. After staring for a moment at Mirya and Christopher, he turned to run, but his escape was blocked at the transept doors by a half dozen village women who had seen too much killing in the last few minutes to be bothered with the fact that they were facing a man with a sword. Between him and the west door, though, stood only Vanessa and Charity. The old weaver was unarmed. Vanessa had but a candlestick.

He lunged for them, sword flashing, looking for something to kill. Vanessa stepped in front of Charity, raised her weapon. Christopher shouted for them to get out of the way, but the girl stood her ground; and as the big man rushed at her, she prepared to strike.

But when the sword fell, Charity threw herself on Vanessa, shoved her out of the way, and took the heavy blow herself. Blood was suddenly everywhere, bursting from the gash in her head, flooding from her mouth. She fell, twitching, eyes glassy, dead before she hit the floor; but she had slowed the soldier's run sufficiently for Mirya to catch up with him and plant her sword in the middle of his back.

He staggered on a few more paces, then tumbled to the floor in a clatter of metal and leather. Mirya herself, her dispassion and tranquillity gone, dropped to her knees beside the body of the old woman, put her bloody hands to her face.

"Ai, Elthiai!" she sobbed. "Once . . . I could only save you once, and now . . . oh, Charity . . ." The Elf looked up, and her streaming eyes found Christopher. "Many years ago, she told me that she had . . . things to do. "I . . . did not foresee that this would be among them." Her eyes closed in pain. "I did not foresee anything."

Vanessa was cradling Charity's gashed and lifeless head in her lap. Her homespun was heavy with blood and smears of brains. Her head was thrown back, her face contorted, and Christopher knew that, behind her clenched eyes, Vanessa saw nothing—no patterns, no futures, no peace— nothing save the ending of the haven that she had found for a time, a little time, in Saint Brigid.

Other men and women of the village were arriving at a run, their wooden shoes and leather shoes clattering down the length of the too-silent nave. Some recognized their sisters and children among the living, some found them among the dead. Abel saw what was left of his mother lying in Vanessa's lap.

He knelt and, shaking, touched the blood-smeared face. Vanessa regarded him mutely, her voice silenced by sorrow, and he put his free arm about her shoulders. Blond and dark, fair and swarthy, they put their heads against one another, and wept.

Christopher, drained, bit back curses and shrieks and let the living grieve for the dead without accompanying antics and capers. Paul delMari had left his doddering humor behind in Shrinerock; and in the blood-soaked church of a village with which he was linked by fate, history, and elven intervention, Christopher delAurvre left his madness.

But Mirya bent, kissed Charity's bloody face, held Vanessa and Abel for several minutes. And then, to Christopher's surprise, she rose and approached him.

"Did you say once, my lord, that other barons had joined you in your efforts?" she asked. Tragedy screamed from her eyes, and though her voice was controlled, even, there was a weight of terrifying purpose behind it.

"Yes." Christopher's voice was hoarse. "They're gathering at Shrinerock. I hope."

"It is in Saint Brigid that they are needed, messire."

Surrounded as he was by the blood and bodies of the innocent, his ears filled with the cries of grieving men and women, Christopher wanted to strike her for her complacent truism. "You don't think I know that? I'd fetch them in a heartbeat if I could get out of this town."

Mirya shook her head. "I . . . will take you to Shrinerock."

"But . . . the sentries . . . the soldiers . . . Berard's got the fields crawling with them."

Jaw trembling, the Elf met his eyes. "I saved the Free Towns from your grandfather's plots, and I made sure that he could not further them. Berard's meshes are but loosely woven in comparison, and my debt to you is as yet unredeemed."

Christopher stared, stunned, unable at first to grasp what she was telling him.

"I will take you through the free company camp tonight," said Mirya slowly. "And then we will journey to Shrinerock."

CHAPTER 28

With the coming of night, the streets of Saint Brigid were silent and empty. Chains spanned the intersections, guards kept watch at the crossings. On the wall, anxious men strained their eyes and ears into the darkness that lay between the town and the deeper darkness of the forest, searching for movement or sound. Within the houses, women cared for the dead, sewing shrouds, waking the bodies of husbands, sisters, sons, daughters, friends, singing softly over the still forms the long, slow melodies of plainchant.

Charity's house was empty and still. Christopher could hardly believe that a single, aging woman had been able to fill a home with so much life and light, but it was true. With just Vanessa and himself within its walls, it was as a husk, an empty shell.

Vanessa was angry, crying, and he held her while they sat by the fire. "They killed her, Christopher. They just killed her! They killed them a'. There wan't any reason for it. They just wanted to kill!"

Her face was pressed to his chest, and that was good, for he did not want her to see how utterly helpless he felt. In a few minutes, Mirya would come for him, and she would lead him through the rings of eager-eyed robbers that surrounded the town, but there was no smack of empowerment to that particular turning of his personal and ephemeral maze, for it was by an elven hand that he would escape Berard's snares.

The same hand that had struck down his grandfather.

"I ha' to do sa'thing, Christopher." Vanessa spoke with clenched teeth and clenched fists. "I can't let them do tha' and get awa' wi' it."

"Shh," said Christopher. "There's nothing we can do here. We'll just have to hope I can reach the alliance."

"I've got to do sa'thing. I wi' do sa'thing. I can . . ."
She lifted her head and stared at the fire. "It's just patterns
. . . in't it? Just . . . patterns . . ."

There was a light in her eyes that terrified him. He pulled
her head against his chest once more. "Shh . . ."

A tap at the door, and Mirya and Natil entered. The
harper bowed formally to Christopher. "I ask leave, my
lord, to stay in Saint Brigid. There are folk here who require
my skills."

Christopher stood up. He might as well have held a hungry lion on a two-foot tether as command an Elf. "Natil,
enough of this charade. I never really had you in my service." He glanced at Vanessa. She trusted these beings im-
plicitly, would have done anything for them. And he himself
had told Natil that he trusted her with his life. Did a del-
Aurvre say things like that so lightly? Was the sperm getting
that weak?

"You'll always have a place of honor in Aurverelle, Natil," he said. "You'll always be welcome. But I can't give
you orders. And I won't. Stay if you need to. Mirya will . . ."
He hesitated, stumbling over the past.

But Mirya bowed deeply. "I will take you to meet the
forces of the alliance, Baron Christopher. But we must go
now." She turned to Natil, embraced her. "Farewell, my
sister. *Alanae a Elthia yai oulisi.*"

Their heads were pressed together, and there was urgency
in their faces. Natil's lips moved almost soundlessly: *"Manea."*

So like humans. Were they really that different? His eyes
aching, Christopher stooped and kissed Vanessa. The light
was still in her eyes, and it reminded him unnervingly of
the radiance that he saw in Mirya and Natil. "Adieu,
sweet," he said. "I'll be back. And then . . ."

She shook her head, laid her finger upon his lips. "Dan,"
she said urgently. "Dan make plans, Christopher. Patterns
can change i' a heartbeat, an' you might na wan' me after."

Her words were grievous, but his signet was still on her
hand, and her pendant—elven or not—was about his neck.
He held her greedily, possessively, just like the delAurvres
always held their women. "I'll always want you, Vanessa.
No matter what. I'm not going to let you go again."

But it was he who had to go now, and a few minutes later,
Christopher and Mirya slipped over the edge of the village

wall and lowered themselves to the ground in the deepest shadow they could find.

Mirya's impenetrable calm had returned. Christopher sensed that she was examining the encampment of the free companies as though it were an opponent in a hand-to-hand fight. Christopher heard shouts and laughter, but he could see nothing save faint variations in the darkness of the forest and the light from the torches and lamps that illuminated the free company camp. He was reduced to holding Mirya's hand—clasping the same flesh that had wreaked profound change on his grandfather—when they left the shelter of the wall and made for the ditch.

The ground turned soft beneath Christopher's boots, and he slipped in something fetid and slimy that he was glad he could not see. They descended, but though the Elf, as usual, moved noiselessly, Christopher found that the mud sucked at his boots with a sound that his tension magnified into shouts and thunderclaps.

Mirya put her lips to his ear. "Be easy," she whispered. "The sentries are not close to us here. The difficulties will begin in earnest after we have passed the palisade."

Christopher wondered whether she knew that, in reality, his difficulties had begun in earnest the moment she had revealed herself to be the Elf who had struck his grandfather.

Peach trees. He kept thinking of peach trees.

But he crossed the ditch with her, climbed the bank, and approached the palisade. It was badly broken, and they had no difficulty passing through. But as Mirya had said, they were now closer to Berard's sentries, and the entire area was ringed with guards and the horses and tents and equipment that inevitably accompanied the movement of nearly four thousand men.

"Hold," Mirya whispered suddenly. "Hold still."

Christopher froze. His hand started for the grip of his sword, but he stopped instantly when he realized that Mirya's order had doubtless included even such comparatively trivial actions.

"A moment, my lord," said the Elf, and she slipped away.

Christopher stood motionless, stranded, blind, forcing himself to believe in the Elves and in their good will as he had once forced himself to believe that, yes, a man could walk from Nicopolis to Aurverelle.

And he had so walked. Truly, a man could journey a thousand miles on foot; and, to be sure, the Elves could bring healing and assistance. But where did that leave Roger? Had he been sick? That depended upon one's point of view. Had he been healed? A matter of opinion. What the devil *was* healing, anyway? What was help?

A stirring, a sense of sagging, then silence. In a moment, Mirya was back at his side. He felt her take his hand again . . . immortal flesh, magical flesh . . .

. . . help and healing . . . like Vanessa . . .

. . . like his grandfather?

"Let us go," she whispered. "If we are silent, we can gain the trees and cut through the forest, thereby saving time."

Christopher glanced at her. "Mirya, the forest is on fire."

"Haste is imperative, messire," she said. "Berard will renew the siege tomorrow. I will deal with the fire."

Christopher was baffled. "How?"

He sensed a smile. Then: "Elves are known for being ingenious."

Together, they slipped toward the fields, dropped on their bellies, crawled under cover of what crops had not been entirely burnt flat by the drought or ground down by the passage of Berard's troops. Minute by slow minute, they inched their way forward as the stars wheeled and the moon threatened to rise.

A horse cantered across the fields, its rider holding a torch high. Mirya hissed a warning, and they both flattened themselves among the furrows. The Elf took a long, slow breath, tensed. Christopher sensed that she was doing . . . something. The rider passed. Mirya sighed.

"I did not foresee that," she said.

"You're not foreseeing much these days," said Christopher, but he felt the Elf flinch.

"Our time is over," she said softly.

He might as well have struck her. "I'm sorry. I shouldn't have said that."

He caught a flash of her eyes. "There are many things we do that we later regret," she said.

He knew what she was referring to. He struggled with words, but he knew none that could bear a sufficient weight

of double meanings, uncertain emotions. "Mirya . . .
I . . ."

"Peace. Let us go."

They worked their way across the field, stopping frequently while Mirya examined the obscure patterns of the
world, then continuing on. A waning moon was rising by
the time they reached the cover of outlying bushes and the
first ranks of trees, and Christopher looked back at the village, faint in the faint light. Fifty years ago, were it not for
Mirya, the Free Towns, Saint Brigid among them, would
have ceased to exist. The Inquisition would have come and
gone, and Roger would have taken the human gleanings of
what it left. There would be no tolerance today, no clasping
of elven and human hands, no safe place in which a girl
from Furze Hamlet could find the help necessary to free
herself from her torment.

He put his hands to his face. "Oh, dear Lady . . ."

"May Her hand be upon you, Christopher." There was
a hint of benediction in Mirya's tone, but she turned and
led him off into the trees.

Blindly, Christopher stumbled after her. He wanted to
hate her, but he had begun to despise himself for that very
reason.

Jerome was busy these days, for in the absence of both
the master and the seneschal of Aurverelle, all the admin-
istration of the estate fell into his hands; and these matters,
difficult enough in the best of times, were further compli-
cated both by the drought and the current absence of almost
every man who could wield a weapon.

He coped. That was his duty. As a man of humility and
honesty, though, he freely admitted that the women of the
barony were assuming the tasks of the men with astonishing
spirit. Raffalda was showing a gratifying talent with large-
scale accounts and organization, and the townswomen and
countrywomen were picking up spades and hoes and tending to the job of providing water to the parched fields with
fruitful determination.

But in the east, as though to mock their efforts, the fire
that was eating its way through Malvern grew and advanced,
spreading, stretching far to north and to south. The odor of
burning leaves and wood was a constant presence, and
driven by the strong east wind, smoke occasionally puffed

across the treetops like a patchy fog. If the fire reached the western edge of Malvern, the fields and villages of Aurverelle might well follow the trees into charred uselessness, but at times that seemed to be but a small thing when compared to the magnitude of the destruction that was overtaking league upon league of the parched forest.

Deer, panicked and disoriented, were appearing regularly in the fields close to the trees; likewise wild swine and bear. Birds fled in flocks to the safety of the Aleser. Badgers staggered out of the smoky haze that lay thick on the forest floor and lay wheezing among the dry furrows. Squirrels bounded up the road to Aurverelle as though to implore human aid. Everything that could creep, fly, or run was moving to the west, away from the fire, out of the forest.

And there were others, too. . . .

One of the village girls who was helping the understaffed castle by acting as lookout and messenger came running into Jerome's office late one afternoon, skirts and hair flying. "Lord Bailiff," she said, eyes wide, "there are people coming out of Malvern!"

Jerome was on his feet in a moment, thoughts of brigands flashing through his old, methodical mind. Brigands. And only a few guards to defend the castle. Well, there were still old men, women, and girls left, and all of them were Aurverelle folk: the robbers would soon find out that they were not dealing with a bunch of flatlanders.

But as he was mentally sorting through what orders he should give, one of the remaining guards showed up with the news that the strangers were unarmed, that there were many women and numerous children among them. The smoke, he said, was pursuing them like hounds, and many had fallen gasping at the edge of the fields.

Brigands? No, something else. Something possibly even more urgent. "For God's sake, gather the men and women and go help them out," Jerome snapped, and then, after blinking at the wall for a moment, wondering who on earth would have been in the forest besides hermits, he caught up his habit and ran down the corridor, down the steps, and outside, calling for a horse as he went.

His questions were answered when he reached the edge of the forest and joined the small group of field workers who were endeavoring to help the strangers. The latter, as reported, were many, and, yes, there was a sizable number of women, young mothers, and children among them, as well as a number of guards bearing the gryphon and silver star of the delMari family.

Shrinerock. What?

"My good Brother Jerome!" Martin Osmore was approaching. The lad was stripped to the waist, his skin was smeared with dirt, and his dark eyes were red with smoke. An older man leaned on his arm, and both looked infinitely tired.

Jerome froze. What, indeed? Perverts in the forest?

But the older man patted Martin on the shoulder and, a little unsteadily, went up to Jerome. He offered his hand. "Brother Jerome? I'm Baron Paul delMari." Jerome took his hand absently, his eyes wandering back to Martin. A sodomite . . .

Paul frowned. He attempted to clear his throat disapprovingly and wound up coughing for the better part of a minute. "Master Bailiff," he said at last, "my castle has been taken by brigands, and Malvern Forest is burning because they fired it in an attempt to kill all of us. We ask for succor."

"Yes . . . yes . . . of course . . ." Jerome was confused. Baron Paul and Martin? And the forest . . . deliberately fired?

About him, the women who had been working in the fields were attending to the refugees. Some carried women and children away from the haze of smoke and into the clearer air. Others banded together to support a group of Benedictine monks who were almost unconscious. Cries of *Some water over here, please,* and *Give her air* and *Breathe, child, breathe* tossed back and forth like wind-driven branches. A short distance away, a young woman appeared to have gone into premature labor, and an Aurverelle midwife was just now arriving on pillion behind one of the castle guards.

It was noise and confusion, the racket and din and dust of human beings. Perhaps three hundred people had staggered out of the forest, and most of them needed immediate attention.

Jerome tore his eyes away from them and found himself looking again at Martin's naked torso. The lad was as streaked and dirty as a laboring man, and the friar realized that, regardless of what had been done with that pale body in the past, it had most recently been used for work that was more honorable than any other.

He got down off his horse and bowed to Paul. "Aurverelle is open to you and your people, Lord Baron. Enter and refresh yourselves. I . . ." He stole another glance at Martin. Sodomites in Aurverelle? Honorable or not, what was the world coming to? ". . . cannot but believe that Messire Christopher would have it so."

Martin looked as though he guessed the reason for Jerome's hesitation, but he seemed determined to ignore it.

"Terrill!" One of the women was kneeling over the crumpled form of a child. "She's stopped breathing!"

A young man who had been helping the last of Paul's people out of the trees dashed to her side. After examining the girl for a moment, he opened her mouth, set his lips to hers, and pumped her lungs full of his own breath. He repeated the treatment once, then again.

Paul watched for a moment, then sighed, passed a hand through his sooty hair. "Thank you, Master Bailiff," he said. "We are grateful to you for your . . ." He glanced at Martin knowingly. The lad's mouth was set. ". . . kind offer. But many of us won't be staying long. If you would be so kind as to provide me and my men with horses and equipment, we'll ride to join with the alliance." His face was one that had seen a good deal of laughter, but it was lined with care at present, and as Jerome watched, it darkened with anger. "And we will go and deal with these criminals."

Martin looked at Paul. "You're not going without me."

Paul wrapped an arm about the lad. "Never, Martin. If Jerome is willing, we'll not be here any longer than it takes to clear our lungs, eat, and take a bath."

At the edge of the trees, the young man who had been tending the fallen girl straightened. The child stirred, gasped, breathed; and the mother, weeping, threw her arms about the neck of the unorthodox physician. He suffered her thanks for a moment, then kissed the child, stood, and bowed to them both.

"Terrill," called Martin. "We're going to Shrinerock."

The young man looked up at Martin's words, then approached. Clad in green and gray, a sword at his hip, he seemed untouched by the smoke and the dirt. His face was womanly, and his gray eyes held more than a measure of unearthly light.

"Terrill," said Paul, "this is Brother Jerome, Messire Christopher's chief bailiff. Jerome, Terrill of Malvern."

Jerome noticed that the introduction had accorded Terrill the higher honor, but he reminded himself that he was but a friar, and that therefore he should not be concerned about such things. Nevertheless, it was curious. And those eyes . . .

Terrill bowed. "I am honored to meet you, Brother Jerome." But he turned to Martin and Paul. "Why do you wish to go to Shrinerock?"

"To . . ." Paul looked disconcerted. "To join with Christopher against the brigands."

Terrill nodded. "You may find Messire Christopher at Shrinerock," he said, "but you would do better to ride directly south, for the free companies are besieging Saint Brigid."

Paul stared. "You're sure of this?"

"My beloved and I are as one in many things," said Terrill. "She is at present guiding Christopher to meet the alliance at Shrinerock, so as to bring them to the companies."

Paul suddenly acquired a crafty look. "And so, if we take our men, and come down from the north . . ."

Martin started to laugh. "And the alliance strikes from the east . . ."

"Then we hit them with two fists at once!"

Terrill's expression—calm, evaluating—had not changed. As far as Jerome could tell, he regarded any thoughts of approaching battle with perfect neutrality. But that was, perhaps, to be expected, for given his demeanor, the light in his eyes, and his uncanny knowledge of what was occurring many miles away, it was obvious that the young man was not human.

Unconsciously, Jerome stepped away from Terrill. There were old stories . . .

Martin stopped laughing, examined the friar critically. "Fra Jerome," he said with some impatience, "sodomites and Elves have come to your door, and I'm afraid that you'll just have to get used to them both."

Elves. Jerome was speechless. His spies of the intellect had deserted him utterly.

"Spoken like a delMari," said Paul. "And thank you, Terrill, for your help. Will you be coming with us?"

"I have kin in Saint Brigid," said the Elf dispassionately. "I would not willingly let them suffer at the hands of such as threaten them." He turned his head towards Malvern and, after a moment, shut his eyes as though in pain. "Or burn our home."

"Well, Jerome?" said Martin.

Jerome floundered, at once outnumbered and out of his depth. "You are . . . all welcome," he said slowly. "And you shall have whatever you need, my . . . uh . . . son."

Paul shook his head, tightened his arm about Martin's shoulders. "No, Jerome," he said. "*My* son."

CHAPTER 29

Mirya appeared determined to reach the alliance forces as quickly as possible, and to this end, she had struck off directly across Malvern, heading straight for the still-spreading forest fire. As the night and part of the first day passed, the smoke grew palpably thicker, and by afternoon, though Mirya seemed unaffected by the foul air, Christopher was coughing.

"We need to stop," she said when the sun was directly overhead. "You must rest."

Christopher decided that he needed pure air far more than rest. In fact, with the trunks of the trees now distinctly washed by a gray haze, he had no confidence that, if he went to sleep, he would ever wake up.

"I understand," said Mirya.

Christopher hacked uselessly, his lungs full of what felt like burning wool. "I wish you people wouldn't read my mind. I've got some thoughts that I'd like to keep private."

Mirya half smiled. "Are you referring to the lustful ones regarding Natil? I assure you: she was flattered."

Christopher glared at the Elf, but she indicated that he should lie down.

"Rest. Sleep," she said. "You are safe here. I am sorry that I have so taxed you."

Christopher remained on his feet. "It's necessary."

"That is true." Mirya maintained her irritating tranquillity. "But it is also necessary for your kind to rest, and though I have no excuse for such a lapse, I sometimes forget that. I will shield you from the smoke."

Christopher stiffened. There it was. Peach trees. "You're going to work magic on me, aren't you?"

Behind their calm gleam, Mirya's eyes were compassionate, even kind. "I only wish to help."

His jaw clenched. Then: "Like you helped my grandfather?"

The Elf dropped her eyes, sighed.

"What did you do to him, anyway?" The words came easily: at last he could ask. "Take his soul?"

Mirya pressed her lips together, fixed him with her gaze. "Do you ask for him, Messire Christopher? Or for yourself?"

"What do you mean?"

"Did you want to be your grandfather?"

She had laid her finger directly on it, and suddenly, all that he had ever admired and abhorred in Roger bubbled up in a geyser of conflict. "No!" he almost shouted at her, "I didn't." Stung, he looked for something with which to strike back. "Did you take care of that, too?"

But Mirya only shook her head. "You make your own choices, Christopher."

"Of course," he said, "after you've set up the patterns to suit yourself, I can make all the choices I want, can't I?"

She merely looked at him, and Christopher remembered that her race was fading, had already faded. Choices? Patterns? Did he want to speak of them? What choices were left to Mirya and her kind after nearly fourteen centuries of active persecution?

After a long silence, she finally spoke. "I did the best I could, messire. I can only say that I did not act out of anger, but out of a desire to preserve."

"Saint Brigid?"

"It is so."

And Christopher, also trying to preserve Saint Brigid, was groping towards his goal with all the surety of a blind man on a battlefield. But Mirya had accomplished her ends by striking a single individual. Christopher, on his part, was determined to slaughter thousands.

Who was right? Who was wrong? His lungs burned, and he hacked again, but they refused to clear. "You're making me crazy."

She shook her head again. "Now you begin to see as do we. Once, the Lady reminded me that I had no sovereignty over all the patterns." Her voice turned sad, bitter. "Now, for the most part, I cannot even see them."

His head ached, and his lungs burned. He gave up and slept. When he awoke, they ate and continued on. The smoke grew thicker as they walked. Another few miles, and he was staggering. He must have blacked out and fallen then, for he was suddenly on his back, and Mirya was bathing his face with water from a skin she carried.

"It's hard going," he said hoarsely. His lungs ached in protest at the poison he was pumping into them.

She nodded somberly, her face drawn and pale. She looked old. "It will get worse ahead, I fear. I will do what I can."

With her help, he got to his feet, but his pride won out then, and he refused her arm. Her face still pale, she nodded, turned, and set off once more. Christopher plodded doggedly after her. Soon, the smoke turned from a drifting fog into a solid presence. They might have been walking along the bottom of a milky lake. And now the heat of the approaching fire added to the pervasive oppression of the drought.

To Christopher's eyes, the world was ashimmer with smoke and smoke inhalation, but he was nonetheless surprised that, somehow, he was staying on his feet. This souplike atmosphere of smoke and dust was fit for no one. At least—and he eyed Mirya who, head down and stoop shouldered, was trekking onward—no one who was human.

But as they continued on, as dusk fell and the smoke, thickening, blotted out details smaller than a tree, it struck him that, indeed, no one who was human could do this at all. With a sense of cold in his heart, he stumbled forward, grabbed Mirya's arm. "What are you doing to me?"

She turned a corpse-white face on him. The fading light showed that her eyes were sunken, her lips pale and cracked. "I have little," she said hoarsely. "What I have, I will give. Please accept it, Messire Christopher."

His sense of cold deepened. "But what the hell are you doing?"

"I am giving you the strength to continue. I am altering all the patterns of which I still have any cognizance so that you may continue to breathe. Come, the flames are close, and the way through is treacherous."

She took his hand—her grip was like ice—and led him on into the night. Time was passing, the fire advancing. Saint Brigid and all who were willing to call the Elves friends were in danger.

And then Christopher heard it: a long, sustained roaring

in the darkness, like that of a great hearth, or a forge. The fire.

Smoke was driving into his face as though fanned by the hand of a giant, and his eyes were streaming. He fought for breath, but he knew that with every lungful he took, the Elf weakened. She had little to give, but she was giving it unstintingly.

Again, he dragged her to a halt. "We can't go on."

"We cannot go back. The fire has lapped about behind us."

"We're in the middle of it?"

"It is so. The only way out is to continue." Her face had turned gaunt with effort, its flesh clinging closely to her skull, but her voice maintained its calm. "I have examined the patterns. There is a chance—a chance that I will do my best to make better—that the line of flame ahead will break long enough for us to slip through."

With a jerk, she pulled him forward. The heat increased, the smoke thickened. Christopher blundered into withering trees, tripped over wilted bushes, went sprawling over felled trunks. Mirya drew him on, picked him up when he fell, encouraged him in a soft contralto that never deviated from dispassionate tranquillity.

Blind, stifling, Christopher clung to the hand that had transformed his grandfather as the roaring of the flames grew into a frenzied crescendo of destruction. Eyes closed, teeth clenched, he drove himself against all instinct into regions of thicker smoke, greater heat, and at last found himself facing a red and yellow wall of flame that stretched from the glowing forest floor to an inferno of burning leaves high above.

Mirya stopped at the sight, put her free hand to her face. "My home . . ." Her voice broke, turned heavy, sobbing. "My home . . ."

Christopher had been clinging to her tranquillity as much as her hand. "It's not all gone."

"It is fading . . ."

Shaking, he grabbed her by her tunic. "There's Saint Brigid, and Vanessa, and all those people out there. *It's not all gone.*"

But her eyes, green as emerald, were hollow. She had given all her strength to the baron of Aurverelle. She had kept none for herself.

The flames advanced. Elf and human, clasping hands, stood before them.

"It is here," said Mirya. "It *must* be here." Her eyes were clenched. She was still working magic, still funneling her will into the patterns, reweaving them, shaping them to her own ends. She had changed Roger with this power, and she had helped Vanessa. Now she was altering the world.

But her face and grip went suddenly slack, and her knees buckled. She fell, her head hitting the ground with a thump. Her fingers were strengthless: Christopher might have been gripping the hand of a corpse.

Freed from Mirya's magic, the fire blasted and stung his face. Embers sifted down on his clothes, smoldering, working their way even through his mail. He dropped to his knees beside the Elf. "Mirya!"

No answer.

His face blistering, his hair all but on fire, his clothes smoldering slowly, he looked up to curse the fire, to curse the patterns that had collapsed and taken his world with them, to spew his hate at the maze that brought him to this abrupt and incontrovertible dead end. But he uttered not a sound, for he noticed that, not twenty feet away, the flames had split.

Beyond the gap was a dark waste of charred earth, ruined trees, smoldering ashes. In the night, it virtually glowed with the recent passage of unspeakable heat, but it looked to Christopher like a hand offered in gracious salvation.

The gap widened, paused, started to narrow again.

He had to move. The fire could consolidate at any moment. If he ran, unencumbered, he might make it. But . . .

. . . he was still holding Mirya's hand.

His lungs were fighting against the searing and polluted air, but he looked into her still, pale face. This was the being who had altered his grandfather. This was the being who had, indirectly, sent him off to Nicopolis, pushed him into despair, driven him into madness. But this was also the being who had healed Vanessa, who had provided a haven for her, and who had most recently given everything of herself . . . for him.

Determined, angry, with a pigheaded stubbornness that he was certain would have made even the most willful of his ancestors proud, he bent, slung the limp body of the Elf

over his shoulder, and staggered towards the fast-closing
gap.

"Tut," said Ruprecht, "I have the best armor in the
world."

The barons of Hypprux and Maris had assembled, with
their vassals, men, and equipment, a few miles from Furze;
and they had set up an encampment to the southwest of the
city. There, in pavilions of silk and velvet, with pennants
flying and the sound of fine steel meeting grindstones, they
spoke of battle and chivalry, and bragged of their accouter-
ments.

Yvonnet was not to be outdone. "I'll remind you of my
horse, cousin," he said, reaching for another half of a
chicken from the heap piled on the long dinner table before
him.

In other parts of the camp, cooking fires smoked and
crackled as men-at-arms gathered for their ration of meat,
cheese, and bread; but in the wide space at the center of the
baronial pavilions, the nobles of Adria, from the great lords
of Maris and Hypprux on down to the barons of such small
towns as Friex and Kirtel, were served at a long table set
beneath a sky-blue canopy.

Today, it was Yvonnet's chef who was showing off: gilded
meats, subtleties, nuts disguised as haslet, beef disguised
as fish, fish disguised as beef. Servants in the livery of Hypprux milled, honey sauces and saffron were everywhere,
and silver trumpets announced the appearance of the most
splendid of the courses.

Ruprecht examined the girth of his fellow baron with a
lifted eyebrow. "Yes, yes . . . I must say, he's more than
likely a splendid beast."

The small barons looked nervous. At the far end of the
table, Pytor, seneschal of Aurverelle, commander of the
forces of the estate and yet for all that a poor and despised
relation at this commingling of nobility and display, fretted,
picked at his food, watched the sun drop toward the burning
forest. Furze was all but destroyed, Shrinerock was unin-
habitable, the free companies were loose—somewhere—and
Yvonnet and Ruprecht had passed three days in sparring and
braggart revelry.

Now the daylight was reddening in preparation for yet

another sunset the color of a bloody wound. "I wish that my master were here," he said slowly.

Ruprecht stared at him. "I wish exactly the same, Pytor." He insisted upon calling the seneschal by given name rather than by title. It was an insult, but having no illusions about his status, the good Russian peasant was immune to it. "If you think I enjoy living in these wretched surroundings, I would seek to correct you."

At a gesture from Ruprecht, a servant ran up, his feet soundless on the thick carpet, and filled the baron's silver goblet from a brimming ewer.

"He's the best horse in the world," Yvonnet insisted loudly.

"I will admit," said Ruprecht, "that you're amply provided for."

"As are the coffers of Avignon," Yvonnet snapped. Ruprecht stiffened. Pytor winced: of all things to bring up, papal allegiance was undoubtedly the most idiotic. "But if those wretched brigands show their faces . . ."

Ruprecht's eyes narrowed. Pytor winced again. Wretched brigands! It was Yvonnet who had brought them into Adria in the first place!

". . . I'd show you what a horse is made of. He bounds from the earth. He leaps about as though he had rabbits for guts! He trots . . . well . . . he trots . . ."

"Very well," prompted one of the small barons.

"Well . . . yes," said Yvonnet. "Very well."

A cry of sentry in the distance, and a challenge. Pytor recognized the voice of one of the Aurverelle men, and he listened hopefully, but, no, nothing more.

A young page appeared at Pytor's elbow. "Is there anything I can get you, my lord seneschal?"

"Yes," said the Russian heavily. "A monkey."

The boy looked confused. "I'm . . . sorry, my lord. I don't think we have any of those."

Pytor nodded, lifted his arms dramatically. "Then we are lost."

Ruprecht glared at the seneschal. "See here, my man, I'm tired of your gloom. If you can't say pleasant things, then go and eat with the servants."

A number of the small barons murmured. Pytor might not be noble, but he was still the seneschal of Aurverelle. Ruprecht was being deliberately rude.

But Pytor stood up. "I am gloomy, lord baron of Maris, because I am Russian. We Russians are always gloomy . . . except when we are gay."

Ruprecht flushed above his black beard. "You're being impertinent, Pytor. I don't like impertinence."

Pytor kept wishing for monkeys and apples. "I am attempting to civilly remind the honored gentlemen that we have a purpose for gathering here."

Ruprecht sat back, stuck his eating knife into the table. "What do you want, serf? Command of the army?"

Pytor was becoming a little angry. "I would remind the baron . . ."

"That you're seneschal of Aurverelle? I assure you, I know that."

". . . that I am not a serf. I am a slave."

Ruprecht's eyes were the color of flint. "Yes, Pytor. I think we all know that. And I'm sure you know that Maris is a member of the Hansa. As is Novgorod. There's a price paid for escaped slaves, isn't there?"

Pytor felt his jaw tighten. It was true.

"Sit down, Pytor."

But another voice, one that rose from beyond the canopy, called out: "No, Pytor, stay on your feet: Mirya here needs your chair."

Pytor whirled to find Christopher approaching the table with a woman on his arm. His face was blistered and black with soot and dirt, his hair was charred in places, and his clothes had been half burnt off his back. The woman with him was like none that Pytor had seen before, for though her face was pale and gaunt, her eyes seemed overly bright, and she was dressed in some outlandish imitation of men's garb.

Pytor ran to Christopher, fell on his knees at his feet, kissed his hand. "Master!"

"Up, Pytor," said the baron. "These . . ." He eyed the assembly in their silks and finery. ". . . gentlefolk don't know the intricacies of the Russian character. I'm afraid they'll think ill of you for being so steadfastly loyal."

"But where has master been?"

"Running through forest fires," said Christopher. "Where does it look like I've been?" Gently, he conducted the woman to Pytor's chair and eased her down. She nodded bleary thanks, and Christopher himself poured a cup of wine for her and put it into her hands. "My thanks, my dear Mirya. My infinite, infinite thanks."

Pytor stared.

Mirya nodded mutely, drank. Christopher turned to Pytor. "You remember Mirya, don't you, Pytor? One of the kind . . . ah . . . physicians who healed Vanessa? Well, now she's saved my life, too."

Ruprecht was on his feet. "What is the meaning of this, Christopher?"

Christopher patted Mirya's shoulder and strode alongside the table until he faced Ruprecht and Yvonnet across three feet of laden trenchers and platters. "The meaning of this, my good lords, is that the free companies are besieging Saint Brigid. All of them."

"Saint Brigid?" Yvonnet looked to Lengram.

Lengram's brow was furrowed for a moment, but then: "One of the . . . ah . . . Free Towns, my lord."

"The Free Towns? *Them?*"

"Ah . . . yes."

Yvonnet pursed his lips, reached for another chicken. "Do you really expect me to worry about the Free Towns, cousin? I told you before: they've never paid a penny to *me*."

With a flick of his wrist, Christopher sent the chicken flying the length of the table. It fell into a tureen of soup and sent a splash of beef broth into the lap of one of the small barons. The man laughed, apparently more enthused at Yvonnet's discomfiture than concerned about his clothes.

"I'm expecting you to worry about Adria, *cousin*," said Christopher.

Ruprecht had sat down, plainly distressed. "We came all this way to fight for the Free Towns? But they're not even ours!"

"They're ours," said Christopher, "because they're Adria's. The free companies are ours because they're our problem." He glared at Yvonnet. *"Aren't they?"*

"Oh, for God's sake, Christopher," said Yvonnet, "I'm not going to waste my time and money fighting for the Free Towns. Let the companies come to one of the big cities, like . . . ah . . ." He glanced at Ruprecht. "Maris, for example."

Ruprecht yelped. "Maris!"

Yvonnet sniffed. "It would be God's justice."

"And what is that supposed to mean?"

"Bunch of whores of Avignon."

"You . . ." Ruprecht was on his feet. "You schismatic swine! You asslicker to that parasite of Rome! How dare you!"

Yvonnet was standing up also . . . and he was reaching for his dagger. But Christopher, blackened and scorched, folded his arms. "I spoke with Martin Osmore the other day, Yvonnet," he said casually.

Yvonnet's face turned white.

"Sit down, both of you," said Christopher.

They sat. Pytor shook his head admiringly. "My master is a splendid man."

"He is, indeed," said Mirya quietly. "I have met the grandson of my enemy and found him to be a friend."

Pytor looked at her.

"He saved my life, also," she said.

But Christopher could make no headway against the intransigence of Ruprecht and Yvonnet. Faced with his demand that they defend an inconsequential little village of southern Adria, they were balking. Although far apart on the question of the schism, they concurred on the matter of the free companies: let them come to a reasonable city, one that belonged to a member of the baronage.

"But what about Shrinerock and Furze?" said Christopher.

"Shrinerock and Furze," said Ruprecht, "are over and done with." He cleared his throat. "I never really trusted Paul delMari, anyway. He was a queer one from the beginning. Odd ideas. And he said he was for Rome."

Yvonnet growled again. "*I'm* for Rome, you—"

Christopher seized the tablecloth and sent the dishes and food flying. "Shut up! Both of you!"

Wide eyes turned towards him. Sooty, burned, filthy, and unshaven as he was, Christopher seemed the perfect madman.

But his voice was clear and lucid . . . almost frighteningly so. "There are four thousand enemies in Adria," he said slowly. "Four thousand. They've got more men than we do. They've got better equipment than we do. They've taken one castle and sacked one . . ." He glanced at Yvonnet. ". . . no, two cities."

"Good riddance," Yvonnet grumbled softly.

"It's only a matter of time," Christopher continued, "before they come for the rest of us. If we can't stop them now, we'll never be able to stop them."

Ruprecht leaned across the bare table. "And I repeat, Christopher: let them come to Maris. Let them come to Hypprux. Then we'll destroy them. But . . ." He straightened, laughed. ". . . Saint Brigid? Good God, man: do you know what these armies cost?"

Yvonnet laughed also, but Pytor noticed that a number of the small barons at the table were examining Christopher thoughtfully.

Ruprecht and Yvonnet, however, were adamant. They would not follow Christopher to Saint Brigid, and in fact, they were angry at him for even suggesting such a course.

Christopher was desperate. "You're just going to let them die?" he cried.

Yvonnet rose from the table, beckoned to Lengram, turned to go. "What's the matter, cousin?" he said over his shoulder. "Find another little village wench to fuck? It's in the family, after all."

Christopher's hands clenched into fists. "Thank the Lady it's not something else, Yvonnet."

The baron of Hypprux stopped as though a hand had closed about his throat. He took a deep breath. "I don't know what you can be talking about, dear cousin. But I'm sure that, should you make any rash accusations, it won't be me who suffers. Do I make myself clear?"

Christopher was silent.

Yvonnet left. Ruprecht went back to his pavilion. Pytor heard them giving orders to break camp the following morning and return home.

But the small barons, who had for the most part remained silent during the argument, gathered in a small group to the edge of the pavilion. They murmured among themselves. Low voices. Concerned faces. Christopher eyed them for a moment, then shrugged and sat down on the edge of the dais.

Pytor examined his master's hands and face. Deep burns, numerous blisters. "Master needs a physician."

"What do I need a physician for?" said Christopher bitterly. "I've got an Elf." He put his hands to his face and wept. "I'm afraid it was useless, Mirya. It's Nicopolis all over again. I might as well have argued with Jean de Nevers and the Comte d'Eu.''

But Mirya shook her head. ''It was not useless,'' she said in a soft voice. ''You took my hand, and I took yours, and we righted a part of the patterns that I put awry a half century ago.''

Pytor was baffled. Mirya could be no more than eighteen by the look of her. But the group of small barons had apparently reached some kind of agreement, for there was a sudden shaking of hands accompanied by a hum of approving murmurs. Two or three then nodded to the others and approached Christopher.

Their finery was considerably less exuberant than that of Ruprecht and Yvonnet: a wealthy merchant could have bested them in ornament and grandeur. These were men who had little enough by way of income and property that they had to look carefully to it, hoard against possible future scarcities, invest in the welfare of their peasants and free-holders in hopes of a future return of work and loyalty. At times, only their blood made them noble, for their hands occasionally showed the usage of more menial implements than swords.

''Lord Aurverelle,'' said one. ''A number of us think that your counsel is wise.''

Christopher lifted his head.

''You're a strange man, sir,'' the spokesman continued with a bow, and Pytor saw that his lap was soaked with beef broth, ''but we perceive that you're honorable and fore-sighted. Therefore, what men and . . .'' He coughed with embarrassment. ''. . . and very few knights we have—too few and too humble for your taste, we fear—we offer to you. We'll accompany you to Saint Brigid, and we'll endeavor to raise the siege.''

His face full of wonder, Christopher stood up and took the man's hands in his own. ''What is your name, messire?''

''Baron Jamie of Kirtel, Lord Aurverelle.''

''Baron Jamie,'' said Christopher. He struggled with words, his voice breaking. ''Baron Jamie, you . . . you are my friend.'' His cheeks were damp, and when he grinned, the blisters on his face broke open and redoubled the wet. ''And so are you all.'' He took their hands then, embraced them, grabbed cups and wine from the remains of dinner and toasted them.

Mirya, too, lifted a cup. "To Aurverelle," she said softly. "And to the lady of Aurverelle."

Christopher heard, blushed beneath his burns. "What . . . lady are you referring to, Mirya?"

She shook her head. "The patterns are unclear, my lord."

But a shout from the sentinels halted the thanks and pledges, and this time a clamor arose from the edge of the encampment: men shouting challenges and answers.

"Halt, or I'll strike!"

"I'm looking for Christopher delAurvre."

"Give me your sword and I'll take you to him."

"I'll not give it to you. Strike me if you want: you'll not strike again after, I assure you."

And along the avenue that lay between the rows of tents and supply wagons came a young man who was as blond and fair as Christopher himself. He was wearing nothing more than a simple coat of mail that was rusty with hard use; but, prideful and determined, disdainful of the rabble of guards and watchmen who followed him, he recognized Christopher, strode directly up to him, and, standing tall, clapped his hand on the pommel of his sword.

"I'm Jehan delMari," he declared. "Paul's son."

Christopher bowed slightly.

But then Jehan sighed, wilted, looked shamefaced at those about him. "And . . . well . . . I . . . suppose I'm a kind of traitor."

CHAPTER 30

Four days of constant siege, and Saint Brigid was still holding out. Berard's guns had exploded, his mines had been countermined, his assaults had been repulsed. Catapults snapped ropes unexpectedly. Siege towers collapsed. Greek fire . . . would not.

To be sure, the villagers had lost men. Berard's archers insisted that they had accounted for at least twenty dead, and the men who had mounted the assault ladders and towers spoke of that many more. For such a small village as Saint Brigid, this was a grievous loss; and yet every day, the villagers took to the walls and responded to any hostile advance with arrows, stones, pikes . . . and an undiminished quantity of pluck. Berard could not understand it.

What he did understand, though, was that he was losing men. Every accident in his camp had maimed and killed, and the villagers, though but farmers, were unnervingly handy with scythes, billhooks, hatchets, and pitchforks. The Fellowship had buried over a hundred of its own, and twice that many lay incapacitated with wounds inflamed by heat and drought.

And all this . . . because of a single, tiny village.

It was Christopher. It had to be Christopher. Only the baron of Aurverelle would have the courage and the imagination that bordered on madness to defend himself and his people with such audacity. Only he would be willing to face down an attacking force that outnumbered by a factor of ten the entire population—*including,* for God's sake, the women and children—of the besieged village. Only he could hold out the hope of actually winning against such ridiculous odds.

Christopher preyed on Berard's mind. Berard saw him always: capering on the village walls, flinging yet another bag of shit, sticking his tongue out at the Fellowship. The baron obsessed his thoughts, haunted his dreams, and during the daily strategy sessions in his tent, Berard caught himself muttering over and over, like a litany: "That damned monkey. That damned monkey."

Christopher had to die. The rest of Adria was as a plum ripe for the picking, but Christopher delAuvrne was a thorn among the fruits . . . and a poisoned one at that. If, Berard reasoned, the baron of Aurverelle could, somehow, turn doors and windows to stone and, by his mere presence, inspire a simple village to such valor, what could he do with an army of knights and nobility behind him? No, Christopher had to be stopped now, for Berard saw that the very existence of the Fellowship depended upon it.

Others in his company were not so sure of this. Christopher, they said repeatedly, was but a single man. How much could he do?

"Plenty," said Berard, "Remember what happened to Shrinerock."

"But Berard," said Jaques, "we've lost men, and we're losing more every day . . . and what'll we have to show for it?"

Berard thumped the maps and tallies on the table. "We'll have Christopher."

"The men want loot."

"They'll get their loot . . . later. After we dispose of Christopher."

"Berard . . ."

The captain stood up, struck the maps and tallies to the floor. "Damn you all! Are you all so blind that you can't see it?"

He realized in the next moment that they probably saw much too well. Since the bizarre happenings at Shrinerock, the possibility of magic had stuck in everyone's mind like a foul odor. If Shrinerock, then . . .

He's just a man. He can die. He can be killed. Berard sat down again, glared, cleared his throat. "I trust that you all are not."

Glances among the men: furtive, worried. Berard suddenly felt as though he were back in Italy. Raoul: was he Bologna? Jaques: maybe he had decided to be Florence today. Marcus, Ravenna. Old Gonzago, who had been the leader of the successful assault on Ypris, could be none other than Milan, the Visconti viper.

What were they thinking, all of them? Open rebellion? A dagger in the heart one fine morning?

Sweating, Berard bent, retrieved the maps and tallies, spread them out again on the table. "We're . . ."

Again, the glances. *Oh, yes, well he's off on his damnable obsession again. Raoul, will you see that his wine has a little something extra in it tonight? There's a good fellow.*

He swallowed, forced himself to go on. So far, nothing had happened. Bonds of loot and women still held them to his will. It was not too late. If he could take Saint Brigid . . .

". . . we're losing too many men. Now, I suggest a diversion that will make all of this relatively easy." He indicated a portion of the village wall. "Gonzago, Raoul, Jaques: tell me what you think of this. . . ."

Shrinerock by starlight was a darkness against the dark sky without a shred of homeliness or cheer about it. Its stone windows, pocked by holes where Berard's men had battered through, stared out at a night landscape of burned villages, and a sense of uncanny power lay heavily about it, one that could not but be increased by loneliness, abandonment, and the constant, unwavering roar of water from the spring far below.

Jehan, Mirya, and Christopher rode up the road from the flatlands, dismounted, and approached the gate. Jehan set fire to a torch, and as the light flickered over the walls like the uncertain fingers of a blind man, the young man's face, already a mask of despondency over his drunken betrayal, turned dark with self-accusation.

"Seen enough?" said Christopher.

Jehan shook his head. "You have to understand, Messire d'Aurverelle: this was my home."

Christopher looked at Mirya. The Elf, drawing on sources of strength unavailable to humans, was recovering quickly from her exertions in the forest, but her renewed vitality had not taken the bleakness from her eyes. She stood, arms folded, watching the distant flames that were devouring Malvern. She knew all about losing one's home . . . or one's world.

He touched her shoulder. "I'm sorry, Mirya. I'm truly sorry."

She nodded. "My thanks, dear friend."

He blinked. Friend? Now he was a friend of the Elves? What was next? Sleeping with them?

But Jehan was stalking deliberately towards the hole that had been rammed through the gate. "Are you two coming?"

Mirya started off, but Christopher put a hand on her arm. "Is this wise?" he said. "Jamie and the others are going to be wondering what the hell we're doing up here. They've made a generous offer: I don't want them to think I don't give a damn about it. And the longer we delay, the more time Berard has to breach the walls."

"The barons trust you," Mirya replied. "They and their men are already on their way to Saint Brigid. They can go no faster. And as for Jehan . . ." She looked at Christopher meaningfully. "It would not be wise to leave alone one who is so close to despair."

Fretful though he was, Christopher understood. Jehan resembled at present a certain baron of Aurverelle who had returned from crusade with a soul full of ashes. "Yes . . . yes. I know."

"Come then."

They followed the young man through the gate and across the courtyard, entered the residence, ascended the stairs to the bedrooms and living quarters. The rooms were essentially intact: the free companies had doubtless enjoyed the appointments of a well-furnished castle.

Jehan turned, lifted the torch. Vaulting, beams, torn tapestries. An overturned table and an occasional pool of dried vomit witnessed the excesses of Shrinerock's most recent inhabitants. "It's been over ten years."

Christopher shook his head. "It's gone, Jehan."

"Maybe . . ." The young man looked down the corridor. "There are other stairs, other rooms. I want to look."

Jamie and the barons were waiting. Saint Brigid and Vanessa were waiting. "Dammit, Jehan! For what?"

"Something I've lost."

Down one hall, then another. A stone door with a hole battered in it. Jehan poked his torch in, then stepped into the room beyond, leaving his companions in the corridor.

It was an ordinary enough room. Besides a bed, there was a table, a desk, a bookcase well stocked with leather bindings. Clothes still hanging in the wardrobe were set into eerie motion by the flickering light.

"This was my room," said Jehan, his voice echoing down the hall. "They didn't keep it for me. They gave it to Martin."

Christopher kept his impatience in check. "I'm sorry, Jehan."

"For what, messire? I believe the better man won."

But as Jehan brooded on the room, Christopher realized that Mirya was standing stiffly, staring, her sight apparently turned inward. Christopher had seen her so before, in the forest and elsewhere, but she had always seemed at ease with her inner vision. Now, though, she looked almost frightened.

"What is it?" he said. "Mirya!"

"Something is happening," she replied distantly. "Something is changing. The patterns . . ." She gasped suddenly. "Dear Lady! It is Vanessa!"

Christopher understood nothing. "What? What's she doing?"

"She is . . . changing the patterns."

He goggled at her. "Can she do that?"

"She has before. But . . . this time . . ." The look of distance and fear deepened.

She fell silent again, closed her eyes. Christopher grabbed her arm. "This time what?"

No answer.

"Mirya! What the hell's going on? What's happening?"

The Elf opened her eyes, spoke slowly. "Vanessa has altered the patterns. And . . . perhaps herself."

Christopher felt cold, sick. Vanessa? Altered? "What are you talking about?"

Mirya shook her head. "Vanessa has the blood. We sent it to sleep, but I fear it has awakened again. And . . . there is more that can happen." She sighed, smiled with a sense of the bittersweet. "Under certain circumstances, the blood can transform. It has . . . happened before."

"But what did she do?"

The Elf shook her head. "I am not certain. It is all . . . confused."

Dan, Vanessa had said at their parting. *Dan make plans, Christopher. Patterns can change i' a heartbeat, an' you might na wan' me after.*

Christopher felt his jaw clench. "Always, Vanessa," he murmured to himself. "I'll always want you. I'm . . ." He thought of the free companies surrounding Saint Brigid, thought of the pathetically small force he was going to lead against them. "I'm not going to let you go again."

Vanessa's family, Etienne of Languedoc, Berard of Onella: the idiotic twists of the patterns that had chained Vanessa to a life of helpless torment just as Roger of Aurverelle had once chained village girls to his bed. But Vanessa had fought, and she had freed herself. And now Christopher was fighting, too: fighting Berard, fighting Roger, fighting the patterns.

I'm not going to let you go again.

Jehan stepped out of the room, his movements distant. Christopher, still shaken, eyed him impatiently. "Are you finished?"

Jehan's voice was toneless. "There is something I need."

"Can't it wait?"

"I think not." Jehan fixed him with a dull eye. "I think you might do well to come with me, Messire d'Aurverelle. This castle has many armories. I seek one of them. Given your plans and desires, you might wish to replace your light mail with something more appropriate to knightly combat."

There was wisdom in Jehan's words, but the lad's allusion to chivalry rankled Christopher. "You know, Jehan, if I could kill them all with a cask of poisoned wine, I'd do it."

Jehan nodded. "I know you would, messire. I don't know whether to laud you or weep."

But as he led them back towards the stairs, he paused at a stone door. Like many in the castle, it had a ragged hole in it.

"What is it now?" said Christopher.

"This was my parents' bedroom."

"Fine. Fine." *Just go on, will you?*

Jehan turned and started down the hall again, but a low moan from the room beyond the door made him whirl. Christopher also turned, his sword in his hand, but Mirya cried out and plunged through the hole. In a moment, the moan turned to sobbing. "Water, quickly," the Elf commanded. "In the name of *Elthia*, water!"

For an instant, Christopher and Jehan stared at one another. "There's water in the kitchen," said Jehan. "Follow me." But when, simultaneously, they turned for the stairs, they crashed into one another and fell on the floor.

Jehan got to his feet, pulled Christopher up after him. He glared at the baron. *"Follow."*

Christopher followed, and in a minute they had found the kitchen and returned with a brimming pitcher. In the fetid darkness of the baronial bedroom, they found Mirya bending over an emaciated figure. Jehan lit the candles in a wall sconce, but a soft radiance born of no torchlight illumined the Elf, and her hands lay lightly on the face of the—girl, was it?—who lay on the bed.

It was indeed a girl, but thin and gaunt as an old woman, the scanty garments that she wore—under the circumstances, more horrifying than titillating—seemingly the shroud of a corpse. And when Christopher brought the pitcher to the Elf and held it ready, he stared, stricken, for he saw that the girl had been chained to the thick bedpost.

His grandfather . . .

But Mirya took the pitcher and poured the water into her cupped hand while the girl, still sobbing, lapped weakly. The radiance about the Elf seemed to turn the water into palmfuls of light. "Be cleansed," she said. "Be changed. Be healed."

As Christopher watched, the gauntness left the face of the girl, her flesh plumped, her eyes lost their glassy stare—and at last she appeared to come to a cognizance of more than a guttering existence. She cried out and put her hands to her face, and Mirya thrust the pitcher at Christopher and gathered the whimpering, sobbing child into her arms.

"She has been here for days," said the Elf quietly. "Berard had her for his sport. He did not think to free her when he left."

Christopher looked at the pathetically tiny ankle that was held by a thick iron chain. "He just . . . chained her up? And left her?"

Mirya nodded.

Christopher set the pitcher aside, passed a hand over his face. Berard and Roger, like Christopher and the monkey. The monkey, though, was dead. Berard . . .

He clenched his fists, swore inwardly. Mirya had attended to Roger, but that was in another time, another world. He himself would deal with Berard.

"What's your name, child?" he said softly.

The girl's mouth worked. "Joanna," she whispered.

Christopher knelt beside the bed. There had been nothing

noble about his grandfather, nothing save the planting of a few peach trees. "Joanna," he said, "you're among friends. You're safe."

"I don't know you," she said. "Who are you?"

"I'm Baron Christopher of Aurverelle. And this is Mirya of Malvern. She's a healer . . . and . . ."

Mirya looked up, looked at him.

". . . and . . . she's my friend."

Mirya smiled through sudden, silent tears. Joanna shuddered, sobbed quietly. The Elf rocked her.

Christopher clasped the Elf's hand. It was over. Roger's ghost had been banished. Other tasks lay ahead.

But when he rose, Jehan was gone. "Where the devil . . . ?"

"Jehan is on the next level up," said Mirya as she rocked Joanna. "Down the corridor about twenty paces to the right of the stairwell. There is no door: a section of wall should be open."

"You know where he is? The patterns?"

"The patterns say less and less, my friend. But in past years, my kind came here often. I can guess."

Christopher nodded. Less and less. Fading. But before he left, he drew his sword and put all the strength of his shoulders and hips into a strike that smashed through the bedpost to which Joanna was chained. Reaching out, Christopher slipped the ring from the wooden stump and put it into the girl's startled hands.

"Be free," he said. "Be healed."

Mirya's cheeks, he saw, were damp.

"I'll find Jehan."

Taking a candle, bearing light into the darkness of a deserted castle, he left the room, climbed stairs, turned to his right, and followed the upper corridor toward the ruddy flicker of torchlight.

Yes, Jehan was here. A section of wall had, by hidden mechanism and secret prompt, swung back, and Christopher, passing through the opening, found himself in a kind of armory. Here, though, were no common weapons of base metal, for the swords he saw gleamed with gold, the pikes and spears with silver. Mail and plate sparkled with gems.

At his approach, Jehan looked up from a surcoat he was holding. "Take what you want, Messire d'Aurverelle," he said, sweeping out an arm. "Go and battle your enemies . . . and mine."

The surcoat in Jehan's hands, agleam with jewels and embroidery, was blazoned with the delMari gryphon and silver star. Jehan held it up, regarded it solemnly. "It was for my adubbement," he explained. "My father . . ." He bent his head. "My father so wanted me . . ."

Christopher did not know Paul delMari well, but he knew him well enough. "He still wants you."

"No . . . no . . ." Jehan shook his head, his eyes hollow. "He has Martin now." He examined the surcoat again. "But . . . I'll take this."

His mouth set, he clutched the garment to his chest.

"It's all that I'll need," he said.

CHAPTER 31

Martin Osmore, resplendent in the livery of a knight of Aurverelle, leaned across the immense desk and seemingly transfixed the mayor of Saint Blaise in his chair. "How many men? All you have."

Paul delMari did his best to suppress a smile. Folding his arms, he leaned against the wall near the door of the office, content to watch from a corner the confrontation between virtual noble and ostentatious peasant.

"Ah . . ." Matthew was a stout man, and his dark hair was suddenly damp with sweat. ". . . see here, Martin. I can't just go and authorize the departure of all the city's men-at-arms."

"Why not?" said Martin. "As you've been telling me all my life, you're the mayor."

Matthew seemed to inflate a little at the reminder of his office. "There you go again, Martin. I'm afraid you've not much of a head for figures. Never have. That time in Shrinerock didn't do a thing for you in that department—"

Martin glanced at Paul. Smiling, Paul lifted his eyes to heaven, spread his hands.

"—and that's why your mother and I want you to marry Agnes Darci," Matthew continued. "She's a nice girl, very practical—knows a groat from a penny, you know—and she's got a head for figures. Good hips, too! You'll need her if you're to amount to much, you know."

"Right now," said Martin, "I need soldiers. Saint Brigid needs soldiers."

"And . . . this Saint Brigid stuff. I can't send all the men-at-arms to Saint Brigid with you."

Martin glanced again at Paul, this time with a look that said: *You see what I have to deal with? Can you blame me?* But Paul winked and nodded.

Give it to him, son, he thought. *Give it to him.*

Martin turned back to his father. "I'd like to know why."

"Well," said Matthew, "they're . . . just not our people, you know. They're rather queer."

Martin's eyebrows lifted, his dark eyes widened. "I'm sorry: I didn't realize that."

"And that's another thing—" Matthew began, but Martin's mailed fist crashed to the desk, stopping him in midsentence. Matthew stared at the fist, then at Martin. Paul delMari smiled. Yes, that black Aurverelle livery was rather impressive. Just like Martin himself.

"Lord Mayor," said Martin, "the Messire d'Aurverelle, at great risk to his life, is attempting to put an end to the threat of constant pillage and violence that hangs over all of Adria." The lad whacked out the words as though he were driving wooden pegs into a plank. "I am on my way south to help him." Whack! "I'm asking for men." Whack!

Matthew stared.

"Will you . . ." Whack! ". . . give them . . ." Whack! ". . . to me?" Whack!

Matthew tried once again. "Martin, I ask you, give up this foolishness. We have plenty of men to guard our city . . ."

"That's why I'm asking you to lend me a few."

". . . and there's no reason you have to go off and meddle with other people's affairs. It's . . . well . . . it's not good business." The mayor nodded as though he had just demonstrated a geometric proof. "You need to stay here and marry Agnes."

Paul saw the anger building in Martin, tried to head off the explosion. "Son . . ."

"Not now, Father," Martin snapped. Paul took a step back, eyes wide, lips pursed . . . but silently applauding. Spirited!

Martin went back to Matthew, who seemed convinced that he had dealt with the problem. "I'm not going to marry Agnes Darci," he said flatly.

Matthew's eyebrows went up. "You certainly will."

"It's impossible . . ."

Matthew blinked. Paul gritted his teeth. Here it was . . . look out . . .

"I don't like girls," Martin continued. "At least, I don't like to sleep with them."

Matthew stared, uncomprehending.

"I like men. I like to sleep with *them*."

Matthew paled. "Surely you can't—"

Martin's fist thudded to the desk once again. *"I like to fuck them!"*

Silence in the office. Outside, a street vendor was hawking pies, and a pair of girls ran down the street, giggling at some incomprehensible joke. But Matthew only sat, not moving, not saying a word. His hair was lank with sweat, and his skin had turned the color of a fish's belly.

Finally, his lips quivered, moved. "H-how?" he said in a whisper.

"Up the ass!"

Matthew was gray. "You're a—"

"Sodomite," said Martin. "Faggot. Queer. A hunk of meat for the Church's fires. Tell me, my lord mayor, how do you want me? Rare? Or well done?"

Matthew struggled to his feet, shaking. "I do believe you're proud of your sins," he said.

Martin sighed. "Dear Lady . . ."

"Get out," said the mayor. "Get out of my house. Get out of my city. Get . . ." He looked on the verge of incoherent screaming. "Get out!"

Martin stood his ground. "I want two hundred and fifty men, armed and armored."

Matthew's jaw quivered. "Take them. Take them and go. Get out! From this day forth, I have no son."

Martin shook his head. "No, my lord. You had no son the day I went to Shrinerock. And as for me: I have another father."

Leaving Matthew gaping, Martin turned and stomped out of the room, bawling for the head of the city guards. "Two hundred and fifty men, Caspar! Ready to ride in an hour!"

Matthew was glaring at Paul now, but Paul only smiled. "Quite a man, that," he said cheerfully. "My son, you know." Matthew's glare turned puzzled, then enraged. "Ah . . . did you want to draw up a bill of sale, lord mayor?"

It was unseemly for a baron to flee when a commoner made to throw something at him. But Paul fled anyway, bounding down the stairs like a boy, laughing.

Five hundred against four thousand: the odds were not encouraging.

Christopher was well aware of the idiocy of his proposed

campaign, but insistent, driving, he pressed his small company of soldiers and knights southward. He intended to strike immediately upon reaching Saint Brigid. No formal challenges, displaying arms, and miscellaneous flummery here, just a sudden attack and a fervent prayer that Berard would be taken by surprise . . . or at least that his sentries would be a little lax that morning.

Jehan, caught up in his chivalric dreams, would have hated the plan, and for that reason Christopher had not told him of it. But Jehan disappeared sometime during the second night on the road. He took only his horse and the splendid surcoat.

"Does master think that he has gone back to the free companies?" Pytor asked dourly as the company ate a quick breakfast. "That would be very bad indeed."

"I don't think so," said Christopher. Joanna, a servant now among the servants of Aurverelle, brought him an uncut loaf. He thanked her, wished her a good morning, then stuffed his mouth, chewed, and swallowed. He wanted to be on the road again. Eating had turned into a chore.

"Perhaps he's ashamed," said Baron Jamie. "It wouldn't surprise me."

"Jehan? Run away?" Christopher shook his head. "No, it's something else."

Just another part of the patterns that shifted and blurred regardless of what one did or did not do. Vanessa had apparently tried to alter them, but how could one alter anything so ephemeral and yet so powerful?

But the Elves altered them, and Mirya, an Elf, had said that Vanessa had altered herself. . . .

He recalled her last words to him and suppressed a shudder. *Always, Vanessa.* "But it's bad enough, whatever his reasons. We've got to all be crazy to attack Berard with only five hundred, and without Jehan, that's one less."

Jamie's eyebrows arched. "I have heard tell," he said slowly, "that the baron of Aurverelle is mad."

Christopher shrugged.

About them, the men were finishing up their morning meal. Jamie watched them for a time, then: "God be praised, so are we all."

As usual, Mirya appeared at Christopher's side without announcement or sound; and, as usual, Pytor and a number of the men at the table crossed themselves fervently. Elves! Dear God . . .

"My lord baron," she said, "you have more than five hundred."

Christopher looked around the camp, saw nothing more than he had seen the night before. "You, of course, would like to explain that statement, Mirya."

The Elf permitted herself a small smile. "Paul delMari and Martin Osmore reached Aurverelle safely—"

"Thank the Lady!"

"The Lady . . . and Terrill. But hear me: not content to remain in your castle, Paul and Martin and the men of Shrinerock armed themselves and took the south road. They are on their way to Saint Brigid, gathering men and supplies as they come."

Jamie looked nervous. "How . . . ah . . . do you know this, Fair One?"

Mirya bowed. "My beloved is with them. I know."

"I told you," said Christopher. "She reads minds." But his fists were clenched. Patterns were indeed altering. The maze was proving more ephemeral than he had ever dreamed. Maybe . . . maybe Vanessa . . .

You might na wan' me after.

After what? What had she done? He felt at once jubilant and cold. "How many?" he said.

"Four hundred seventy and five," Mirya replied. But the wind shifted, and the odor of smoke drifted through the camp. Mirya stiffened, her gaze going to Malvern. The trees were dry, the leaves were brown . . .

. . . and the fire was still spreading.

"Forgive me," she said softly, and she turned away to the forest, her hand to her face. Suddenly, despite her powers and her age and her actions against Christopher's grandfather, Mirya seemed too fragile ever to survive in a world that contained such things as swords and fires and mass slaughter.

Fading . . .

You might na wan' me after.

Christopher shook the thought away violently. "Let's go," he said. "I want to be in position by tonight. The Lady willing, we'll make it without being noticed."

"The Lady?" said Jamie.

"Yes," said Christopher. "The Lady of the Elves."

Mirya had reached the trees. She put her arms about a gnarled trunk, rested her head against the bark.

Fading . . .

Jamie was nodding slowly, thoughtfully. "You'll forgive the rest of us, Messire Christopher, if we hear confession and receive the Sacrament the night before we face the free companies."

Christopher was watching Mirya, feeling with her, as much as he could, the loss, the ending. Malvern was but an outward sign. "By all means, Messire Jamie. But . . . if you please, I'll have the ordering of the battle cry for to-morrow."

"And that is?"

Mirya was weeping. He knew she was weeping. "It will be: *Elthia.*"

Berard ordered not just one mine, but many; and at the same time, he planned a multiple scaling of the village walls. But, very deliberately, he refrained from making any final decision regarding the main thrust of the attack. It might be the mines, it might be the siege towers and ladders. Anything could happen; and since Christopher seemed all too adept at second guessing him, this time, he would let the baron wonder what he was up to, for he in fact would not know himself until the last instant.

The Fellowship, though, in the course of these last four days of constant, maddening work—work plagued by mishaps, heat, absurdly coincidental accidents, and constant outbreaks of temper—had splintered badly. Only with the most profound eloquence and lavish promises had Berard managed to persuade his captains to give him this last chance . . . and then they could go and raid the countryside, burn villages, rape women, gamble—or, for that matter, keep chickens if it pleased them—with his blessing. Just one more chance. Just a few days more. That was all.

His luck, so far, had held. Eustache de Cormeign, to be sure, had thrown up his hands and departed with his *kata-phraktoi*, but the Fellowship—dissatisfied, bickering, increasingly rebellious—had stayed with him. The mines had crept towards the village walls, the siege towers had risen from their wooden platforms, the men had sharpened their swords.

On the morning of the fifth day, all was ready, and the

sun was just beginning to fight its way though the welter of
smoke sent up by the forest fires when Berard rose from his
bed. He called for water with which to wash, ate breakfast
with his captains, and debated some last points of battle
order. Outside, the men were forming up. Every available
man was going into battle. Berard had even called in the
sentries and the scouts.

After breakfast, he shook hands all around, slapped a few
backs, exchanged a few jokes and pleasantries that no one
really meant. The captains went off to arm themselves, and
Berard called for his servants. He was going to wear his
best plate today, for though he was not worried in the
slightest about any combat the villagers might offer him, he
nonetheless wanted to look as formidable as possible when
he met the baron of Aurverelle.

Afterwards . . . well, afterwards, he might settle into
Saint Brigid and raid the Free Towns, or he might decide to
return to Shrinerock. Baron Berard: yes, indeed, it had a
good sound.

But as he donned his quilted undervest, there was a stirring at the flap of his tent. A slender figure was suddenly
standing in the doorway: blond, gray-eyed, wrapped in a
ragged cloak.

Jehan.

The servants stood, the cuirass still in their hands. Berard
motioned for them to set it aside, hid a frown. This was not
good at all. This could, in fact, prove to be quite unpleasant. What did Jehan want? And of all the times for him to
show up!

But Jehan smiled. "Hello, Berard. I hope I'm not too
late."

Too late? "Ah . . . it's good to see you again, Jehan."
Berard tried to put into his voice a certain casual jollity, but
he made sure that, yes, his dagger was still in his belt.
"What do you mean . . . too late?"

Jehan smiled. "I wanted to arrive before the village fell."

This was promising! But Berard was still glad of the dagger in his belt. "You want to help?"

"As I can." Jehan shrugged within his cloak. "I did
some thinking after I escaped. You were always right, Berard. I got myself caught up in so many thoughts about chivalry and knightly behavior . . . it just got in the way. It

made me useless for anything. I think that . . . now . . . I'll be better off.''

There was something about Jehan, something that Berard did not quite trust. Could disillusionment turn someone so completely around? Never having been disillusioned in his life, Berard was not sure. He supposed that it was . . . possible.

But if nothing else, Jehan's return would allay some of the resentment among the men of the original Fellowship. It would be just like the old days . . . and there would be time enough to get rid of him after Saint Brigid fell, when Berard could be sure once again of loot, lust, and, therefore, loyalty. Until then, why, friends were friends, Jehan! Good fellows all! Welcome and well met!

A good plan. A little too deviously Italian perhaps, but then, sometimes one had to compromise. With an inward shrug, therefore, Berard opened his arms and stepped forward to embrace the prodigal. ''Then welcome back, Jehan! So sorry about your father's castle—''

But Jehan loosed the fastening of his cloak, and with a rustle and a thump, the ragged garment dropped to the floor to reveal a glittering surcoat, embroidered and bejeweled, blazoned with the gryphon and silver star of the house of delMari.

Jehan's sword came out of its sheath with a shrill hiss. *''God and Saint Adrian!''* he cried, and Berard had only a moment in which to stare, dumfounded, before the lad struck.

Jehan was quick and sure, and fire as hot as that which was devouring Malvern was suddenly spreading up Berard's side like sheet lightning. He felt a gush of wetness, and sounds abruptly turned distant and echoing. The world spun and darkened.

He staggered back, helpless to prevent another slashing blow. Groping, dizzy, he tried to reach for his dagger, found that he had nothing with which to reach for it: his right arm was hanging by only a few shreds, and blood was pouring out of a stump that terminated a hand's breadth from his shoulder.

His servants, though, were catching up knives and swords and spears, surrounding Jehan, striking, lashing out. One leaped upon his back as another laid open his side. Lacerated a hundred times, bleeding and concussed, Jehan fell quickly, and the servants rushed to carry Berard to his couch. Someone was calling for water, someone else ran off screaming for a physician; but dizziness and darkness were growing on Berard, and from short, flickering glimpses of the faces of his servants—all he could see now—he judged that he was beyond the help of any leechcraft.

The rank, metallic taste of regurgitated blood was welling up in his throat along with his breakfast bread and wine as Berard flailed out with his good hand, batted the servants away, staggered to his feet. The flat carpet bucked and fought his feet treacherously, but he lurched to the tent flap and pushed outside. Close by, he knew, were the men, assembled and ready for the assault.

He was almost blind now, and he did not know whether his blood-filled throat would be able to shout, but he sucked air into his lungs and forced it out again:

"Fire the mines! Full assault! Straight up the middle!"

The ground tipped, and his useless arm flapped like the piece of dead meat that it was. He fought to stay on his feet, but his legs rebelled against him, and he spun in little circles like a crippled dog. He could hear shouts, cries of confusion. Were they giving up?

He tried to shout, to curse, to repeat his orders, but his words, drowned in his own blood, burbled and wheezed out in a crimson froth.

There was a roaring, then: a sudden blare of horns and hoofbeats and challenges. Berard managed to focus on a black banner streaming in the east wind. It was approaching him quickly, like the urgent herald of a King coming into his Kingdom, and though he could not see who bore it, his failing sight gave him a last, fading glimpse of what was on it: the figure of a standing knight lifting a sword against an attacking lion.

Aurverelle.

He stared, but the blood loss overwhelmed him then and left him in a sightless world. He felt the ground come up to meet him like a fist, felt his breath flutter to a stop, felt the fires of his wounds go cold. And all that penetrated the husk that he was, all that stirred it into a momentary recognition and remembrance of life and living before it slid into finality was the sound of a battle cry that rose from many throats as from one:

"*Elthia!*"

CHAPTER 32

Unfurling banners and pennants and shouting out their challenge, the forces commanded by Christopher and Paul swept down from the east and north, charging out of morning mist thick with the smoke of the forest fire, driving straight into the startled ranks of the free companies.

Spears hit their mark, striking deadly and centered upon steel carapaces. Horses reared, lashing out with their hooves, pummeling and battering the archers before they had a chance to nock an arrow. Axes and maces and swords lifted and fell . . . and Berard's men fell beneath them.

But even in the midst of the initial charge, Christopher had realized that there was a strange sense of indecision and hesitancy about Berard's men. Some had been arguing, shouting, gesticulating animatedly. Servants had been running in and out of Berard's tent. A few groups of soldiers had appeared to be actually walking away.

It was too good to be true, and to Christopher's utter surprise and shock, it remained too good to be true. The forces of the Aurverelle alliance met with startled faces, a complete lack of morale . . . and little else. They plowed and furrowed the human field with which they were presented and left behind a scattered mass of panic.

Dismounted for the assault, hemmed in by the village and the forest, Berard's men had no chance whatsoever to fight before they were ridden down, hacked, spitted, and crushed. Christopher, resplendent in the golden armor he had taken from the Shrinerock armory, found himself surrounded by men who were not so much running or fighting as floundering like so many stranded fish. The outcome of a battle, it was said, could be determined by the loosing of the sixth arrow, but here there were no arrows—the archers had been among the first to go down—and the outcome, it seemed, had been determined even before the charge.

No quarter had been asked, and none would have been given in any case, for Christopher had pronounced sentence upon the free companies nearly two weeks ago. The business of killing, therefore, turned into hot, revolting work; and since his spear had broken after his third charge, Christopher now used the plain, unadorned sword that had replaced the relic-laden wonder he had lost, along with his illusions, at Nicopolis.

He still had no illusions. The French, he knew, would have issued a challenge and waited politely while the free companies formed up—or perhaps negotiated. Not so Christopher. Surprise, like thrown apples or breaking into noblemen's bedrooms, was unchivalrous, but effective. Still, though, what he was seeing as he stood up in his stirrups and smashed his weapon down on the steel helmets and visors of men who wept and cried out and struggled ineffectively was much more than surprise alone could account for. Something else had happened.

Across the field he saw Martin and Paul delMari, both clad in Aurverelle armor, fighting side by side through the shuddering mass of milling, frightened man-flesh. Martin was young, strong, and, yes, by the Lady, he could indeed fight. There was no mincing nervousness or sense of craven apology here, just strong shoulders, an obviously cool head, and regardless of his choice of bedmates, a lusty, male swagger.

The three met in the middle of death. As his horse pranced spiritedly among the armor-clad bodies lying thick on the ground, Paul raised his visor, lifted his sword in salute. "The baron of Furze and his son greet the baron of Aurverelle!"

"Compliments to you both!" Christopher shouted above the cries, the clanks, the screams. He stared at Martin. Son?

But Paul and Martin had already turned, spurred their horses, and struck at the heart of a body of brigands who were attempting to mount some kind of concerted defense. Abbot Wenceslas led another party in from the other side, and just then, Abel and perhaps two score Saint Brigid men armed with swords and axes swung down from the village walls on ropes, assembled, and stormed across the intervening ground.

The defense collapsed. Berard's men broke and fled. Even the bravest, who seemed ready to stand their ground, seemed to reconsider when it became obvious that their valor would consist of nothing more than being dismembered.

Flight, however, consisted of little else. This was not battle. This was rout. This was slaughter. This was easy killing, pathetically easy. Berard's men screamed, ran . . . and died. One or two of Christopher's people fell, dragged down by the brigands more for their horses and possible escape than for any hope of combat; but on the whole, the Aurverelle alliance reaped its way across the field, turned, and reaped its way back, unhindered, unopposed.

Within a half an hour, it was over. Silence fell, the clouds of dust dissipated. The knights and men of the alliance dismounted, wiped and sheathed swords, and, almost puzzled by what they had done, stared at the carnage. Christopher, too, slid from his saddle in the eerie stillness, wondering at the dead who lay tumbled like logs left by a flood.

A grinding of metal as a body shifted. Footsteps. A muffled voice. "It's ridiculous," Jamie was saying to someone, perhaps to no one in particular. "They didn't even put up a fight."

"I won't complain," said Christopher. But he had been expecting a fight. His blood had been—was still—pounding. Within his armor he was damp and acrid with nervous sweat. And this . . . simple butchery. He almost felt cheated.

"Master! Master!"

"Over here, Pytor."

The seneschal, wearing mail covered with dirt and blood, ran to him and, after bowing, began trying to help him out of his armor. "It is hot," he said, "master will suffer."

"I'm all right, Pytor. Really."

Jamie was still perplexed, and he scuffed towards Christopher, his visor up. "But where's the glory in this?"

Angered, Christopher stepped away from Pytor, threw down his sword. It struck the ground point first, quivering. "Dammit, where's the glory in anything? They're dead! They're just dead, that's all! That's what we wanted, wasn't it?"

Chagrined, Jamie groped for words. "I mean . . . I . . ."

Christopher shook his head. Yes, he felt cheated. Something had happened. "I know what you mean." He prodded a crushed and bloody body with his foot, then looked up suddenly. "Where's Berard? Where *is* that son of a bitch?"

"We have been looking," said Pytor. "No one has seen him."

"Did he escape?"

"Master knows that it is possible."

Christopher's anger seethed again, and he grabbed his sword and stomped across the battlefield, turning over bodies, peering into dead and bloody faces. But not until he reached the free company camp did he find what he was looking for. Berard was lying on the ground just outside his tent, face down and unarmored. His side was open, one arm was gone, and the flies were clustering thickly about him.

A few feet away, Jehan delMari also lay dead. A sword was in his hand, but the gilt of the delMari surcoat was tarnished and thick with blood and dust. What had happened was obvious.

"God of my fathers," said Pytor. "It was Jehan."

"He did us a great favor," said Jamie.

Christopher nodded. Jehan had found his own solution to the maze of patterns that had surrounded him. "It's . . . incredible, though," he said. "No wonder it all went so easily. If there were a more precise way to break the free companies, I can't think of what it would have been."

With Pytor's help, he unbuckled his helmet and dropped it on the ground. The heat was insufferable, and the weight of metal encasing him seemed suddenly to be more than he could bear. But it was not the heat or his armor that suddenly made him stagger. It was everything else. The siege had been broken. Saint Brigid was safe. His grandfather was, finally, dead.

He looked down at Berard. Incredible. It was all incredible.

"Christopher?"

He recognized the voice . . . or so he thought. Turning, he saw that a slender maiden was stepping towards him. Her hair was dusty, her clothing only of homespun, but she picked her way though the desolation of the battlefield and the overturned camp as though at once utterly untouched by it . . . and yet stricken by its very existence.

He stared. Something about her . . . "Vanessa?"

"I . . . I think so."

And when she stood before him, he understood the reason for her hesitancy. This was Vanessa, true: the same blond hair, the same brown eyes, the same curiously defiant set to her fine chin. And yet it was as if a veil had been torn from a window so as to let the sun stream through unimpeded. She seemed luminous, light, and there was a radiance in her eyes.

Christopher stared, then, almost afraid, reached out to her, touched her shoulder. Solid flesh and blood, but . . . something else, too.

"I did it, Christopher," she said, and he heard in her voice another accent than that of Furze Hamlet. "I did it."

"What . . . what did you do?"

She struggled with words, struggled seemingly with her body. "I changed the patterns," she managed at last. "I did it like Mirya showed me . . . but this time I changed them for everyone . . . and I . . ."

She was shaking. She lifted her hands, stared at them.

"There were stars out there . . . and I used them . . . and I did something . . . to myself, too. . . ."

She was lovely and frightening both. Jamie was staring. Pytor unconsciously crossed himself.

Vanessa looked up. "I told you not to make plans, Christopher. I told you that you might not want me after."

Christopher was rooted. "What. . . ?"

Vanessa forced herself to say the words, slowly, carefully, all the while shuddering as though the sound of the alteration in her voice was itself a horror. "It was I who made Jehan decide to kill Berard. He was almost upon the decision himself, and when I shifted the patterns so that the siege would not be anymore, he chose."

Christopher stared into eyes that seemed to reflect too much light, into a face that was touched with elvishness. "No . . ." *You might na wan' me after.* "No . . . it's just a coincidence."

She shook her head, shook her hands to indicate herself. "Is this a coincidence, Christopher?" Her eyes were streaming. "Too much starlight . . . too much starlight." She put her hands to her face, jerked them away as though recoiling from the touch of the near-luminous flesh. Her resolve broke then, and she cried out: *"Dear Lady, Christopher, I do not think I am human anymore!"*

The free companies were destroyed. Many were dead, many were wounded, many more were prisoners.

The sun rose through the roiling smoke of the forest fire,

the fields grew hot even to the unarmored, and the sky remained a rainless blue. The villagers and the men of the alliance buried the dead—Dom Gregorie blessing the graves of brigand and ally alike with sad but divine impartiality—and the women of Saint Brigid tended the wounded.

Christopher watched from the shadow of the forest. Out there were the dead and the wounded, but here, at his side, Vanessa was a casualty, too. Though she was sitting on the ground, speaking haltingly with the Elves, the sound of her voice and the radiance of something beyond health that was about her told of a wound more profound than any that could have been given by sword, arrow, or spear.

Angered by the death of Charity, her teacher and her friend, threatened with the loss of the village that had become her home after she had been driven from her birthplace, Vanessa had fought in the only way she could. She had known something of the patterns, she had known that they could be changed, and so she had changed them.

But in altering reality, she had altered herself. She perhaps could not be considered entirely elven now, but as she had suspected—and as Mirya, Natil, and Terrill had reluctantly confirmed—she was no longer quite human.

Still gripped by an aching weariness that seemed about to wring a sob from his heart, Christopher stared out across the battlefield, watched bodies being taken away, wounds being dressed. A casualty. She had tried to fit in, she had tried to be simply, mortally, wonderfully human . . . and now both were forever beyond her.

And perhaps beyond him.

"Can I na . . . not undo it?" Vanessa was asking Mirya. "I mean, after all, I did it to begin with."

Mirya shook her head, her green eyes sad. "Consider," she said, her voice as soft as the whisper of the dry leaves above her head, "Abel can take ore from the earth, and he can smelt it and turn it into steel. But he cannot turn that steel back into ore. The steel remains steel."

Yes, that was it. Vanessa was steel. Pure steel. But though Christopher smiled at the rightness of the thought, he wondered whether his resolve was firm enough to clasp that metal to his heart.

Out across the fields, he saw Paul delMari. The baron of Furze was helping Martin direct the burials. Paul had fought with the strength of a youth that morning, but his manner with the vanquished was now polite and businesslike. But as Christopher watched, Paul seemed to consider, and then he suddenly beckoned Martin to his side.

The bond between Paul and Martin had grown. Paul grieved for Jehan, for all the foolishness of his son's brief life, and for his own errors and misjudgments. Martin still agonized about his homosexuality and the uncertainty of his future. But they were indeed father and son now, and they were both determined to shape the patterns of the future to their desires.

Vanessa bent her head, Natil put her arms about her. "You have always been a kinswoman, Vanessa. Now there is a greater tie between us."

Vanessa shook her head, half-sorrowful, half-puzzled. "I am sorry, Natil: I just wanted to be human."

Paul was calling to Jamie and one or two of the other barons who were nearby. Martin stood before him, looking perplexed. But when Paul was surrounded by his peers, he spoke in a stern voice, a voice that carried clearly across the fields. "Kneel down, Martin."

Seemingly in shock, Martin knelt.

"Some," Natil was saying, "will always be more than human. That was foreordained from the first sharing of love between immortal and mortal."

Paul drew his sword. A touch of the blade to Martin's shoulders, a light tap of Paul's fist on his chin—old Roger, in accordance with delAurvre tradition, had nearly struck Christopher to the ground—and it was over.

The assembled barons were smiling. Paul's voice came again: proud, clear. "Rise, Messire Martin of the house of delMari!"

For Martin, embraces, smiles, congratulations to one who had just taken his place in a brotherhood of arms. No one in the little group doubted his worthiness. Peasant blood? That had just been done away with, and Paul delMari's reputation, particularly this morning, was such that no one would ever doubt his ability to make knights . . . or sons.

But Vanessa was staring at her hands, examining fearfully the work of her own blood. The change was subtle, but profound. No one who had known her could have any doubt. "I just wanted to help," she said. The grief in her voice was deep. "I just wanted to do something."

Christopher knelt before her. "You did. If you hadn't

changed the patterns, we might well have lost. You saved your village. You saved all of us.''

Vanessa closed her eyes. ''But now . . . there are stars in my head—I can see them—and now I d-do not have a village at all.''

''You've still got Saint Brigid.''

She shook her head. ''They knew me before, Christopher. They are good people, and they would take me in, but they would know, and what is worse, I would know. It just cannot be the same.''

Christopher touched Vanessa's cheek with his gloved hand. Her voice and speech and manner had changed. Her face, though, was just as sweet, her heart just as valiant. A fighter. Just like every delAurvre who had ever borne the name.

And that included himself, he realized. A fighter. And he had, in the end, conquered even his grandfather. Perhaps, just perhaps, such a feat granted one certain privileges . . . such as the planting of a few peach trees. Preferably—and he found himself thinking it without hesitation—with his beloved at his side.

You might na wan' me after.

Elven blood in Vanessa. Elven blood in many. Fading, but lingering. And in that legacy of sleeping blood, perhaps lingering forever.

In the beginning, Natil had told him once, *people needed Elves to help them. Later on, they needed Elves to believe in. Then they needed something to fear. And now they need something to hate.*

Yes, and now they needed the Elves to fade, to take with them the knowledge of the patterns and the luminous wonder of the world. Their immortal blood, though, would spread throughout humanity: maybe people needed that, too. And maybe someday they would need it to wake up again.

He looked at the elven faces: Mirya, Terrill, Natil. Friends. Fading friends. There was a transparency about Mirya and Terrill, and Natil's solidity seemed poised on the edge of a sword. Fading. And soon . . .

Always, Vanessa. Always.

Always. He wanted to tell her that, wanted to hold her, take her hands, feel flesh against flesh . . . mortal or immortal it no longer mattered. But his gloves—noble clothing again—were in the way, and though he started to pull them off, he stopped halfway through and stared at his right glove, weighed it in his hand.

His glove.

He looked up. Paul and Martin, arm in arm, were walking off towards the village.

"Nothing c-can be the same," Vanessa was saying. The elven accent was irresistible, but it lay still awkwardly on her tongue. "I do not know what to do . . . I dan . . . don't . . . d-do not know where to go."

His glove. The baron of Furze could make knights. What about the baron of Aurverelle? What could he make?

Christopher knew. Still kneeling, he held out his glove to her, offering it, offering himself. "You could . . . you could come to Aurverelle," he said softly.

Vanessa stared at him. "But . . ."

He took her hand, put his glove into it. Roland had his God, Christopher had his lady. "You could come to Aurverelle," he said again. "And . . . live with me."

Her voice was full of tears and wonder both. "Do you still want me, then? Even though—"

He put his bare hand lightly to her cheek, as though he touched a sunbeam. "Even though, my lady."

The Elves were silent. Paul and Martin had reached the village gates and had vanished into the world of streets, houses, mortal men and women. In the distance, Malvern continued to burn, the smoke rising into the air, streaking away to the west to redden the sun that was already dropping down toward the peaks of the Aleser.

Vanessa still stared at the glove as though afraid to close her hand on the pattern it represented. "I am just a peasant girl, Christopher. . . ."

He shook his head. Her lineage was far older than his, stretching back as it did to the first dawning of a new-created world, and therefore it was he himself who begged for grace, for a chance to care for and sustain what small fragments were left of an ancient order, until . . . someday . . . perhaps . . .

". . . but . . ." Her hand shook, but it, at last, closed. "Yes," she said softly. "I will come."

She sobbed again, broke, and cried as helplessly as Christopher. But he gathered her into his arms, wondering still at the lightness about her. She had been a symbol for him, and then she had become human, and now she was both . . . and yet neither. But he had been graced, indeed. He had been graced by the Elves, by Vanessa, and (though he was surprised to think of it in just that way) even by his grandfather.

Yes, he thought. He would plant peach trees. If Roger of Aurverelle, swaggering and violent, docile and doddering, had taught him nothing else, he had taught him about peach trees.

Don't miss

SHROUD OF SHADOW

by Gael Baudino

coming soon from Roc Fantasy

CHAPTER 1

Ante diem festum Paschae, sciens Jesus quia venit hora ejus, ut transeat ex hoc mundo ad Patrem . . .

Easter was late that year. So was spring. Out in the Bay of Maris, the water was cold and gray, the breakers washing whitely the feet of the steep headlands that guarded the harbor. Gray water, gray sky, gray rock. The foam was the color of milk . . . or of death.

And Omelda was washing the floor of the Betancourt mansion.

. . . cum dilexisset suos, qui erant in mundo, in finem dilexit eos.

The water in her bucket was gray, and it foamed whitely as she sluiced it across the gray stone floor of the kitchen. Spill, slosh, scrub. Omelda's knees were sore, and her back was sore, too. Her hands were dry and cracked from weeks of scrubbing and laundering and cleaning, and her hair hung in sweaty tendrils despite the cold that whispered winter's parting words at the windows and the chimney and the doors.

. . . sciens quia omnia dedit ei Pater in manus, et quia a Deo exivit et ad Deum vadit: surgit a coena, et ponit vestimenta sua: et cum accepisset linteum, praecinxit se.

Holy Week. Maundy Thursday. Vespers. The house was silent, with no stump of the polished, mercantile boots of Nicholas Betancourt himself, no patter of the steps of his prim and pretty little wife, no unctuous tread of his servants. Everyone was at church in the great cathedral. There, and in a hundred smaller churches and private chapels in the city, the mysteries of the Passion and Death were being commemorated even now: choirs singing the gospel and antiphons, men—sad-eyed men, avaricious men, men whose hands knew the slick feel of gold and the chill of silver, men who had been born into sheets of linen and silk—baring their feet as their priest, whether mitered bishop or humbly tonsured friar in orders, knelt to wash them in memory of another washing, now fifteen hundred years past.

And Omelda washed the floor. Alone.

Mandatum novum do vobis: ut diligatis invicem . . .

More water—on the feet, on the floor, against the cliffs.

Beati immaculati invia . . .

The cathedral and the churches were distant, but Omelda
knew exactly what the cantors intoned and the choir sang
in reply as the water trickled over bare feet. She knew because she heard it. She was a mile away from the nearest
service, but the words and the melodies, made a part of her
by over twenty years of cloistered monasticism, rang in her
mind, shouldered her own thoughts aside, blurred her washing of the kitchen floor into the washing of the feet.

Postquam surrexit Dominus . . .

It was always this way. The music had long ago become
an inescapable part of her nature, and whether she was an
obedient nun—a prisoner of custom, enclosure, and church
law—or a contumacious and apostate scullion, *de facto* excommunicate for her absence and her lack of repentance,
the music was still there, an incessant, intrusive, violating
presence.

She had fled the nunnery to escape the melodic possession. But though she could climb walls, and though she
could elude the beadles and sheriffs and searchers, she could
not so escape from her own mind. For two years, she had
run, hidden, prayed for relief. To no avail.

Every night, she would awaken to a ghostly choir of
memory and habit singing matins and lauds, and she would
lie sleepless until they were finished. With the sunrise would
come prime, and then mass . . . all in her mind. And
whether, during the eight periods of monastic prayer and
worship that occurred each day—the Hours of the Holy Office—she ran errands, washed dishes, cooked food, or, as
now, scrubbed the floor, she did so to the inner accompaniment of plainchant. In her mind, the psalms ran their full
course each week, the feasts and holy days came and went,
and the special antiphons that the Benedictine order zeal-
ously kept separate from the body of the Church sounded
quietly and austerely.

Dominus Jesus . . .

Her inner cantor intoned the first words, and then as the
waves of the North Sea rose up to batter the cliffs about the
harbor, so the choir's response, plexed, multi-voiced, rose
in a wave of song and flung itself against the private thoughts

and conscience of Omelda the nun, Omelda the apostate, Omelda the damned—

. . . postquam coenavit cum discipulis suis . . .

—and she had at last reached the conclusion that it would never end. No amount of labor, physical privation, mental discipline, or distance from her cloister would ever banish that invisible choir, would ever give her the inner silence that she craved. Two years now, and nothing had changed about the endless violations save her will to endure them.

. . . lavit pedes eorum, et ait illis . . .

She dropped the brush she was holding and put her soapy hands to her ears. But the voices were within her, and they continued, unperturbed:

Scitis quid fecerim vobis . . .

"Stop," she murmured.

. . . ego Dominus et Magister?

"Please . . ." Aching with the defeat and the utter futility, she bent her head. Cold water trickled down her cheeks, mingled with her hot tears.

Exemplum dedi vobis, ut et vos ita faciatis.

"Dammit! Stop!"

Her words echoed off the roof, fell into silence amid the rustle of embers in the hearth. The wind answered her, the wind and the voices in her mind:

Credidi, propter quod locutus sum . . .

She wept, but she did not scream again. It was dangerous to scream, for the fact that she was not at church, that she kept instead behind closed doors and windows and labored alone into the evening could not but engender questions. What kind of heretic was she? A Lollard? A Waldensian? A Hussite? And if she were none of these, then why was she not in church like a good Christian?

No one would understand her tale of the creeping madness of melody that was stalking her, that forced her to absent herself from services of any kind lest, so encouraged, its tyranny become absolute. No one, indeed, would sympathize with an apostate nun whose presence, if discovered, would bring the whole city under episcopal interdict. And certainly no one would heed her protests against being returned to her cloister, there to face an interior horror that would make any discipline ordained by the abbess seem paltry and trivial both.

No, it was very dangerous to scream, for screams would

bring the beadles and perhaps even the Inquisition . . . and the voices in her mind never listened to her screams, anyway. But dangerous and futile though they were, the screams bubbled within her, now and then rising to her lips only to be choked off in a spasmodic whimper. And thus she washed the kitchen floor.

Standing at last, shaking, her frustration turning her heedless, she opened the shutters and let the cold April air smack into her face. Evening had fallen, and the grays of the city were shading into black. Silence: only the bloodless sound of the wind and the intrusive plainchant in her mind.

Dead to the world, they had told her. Dead to everything. No man, no children, no family. Dead. And she had fled it. But whether she considered her mind, shackled by the ritual that rang unceasingly in its depths, or her body, numb and unresponsive, she was still dead.

And here, on this Thursday of Holy Week, with the spring late and the wind cold and the evening gray as a stone, she could no longer think of a reason for continuing with this parody of existence.

The house was a tomb. The city was a tomb. She was, she reflected, damned already: would suicide make that much difference? At least she could ordain her own physical death.

Ubi caritas et amor, Deus ibi est.

She put her arms on the sill, cradled her head. "Love me, God," she said. "Just love me. I'm going to do it tonight. Please love me anyway."

And still the choir sang on: *Et ex corde diligamus nos sincero.*

Maundy Thursday. Feet were being washed throughout Europe.

The central mystery of Christianity was but three days away, but the body had to die before it could rise again, the exalted had to be humbled . . . and so feet were being washed. Touched. Handled. Water trickling over toes and insteps, tinkling into basins all agleam with the light of a hundred candles.

Fifty leagues to the southwest of a window out of which a young woman stared into the night and contemplated suicide, in a shabby little church in a shabby little city, Siegfried of Magdeburg, a friar of the order of Dominic, took into his hand the foot of a man named Paul Drego. An acolyte held a pewter basin ready as another handed Siegfried a pitcher of water, but Siegfried's eyes were not on basin or pitcher or foot: they were on Paul's face. He was wondering what he saw in Paul's face.

As the water trickled over Paul's foot, as Siegfried's hand mechanically registered the fleshly fact of bones, sinew, skin, and hair, the friar wondered. There were so many layers to a human being, so many levels of deception and self-deception, so many lies and masks that made up a mortal life. And as Siegfried was Inquisitor of Furze, it was his constant business to look beyond those layers and levels and deceptions and masks, to examine every flicker of every emotion over every face with which he was confronted, to spy out—vigilantly, indefatigably—what lay beneath, what lurked in the dark recesses of conscience and private thought.

Washing feet on a Maundy Thursday, holding a pitcher of water, staring into the face of a man who made hats for a living . . . he was yet the Inquisitor. And so he paused with his hand cupping Paul's heel, weighing his bare foot, considering, for a moment, what methods might be required to lay bare the hatmaker's inner world. Here, for example, just below the ankle, was a place in which to put a needle. Not quickly, mind you, but slowly. There were certain boots in certain rooms of the House of God (it was just down the street, one would reach it in the space of time it took to say a *Confiteor*) made just for that purpose, with straps to hold the foot steady and a screw thread on the needle so that it could be inserted hair's breadth by hair's breadth.

Or the toenails. Or this tendon. Or here . . . or here . . . or here . . .

Siegfried knew that strangers had taken shelter in Paul's house, had stayed a few days, and then had departed. Peddlers? Beggars to whom the hatmaker had, in Christian charity, offered the hospitality of his house? Representatives of the Aldernacht firm who had come down from Ypris to further the plans that Paul and his friends had formulated, plans to bring gold to Furze and revitalize the moribund economy?

Perhaps. It could be. Or perhaps it could be . . . something else.

What lay behind Paul's wide eyes? What lay behind the

lies that made up his life? A little fear, maybe? A little guilt? Those strangers, Paul. What about those strangers? *Barbes* uprooted by Cattaneo's valor in the Alpine valleys? Some Fraticelli come out of the Apennine fastness? A Lollard or two with a Bible in the vulgar tongue and a collection of pious aphorisms? Something else?

Layers. Masks. It was all layers and masks. Siegfried himself was at one with his thoughts, and his personal lack of inner duplicity, he knew, added to the fear that his office evoked in those who had enmeshed themselves in a web of heresy. They knew him for what he was, and he—a joining of the cornerstones of will and spirit so perfect that a scrap of gold leaf could not slide between them—would inevitably find out what they were.

Up near the altar, Bishop Albrecht cleared his throat, a gentle, supposedly unobtrusive prompt for Siegfried to proceed with the rite. And Albrecht, too, had his masks and layers: dazzled and deluded by his fruitless dreams of new cathedrals in old cities and his belief in a naive piety that would triumph over the pernicious evils of the world, the bishop had essentially ignored Siegfried's twenty years of constant, exhausting work against heresy in Furze.

Lies. Lies to oneself, lies to others. Again, Albrecht cleared his throat. Siegfried sighed, frustrated, but he reminded himself that the work went on, that Albrecht's dreams had not, could not, interfere with the Inquisition; and therefore, his eyes still on Paul's face, he dried the hatmaker's foot, gave him a thin smile and a quick squeeze of the ankle, and moved on to the next man.

The wind came in from the sea like a black knife, and it stuck its cold point through the threadbare places in Omelda's cloak as she made her way toward the wharves. It was night, the services were over, the Betancourt family was abed, and the streets of Maris were empty save for this runaway nun who was taking the road to the sea and to death.

Her goal was not the wharves or the shore. That kind of ending would be too slow, and her body, losing courage, might drag her back to life. No, she needed something quick. If she could actually get out of the city, there were cliffs to the north. A steeling of the nerves, a quick plunge, and that would be the end of it. God could judge her then.

With the ending of formal services in the cathedrals and churches and monasteries, her inner plainchant had subsided. It would, to be sure, begin again in the pre-dawn hours with matins and lauds, but for now she leaned against the wall of a salt-stained warehouse and peered out toward the water and the sea with a silent mind. She could wade out, pass the chains that locked up the harbor at night, and gain the outer shore, thereby avoiding the city wall with its gates and its guards. From there, she could climb to the cliffs. She would have silence until just past midnight. And, if she actually reached the cliffs, she might have silence forever.

She pushed on, and she had almost reached the water when a large hand seized her cloak and pulled her back into a pair of muscular arms.

"Well, what have we here? A li'l barnacle, looking for som'ting t'fix on?"

The man laughed, and his companion—yes, there were two—joined him. Omelda was square and stocky, but she might have been as slender as Nicholas Betancourt's pretty wife as she was whirled about and sized up by the two watchmen.

"What're you doing here?" said the second.

Omelda glanced out at the waves, at the distant cliffs that she could more sense than see. "I'm taking a walk."

The men laughed. "You're up t'no good, girlie," said the one who held her. He scratched the stubble of a black beard on his shoulder. "What sha' we do with you?"

"You can let me go," she said. Here she was, standing and gabbling at these men, wasting precious minutes of mental silence. But she had no choice. Thirsty though she was, fate had snatched her water away.

The second man folded his arms and eyed her up and down. A crafty look had crept into his face, one that she had seen often, and she was not surprised at all by his next words. "What'll you give us to let you go?"

The look, the tone of his voice: she knew precisely what she could give them. In any case, they would take it whether she offered it or not. That they were willing to bargain at all was an unexpected stroke of luck. "Whatever you want, sir," she said, and though she felt the dull numbness already creeping through her groin, she was grateful that she

could do something that would, in the end, make them leave
her alone.

They took her to a dirty lean-to, laid her down on a pile
of sacks, and took turns pumping her full of sperm. But
though Omelda's body was occupied, her mind was relish-
ing the silence in which the men left her while they grunted
and strained and satisfied themselves: the silence within her,
the silence they could not touch.

When they were done, they let her go, and she waded out
into the sea. The water—rank, stinking with sewage, clotted
with the pitch that the aging Hansa boats persisted in throwing off like shit from diarrheic cows—weighted her garments, and she half staggered, half swam out to the pilings
that held the harbor chains. Low tide. She was still in luck.

In another two hours, she had reached the shore outside
the walls of the city and climbed the rocky path out to the
cliffs. The viscous sperm dribbled out of her in clammy
rivulets, and the wind turned her damp garments to a shroud
of cold, but the chants were still, for the moment, silent;
and now the ruins of the old fishing village that marked the
tip of the precipitous headlands were in sight, shimmering
in the bright gleam of a moon just past full.

Spring was indeed late: not even a handful of grass or
wildflowers softened the hard earth and clumped boulders
of the cliffs. A hundred feet below, the North Sea raged and
flung itself at the base of the rocks as though determined to
have them down, but Omelda, worn out as much by the
men's use of her body as by her long trek, sat down at the
edge of the drop and, wrapping her sodden cloak more
tightly about her shoulders, bent her head.

The world hung at midnight, passed, and in the dim corners of her mind, she heard a whisper, like a child's voice
starting up out of a tomb:

Astiterunt reges terrae, et principes convenerunt . . .

She could not thrust it away. In her old convent, in all
convents and all monasteries, those consecrated to God had
begun the first office for Good Friday. And Omelda, if she
allowed herself to live, would hear it all. Antiphons. Psalms.
The Lamentations of Jeremiah. The Mass of the Presancti-
fied. Chanted, hymned, and intoned, the Hours would progress through matins, lauds, prime, terce, sext, nones,
vespers, and compline, and Omelda would be, as she had

been since her father had deeded her body to the Church when she was three, an unwilling participant.

And she had so wanted to die with her own mind.

She put her hands to her face, felt the grit of salt and sand. Her vulva was burning: the men had been rough enough to make her bleed. It should not matter. It really should not matter. A brief pitch forward into the wind, and it would all be over.

Quare fremuerunt Gentes, et populi meditati sunt inania. Would that be Hell? Would that be the particular flavor of eternal punishment—divinely fitted with excruciating exactitude to her crime—to which she would be condemned? Never to hear silence? Never to experience anything save an endless round of chants and psalms and hymns and adorations and processions that would go on and on until her soul, plunged into a dementia from which there was no escape—

A lull in the wind. She heard a harp.

Only a note, two notes, and then the sound was drowned once again in the rush of air. But before that soft chime of bronze strings, the voices of her inner choir had faltered, and for a moment, Omelda stared stiffly out at the roiling, moon-gleaming ocean, not knowing whether to be startled, frightened, or grateful.

She turned around to the heaped ruins of the fishing village. There was a light there, very dim—Omelda did not wonder that she had not seen it before—and, in another lull, the harpstrings rang again, and again they scattered the chanting voices that had come creeping back into her consciousness.

She rose and followed the sound and the light; and as she approached, she heard the harp more clearly. Now the sound of plucked wire, soft and dulcet though it was, was cutting through the howl of the wind and the crash of the breakers . . . and it was cutting through Omelda's heart and the voices in her head, too.

She had never heard such music before. Upheld firmly by a counterpoint of open fifths, its notes constantly changing durations and inflections, it flowed like speech, or like a river. The notes rang, wove in and out, cascaded in sparkling arpeggios, all the while speaking with unalloyed clarity of sunlight and good weather, of azure sky and blue water.

And the voices in Omelda's head wilted before them.

She followed the light and the sound to a tumbled-down house that still possessed an intact chimney and a single room. There she peered in through a window that had long ago lost its shutters and saw a woman sitting before a fire. A small harp was in her lap, and her fingers were on the strings. Her long dark hair, shot with much silver, was uncovered and unbound save for a single, small braid in which was tied what looked like an eagle feather, and her clothing was such a patchwork of outlandish and foreign garments that Omelda could not but wonder whether this were one of those fabled women who had forsaken their homes and their families to run off with the gypsies.

But it was no exotic gypsy strain that the harper played. The music—at once shining and humane, comforting and sympathetic—was like a warm hand; and Omelda, leaning against the weathered sill with blood and sperm running down her thighs, wept. Whoever this harper was, whatever she was doing, she had the power to still the voices.

But after a time, the harper stopped, bowed her head, sighed. Her hands fell to her lap.

"Please," said Omelda. "Please play some more."

The harper gasped, turned. Startled blue eyes fixed themselves on Omelda. "Dear Lady . . . I had no idea."

Omelda clutched her cold cloak about her cold shoulders. "I'm not a lady. I'm just a woman. Please . . . please play."

The harper was silent for a moment, and then she nodded slowly. "Of course, beloved. Of course I will play for you. Come in and share my fire. You must be frozen." There was no suspicion or caution in her voice: the offer of a fire and of music was wholehearted, without reservation. "But what are you doing out in this weather?"

Omelda pushed in through the rickety door, swung it to behind her. The voices were bubbling up again, and she plunked herself down by the fire without answering. "Please . . ." she said, "just play. It's been so dreadful, and . . . you're the first to . . . to . . ." She shook her hands gropingly. There were no words for that long, awful running.

The harper regarded her calmly. "What is your name, child?"

"Omelda. Please play."

The harper nodded slowly. "My name is Natil," she said. And then she played, and the music rose up like a wave, swept away Omelda's inner choir, and left behind only a quiet, dark silence.

If you and/or a friend would like to receive the *ROC Advance*, a bimonthly newsletter featuring all the newest and hottest ROC books and authors, on a complimentary basis, please fill out this form and return it to:

ROC Books/Penguin USA
375 Hudson Street
New York, NY 10014

Your Address
Name _____
Street _____ Apt. # _____
City _____ State _____ Zip _____

Friend's Address
Name _____
Street _____ Apt. # _____
City _____ State _____ Zip _____